A former deputy district attorney, Alafair Burke is an Associate Professor of criminal law at Hofstra School of Law and lives in New York City. She is the daughter of acclaimed crime writer James Lee Burke. *Dead Connection* is her fourth novel, following the highly praised Samantha Kincaid series of thrillers, *Judgment Calls*, *Missing Justice* and *Close Case*.

# DEAD CONNECTION

Ellie Hatcher is working in Manhattan's detective bureau when she is pulled into a homicide investigation. Two women are found murdered precisely one year apart, and there appears to be only one connection — both were members of the same online dating site. And when a third victim is uncovered, it becomes clear that there is a serial killer using the internet to find his victims . . .

Books by Alafair Burke
Published by The House of Ulverscroft:

JUDGMENT CALLS
MISSING JUSTICE
CLOSE CASE

ALAFAIR BURKE

# DEAD CONNECTION

*Complete and Unabridged*

# CHARNWOOD
*Leicester*

First published in Great Britain in 2007 by
Orion Books
an imprint of The Orion Publishing Group Ltd
London

First Charnwood Edition
published 2008
by arrangement with
The Orion Publishing Group Ltd
London

British Library CIP Data

Burke, Alafair
    Dead connection.—Large print ed.—
Charnwood library series
1. Women detectives—New York (State)—
New York—Fiction 2. Online dating—Fiction
3. Detective and mystery stories
4. Large type books
I. Title
813.6 [F]

ISBN 978–1–84782–038–9

Published by
F. A. Thorpe (Publishing)
Anstey, Leicestershire

Set by Words & Graphics Ltd.
Anstey, Leicestershire
Printed and bound in Great Britain by
T. J. International Ltd., Padstow, Cornwall

For Sean Simpson
I can't believe I found you
on a computer.

# PART ONE

# PLAYING WITH THE BIG BOYS

# 1

The man's first look at the newspaper item was a casual one, followed immediately by a more deliberate perusal. But it was the photograph accompanying the story that had him transfixed.

Caroline Hunter had preoccupied his thoughts in recent weeks, but this was his first opportunity to reflect on her appearance. To his surprise, she reminded him of a girl he had worked hard not to think about for a very long time. So proud. So uppity. Caroline Hunter had the look of a woman convinced of her own intelligence, a woman who assumed she could do whatever she wanted — get whatever she wanted — without any repercussions.

The man wondered if Caroline Hunter had any regrets as those two bullets tore through her body. Maybe for some women it took dying in the street like a dog to reflect upon one's decisions and the effects they have on others. He felt his muscles tense, crumpling the pages of newsprint in his hands.

Then he placed the paper neatly onto the breakfast table, took another sip of tea, and looked down at the muted traffic in the street below the window. He smiled. Fate was presenting him an even more promising opportunity than he had understood when he first spotted the article. Details remained to be worked out, but he was certain of one thing:

Caroline Hunter was only the beginning. There would be more stories, just like this one, about women just like her.

\* \* \*

Three hundred and sixty-four days later, Amy Davis finished a second glass of red wine, pondering which excuse she should exploit to call it a night. She should have known better than to agree to a first date that started at eleven o'clock. Even by New York City standards, such a late invitation was an unequivocal sign that the guy wanted to avoid the cost of dinner but leave open the possibility of a spontaneous one-nighter.

But then the guy — he claimed his name was Brad — had suggested meeting at Angel's Share, not one of the usual meat markets. Amy still thought of the cozy lounge as her secret oasis, tucked so discreetly inside a second-floor dive Japanese restaurant on Stuyvesant Street. She decided to take Brad's awareness of the place as a sign. Then she looked out her apartment window and saw the snow, the first of the season. To Amy, the first flakes of winter were magical, almost spiritual. Watching them fall to the quiet square of grass beneath the oversized bay windows at Angel's Share would be fantastic, much more satisfying than observing them from the fire escape of her fifth-floor Avenue C walk-up.

And so Amy had taken a risk. None of the previous risks had panned out, but that didn't

4

mean that Brad wouldn't. Besides, all she had to lose was another night at home with Chowhound the Persian cat, falling asleep to the muted glow of her television. Three weeks earlier, she had committed herself to this process, and nights like this were the price she would have to pay if she were ever going to find The One.

She knew the date was a mistake precisely one second after she heard the voice behind her at the bar's entrance. '*Are you Amy?*' It was a nice voice. Deep, but not brusque. Friendly, but calm. For exactly one second, she was optimistic. For that one second, she believed that Brad with the good voice, who was familiar with Angel's Share, whose first date with her fell with the first snow, might just make a good companion for the evening, if not more.

Then the second passed, and she turned to meet the man who went with the voice. The truth was, Amy did not care about looks. People said that all the time, but Amy actually meant it. Her ex-boyfriend — perhaps he had never become a boyfriend, but the man she'd most recently dated — had been handsome as hell, but by the time they were through, she found him repulsive. This time, she was putting looks aside to focus on the qualities that counted.

Brad's face was not unattractive, but neither was it familiar — a surprise to Amy since they had exchanged multiple pictures over the last week. Internet daters posted photographs, so, even though Amy did not particularly care, she looked. It was nice, after all, to have a visual image to go with the instant messages and e-mails. This face in front of her, however, did not match the image she'd carried.

As Brad squeezed through a small group of people to ask the host for a table, she mentally shuffled through the pictures he'd sent and realized that in most, his face had been obscured — sunglasses on both the fishing boat and the ski slopes, a hat on the golf course, a darkened dinner table at some black tie event. One head shot had been pretty clear, but even a toad could eke out one good picture. In retrospect, she realized she had used that one good picture to fill in the blanks on the rest.

Once they were seated, Amy tried to put her finger on precisely what was different. The face was puffier. Older, too. In fact, Brad looked much older than the thirty-eight years he claimed in his profile. Sure, she might have shaved off a couple of years herself, but she was talking *much* older in his case. She realized there was no point in getting bogged down in the differences. He looked completely different than she had envisioned, and that was that.

By the end of the first glass of wine, she knew it wasn't just Brad's face that didn't match up to his online counterpart. According to Brad's profile, he was a gourmand and a red wine junkie. She allowed him to order first, afraid she might embarrass herself with a passé selection. After he requested a cheap Merlot mass-produced in California, she proceeded to ask for a Barbera d'Asti. If Brad was going to lie, then she was going to rack up Piedmont prices on his tab.

He talked about work while he drank, pausing only to take big gulps from his glass. Commercial litigation. A motion for summary judgment. Something about jurisdiction and somebody who lacked it. An appeal. His monologue would have been boring at eleven thirty in the morning, but Amy found it sleep-inducing at this late hour.

She tried shifting the conversation, resorting to all of the subjects he'd gone on about in his e-mails — independent films, running, his photography hobby. Each topic was a bust, sparking nothing other than a brief expression of surprise on Brad's unfamiliar face. Reaching for her coat, Amy did not see Brad order the second round until it was too late.

Nearly an hour into the date, Brad finally took a break from his running legal commentary. 'I'm sorry. I've been working so hard it's tricky to turn it off sometimes. I should ask you about yourself.'

The brief glimmer of hope Amy allowed herself was dashed when he proceeded to make good on his perceived obligation. 'So which publishing house do you work for?' he asked.

'Pardon me?'

'You're an editor, right? Which house?' Her confusion must have been apparent. 'Oh, right. No, you're a . . . a fund-raiser. For the Museum of Modern Art, right? So how's that going for you?'

It was going, she thought, much better than this date. The jerk had actually mixed her up with some other stupid woman he was duping online. The wine was good, and the view of the snow was wondrous, but nothing was worth this humiliation.

She selected her excuse and went with it. 'I know I said I was up for a late night, but I took a painkiller earlier for this problem I'm having with my rotator cuff.' She rubbed her right shoulder for effect. 'With the wine on top of it, I'm feeling a little loopy.'

'Let me walk you home,' Brad suggested brightly, clearly spotting an opportunity in her feigned high.

'No, really, I'm fine. I'm just around the corner,' she lied. She might be an idiot for signing on to this endeavor, but she knew better than to tell any of them where she lived.

Amy didn't bother waiting once he signaled for the check. She yawned conspicuously and began to maneuver out of the booth as she pulled on her coat. Before Brad could rise for the awkward good-night peck, she shook his hand abruptly and thanked him for the wine he had yet to pay for.

Then, after a quick scramble down the narrow staircase, through the exit of the Japanese restaurant, she was out of there. She was alone, free of that lame excuse for a date. It struck her then that two or three times a week, for the last three weeks, she had reached the end of the evening with this same feeling. She had made a ridiculous pact with herself to 'get out there,' to finally meet a man she could see for more than a month, to finally meet a man she could trust and even love. But, at the end of a night like this, she was always happier once she was able to get *out of* there. After an hour with Brad, the idea of watching snow from her fire escape didn't sound half bad.

Amy walked through the East Village, smoking a Marlboro Light, with a new appreciation of her solitude. She was a thirty-one-year-old woman living in Manhattan. She had a painless enough job in a kickass museum. She got to see mind-blowing art every day. She had fifty-one different delivery menus in her kitchen drawer and really good hair. She had a big fat Persian cat named Chowhound. Tomorrow she would treat herself to some street shopping, where only in this city could twenty bucks buy you a seemingly authentic designer handbag. There were worse things in life than being on her own.

The snow was starting to stick by the time she reached the alphabet blocks on the Lower East Side. Amy's father still didn't approve of her choice of neighborhoods, but her parents had been overprotective ever since that problem back home. She kept telling him that times had changed since he formed his impressions of the city. Every location in Manhattan was safe now, and the Lower East Side was all she could afford.

She had her key ring in her hand and was already unzipping her coat when she heard the noise from the alley. *Mew.*

'Chowhound?' she called out, peering into the dark void between two buildings. She looked up at her fifth-floor window above, left open during the last cigarette before she walked out for the night.

*Shit. I've got to quit smoking.* She always made sure to lock the other window, the one by the fire escape. And it would take Jackie Chan to leap from the fire escape to her smoking window. But she forgot that big fat Chowhound was 50 percent fur and had the uncanny ability to squeeze himself through tiny spaces if he knew freedom awaited him on the other side. And Chowhound, in spite of his plumpness, was freakishly aerodynamic. When it came to a pounce to the fire escape, Jackie Chan had nothing on him.

'Come here, Chowhound. Come here, baby.' Amy could see she was going to have to tear him away from whatever disgusting thing he was eating next to the Dumpster. She looked up and down her street. There was no one within a block. She'd be quick.

As she reached down to grab the cat, the man pinned her from behind. She felt arms around her waist, then latex hands around her neck. She felt the frame of his body pressing against her and she knew it was happening. It was real. The moment Amy had always feared — that every woman, at some level, always fears — was happening.

Amy was strong. She fought back. She was not going to make it easy for this son of a bitch. She kicked and twisted, punched and clawed.

But everything she managed to grab — sleeves, coat, collar, gloves — only protected her attacker. Her range of motion was limited by

10

her winter parka. The ground was growing slick now. She could not find the leverage she needed.

*Please, God, no.* He was no longer just squeezing her neck with those latex-covered fingers. He was crushing her throat. Her tongue was swelling. When he had forced the full weight of her body to the concrete, he placed his head next to hers and gazed into her face.

*I know you.*

Amy heard the words in her mind, but could not speak them. She knew she had enjoyed the last breath of air she would ever take. As she finally succumbed, she tasted blood, bile, and Barbera d'Asti. It was the taste of death.

With a gloved hand, her killer placed a single piece of paper in Amy's coat pocket, satisfied with the puzzled and panicked look that had crossed her face in those final seconds. It was a look of recognition. It was a look of profound regret. It had been precisely as he had wanted it. He wondered if the others would flow so smoothly. *How many more until they notice?*

# 2

Detective Ellie Hatcher was certain that something was wrong with the victim's story. She'd spent the last fifteen minutes in an interview room of the NYPD's Midtown North Precinct working through the man's report. He hadn't wavered from his bogus story yet, but she knew she was getting close.

But now it appeared from a loud rap on the door that she had a different problem looming. She turned to find the towering bulk of her lieutenant, Randy Jenkins, filling the door frame. He beckoned her with an upward tip of his prominent chin.

'Hatcher, we need to talk.'

'I'll be right in, boss.'

'Wrap it up.'

'Five minutes,' Ellie said. She looked at the man sitting across the table. He was still holding the pack of ice to the side of his head. 'We're just about done here, right?'

'Five minutes,' Jenkins emphasized before closing the door.

'They gave you one nasty bump, huh, Mr. Pandey?'

'I am sure that in your position you have seen others who faced far worse.'

'Not too many. I'm still pretty new to this.' Ellie smiled shyly, but then quickly tucked her expression away, pretending to look over the notes she had been compiling. 'I'm sorry. Can you run over the timeline again — just to make sure I haven't missed anything?'

As Samir Pandey related his story for the third time that morning, Ellie searched for the flaw. Car-for-hire drivers were rarely robbed — far easier for the bad guys to go after the yellow taxicabs that deal only in cash and stop on demand for the nearest waving hand. Tack on Pandey's claim that a man in a ski mask popped out of nowhere, pulled open the back door, and conked him in the back of the noggin at six in the morning while he was driving on the West Side Highway, and the story was about as convincing and original an explanation as *I don't know. Some black guy did it.*

'Can you excuse me for a moment, Mr. Pandey?'

Escaping the watchful eye of a suspect always helped Ellie collect her thoughts. She turned the facts over again in her mind as she paced the narrow hallway adjacent to the interview rooms. According to the car service's dispatcher, Pandey had picked up his last scheduled fare from the Times Square Marriott at five in the morning and dropped her off at her Bronx apartment thirty minutes later. Pandey was late returning to the garage, then called in shortly after six fifteen, groggily reporting that he had just come to after the assault and robbery he suffered on the drive downtown. He was only missing the fifty bucks from that last fare, and he would have had to have knocked himself in the head to get it. Ellie had seen the bump. He wasn't messing around.

Looking at the old-fashioned, round clock that hung at the end of the hallway, Ellie evaluated her next move. She knew what her training detective would have said during her probation period. He would have told her to save her energy because this was how the system worked: An employee pilfers cash, then blames it on a robbery. The employer uses the police department as a bullshit detector by requiring a report. Sometimes the employee caves and retracts the allegation, afraid of getting in trouble for filing a false statement. More often, he calls his boss's bluff, knowing the cops are too busy to pursue a robbery complaint with no leads. Ellie knew that a good, efficient detective — one who could prioritize her limited time in sensible ways — would act as a transcriber, file the report, and move on to the real work.

Efficiency, however, had never been Ellie's first priority. She knew that Pandey was lying, so that made him important — to her at least. She didn't especially care about punishing the man. He seemed decent enough. What she needed was an explanation for *why* this decent-enough person would bother. *Find the motive,* her father used to say. Until she understood Pandey's motive, this inconsequential robbery report would continue to nag at her.

She was telling herself to defer to efficiency, just this once, when a uniformed officer informed her she had a visitor. A dark-haired, dark-skinned woman in a multicolored maternity sari was waiting down the hall near the entrance to the detective bureau. From the looks of her girth, the baby she carried in her stomach was just about done.

'I'm here about my husband?' the woman explained. 'Samir Pandey. I called his employer when he was late coming home. There has been a robbery?'

'He's fine,' Ellie said. 'Just a little rattled. Nothing to worry about — especially when you've got enough to keep your mind on. When are you due?'

'One week.' The woman beamed proudly. 'A daughter.'

'Well, congratulations. If you want to have a seat, your husband will be out shortly. We're just about done with his report.'

'Hatcher, aren't you supposed to be in here?' Jenkins scrutinized her from the doorway of his office.

'Just one more second, boss,' she said, smiling.

It was more like ninety seconds. Ellie found a comfortable chair for Mrs. Pandey in the cramped waiting area, then stopped at her desk. A quick call to the car service's dispatcher, followed by a few keystrokes on her computer, and she had her answer. She darted to the bureau's communal printer, removed the spooling page that awaited her, and shook the printout excitedly as she headed back to the interview room.

Pandey wasn't just out the fifty bucks. He was also out forty-five minutes. Forty-five minutes when his extrapregnant wife was waiting for him, wondering why he hadn't come home. She knew Pandey's reason for lying, and she had the piece

15

of paper that would persuade him to come clean.

The photograph of Sandra Carr, the woman whom Pandey had driven to the Bronx as his last fare, had been taken courtesy of the New York Police Department after Carr was busted for solicitation a year earlier. Pandey's face fell when he saw the picture slip to the table from Ellie's fingertips.

'Forty-five minutes,' Ellie said to her robbery victim. 'You were missing the cash from your fare and the next forty-five minutes.'

'Please do not tell my wife,' he said. 'It is our first child. I have never done such a thing until today. I almost made it. Just one more week for the baby, then the doctor says we must wait six weeks after that. When I went upstairs with the lady, I could not even — '

Pandey pushed the photograph away, and Ellie thought she heard a sniffle. She understood why he was here. A few lies — even the self-inflicted head injury — were to this man a small price to pay to put this morning's activities in the past.

'Mr. Pandey, I think we can mark your report as unlikely to be solved if you can behave yourself for the next seven weeks. I hear you've got a little girl on the way.'

The driver was still thanking Ellie as he walked out of the station with his wife.

\* \* \*

'Hatcher. Get your ass in here.' Jenkins had stepped from his office doorway into the detectives' room.

16

'The interview went a little long, boss. Sorry.' Ellie followed Jenkins into his office and rested a hip against a two-drawer file cabinet.

'Seems to happen to you a lot. You ought to be careful about that curiosity,' he warned. 'You're either going to wind up a hero, or dead.'

'Or both.'

'Yeah, well, either one's a bitch.' Jenkins lowered his dense, muscular frame into his chair, working his jaw like he was still mulling something over. 'We have a situation. And I'm not saying anything until you take a seat. You've got too much energy, Hatcher.'

Ellie did as she was told, but Jenkins's jaw was still grinding. The lieutenant did that a lot. Hatcher suspected he maintained that stoic facial expression and the close shave of his dark black skull for a reason. His look was unambiguously serious. Authoritative. One eyeful of him, and the largely white detectives he supervised knew he was the real deal. No handouts when it came to Jenkins. But Hatcher had realized about a month into the detective bureau that the movement of Jenkins's jaw gave a hint at what went on beneath the hardened exterior. And now it was telling Ellie that he was bothered.

Jenkins was bothered, and she was in his office. Sitting, not standing. Something was definitely up.

'I got a call from a homicide detective this morning.'

'Is everything all right?' She could hear the alarm in her voice. Ellie's job had nothing to do

17

with the homicide division. She'd made detective just thirteen months earlier and was lucky to work scams and robberies. The one and only time she'd received a surprise call from the police about a dead body, she had been fourteen years old, and the body had been her father's.

'I suppose that depends on what you mean by 'all right.' A detective over there has a couple of dead women on his hands and seems to think you can help figure out who might have put them there.'

'Excuse me?'

'No offense, but I was surprised too. Apparently someone's got himself a theory and thinks you're in a unique position to help him. You've got a special assignment.'

'To homicide?'

'Now don't go getting that tone. It's an assignment. Temporarily. You'll help out as you can, and then you'll come straight back here when you're done playing with the big boys.'

'Of course. It's just temporary.'

Jenkins looked through the window that divided him from the detectives, working his jaw. 'You don't want it to become more than that. No matter what they say, it can't come easy. Not to me, and not to you. You better deserve it twice as much as they do. You get what you want too soon, and you won't be seen as earning it.'

Ellie knew precisely what he meant. She had made detective quicker than most, after four years on patrol, and the assignment had coincided with the wave of media attention thrown her way that year. She knew other cops speculated she got a leg up either because she was female, because of the press, or both.

'Yes, sir. Thank you. I still don't understand, though. Who's the detective?' Not that it made a difference. Ellie didn't know anyone in homicide.

'Flann McIlroy. You ever heard of him?'

'By name, sure.' The truth was she usually heard Flann McIlroy referred to by a slightly different name. McIl-Mulder, as he was called, was a colorful subject of discussion — usually complaints — among other career detectives who resented the singular adoration he appeared to enjoy. In the case that sealed his status as a media darling, a clinical psychiatrist had been pulled from the elevator of her Central Park West building when it stopped at a floor that was supposedly closed for construction. She had been stabbed eighty-eight times. The M.E. couldn't determine whether the rape came before, during, or after.

'Well, apparently McIlroy thinks he knows something about you,' Jenkins said. 'Face it. You've gotten more press lately than most of us experience in a career. What the hell that's got to do with two bodies in New York is for you to figure out.'

Ellie would have loved to explain that she did not want the attention. To start with, the news stories weren't about her. They were about her father. No, not even. They were about the man her father had hunted — the man who may have killed him. She was a mere human-interest sideshow, the daughter who followed in her dead daddy's footsteps, who still believed in him.

Instead, she nodded silently. A homicide detective read about her and for some reason thought she could help him. Two dead women, and a role for her in the investigation. Only one explanation for this temporary assignment came to mind: The women were working girls, and the department needed a decoy. She had a sudden image of herself in a sequined tube top and capri pants, roaming Penn Station.

She'd managed to avoid decoy work as a patrol officer, even though her male colleagues had always made a point of reminding her that she was an obvious candidate for a job in vice. She was thirty years old, but heard all the time that she looked younger. She had thick, shoulder-length honey blond hair and pool-blue eyes. Her five-foot-five frame was naturally curvy, but with some added muscles thanks to kickboxing and light weight training. Despite her current job, New Yorkers never seemed surprised when she confessed with embarrassment that she was once first runner-up in a Junior Miss Wichita beauty pageant. She'd been told a few times she was a real 'Midwestern knockout.' For some reason, they always threw in that regional qualifier.

She wasn't doing tube tops, though. Spaghetti straps would have to suffice.

Jenkins had a different kind of advice for her. 'This won't go over well with some people. McIlroy's got favor with the higher-ups, but his own people? The people in his house? They won't like this.'

'From what I read about that psychiatrist case, the guy's smart. Maybe that'll be enough to protect me.'

Ellie remembered the case from the news. The primary detectives focused on the building's construction crew because the workers had access to the closed floor. McIlroy, on the other hand, got wrapped up in the fact that the murder was on the eighth floor, and the victim was stabbed eighty-eight times. He even studied photographs of the bloody smears of the crime scene until he was convinced they were shaped in a chain of number eights. The rest of the homicide task force wrote it off as another crazy McIl-Mulder theory, but McIlroy hit the neighborhood homeless shelters and found a paranoid schizophrenic who'd been treated by the victim two years earlier while he was on his meds. Off his meds, he'd been walking the streets on the Upper West Side mumbling to whoever'd listen about the number eight.

Jenkins ran a palm over his head stubble. 'I think some people would say he's lucky. And they'd also say it was bad form, working another team's case. But what really pissed the task force off were the department's press releases. McIlroy looked like a lone hero.'

'And we know how that must've gone over.' Ellie thought of the barbs about McIl-Mulder she'd overheard among older detectives. She wasn't sure which seemed to bother them more — his supposedly half-baked theories or the astonishing coincidence that the press always seemed to have a heads-up on the inner workings of his investigations.

Jenkins shrugged. 'He's still the favored boy there, at least with the brass. But he's got a reputation — well, it sounds like you've heard about it. I could tell them I need you here. I can keep my own people when I need to.'

'No, sir. If I can help there and come back when I'm through, that's what I'd like to do.'

'I didn't have a doubt in my mind that you'd say precisely that.' He handed her a slip of paper with McIlroy's name and an address scrawled on it. The tell in his jaw was gone. Ellie took it as a sign of something Jenkins would never say aloud — he had been worried about her ability to handle the scrutiny that would come with the assignment, but he no longer was.

It took Ellie only ten minutes and one box to pack up her desk, and the box was only half full. A picture with her mom and brother taken two Thanksgivings ago back in Wichita, a handful of hair clips, her favorite water glass, a jar of Nutella, a spoon, a cigarette lighter, and the potpourri of pens, Post-its, Jolly Ranchers, and other crap that fell out of her top desk drawer. That was it. All she had gathered in thirteen months.

And somehow those thirteen months had led her to a murder assignment.

# 3

Ellie Hatcher never thought she'd be a cop. Sure, like any little kid modeling herself after a parent, she'd thrown around the idea. But *police officer* had fallen somewhere on the list between fashion designer and astronaut. Then, after her father died, she believed she'd lost every positive feeling she had about law enforcement. Her father literally gave his life to the job, and it left his family with nothing. No money. No support. Not even answers about his death.

It also left her without the luxury of dreams about her future. When her older brother, Jess, ran off to New York to become a rock star, Ellie and her mother had been on their own. Even if Ellie had been willing to leave as well, the scholarship money she earned in B-level beauty pageants fell far short of out-of-state tuition. That left Ellie as a part-time waitress and a part-time prelaw student at Wichita State University.

She'd probably be a lawyer in Kansas now if it weren't for Jess — or at least for her mother's inability not to worry about his pattern of mixing alcohol (and most likely other substances) with a general penchant for recklessness. After two years of watching her mother age ten, Ellie realized the best thing she could do for her mother — and herself — was to leave Wichita to look after her brother.

Then a strange thing happened. She fell in love — not with a man, but with New York City. Young people, living beyond their means in cramped apartments, walking to the corner deli for takeout — tiny specks moving intently, carving out their own patterns among the chaos. Life in the city was exciting and unpredictable, exactly the opposite of the endless enclaves of ranch homes she'd known as a child. She was turned down for every paralegal job she applied for, but she learned not to care. Waiting tables paid more anyway, at least on the good nights.

Then a stranger thing happened. As is inevitable in any relationship, Ellie started to notice the darker side of the city she loved. Beneath the tall buildings, upscale boutiques, and bright lights lived signs of a seedier and more harsh New York. A woman with fading bruises, pausing discreetly at the garbage can outside of the bakery, eyeing the half-eaten croissant lying just under that discarded cigarette butt. A homeless man tucking himself more tightly beneath urine-soaked cardboard boxes, hoping to avoid a roust to the shelters that would not permit his one and only possession — the matted beagle snuggled into the crook of his knees. Too many men waiting at the Port Authority for the young girls who arrive from faraway towns with big dreams but nowhere to sleep.

Ellie tried to look away — to ignore the signs like everyone else. But as she strived for blissful ignorance, the problems only grew more glaring. She realized that only one job would allow her to love this city the way she wanted to: She could be the person who stopped to help instead of looking away. It took three years of part-time classes at John Jay, but she finally became a cop. Then after four years of hard work, she made detective. One serious boyfriend had come and gone along the way, but she still had New York. And she still had her job.

Now that job was taking her to the Thirteenth Precinct, home of the Manhattan South Homicide Task Force, a boxy six-story building on East Twenty-first Street between Second and Third avenues. At the front desk she asked one of a handful of uniformed officers for Flann McIlroy, and he escorted her to the task force offices on the third floor.

'Fourth desk back, on the right,' the officer instructed, pointing across a room crammed with desks, shelves of notebooks, and men. The male-to-female ratio among the detectives here was even higher than what she was used to at Midtown North.

Walking the gauntlet. That's how it felt. Eyes intentionally followed Ellie and her half-filled brown cardboard box. The eyes' owners exchanged knowing smiles. Each whisper grew bolder than the last. *That must be McIl-Mulder's Date Bait.* Another said something about Scully being a blond. And having a box. A big box.

Ellie pretended not to hear their remarks or notice their lingering glances. In a way, she appreciated them — or at least what they represented. Offensive jokes, lewd gestures, and the open resentment of outsiders often defined the working atmosphere of cops — at least for those who were not yet a part of it. But the veneer served an important purpose. Reinforced daily in small ways such as these, it protected the bonds that lay beneath the thin but often impenetrable cover.

On this specific occasion, the jabs were aimed at her, and she understood why. She'd suffer through until the comments had served their purpose — a purpose that would ultimately benefit her, once these men came to realize, as others had before, that Ellie was no creampuff.

At the fourth desk back on the right sat a man Ellie thought she recognized from various departmental press conferences. He didn't fit Ellie's stereotype of a pseudocelebrity law enforcement stud. The NYPD had bred its fair share, and they usually fell into one of two molds — the good-looking buff Italian, or the good-looking buff Irishman. Different coloring, distinguishable jawlines, but the looks were always off the charts. Flann McIlroy, by contrast, resembled an older version of the Lucky Charms leprechaun. He was not unattractive, but he had the look of a child star, decades later — in his forties, but forever destined to resemble a fourteen-year-old redhead with a gap in his teeth.

'Are you Detective McIlroy?'

'Does Keith Richards pick coconuts?' McIlroy's eyes remained on the report he was reading.

'I think the surgeons might've removed that

impulse while they were fixing the rest of his brain.'

'Ah, very nice. A woman who keeps up with her pop culture.' McIlroy rose from his chair and offered a thick hand. 'You must be Ellie Hatcher.'

Ellie shifted her cardboard box for a handshake, and McIlroy quickly relieved her of the parcel, setting it on his desk. In a framed photograph that he pushed aside, Ellie recognized the men on either side of Flann McIlroy as Rudy Giuliani and Bill Bratton.

'That's me,' Ellie said, 'reporting to duty. Thank you for bringing me over.'

'You make an excellent first impression. Most of my colleagues don't get my rhetorical questions.'

'Aging rock stars, I get. Throw out any allusions to French literature, and we might have some problems.'

'You must be wondering why you're here.' McIlroy had a gleam in his eye.

'I go where I'm told,' Ellie said matter-of-factly.

'I got permission from the assistant chief to work a single case exclusively.'

Ellie did her best to conceal her surprise. Lieutenant Jenkins said McIlroy had suck with the brass, but the assistant chief was extremely brassy — he ran the entire Manhattan detective borough.

'My lieutenant's not particularly happy about it, so the freedom may not last. He's already threatened to pull the plug tomorrow if it doesn't go anywhere, but he's mindful of the politics. If nothing breaks — the case, you, me — we all turn back to pumpkins. So let's just say you better not unpack this box quite yet.'

'Not a problem. Desks are overrated anyway.' Ellie tried to sound like she was taking it all in stride.

'Unless you've got a hearing problem, you probably noticed some comments as you walked in.'

McIlroy hadn't bothered to lower his voice. Nearby detectives shifted their eyes back to their work.

'No hearing problem, sir,' Ellie said.

'And none of this 'sir' stuff. Call me Flann.'

'And call me Ellie. Or my friends just call me Date Bait.' She threw a look to the younger detective at the next desk, and he laughed aloud and smiled. *One down, the rest of the room to go*, Ellie thought.

'Let's talk while we drive,' Flann said. 'I want you to see something.'

\*   \*   \*

'Friday night, around three in the morning, two men found a woman's body in an alley off of Avenue C.' McIlroy flipped down the sun visor on the department-issued Crown Vic as he hung a left onto Third Avenue, followed by another quick left onto Twentieth Street to take them to the far East Side. 'The girl's name was Amy Davis. She lived in the adjacent building. We've already determined she was walking home from a date when the bad guy grabbed her. Strangled.'

He pushed a manila folder across the seat toward Ellie. She opened it and removed an eight-by-ten photograph. Amy Davis lay on a metal slab. A white sheet was pulled up to her shoulders, but the rest of the picture told the story. Her face was scarlet. Dark contusions discolored her neck and throat, her eyes protruded from their sockets, and her swollen tongue peeked out from encrusted lips. Ellie could tell from the many marks between Amy's jaw and clavicle that the killer had used his hands. She had definitely struggled.

'How do you know the date didn't walk her home and do all of this himself?'

'We called his cell right after we found *this* in the vic's coat pocket.' McIlroy handed Ellie two sheets of folded white paper from his own jacket. 'That's a photocopy, obviously.'

Ellie read the string of e-mail messages from the bottom up, starting with the earliest. The first message was sent a week ago, from CameraMan to MoMAgirl: *I saw your profile. We seem to have a lot in common. Maybe between my photography and your love of Warhol, we can take the artworld by storm. Check out my profile and let me know. My name's Brad.*

MoMAgirl responded two hours later: *You don't look too bad yourself. What kind of stuff do you usually shoot? Amy (aka MoMAgirl)*

The two had e-mailed each other once or twice a day for the next few days, until Brad finally suggested on Friday evening that they meet for a drink that night at eleven o'clock.

'Eleven o'clock on a Friday night? What a cheese ball,' Ellie muttered under her breath.

'The cheese factor, as you put it, gets considerably worse,' McIlroy said. 'But he's not our guy. I called his cell at three thirty in the morning, after we found the e-mails. I think I hit redial six times before he finally picked up. By that time, he was in bed at another woman's apartment. According to the bedmate, our playboy Brad called her around midnight saying he was in the neighborhood.'

'He could have made that call after the murder to give himself some semblance of an alibi.'

'Except the girl remembers bar noises in the background, and the waiter at Angel's Share remembers Brad on his cell phone when he signed for the check. Apparently he was pissed off about the price of the wine Amy was drinking.'

'Did you check the call records on Brad's cell phone?'

McIlroy nodded. 'They're consistent: Two back-to-back calls around midnight. One to a woman in the West Village, which went unanswered. Then another call, which his overnight companion picked up.'

'And he couldn't have killed Davis between the phone call and the booty call?'

'Nope,' Flann said, smiling. 'The booty call, as you so aptly described it, took place next to the Flatiron Building. The security camera in the elevator has him arriving ten minutes after the cell phone call.'

Ellie finished the chain of reasoning. 'And it's impossible to get from the Village to Avenue C, then back up to the Flatiron in even twice that time.'

'I was impressed he made it to the Flatiron in ten minutes.'

'When sex awaits,' Ellie said, refolding the sheet of paper and handing it back to McIlroy. 'So the victim had a date that night, but it's got nothing to do with her murder.'

'Now *that* I'm not so sure about. Here's my hunch.'

Ellie raised an eyebrow. According to her lieutenant, one of McIlroy's misplaced hunches could tarnish her reputation for years.

'Don't worry,' Flann said, catching her expression. 'It's one notch stronger than a hunch — I guarantee. Did you notice how our victim met this courtly gentleman, Brad?'

'On the Internet. Very Twenty-first Century.' The e-mails had been sent through a company called FirstDate.com. Ellie had recognized the name. From what she could tell, FirstDate was one of the biggest online dating companies around, at least in the New York area. She could hardly ride the subway or pass a bus stop without spotting an ad announcing that true love was waiting for her somewhere out there in cyberspace. If the men on the service were anything like Brad the bed-hopping Camera-Man, then Ellie had no remorse about resisting her occasional curiosity.

'I read that you've got an interest in high-tech law enforcement,' Flann said. 'I'm hoping that's

31

going to come in handy.'

It was Ellie's first confirmation that McIlroy knew about her fifteen minutes of fame. In retrospect, Ellie regretted giving any interviews. She'd done it for her mother, hoping that a profile piece might bring more attention to her case against the police department back in Wichita. The strategy hadn't worked. The case was still pending, the police department was still calling her father's death a suicide, and her mother was still broke.

'Don't get your hopes up,' Ellie cautioned. 'I said I was interested in it, not that I was an expert.'

'Do you remember this murder?'

McIlroy handed Ellie another folded piece of paper. It was a photocopy of a newspaper article, dated just over a year earlier, about the discovery of another young woman's body — this one shot to death in NoLita, just north of Little Italy.

An aspiring psychologist and author who devoted herself to the study of interpersonal relationships died alone early yesterday morning after she was shot in the trendy NoLita neighborhood in downtown Manhattan, a police spokesman said. Caroline Hunter, 29, was killed on the corner of Spring and Elizabeth shortly after 2 a.m. in what police investigators believe was a botched robbery attempt.

Hunter was pursuing her Ph.D. in social psychology at New York University, where her dissertation examined the role of online relationships in contemporary society. She had just signed a significant publishing contract to write a book summarizing her findings for a broader audience.

'Carrie, without a doubt, would have emerged as one of the most significant sociological voices of her generation,' said her editor at Penman Publishing, Joan Landers. 'We have all lost the opportunity to learn from her.'

The gunshots interrupted a telephone conversation Hunter was having with her mother.

'She often called late because of the time zones,' said Barbara Hunter, of Yakima, Washington. 'She'd say good night and let me know all was well. She was in the middle of telling me about a meeting she had with her editor when I heard some kind of scuffle, then two loud bangs.'

Mrs. Hunter believed her daughter may have been walking home to her East Village apartment from a meeting arranged on an Internet dating Web site as part of her ongoing research. Police say they have confirmed that Hunter's dinner companion was not involved in the shooting. Witnesses have reported seeing a lone man flee with Hunter's purse. Police had no comment on current suspects, but said the investigation continues.

The photograph accompanying the article jogged a memory somewhere in the recesses of

Ellie's mind. Every once in a while, one of the thousands of gorgeous young women in New York City with a professional head shot fell prey to the random violence of the city. Those were the crime stories that the local papers took hold of. Caroline Hunter had been famous for a few days, then relegated to the unsolved murder files.

Ellie told McIlroy that she had a vague recollection of the story.

'So did I. And when I caught this case and saw how pretty Amy Davis was, I immediately pictured the tabloid headlines. That got me thinking about the last time the media glommed on to one of these cases. Out of curiosity, I pulled the file. Caroline Hunter. Notice anything?'

'Kind of hard not to,' Ellie said. 'According to this article, Hunter was shot on the way home from a date she'd arranged on the Internet. She was even writing her Ph.D. on online relationships.'

'Anything else?'

'Two women, both attractive. Both in downtown Manhattan. Approximately the same age. One strangled, though; the other shot.' Ellie knew, however, that killers could change the way they killed, as long as the method itself was not an important part of what they considered their M.O.

'What about the timing?'

She calculated last Friday's date in her head, then saw what McIlroy was getting at. 'Exactly one year apart.'

'To the day. Now you know why I said it's

more than a hunch.'

'I believe you said one notch more,' Ellie added.

'Still, it's more. And that's why we're going to Amy Davis's apartment. Your charge, Detective Hatcher, is to find me something that says we're on the right track.'

# 4

Amy Davis had lived in a prewar walk-up apartment on Avenue C. This was the Lower East Side, not to be confused with SoHo, Tribeca, or some other fame-infused bastion of downtown coolness. In Alphabet City, gentrification had hit only building-by-building, block-by-block: The gamut ran from unmarked needle-exchange counters to Glamazon-infested martini bars. Davis's building fell on the shabby end of the neighborhood's spectrum.

McIlroy pressed one of the roughly twenty doorbells lined up at the building's entrance. A voice blurted through a speaker under the buzzers. 'Dígame.'

'Policía. Estamos aquí con respecto a asesinato.'

Ellie was able to make out a few of the words. They were the police and were here about *something*. Her Spanish vocabulary could use an influx of nouns.

The door was opened by a man in faded jeans, an oversized flannel shirt, and a coarse goatee. 'You speak some pretty good español, man, but I'm fine with English.'

McIlroy took care of a brief introduction. The superintendent's name was Oswaldo Lopez. His friends all called him Oz, he added, checking out Ellie as he said it. The detectives followed him up the steep, zig-zag staircase that ran through the center of the building.

'How long have you been the super here?' McIlroy asked between deep breaths, already starting to fall behind.

'Around eight months.'

'What can you tell us about Amy Davis?'

'Pays her rent. Comes and goes. Keeps to herself, at least around the building. Like everyone else. It's that kind of place.'

'Any regular company?' Ellie asked.

'Not that I noticed. But I'm not a doorman in a white-glove high-rise, you know what I'm saying?'

Ellie knew exactly what he was saying. Oz probably responded to about half of the tenants' complaints, based on who was most generous or persistent. He did not, however, make friends or keep tabs. It was, as he said, *that kind of place*.

'When can we start showing the apartment?' Oz asked.

'Sometime after we've put its current tenant in the ground,' McIlroy said without missing a beat.

'No disrespect, man. The owner wanted to know.'

'If Davis paid her rent, he doesn't have anything to complain about until the end of the month. Now does he?'

'Like I said, no disrespect.'

When they reached the fifth of six floors, Oz removed a key ring from his belt and unlocked a door in the back corner of the hallway. Ellie and McIlroy entered, and Oz followed. McIlroy looked annoyed but too out of breath to express it.

'I think we'll be fine here, Mr. Lopez,' Ellie said. 'We'll let you know when we're finished.'

The super paused, no doubt wanting to get a first-hand view. Murder-related macabre was simply too titillating for even the most complacent people to resist.

McIlroy thanked her once the door was closed and they were alone. 'My doc says I need to add more cardio into my workout routine.'

'Hey, at least you've got a routine.'

'That's what he thinks,' McIlroy said, wiping a bead of perspiration from his temple. 'I'm surprised you're not wheezing a little.'

'I live on the fourth floor of a converted townhouse. I'm used to it.'

'Nice of you not to mention the fifteen years you've got on me and the obvious fact that you're more fit than I ever was. But I don't smoke.'

'Neither do I.'

'Okay,' McIlroy said after a pause. 'If you say so.'

'I say so.' Ellie took her first look around Amy Davis's apartment. 'So give me some hint why I'm here. What am I going to lead you to that you couldn't find yourself?'

'We'll know when you find it.'

Whatever it was, the search wouldn't take long. The apartment was an undersized studio, just a few hundred square feet. A double bed and a single nightstand were tucked into one corner. A love seat, tray table, and steamer trunk-cum-TV stand occupied the center of the room. A tiny desk was crammed into a poor excuse for a kitchen. Clothes and shoes were stuffed anywhere they fit.

The items in Davis's wardrobe spoke to the double life led by so many city women. The modern business-casual workplace demanded tailored shirts, pencil skirts, and fitted pants — not unlike Ellie's own charcoal gray V-neck sweater and straight-leg black pants. In her free time, though, while Ellie hung out in sweatshirts and Levi's, Davis hoarded low-rider jeans, bohemian tops, and funky boots.

Ellie opened one of the kitchenette's cabinets. No dishes, no pans, no food — just more clothes and shoes. Only two bowls were in sight, and they were on the floor — one filled with water, the other empty, with the word *Chowhound* printed on the side.

'What happened to the cat?' Ellie asked.

'Funny thing about that cat. The first time I came to the apartment, he led me right to the window by the fire escape and started meowing. Like he was telling me something.'

'So where is he now?' Ellie had never stopped to wonder what happened to animals after their people were killed.

'In the bunk room at the bureau.'

'You're kidding.' No wonder this guy had a reputation as a maverick, Ellie thought.

'I tried taking him home with me, but my seven-pound Siamese was a little intimidated. Chowhound's an absolute beast. The guys at the house aren't too happy about the loads he leaves in his litterbox. The vic's parents are supposed to pick him up tomorrow.'

McIlroy took a look around the apartment and shook his head. 'I'll never understand living in a place like this. Some people think the city begins and ends with Manhattan. On Staten Island, this girl could have bought a house and a yard for what she was paying to rent this dump.'

Ellie smiled to herself as she hit the power button to the laptop on Davis's desk. McIlroy moved into the bathroom, out of her view.

'I quit,' Ellie called out to McIlroy as she scrolled through the recently viewed files on Amy Davis's computer. 'Smoking, I mean. I quit. Well, basically. Almost.'

'You don't have to explain.'

Ellie heard rustling and guessed McIlroy had moved on to the medicine cabinet. 'I know. But then I couldn't ask what tipped you off.'

McIlroy chuckled. 'You had a lighter in that box of junk you hauled into the division this morning. Plus you had that way of fiddling with your pen in the car, like you were jonesing for a smoke.'

'I'll have to watch that,' she said, making a mental note. 'We should take this laptop in to get a better look at the files.'

Ellie quickly rifled through the nightstand, the desk, and the kitchen cabinets doubling as dresser drawers. She inspected the printer on top of the desk, then walked to the bathroom. It wasn't big enough for two people.

'Do you mind if I see the e-mails again? The ones between Brad and Amy.'

McIlroy handed her the printout.

'Was the original in black and white like these pages, or in color?'

40

'Color.'

'You're sure?'

'Does Donald Trump need a haircut? Yeah, I'm sure.'

Ellie flipped open the top of the printer, removed each of the four cartridges of ink inside, and confirmed that three of them were bone dry.

'Those e-mails in her coat weren't printed from here,' she said. 'This is an ink-jet color printer, but she's out of colored ink. With just a black cartridge, this is essentially a black-and-white printer.'

McIlroy took another look at the printout. Each message bore a time and date. 'She said right in that last message that she was home from work.'

'I noticed that too. But that e-mail wasn't printed here.' She held up a sheet of paper that was left resting on top of the printer. It was a receipt for a pair of shoes Amy had ordered off the Internet the day before she was killed. 'See? No color.'

'So you think she lied? Maybe she was at a boyfriend's place?'

'I don't think so. There's a glass of water and an open book on the nightstand. She's got hair and makeup stuff scattered all over the bathroom. No. She's definitely been sleeping at home, and there's no signs of a man around. The e-mail wasn't printed out from here because *she* didn't print it out. Think about it: Why would she need to? She clearly knew where the bar was — she said it was one of her favorite places.'

McIlroy looked excited. 'No one can read a

thirty-year-old woman like another thirty-year-old woman. Okay, so now tell me what you think it means if Amy Davis wasn't the one who printed out the e-mail.'

'Well, it might mean there's some perfectly innocuous explanation.'

'Or?' He obviously wanted to hear her say it.

'Or it might mean that someone else printed out the e-mail and deliberately planted it in her coat pocket so the police wouldn't miss the fact that Amy had been using FirstDate.'

'And what would that mean?'

'That someone wants us to know he's out there.'

It meant that, just possibly, Flann McIl-Mulder had much more than a crazy hunch.

# 5

Anonymity. The promise of an unrevealed identity. Anonymity is appealing. Anonymity provides a shield, and a shield provides safety. Ellie Hatcher and Flann McIlroy were learning, however, that a shield could also be used as a sword.

FirstDate was not like an old-fashioned dating service. There were no background checks and no interviews to determine shared interests and values. The company purported to know nothing about its individual members, let alone who was best suited for whom. In fact, FirstDate's refusal to suggest potential matches was precisely what attracted the lovelorn, at least those who believed that chemistry and love were too irrational and unpredictable to be crassly calculated by a computer.

FirstDate left the hunt for these elusive objects to the hunters but made the possibility of a successful end to the hunt seem plausible. It did so by providing a virtual meat market with no geographic or temporal limits. With FirstDate, you could hook up with your next love from your desk, with none of the messiness (or potential lawsuits) inherent in dating a coworker. With FirstDate, you could meet someone on a Saturday morning while you surfed the net in your pajamas in front of the television.

But what really attracted customers to

FirstDate was the anonymity provided by cyberspace. FirstDate users went by pseud-onyms. No addresses, no phone numbers. Not even e-mail addresses. Members contacted each other — at least initially — directly through the FirstDate site, using the FirstDate mailboxes and messaging systems, rather than personal e-mail accounts. The entire system was set up so that careful members could 'meet' and get to know any other FirstDate member without ever disclosing their identities.

Anonymity. Safety. Privacy. It all sounded good. Unless, of course, a killer used the anonymity to ensure safety and privacy from the police.

To find the men who contacted Amy Davis through FirstDate, Ellie and Flann needed access to her account. That simple task was proving to be frustratingly difficult.

The many pages on the FirstDate Web site listed only one telephone number, and that was for members of the media. Everyone else was supposed to make contact via e-mail. Ellie called the number, and a public relations representative eventually put her through to a customer service representative. Much to Ellie's surprise, even after she identified herself and explained the nature of her inquiry, the FirstDate employee informed her that she would need a court order before the company would release any personal information regarding Amy Davis.

'The poor woman is dead,' Ellie protested. 'I think if she were here, she'd be more concerned about the police finding the man who killed her than about her privacy.'

There had been an uncomfortable silence, followed by the comment, 'We at FirstDate assume that our customers value privacy above all else. We will, however, comply with any lawfully issued court orders.'

Anonymity. Safety. Privacy.

After their efforts with FirstDate petered out, they tried the department's computer technicians, but were told the staff was too backed up to look at Amy's laptop. Apparently McIlroy's suck with the honchos didn't trickle down to the crime analysts.

'Aah, why bother? Corporations and crooks take all of the techies worth having anyway.' He and Ellie sat side by side at his desk, staring at Davis's laptop screen. McIlroy picked up the phone. 'I know an A.D.A. who will help us get a court order. We'll force FirstDate to open Davis's account.'

Ellie waved him off. 'That'll take forever. Let me try a few things.'

She pulled up the log-on page at FirstDate. She typed 'MoMAgirl' in the user name box, offered a few random letters for the password box, then hit enter. The computer responded with an error message informing her that the user name and password did not match.

'No shit,' McIlroy said. 'You really think you're going to stumble upon it?'

'Nope.' Ellie clicked on the hypertext beneath the error message: *Forgot your password?*

Ellie smiled when the next screen appeared. The screen contained three prompts: the e-mail address the member had used to register, the member's date of birth, and the name of the member's pet. 'For a company that values privacy, they sure haven't done much to protect it.'

She had seen a few e-mails printed out on Amy's desk at her apartment. They had all listed an e-mail address in her name at the Museum of Modern Art. She typed that address into the first box on the screen, followed by Amy's date of birth, followed by 'Chowhound.' That was a good cat name. Good and memorable.

She hit enter, mentally crossing her fingers. Then she received another message. *Sorry but the information you provided does not match our records.*

McIlroy reached again for the phone. 'I'm going to make that call to the D.A.'s office now. Good thing I didn't bring you onto the case for your computer skills.'

'Don't you dare,' Ellie said, holding up her hand. 'And here I thought you were starting to have some faith in me.'

She pulled up the member profile for MoMAgirl. The photograph of Amy Davis was flattering, but with enough shadows to maintain some mystery. Her dark hair was windblown, and she wore sunglasses. She was smiling, seemingly happy to be wherever she was when the picture was taken.

In the box of basic information, next to her photograph, and above a lengthier statement Amy had written about herself, MoMAgirl listed her height (5'3"), hair and eye color (brown and

46

blue, respectively), body type (athletic), ethnicity (white), and age (29).

'Got it,' Ellie said, clicking back to the password reminder page. 'Amy wasn't twenty-nine, but she wanted FirstDate to think she was.'

Ellie typed in the requested information again, this time shaving two years off Amy's birth year. When she hit the enter key, a message popped up informing her that her FirstDate password had been sent to the member's e-mail address.

'Call MoMA, please? Ask them how employees check their e-mail from home. And make sure you get her log-in information.'

A few minutes later, McIlroy had the information they needed to access Amy's work account. Ellie logged in and found eighty-two messages waiting. The most recent was from FirstDate, reminding Amy that her password for the profile MoMAgirl was 'Colby.'

'Hot diggity,' Flann said, rubbing his palms together.

They were finally where they needed to be, logged in to Amy Davis's FirstDate account. Now it was time to find out just who tried to get to know Amy Davis. Anonymously. Safely. Privately.

★　★　★

At an Internet café in Midtown Manhattan, the man who strangled Amy Davis sipped a cup of coffee and smiled. He smiled because he liked what he saw on the screen of his laptop.

He had been keeping an eye on MoMAgirl's

47

profile. Until Saturday evening, he had seen the words 'active within 24 hours' posted above that pretty picture of hers. Then it morphed to 'active within 48 hours.'

*Patience*, he told himself. *Even the stupidest police officer could figure this one out*. After all, the unsubtle clue left for them in Amy's coat pocket had a purpose. Her e-mails would point the police directly to that insipid poseur she met that night at Angel's Share. He would undoubtedly be of limited intelligence. Even so, sooner or later, he would persuade the cops of his innocence, and they'd start to dig for another suspect.

Now it appeared he had gotten what he was waiting for: another change in the text above MoMAgirl's picture. 'Online now!' the screen declared.

He caught himself smiling, then forced himself to stop. Smiling would bring attention to himself. He didn't want the attention. Not yet, anyway. Not on him.

He read the words again. *Online now*. How thrilling. Amy Davis, of course, could not be the computer user who was online as MoMAgirl. He had made sure of that in the alley on Friday night. It had required more of a fight than he anticipated, but he had put her down for good. And now someone had logged into her FirstDate account. The police had made the connection. The game was on.

He was surprised that he didn't feel at least some guilt. He'd expected some pangs of discomfort. But nothing. In fact, taking out Amy was a piece of delicious karmic balance. More than five years earlier, in a spontaneous act of curiosity, he had Googled the name, wondering what had ever become of Amy Davis. Lo and behold, she was in New York, where he had recently moved himself. It had been a few years since he'd thought about her, but when the moment presented itself, there she was. Still in New York. Still at the museum. Still single and lonely, living in that same apartment. It was as if fate had held her there for him, ready to be used at just the right time.

On further contemplation, he decided there was no reason for him to be surprised at his lack of remorse. The average person didn't truly care whether other people lived or died; they just convinced themselves they did because they were supposed to. He, however, knew better than to assume any kind of ingrained benevolence. In his entire life, he had known only one truly good human being.

He clicked on the Message Me button. He liked this particular function, which allowed FirstDate users to chat on the screen in real time. Spontaneous, but anonymous.

He stroked the keys lightly with his fingertips, mentally composing the text he wanted to send. He allowed himself to type words in the dialogue box: *I know you're not Amy.*

He reread the single sentence, then added another. *I know because I strangled the life out of her.*

He let his index finger rest — lightly — on the Enter key, exhilarated by the possibility.

Sighing, he deleted the letters, one by one, then closed the messaging box. It wasn't time. Not yet. He'd had enough personal experience with police to know they had procedures to follow, clues to chase down, and mistakes to make before the fun could begin. Between Amy Davis and Caroline Hunter, they had plenty of work to do. And he had another love-starved woman to stalk.

★ ★ ★

Ellie turned first to Amy Davis's work e-mail, reading through all of the messages in her in-box and trash can. The only one related to FirstDate was a solicitation she'd received nearly five weeks earlier, inviting her to enjoy a thirty-day free membership on the service. Amy had left the message in her in-box for a full week before taking FirstDate up on its offer. Ellie shook her head, knowing that if Amy had deleted the message immediately, she would be the one sitting in front of her laptop right now.

Ellie closed Amy's museum account and moved into her FirstDate account. She clicked through a random sampling of messages.

'She didn't tell anyone on FirstDate her work e-mail address. She used her first name, and it doesn't look like she told anyone where she lived.' She opened a few more messages. 'Even when things moved beyond e-mails to phone calls, she insisted on calling them. She was being pretty safe.'

'Apparently not safe enough,' McIlroy added dryly.

'Okay, this should be pretty simple.' She directed McIlroy's attention to the computer screen. 'There's a feature here called Connections. When you click on it, the FirstDate site takes you to a page that keeps track of all the other users Amy had contact with. Then you can click on each one' — she clicked on one of the photographs on the screen — 'and it shows when the last contact was with that connection. And, from there, you can click on E-mails to see all the messages to and from that connection. Since she only contacted the online dates through her FirstDate account, we should be able to find all the old messages here. We can compile a list and go from there. What about the first victim? Caroline Hunter?'

'I've got a huge stack of notes that her mother had in storage. They just arrived this morning.'

'You called her mother about this already?'

'I told you — it was slightly more than a hunch. If the same man killed both victims, then working the Caroline Hunter case is a legitimate way to solve ours.'

'So what'd you find out?'

'The mom says everyone loved her daughter, she always knew it had to be someone who didn't know her, that kind of thing. She sent everything, including a list of her profile names and passwords on FirstDate.' He pulled a piece of paper from a file drawer in his desk and placed it in front of Ellie.

'A *list*?' Ellie asked, scanning the names that filled the entire page.

'Apparently you can be twenty different kinds

51

of women online, and Caroline was trying all of them out as research for her book. Different personalities, different photos, different people. She had so many profiles, she kept them posted on a bulletin board above her desk for reference.'

'Let's see if we can even access those accounts now. They've probably expired.' Ellie moved through several screens on the Internet. 'Okay, see how this works. One of her names was new2ny. If you're just some FirstDate user out there in cyberspace and try to search for new2ny, you can't find her. Hunter didn't renew her subscription because — well, you know why. So, new2ny is a dead profile. She can't be contacted. But dead on FirstDate isn't really dead. It just means dead to the outside world. New2ny still has an account that can be logged into with the password.'

She typed in the corresponding password on the list, and Caroline Hunter's smiling face appeared on the screen. According to the profile, new2ny was a twenty-six-year-old fashion publicist who had moved to the city after graduating from Indiana University. In the photograph posted with the profile, Caroline wore her hair pulled back with a paisley headband, making her appear younger than her actual age.

'It's in the company's interest if users can go active and inactive with the same user name,' Ellie speculated. 'They think they finally found that special someone, so they take themselves off the market. But then when they're single again, they can hop right back on, using the same online handle. If you're unsubscribed — '

'Meaning, if you're not paying.'

'Right. If you're not paying, you can still log in to your account, but you can't contact anyone.'

'And other people can't find you or contact you.'

'Exactly. But that's fine for our purposes.' Ellie clicked on the link to new2ny's connections. Hunter had more messages than Amy Davis had accumulated in three weeks, just under this one user name. Depending on the extent of Caroline Hunter's online activities under her other profiles, they could be looking at several hours of work. Less than half an hour remained in her shift, but Ellie knew her borderline OCD wouldn't allow her to stop sifting through the messages until she was done. If she got paid for all the free overtime she'd donated to the NYPD in her five years as a cop, she might actually have a savings account.

'We'll have a list by tomorrow.'

'I'll call my A.D.A. buddy and give him a heads-up. Late morning?'

'Sure.'

When McIlroy left to make the call on his cell, Ellie didn't bother asking where he was heading. By her count, it was McIlroy's third trip to check on Chowhound in the men's locker room since they returned from Amy's apartment. The previous visits had been brief, but this time, he didn't return for nearly twenty minutes.

'We've got a fuller morning than we thought,' he announced. 'My guy's willing to help us out, but first we've got to do a drop by at FirstDate.'

'Did you tell him we already tried?'

'Yeah, but he wants us to go through the drill in person. Tell them we really mean it about the court order. I called the corporate filings office and finally tracked down an address near Battery Park. Maybe they'll cave when they see our smiling faces.' He removed his coat from the back of his chair and pulled it on. 'I'm heading home. I suggest you do the same.'

Ellie assured him she'd be close behind, but for three additional hours, she remained glued to the computer screen, reading every last message in every last one of Caroline Hunter's accounts.

Not a single name overlapped. No one person had contacted both Caroline Hunter and Amy Davis, at least not using the same profile name. Maybe her lieutenant had good reason for his concerns. Maybe McIlroy was seeing shadows. Two women dead, both among thousands of other women on FirstDate. Maybe there was no connection between their murders.

She found herself fiddling with the pen she held between her index and middle fingers. She'd been telling herself that quitting was easy — a self-imposed contract to go cold turkey, the only way to go — but all that energy in her right hand made it clear she was still craving a smoke.

She was about to shut down the computer when she took a closer look at the e-mail message on the screen. It was sent to Caroline Hunter, posing as a thirty-two-year-old pediatric resident who went by the handle BrooklynHeidi, by Chef4U, who — according to his profile — was a thirty-eight-year-old who lived on the

Upper East Side and would love nothing more than to cook a Julia Child recipe for his perfect date. Ellie took in Chef4U's photograph, thinking that it would be nice to go home to a man with moppish blond hair, bright blue eyes, and a pot of beef bourguignon. For now, though, all she had to go home to was an empty apartment.

She picked up the thick binder of notes that Caroline Hunter's mother had sent to Flann and began reading. Interspersed among summaries of dates, quotations from various e-mails, and draft chapter outlines, Ellie found random notes jotted in the margins — Caroline's miscellaneous reminders to herself about hair appointments, phone calls, and grocery lists.

From what Ellie could piece together, the book was shaping up to be less about the men Caroline met online than about her own self-discovery. By creating different personalities on the Internet, she experienced a kind of independence she'd never felt before. At the same time, these desperate, fleeting encounters with men who shared no common social connection made her feel profoundly alone in the world.

Having read Caroline's scribbled words, Ellie somehow felt lonelier as well. Caroline Hunter was smart, reflective, and had something original and provocative to say. She should still be alive. Ellie closed the notebook and finally resolved to go home.

# 6

That evening, in a wood-framed ranch house in Wichita, Kansas, Roberta Hatcher was doing exactly what she did every night. She was watching her shows on a console television set and pouring herself a vodka on the rocks from the bottle of Smirnoff that rested on the tray table next to her reclining chair.

When she married Jerry Hatcher thirty-five years ago, she never expected to be a widow. No one ever thinks about those possibilities when they are young. Even if she had considered the fact that one of them would have to go first, and the statistical likelihood that it would be Jerry, she certainly never would have anticipated that she'd be left a widow so early, with a daughter just starting high school and a son who barely managed to finish.

It had been more than fifteen years since her husband died. That's how she always worded it: Jerry had simply died. The newspapers and the police department said Jerry shot himself. That was the official account, so of course that's what they said.

Ellie, however, always made sure that her father was the object of the sentence, not the subject. At first, Ellie insisted on saying that her father 'was murdered.' Over time, though, even Ellie tired of the reaction those words triggered — looks of sympathy for a fatherless girl of questionable mental health. Over time, Ellie adopted a tamer version of her father's death. He 'was killed,' she usually said.

Last year, when the national news briefly cared about the long-delayed capture of the College Hill Strangler, Ellie had hauled out the M-word again. *I truly believe my father was murdered by William Summer.* She repeated that same sentence to whatever reporters would listen. She willingly played the role she'd come to despise at the age of fourteen — the haunted fatherless child. She even spun the story of a young female cop following in her father's footsteps, as if he had encouraged her in that direction. As if it weren't his son that traditional, conventional Jerry had always pushed to be a cop. As if Jerry had even *noticed* his little daughter desperately offering her own theories about the killer named for his preferred stalking territory in the otherwise quiet College Hill neighborhood south of WSU.

Ellie didn't care whether the papers got her story right. She only cared about one truth. Ellie swallowed her pride, played the game, and did everything she could to get the news, the city, the police department — *anyone* — to take another look at Jerry's death.

At the time, she insisted that she was doing all of this for herself. According to Ellie, she needed to see that son of a bitch William Summer — the man finally connected to the College Hill Strangler pseudonym — take full account for his victims, including Detective Jerry Hatcher. She needed to see her father vindicated.

But Roberta knew there was more to it. Her daughter rarely did anything for herself, and this campaign to declare her father's death another College Hill murder was no different. Ellie was doing it for her family. That is what Ellie had done for nearly as long as Roberta could remember — taken care of her and Jess.

Ellie knew that, more than ever, Roberta could use that money from Jerry's life insurance and pension, long ago denied to her. Suicides, Roberta had been informed, were not in the line of duty. And death by suicide was what they called it.

Her husband was found in the driver's seat of his car, pulled to the side of a country road north of Wichita. A single bullet was discharged from his service revolver, into the roof of his mouth, through his brain and skull, and lodged into the roof of his Mercury Sable. Gunpowder residue was found on Jerry's hands, in a pattern consistent with a self-inflicted gun wound, she was told. *He left no note*, she pointed out repeatedly. That wasn't uncommon, the department's shrink explained. Jerry had, after all, been raised Catholic.

Jerry had also been depressed, the department emphasized. And obsessed. And disenchanted. On these points, Roberta could not argue. Her husband had certainly changed from the man she knew twenty years before his death. She, Jerry, their marriage, and their family had all begun to change on February 2, 1978, when he was called out to what became one of the city's most notorious crime scenes.

58

The dead were a single mother and her two children. All three of the victims were bound, blindfolded, and strangled. Semen on a rag found near the twelve-year-old daughter's body suggested that the killer got to the young girl last and —

Roberta tried to block out the details of the scene as she took another sip of vodka. Unfortunately, the images — and those from the murders that would come later — were far too ingrained in her memory. She could only imagine how they affected her daughter. Little Ellie, sneaking all the time into that damn basement to be a part of her father's hobby. Roberta should have insisted on a padlock.

In theory, Jerry should have stopped working the case when the Wichita Police Department disbanded the College Hill Strangler task force a few years after his last known kill. When the trademark communications and murders appeared to stop, everyone assumed the man was either dead or in prison.

But not Roberta's husband. The files, the photographs, a killer's self-aggrandizing letters to police and the media — the College Hill Strangler investigation itself — continued to decorate tabletops, nightstands, and every surface of her basement walls for another decade. After Jerry's death, the department seized it all. All that Roberta and her children were left with were the memories — of Jerry, and of the case he could never put behind him.

After all these hours of all these nights over all these years, she honestly didn't know what to believe about the facts surrounding her husband's death. But she knew that, regardless of who pulled the trigger on Jerry's gun, William Summer was responsible for what happened to her and her family.

The repeat she was watching of a sitcom about nothing ended, and the network moved on to a drama about police officers who solved crimes by analyzing physical evidence. Roberta changed the channel with a click of the remote control, then took another sip of vodka.

She glanced at the digital clock that sat on the top of the television. Nine o'clock. Pretty soon Ellie would be calling to check in on her. Just as she always did.

\* \* \*

That same night, in New Iberia, Louisiana, another mother was thinking of her daughter. Evelyn Davis sat on a small settee in her art studio, next to her daughter's best friend, Suzanne Mouton.

On further reflection, Evelyn thought, perhaps Suzanne was no longer Amy's best friend. In fact, Suzanne may never have been Amy's best friend at all. Suzanne had been part of Amy's group in high school. That much she was sure of. She remembered how the other members of the group always loved to call this particular girlfriend by her full name. Suzanne — pronounced the Acadian way, Susahn — Mouton. It did have a very nice sound to it. But Suzanne Mouton had always just been one of the crowd,

60

not one of the two or three girls who took shifts being inseparable from Amy.

The reasons Evelyn was close to Suzanne now, nearly fifteen years later, had more to do with the fact that Suzanne had been the only one of Amy's friends to stay in Louisiana. And when Suzanne's own mother died when she was a junior at LSU, Evelyn Davis had stepped in to help her get through it.

Amy's trips home had already begun dwindling back in college. At the time Evelyn assumed that her daughter was just too busy with her classes at Colby to fly all the way down from Maine. But then Amy's visits became briefer, even during breaks.

Evelyn couldn't say she was surprised that she and her only child had grown apart. Amy had always been her father's daughter. Like her father, she would have preferred to live in Houston. Or in San Francisco or New York for that matter. Anywhere but what she called 'da buy-you.' She worked hard to avoid picking up a regional accent, sure it would hamper her once she finally escaped the land of sugar cane and gators.

And her hatred of Louisiana had always translated into resentment toward her mother. Amy knew that Evelyn was the one who insisted that the family stay in the only state she had ever known. It had been a condition when she married Hampton. Evelyn had insisted, ironically, because her own mother needed her.

Something had begun to change in Amy, however, just in the last few years. Possibly it was because she was finally living in a city of her choosing. Or perhaps it was the job at the museum, which Amy loved so much. Evelyn, after all, was the parent who had encouraged her interest in art. Or maybe it was simply the process of growing up and realizing that every story, every person, and every marriage has two sides.

But now all that was moot. Evelyn had to pack a bag, fly to New York, and return her daughter's body to the town she always hated.

'Thank you so much, Suzanne, for being here.' The tissue that Evelyn held was shredded to pieces.

'Of course I'm here.' Suzanne handed Evelyn a new tissue and tossed the other in a wastebasket. 'Are you sure you don't want me to fly to New York with you? I could make J.D. watch the kids for a few days.'

'I'll be fine. Hampton's flying up there from Dallas.'

Suzanne was silent, but her expression said enough. She felt sorry for Evelyn — not just because of what happened to Amy up north, but because Amy's father couldn't cut short the deal he was brokering in Dallas to mourn with his wife. Evelyn had learned not to complain. She, after all, was the one who insisted that he keep his law firm's Lafayette office as home base. Travel was part of his life. He knew it was hard, he explained — for both of them — but it just didn't make sense for him to spend a day traveling home, just to leave again for New York. They'd meet tomorrow at LaGuardia instead.

'If I tell you what I need to bring, Suzanne, can you pack a bag for me?' Evelyn asked. 'I just can't bring myself to leave this room. I shouldn't have changed it. She should have had her bedroom. Her things should still be here. An artist's studio — what vanity.'

Suzanne did her best to console her, but they both knew there was nothing one can say to a mother who has to bury her child. Her only child. Her baby, strangled in an alley and left beside a Dumpster like garbage.

'How could this have happened?' Evelyn was sobbing now into her tissue. 'She was always so careful. Ever since she left for college, she was always so very, very careful. She was in her thirties, and still — '

Suzanne made soothing noises and patted Evelyn gently on the back as she cried. People overused the word *ironic*, but Amy Davis becoming a murder victim was indeed ironic. A statistic. Another woman killed while walking alone at night in an area where others would say that single women ought not walk alone. It was ironic because Amy had always been, as her mother said, so very, very careful. She was so careful about letting men get to know her that she was still walking alone at night.

'All these years, Suzanne, she could never trust anyone. Maybe if that awful business had never happened. Maybe she wouldn't have been in the city. Or at least she wouldn't have been alone.'

Evelyn knew that Suzanne, of all people, remembered the incident to which she referred.

Amy had learned her lesson. She had to be careful. Careful with men. Careful with trust. Careful with the unpredictability of human emotions. These were valuable lessons, but Amy had learned them too young, and she had probably overlearned them. Plenty of women were unmarried after thirty, but Amy had never even had a serious relationship. She was too careful, too untrusting, too unwilling to be vulnerable.

Evelyn's crying had subsided and her breathing was more regular now. She stood, straightened her sweater set, and began to gather the things she would need for her trip. 'I will pack my own bag, but I do need one very huge favor. Can you make room in your home for a cat? He's a Persian. I did my best to lobby Hamp, but he's allergic.'

# 7

Firstdate's corporate offices were housed on the eighteenth floor of a midsize tower on Rector and Greenwich streets in the city's financial district. A red-haired receptionist stood guard behind a sleek black desk that rested between the elevator and a set of double glass doors. Through the glass, Ellie spotted a dozen or so workers clicking away on keyboards in cookie-cutter cubicles on the floor, with a few private offices scattered along the perimeter.

The redhead wasn't much of a guard. She hunched in her highbacked chair, twirling a lock of wavy hair with her fingers, speaking animatedly into her cell phone. A couple of light taps of Ellie's nails against the receptionist's desktop triggered nothing but a nod. A flash of her detective's shield finally caught the woman's attention.

'I'll call you right back.' The redhead flipped the phone shut, straightened her posture, and asked how she could help. McIlroy asked to speak with someone who might be able to assist them with some profile names that had come up in an investigation.

'I'm sorry. We have a firm policy against disclosing information about our users.'

Apparently all FirstDate employees received the same training.

'We were hoping to talk to someone about

that,' McIlroy said. 'We certainly understand the reasons for your policy, but this is a little unusual. Our case is a double homicide. Two women are dead, and they were both active on FirstDate. I'm sure you can see the urgency.'

The receptionist's eyes widened at the mention of a double homicide, a description that wasn't precisely accurate since the two victims were killed an entire calendar year apart. But people mislead for a reason. Ellie watched the woman's fingers move toward a directory of telephone extensions that was taped next to the telephone.

'I'm really not sure how I can help you — '

'We just need to talk to someone who might be in the position to look up a few names for us,' Ellie interrupted. She and McIlroy had agreed in advance that Ellie would play the bad cop if necessary to get to the company CEO, Mark Stern.

'There's only one person I can think of who might have the authority — '

'Why don't you go ahead and call that person?' McIlroy asked.

'He has a very busy schedule. Can you, like, call later to schedule an appointment?'

Ellie stepped in. 'If we have to get a court order and FirstDate ends up on the front page of the *New York Daily Post* as a stalking ground for serial killers, I suspect Mr. Stern will want to know who turned us away when we tried to make a quiet courtesy call. Is this the name I should give him when he asks?' She held up the nameplate that rested on the desk.

As it turned out, looks really couldn't kill. Once Ellie and the receptionist came to that mutual realization, a set of manicured pink nails tapped a four-digit extension into a phone, and, after a terse conversation, Ellie and McIlroy were escorted to a corner office.

'Mr. Stern, these are the detectives who wanted to speak with you.'

The chief executive officer of FirstDate lived up to one's expectations of a man who made his living selling the romantic fantasy of realistic love. He was probably approaching forty and wore a platinum wedding band, a conservative navy blue suit, and a not-so-conservative lime green tie. His hair was on the long side for an executive, with the right amount of gray at the temples. Message: I was young once myself but found the right girl, fell in love, and remained loyal and happy. The silver-framed photograph of his beautiful wife in her beautiful wedding dress, placed prominently on his desk, wasn't exactly subtle, but selling love, after all, was how Mark Stern made his money.

McIlroy handled the introductions, then got to the matter at hand. 'We're investigating the murder of two women — similar ages, killed precisely one year apart. Both women were killed outside of their homes, apparently by strangers. Both women were using FirstDate.'

Stern nodded a few times, taking in the information. 'That sounds quite tragic, detectives, but I'm not sure how I can possibly help you.'

'We have a list of the men who contacted our

victims through your service. We need your help to track them down.'

'If you have a list of suspects, I'm not certain what more I can add. Checking them out sounds like police work to me.'

'A list of user names,' Ellie corrected. 'We have a list of FirstDate profile names and need to know the identities behind them. Coming up with that list, and figuring out that you're the one with our answers — that was our police work.'

Stern smiled, more at Ellie than at McIlroy. 'I'll presume that you accessed the accounts lawfully.'

'We did.'

'And you have an entire *list* of users who contacted both of these poor women before they died?'

Ellie interrupted. 'The two poor women had names, Mr. Stern: Caroline Hunter and Amy Davis. And, no, we don't have a list of men who contacted both of them, but we do have a list of men who contacted *either* of them. And as you know, a single person can use multiple user names. In fact, Caroline Hunter was using your service to do precisely that. We need the names so we can look for overlap between the lists, among other things.'

'Among other things? You mean things like prying into the backgrounds of our users to see who might seem murderous?'

Ellie gave him her best sardonic smile. 'We'll cross-reference it with registered sex offenders, mental patients, gun records. Sounds like you know police work after all.'

68

'Let me see if I can save the two of you some time. From what I gather, you have two murder victims who were both FirstDate customers, and so you assume there must be a connection. That's a logical conclusion only if you assume that the use of my service is unusual. Isn't that how these things work? You discover two victims use the same tiny dry cleaner, and you track down that lead?'

Neither detective spoke, but Stern caught the glance between them.

'Okay, so here's where the logic falls apart. FirstDate's no longer the corner dry cleaner. We have tens of thousands of customers in the New York metropolitan area alone.' Stern was in full-blown sales-speak now. 'People are busy. Dating at work's a no-no. A service like ours has become as common as joining a gym. What you see as a coincidence between two women is yet another indication of just how common First-Date has become in the lives of city singles. It's no more coincidental than if both of these women read the *New Yorker* or bought groceries at D'Agostino's.'

Ellie gave McIlroy a look that said, *Get a load of this guy.*

'We have more than coincidence,' McIlroy argued. 'The killer left us a message.'

The bluntness of the assertion caught Stern off guard. 'I certainly wish we could have started the conversation there. The person who killed these women contacted you?'

McIlroy clarified the nature of the so-called message: the e-mail found in Amy Davis's coat pocket, printed from somewhere other than her apartment. As Ellie heard the explanation through a stranger's ears, she realized how tenuous their theory was.

So did Stern, crossing his arms. 'I'm sorry, officers — '

'Detectives,' Ellie clarified.

'Of course. *Detectives.* I'm sorry, but I'm afraid I really can't help you.'

'Can't? Or won't?'

'Both. With all frankness, it sounds like you're grasping at straws. And, under those circumstances, I can't just let you comb through our records at will. Now, if you come up with individual names, and can offer me some good reason why you need the information, maybe we'd be in a different boat — '

'*Maybe?*' Ellie asked. 'I don't think you understand how this works. We've got a city of eight million people, and we've winnowed our attention down to these few. And we've given you a reason — '

'But not a reason for looking into the lives of every single person on that list. Even if I treat your theory generously, there is *at most* one person on that list who deserves your attention. The rest deserve privacy, which is one of the most important assets FirstDate provides. If our customers can't trust us, we won't have many clients. And our service only works if we have a vast and diverse clientele.'

'Trust? You want to talk about trust?' Ellie pulled two crime scene photos from a manila envelope. 'Caroline Hunter and Amy Davis

70

chose to trust. They took a leap of faith. They put themselves out in front of a world of strangers because your company lures people in with the potential of companionship. Now they're dead, and you're saying you won't help us. You won't help *them*.'

'I'd like to help, but I was hoping you'd understand my dilemma. I'm sorry that you don't.'

'You're sorry, all right.' Ellie muttered the comment under her breath as she turned to leave. McIlroy followed, but Stern stopped them.

'Oh, and detectives. I hope you realize the prudence of keeping this *theory* you're working on quiet. Without more, you might want to be reluctant to send a good percentage of the city's dating population into chaos.'

'You mean you don't want any media coverage sending your company's profits down the tubes.'

Stern, still in diplomat mode, smiled again. 'If you're able to confirm this theory, or find out that one man knew both of these women, please call my lawyers and I'll be happy to help. Until that happens, if I hear anything further on the subject, I think the phone call to the lawyers will be my own.'

On the way to the reception area, Flann suddenly turned on his heel, leaving Ellie in the hallway outside the closed door. He returned a few minutes later.

'You went back in to apologize for my behavior?'

'Sorry. Just trying to smooth the waves, in case we need him later.'

'Don't apologize, Flann. It's exactly what you should have done. Did you lay it on thick and juicy? Call me the B-word? Tell him you can't believe you're stuck working with some quota queen dyke?'

'You're having way too much fun with this,' Flann said, smiling.

On their way to the elevators, the redheaded receptionist asked the detectives if they had gotten the information they needed. Unlike her boss, she sounded concerned.

'Yeah. We found out that Mr. Stern doesn't care that two of the women using his site were murdered,' Ellie said, wondering if she was relishing the bad cop casting a little too much.

The woman looked disappointed, even saddened. Before Ellie walked out the door, she took another look at the receptionist's nameplate. Christine Conboy. The name of one person at FirstDate who might give a rat's ass.

# 8

The Supreme Court building at 60 Centre Street
had seen its fair share of notorious trials
— Lenny Bruce, Son of Sam, a motley crew of
rap stars, mafiosos, and Wall Street crooks to
mark the passing of eras in New York City. In a
small courtroom at the back of the second floor
that afternoon, the show was considerably more
modest — the trial of a bouncer accused of
selling Ecstacy out of a Chelsea nightclub.

Ellie and McIlroy sat two rows behind the
prosecution's counsel table and listened patiently
while the testifying police officer walked through
the chain of custody of the drugs that were
seized from the club's back office. When the
court recessed for a break, the prosecutor leaned
across the railing behind him to confer with the
detectives.

'Who's the new partner?' he asked. His Asian
face was round, almost cherubic, and he smiled
at Ellie. It was a warm, friendly smile, and she
returned it with a firm handshake.

'Ellie Hatcher, and I'm not a full partner. Just
on temporary assignment.'

'Jeffrey P. Yong. And I'm not a full prosecutor.
I just play one on TV.'

'A word to the wise. Never listen to a word
Jeffrey P. Yong says. The man's a born liar. A
thief, too — has about three grand of my
hard-earned salary.'

'That's Flann's way of saying I'm a better poker player than he is, which isn't saying much.'

'You've got a regular poker game?'

'Does Howard Stern enjoy a lap dance?'

Yong, apparently accustomed to Flann's rhetorical questions, didn't acknowledge the remark. 'More like a poker game for the irregular, but, yeah, something like that.'

'What's up with all the chitchat?' Flann asked. 'Jeff usually gets business out of the way before starting in with his bad jokes.'

'If I have such a tell, why do you keep losing your money to me?'

'Why are you avoiding the subject of our court order?'

The frustration in Yong's exhale was obvious. 'I found a note on my chair at lunch.'

Ellie knew to leave the talking to Flann.

'That doesn't sound good.'

'Nope. Not good. Did you see the people at FirstDate this morning?'

'As you asked us.'

'You get anywhere?'

'To the magical land of the pissing match. He told us to pound sand and keep our mouths shut. We made clear there was more to come. So what do you need from us for the subpoena?'

'Tell me again how you think FirstDate can help you?' The look on Yong's face read *problem*.

Flann walked Yong through the victims' shared connection to FirstDate and the e-mails he found in Davis's purse. 'We looked in their FirstDate accounts already. Lots of men, lots of messages. We need to know who those men are.'

'Any common link between the two of them? One man who was e-mailing them both?'

'Not that we know of. But if our guy's smart, he's signing up under different user names to hide his trail. That's why we need to see what's lying behind the user names.'

'Except that the printout of the message would suggest that he wants you on his trail.'

'Why do I feel like I'm getting cross-examined?'

'Because I know what FirstDate's attorneys are going to argue when their business is ruined and they sue everyone involved with this subpoena. Please tell me that you have something else. What did the department's computer wizards say?'

'That I should get in the back of the line. Besides, what do you expect them to tell us? That the Internet's a wonderful thing but with potential dangers? That bad people can use it to commit all sorts of nefarious deeds that we're not sophisticated enough to track?' Flann's tone was growing increasingly exasperated. 'You didn't sound concerned about any of this yesterday. You said to dot the i's and cross the t's, then come down here for our subpoena.'

Yong sighed and placed one hand on top of his shiny black hair. 'That was before the note on my chair.'

'I was wondering when you'd get back to that.'

'The note was from my unit supervisor, and the message apparently came down from above — I can't authorize a subpoena until you have a suspect.'

Flann threw him a skeptical look. 'You're

kidding me, right? Did you miss the part where I explained that the reason we need a subpoena is to help us identify a suspect?'

Yong shook his head. The smile was gone now. 'I know. It's bullshit. It sucks. It ain't right. But having me as your poker partner's not doing you any good on this one. I'm just a cog in the machine — a tiny, powerless cog who knows what a note left on my chair during trial means. I'm sorry, man. If I'd had time, I would have called to save you the trip.'

'How would that kind of message hit your supervisor so fast?'

'I don't know, but you've pissed off someone with some serious suck.'

'Your office has taken off bigger fish than the president of some fledgling Internet company.'

Yong looked just as stymied as McIlroy. 'I thought the same thing. I did a quick Google search to see if Stern was a real player, but I turned up five other guys named Mark Stern before I hit anything on him. I only had so much time to snoop — given this.' He gestured to the courtroom. 'If it's any consolation, when my trial's out, I can sniff around and see where the strings were pulled in my office.'

'And then what?'

'And then you'll know.'

'We need those names. We need to know who contacted our vics before they died. That's what we need.'

'Then you need to find someone above you to go to someone above me, or you need to find another way to get a suspect.'

'And what if I'm convinced that the only way to get a suspect is to know what FirstDate knows?'

'I guess you'd have to find another way to get that information. Maybe an insider to do it for you, without the government's hands on it. But I'm not the one who said that.'

The judge reclaimed his seat at the bench, and Flann lowered his voice to a whisper.

'What happens if I call a contact in the press? Let the story leak — the possible connection between the two women, and a company that won't help the city's finest catch a killer.'

'I doubt any reporter would run it with what you've got — even for you. And if they did, Mark Stern would probably sue the paper, along with the police department and the two of you. I'd strongly recommend against it,' Yong dead-panned. The judge cleared his throat and threw them an impatient look. 'Sorry, guys. Gotta go.'

Following Flann out of the courtroom, Ellie was so dejected at leaving without a subpoena that she barely noticed the man sitting in the back row. She assumed he was there for Yong's case — a friend or relative of the defendant.

She was wrong.

Charlie Dixon was there to make sure of two things. First, that Jeffrey Yong had gotten the message. And second, that the message made its way to the city detectives asking questions about FirstDate. Dixon couldn't make out the entire conversation, but he noticed that the detectives left the courtroom empty-handed. He was pleased, at least for the moment.

# 9

They were greeted at the precinct by a civilian aide, probably just out of high school, holding a plastic cup of soda the size of a bucket.

'There's a couple people waiting here to see Detective McIlroy. I think they're your victim's parents. Something about a cat?' He gestured to an attractive couple sitting quietly on a bench down the hall.

Hampton Davis was tall and tan, with every black hair combed neatly in place. His wife, Evelyn, was petite with a light brown, chin-length bob. They both wore suits — his navy, hers powder blue.

McIlroy handled the introductions. 'Mr. and Mrs. Davis, I'm Flann McIlroy. We spoke on the phone this weekend. This is Detective Hatcher. She's also working on your daughter's case.'

McIlroy led Ellie and the couple to an interview room adjacent to the homicide bureau. The four of them waited in awkward silence to see who would speak first. When Flann finally offered his condolences, Ellie could tell that although he'd no doubt spoken some variant of the same words many times before, he was still uncomfortable with them. He appeared more at ease once he began laying out his theory that Amy's murder may have been related to her use of an Internet dating site.

'There must be some mistake,' Hampton said.

'Our daughter would never use a service like that. She was extremely cautious with men she didn't know.'

'Amy *was* being cautious,' Ellie vouched. 'The service she used is anonymous, and she was very careful not to give out her last name or address.'

Hampton shook his head. 'If you found her listed with one of those companies, then someone else put her there. I've read stories about that. Some crazy person gets obsessed and wreaks havoc on a person's life by posting all kinds of nonsense on the Internet.'

'Amy's had problems like that before,' Evelyn interrupted. A northeasterner would have described the woman's accent as southern, but having been raised in Kansas, Ellie knew that not all southern accents were identical. This woman's cadence was new to Ellie — southern, but not in a way she'd heard before, almost with a touch of Brooklyn thrown in like a hint of cayenne pepper.

'Back in high school, a boy in town wouldn't leave her alone. It went on for months. Don't get me wrong. Amy brought a little of it on herself. I guess this boy changed some grades for her. She was under a lot of pressure. She really wanted to go out of state for college, somewhere nice. Somewhere away from home.'

Hampton placed a hand gently on her forearm. 'Evelyn, the detectives don't need to hear this right now.'

Evelyn gave her husband a firm look. 'What I'm telling the detectives is that Amy learned an early lesson. This boy I'm talking about kept calling her and writing her letters, even after she left for Colby. Then when she came home for Christmas break, he showed up at the mall where she was shopping. You can call her friend Suzanne Mouton to verify. She'll tell you. The whole experience was just awful.'

Ellie realized that Evelyn's story was going nowhere, but took down the number anyway because she understood why this was important to Amy's mother. Evelyn wanted to talk about her daughter in a personal way. She wanted to tell the detectives about a time when she knew what her daughter's fears were, when she was familiar even with the bad things her daughter did as a consequence. To feel close again, Evelyn had to go back to Amy's high school years, when Amy had apparently permitted a troubled boy to alter her transcript so she could escape the bayou.

When his wife finished, Hampton Davis cleared his throat. 'You'll have to forgive us if we seem to dwell on the past,' he said, looking at Evelyn. 'But the experience my wife's talking about was a horrible one. I ultimately had to go to court for a restraining order. The boy was actually arrested after the incident at the mall, and then — well, let's just say things got worse from there. Amy blamed herself for years.'

'Our point,' Evelyn insisted, 'is that our daughter would not have agreed to go on dates with strangers.'

'I'm very sorry,' McIlroy said, 'but we've confirmed that Amy did sign herself up for an account with this service. In fact, she had a date that very night with a man she'd met online.'

'Well, then, that's the man you should be looking at,' Hampton insisted.

'That was one of the first things we did,' McIlroy said patiently. 'We were able to confirm his alibi, but we're continuing to do everything we can — '

'No,' Hampton said, slapping the table. 'You'll have to check him out again. I refuse to believe that Amy would agree to meet men this way.'

Ellie tried to help by explaining how common it was for women Amy's age to use services like FirstDate, but her efforts only served to upset the couple further.

Hampton cut off the conversation abruptly. 'Unless you require anything else of us, Detectives, we'll thank you for your time and let you get back to Amy's case.'

Ellie and McIlroy walked the Davises out, pausing briefly at the men's locker room, from which McIlroy retrieved the makeshift carrier he had fashioned for Chowhound. As Ellie watched Hampton take the awkward cardboard box from McIlroy, she couldn't help but feel that these people were owed something more.

She heard the words come out of her mouth before she'd decided to speak them. 'We're going to find him.'

★   ★   ★

Johnny's Bar on Greenwich Avenue is roughly the size of a typical suburban closet — the walk-in kind with enough room to accommodate

81

the typical suburban wardrobe. In Greenwich Village, however, people are not typical, and Johnny's Bar has just the right dimensions for a kick-ass watering hole.

Ellie wasn't sure how she even knew the bar's name. The sign out front read Bar. She arrived forty minutes after the time she told Jess to expect her. By her brother's standards, that wasn't the same as being forty minutes late. It meant Ellie would have to sit alone for another fifteen. But she'd learned over the years that she needed to be the one to arrive first. Jess couldn't be relied upon to wait. Jess could not be relied upon at all.

The woman behind the bar was called Josie. Josie had long curly black hair, pulled into a giant floppy knot at the top of her head. She wore a black tank top and jeans, accessorized with tattoos and piercings. She managed to look comfortable perched on top of the counter, her feet resting on the bar. She argued with a regular about whether it was finally time for Steinbrenner to go. Johnny's was the kind of place where people talked baseball even with snow on the ground.

It was also the kind of place where a bartender like Josie remembered an occasional customer like Ellie — as well as her drink.

'Johnny Walker, right?'

'Black. On the rocks.'

Josie scooted off the counter and reached for a bottle on the top shelf. 'We don't get too many people in here for the good stuff. Hey Frank, Hatcher here is a full-blown detective on the NYPD.'

'Prettiest cop I ever saw,' Frank grumbled, turning his attention to the television. A football game of some kind was playing.

'Your brother's late again?' Josie was pouring.

'No, I'm early.' Josie turned back to the game, leaving Ellie alone with her thoughts after a long two days.

Ellie let the whiskey warm her chest and stomach, untangling the knots she'd felt since Evelyn and Hampton Davis arrived at the precinct. They were good people, but, like a lot of parents, they knew nothing about their adult child. They still saw her as a precocious little girl, an ingenue just out of college — not as a woman who was already lying about her age on an Internet dating site. They were naive enough to believe their daughter would be safe forever. They thought nothing evil could ever get to her — all because she learned a few lessons in caution from a bad ex-boyfriend after high school.

What the parents from Louisiana didn't realize is that most women have a similar story somewhere in their past — a boyfriend who can't let go, a classmate who sits too close, a coworker who insists despite all reason that he's more than just a friend. Bumping into a creep early in life back in Louisiana simply made Amy Davis a little smarter, a little sooner. It didn't make her safe. Nothing does.

But Ellie could identify with the Davises' grief. Since she was fourteen years old, she had known how hard it could be to accept the death of a family member at the hands of a monster.

For more than fifteen years, she lived with the belief that her father had been murdered, without possessing even an image of the face of the man she hated, let alone a suitable punishment. She had her theories — a white guy, probably in his early twenties for his first kill in 1978. Rigid. Ordered. Bossy, compensating for insecurities. A wannabe cop. One of her reasons for leaving Kansas was her inability to pass a man of a certain age and demeanor without wondering, *Is that the man who shot my father?* To lose a child that way — she could not begin to imagine.

McIlroy had handled the parents the way a homicide detective should. He was compassionate but professional. He gave them the cat they had come for and made sure they knew the department was giving the case its highest attention. But Ellie had crossed a line when she spoke the words you were never supposed to utter: *We're going to find him.* McIlroy wasn't happy about it. He made that much clear after the Davises left.

But Ellie had no regrets, despite the assurances she handed to McIlroy. The Davises might not have believed it, and perhaps neither did McIlroy. Ellie, however, was sure of it. When she made that promise to Amy Davis's parents, she made a promise to herself.

Ellie had just ordered a second Johnny Walker when Jess walked in. She and her brother had little in common. He was brunette, tall, and wiry — hard and dark against her soft and light. They often joked that the Wichita hospital had

84

switched at least one of them at birth.

'Knocking them back again, baby sis?'

'You know me. I've got a problem with the booze.'

They both knew she didn't. Jess might, but they rarely mentioned it. As much as they joked about the hospital switch, the one thing Jess and Ellie had in common was that they were clearly their parents' children. Ellie looked like her mom and acted like her dad. The opposite was true of Jess, and Mom's behavioral genes did not mix well with alcohol.

'You picking up the tab?'

'For a little while at least.' Ellie glanced at her watch.

'God bless the NYPD.' Jess asked Josie for a shot of bourbon with a bourbon chaser and took a seat next to Ellie.

'How's life as a crime fighter?'

Ellie smiled at her brother. He was so predictable.

'What's going on, Jess?'

'Nothing. I can't get with my sister every once in a while for a drink and some chat?'

In addition to being predictable, Jess was also frustrating.

'We'll chat after you tell me what's up.'

'You still got that extra key?'

Ellie sighed heavily and shook her head. 'What happened to your apartment?'

She used the second-person possessive pronoun loosely. Other than a couple of guitars, a pair of work boots, and a gym bag of clothes, very little in this world belonged to Jess Hatcher.

The last she heard, though, Jess had a place to crash in Williamsburg.

'My buddy needed to find a roommate who actually paid some rent.'

'Funny how that works. And the job?' Against her better judgment, Ellie had helped Jess with yet another employment placement, this time as a short-order cook at a diner in the Garment District, not too far from the Midtown South precinct, where Ellie once worked a beat. The seventy-year-old Swede who ran the place always had a weakness for Ellie. Apparently not enough to hang on to the likes of Jess.

'The old man had a few too many morning shifts for me. It's hard to fry up the bacon at six when you're frying up a little rock and roll till four.' He threw in a little air guitar for comedic flair.

'It wouldn't be that hard on you if you did your gig, went to work, then slept later.' Ellie fished the spare key from her purse. She always carried it when Jess asked to meet her.

'Chat time now?' Jess tucked the key in the front pocket of his blue jeans. He gave Ellie the same boyish smile she had been looking up to as long as she could remember. It was the grin of a bashful chipmunk, so out of place on Jess's lined, unshaven face.

'I've got a murder case.'

The shy grin faded. 'I thought you were 'quite happy solving your everyday garden variety felonies.''

It was the line she gave Jess and her mother whenever they worried that she didn't have the psychological makeup to stick it out as a cop. For completely different reasons, it was also the line she used to give Bill, her ex-boyfriend, to settle his completely separate concerns. Bill wondered how long she was going to work her job. Her family wondered how long it would take before Ellie's job started working her.

'I was happy. I *am* happy. But working a homicide — this is different. I stood yesterday in a woman's apartment, reading her mail, smelling her clothing, touching the contents of her medicine cabinet, all the while knowing that someone out there killed her. And then her parents came to the precinct to pick up their daughter's cat.'

'You met her parents?'

Ellie ignored the question. 'Another woman died exactly one year earlier. There are some commonalities.'

'You're working a *serial case*? Ever dawn on you that might not be the best idea?'

'I'll be fine. This is important, Jess. Some guy is out there right now, picking his next victim.'

'That doesn't mean you have to be the one to stop him. You really feel like going down that road?'

Ellie knew what road he was talking about. 'I won't be like that. You can be a good cop without cutting yourself off from every other part of life.'

'And exactly what else do you have going in your life right now, El? You dumped Bill a year ago and have no prospects in sight.'

'Gee, thanks.'

'You know what I mean.' Jess gave her two

months of healing time after she moved out of Bill's apartment but had since been trying to throw Ellie back into the dating world. They both knew the efforts were ridiculous, since most of Jess's friends had the kinds of backgrounds that could land her in the middle of an I.A. investigation. And never mind that Jess couldn't commit to anyone other than his fellow band members.

'Besides, what happens if you actually find the guy? What happens when a man who kills women for sport gets an eyeful of you? Have you thought about that?'

She hadn't, but she also did not want to. She had imagined her father's death too many times. She had pictured him, forced at gunpoint behind the wheel of his car for his own staged suicide. Had he known he was about to die? Had he thought of his family in those last seconds? She did not want to imagine herself like that — outmatched, resigned, absolutely finished.

She sipped her drink in silence, and Jess stopped fighting her. Since Ellie had followed her brother up to New York nearly ten years ago, they had learned to simply accept each other.

'So how's Mom?' Jess finally asked.

'Wondering what you're up to, as always.'

'And the case against the city?'

'Cluster fuck, as usual. The attorney's not getting anywhere, and Summer and the WPD are both still saying there were only the eight victims.'

'The Wichita Police are the same bozos who insisted he stopped at six kills all those years ago.

Now they say it's eight because he confessed to two more. They never would have known about those if that arrogant prick hadn't given them all the information himself. What makes them so sure he isn't still playing games with them? I'm sure he gets off knowing that he's got one more kill in his back pocket they don't know about. A cop, to boot.'

'You're preaching to the choir, Jess. I'm just telling you what I know.'

After the Wichita police finally arrested William Summer, the man formerly known only as the College Hill Strangler, Ellie had immediately retained yet another attorney to represent her mother in yet another claim against the city for her father's pension. For a year and a half, the attorney had been fighting the city for access to the evidence collected against Summer. He had also been fighting the state for access to Summer himself. But until they found proof tying Summer to her father's death, Jerry Hatcher remained a suicide, and the contrary suspicions carried by his family for the past decade and a half remained exactly that. Ellie hated the word *closure*, but she had to hope that an answer about her father's death might snap her mother out of her limbo of grief.

'I'm heading home. Want to come back with me to call Mom?'

'There's an open mic night at The Charleston in Williamsburg.'

'And a ten-minute phone call to Mom will keep you from playing?'

'No, it'll put me in a serious funk and screw

up the rest of my night. I'll pass.'

Part of Ellie wanted to do the same. But while Jess did what he wanted, Ellie did what she thought she was supposed to do. It had always been that way in the Hatcher family. Ellie swallowed down the rest of her drink, then left enough money with Josie to cover a few more rounds of her brother's bourbon.

# 10

Jess had said her life was empty except for her job. The accusation was unfair. Her job was part of her life. It would be like saying Jess's life was empty without his music, or that a mother's life was empty without her children. Remove the things that matter, and any life looks empty.

Jess of all people knew how important her work was. It was precisely because the job was part of her identity that Ellie no longer lived with Bill. Despite what Jess thought, Bill wasn't a bad guy. She'd met him, ironically enough, at one of Jess's gigs in the West Village. Bill was immediately smitten and, after five months, persuaded Ellie to leave her rented room behind and move in with him. He was a hard worker, an investment banker who liked to enjoy the little time off that he had. And what he enjoyed the most — flattering enough — was having Ellie at his side, giving him her full attention. Bill assumed she'd happily leave the job once he offered to take care of her. He assumed that was what every woman wanted. He was envious, in fact, that women enjoyed that as a lifestyle option.

But, despite his every assurance that she didn't need to work, Ellie insisted that she did. After a few months of wrangling, she realized Bill was spending more than a few nights after work having cocktails with a woman in his marketing department. Knowing Bill, Ellie was sure it wasn't a physical affair. But she could see the end coming, so she made way for Bill to have the kind of future he wanted — one that didn't involve the NYPD. She told him she was moving out, and he didn't try hard to stop her. That's what convinced her it was never the real thing. It had been far too easy, for both of them, to leave.

In a switch of roles, Jess was the one who helped Ellie get settled after the breakup. He had an old girlfriend who was grateful for a watch-cop on her Lower East Side sofa for two weeks, and, before Ellie knew it, Jess had found her this sublet of a friend of a friend of a friend. Ellie suspected the original tenant was lying on a beach somewhere in Fiji, but as long as she had a place of her own, she wasn't going to shed a tear for her landlord. It was a big step down from Bill's Upper East Side junior four, but it was all hers, and she could afford it. Barely. It had taken several months and a few coats of paint, but the one-bedroom illegal sublet in Murray Hill finally felt like home.

She nestled herself onto her couch in front of the television, then muted the set and reached for the telephone, ready to get the nightly call to her mother out of the way.

'Hello?'

'Hey Mom. Sorry I'm a little late. I just wanted to say good night.'

'Were you working?' Roberta sounded happy, but artificially so, assisted no doubt by a little vodka. Ellie and Jess called it their mother's nighttime voice. 'Did you make a case on those

92

forged theater tickets?'

'We're still working on it. I just had some paperwork to take care of.'

'Your father used to always complain about the paperwork. Remember how he used to say if he had a donut for every piece of paper he generated in his career, he could feed every cop in America?'

'Did you hear anything else from the lawyer?' Ellie asked, hoping to cut off her mother's muddled trip down memory lane.

'The city told him that Summer kept mementos from all the murders. That's how they linked him to the cases they pinned on him. He also had photographs.'

'Did he tell them we already knew that?'

From the beginning, the College Hill Strangler had a fondness for sharing images of his crime scenes. In one letter mailed to the *Wichita Eagle* in 1981, he included a sketch of one of the murder scenes — so graphic and accurate that police speculated it was drawn from a photograph. After another the next year, he sent the police an actual photograph along with an audiotape of the victim struggling to breathe. For years, that package was the College Hill Strangler's last known communication.

Then precisely twenty years later, a reporter at the city newspaper received an envelope containing a necklace and a Polaroid picture. The necklace was one police had been looking for since 1978 — stolen from the single mother who was the College Hill Strangler's first victim. The picture was of the corpse of another woman, the victim of a still-unsolved murder in 1997. With hopes of revival, EMT's had rushed her immediately from the bedroom where she was found strangled to the hospital where she died. Only her killer could have a photo of her body.

The College Hill Strangler was back. The anonymous mailing was his way of announcing that to the police. While the city was comforted by false theories of his death or incapacitation, he still lived among them, killing. Over the next eleven months, he would dole out six more envelopes of surprises — letters, drawings, even poems. His desire to gloat finally led to his own capture when an alert teenager jotted down the license plate number of a car peeling rubber as it sped away from the neighborhood mail drop.

'They're trotting out the same old story,' Roberta said. 'He was meticulous about his mementos and his diaries. They found evidence linking him to the eight named victims, and that's all.'

'That's bullshit,' Ellie said, quickly apologizing to her mother for the language. It would be just like Summer to gloat to the police about all his other killings, except for the one cop who almost caught him.

'Maybe you could help if you came down here,' Roberta offered. 'I have a hard enough time on my own without all of this going on.'

'Mom, I told you I'd come down once there was a reason to. I'll take as much time off as I have to. If we get access to the evidence, I'll go through it myself, piece by piece. Or if they'd just let me talk to him — '

94

'You know I don't like that idea.'

Ellie recognized that she fell directly in the center of William Summer's preference zone. Right age. Clean-cut. Warm personality. She was convinced that if she had him in the box, he would be unable to resist the temptation to torture her the only way he could — mentally. He would try to torture her by describing what he had done to her father.

'Let's not fight about this, Mom. I promise you: When the time comes, I'll fly to Wichita, and we'll figure out where to go from there — together.'

There was a brief silence on the line, then Roberta asked about Jess. 'I haven't heard from him lately.'

'He's great. He dropped by here earlier. He wanted to talk to you, but his band had a big gig tonight.'

'Good for them. I keep telling the folks around here about Dog Park, but so far no one's heard of them. You know how it takes forever for anything big to make it to Kansas.'

Ellie told her mother she loved her before she said good night. She made a point of telling her mother she missed her. Roberta said she loved and missed Ellie too, then hung up sounding as lonely and helpless as she always did at the end of their calls.

★  ★  ★

The whiskey was still working on Ellie's brain an hour later, along with images of her mother, Amy

95

Davis's damaged neck, and the empty look in her parents' eyes as Flann helplessly handed them their daughter's cat. Her mind's eye leaped back to a memory of her father, sitting alone at the garage sale desk in the basement, surrounded by crime photos, rereading old police reports he had memorized eight times over. Hanging at the center of his gruesome montage was the smiling face of an impish-looking blond woman named Janice Beale.

Detective Jerry Hatcher had been most shaken by that one. By the time Beale was killed, two weeks before Christmas, 1984, the College Hill Strangler had already killed five people. Five people. Three days. Six years. Ellie's father could never shake the guilt that perhaps Beale's death could have been prevented. If they had put the pieces together, if they had warned the public, maybe she would have been spared. That was the thought Ellie's father could never elude.

Like Amy Davis, Janice Beale was single, young, lived alone — a death by strangling. Ellie shook the comparison from her head. She was not going to let this happen. She was not in her father's shoes. Amy Davis had been dead for less than a week. This was not a cold case. If she and Flann worked hard enough, it never would be.

With sleep futile, she climbed out of her bed and reread all of the e-mails Amy had exchanged on FirstDate. She picked the three men who were most interesting. Nothing dangerous. Nothing threatening. Just a hunch about these three. Then she signed up for FirstDate, calling herself 'DB990.' DB for Date Bait, followed by her badge number. She wrote a profile along the lines of others on the site and uploaded a dark, grainy photograph that Jess had snapped of her with his cell phone one night at the Blue Note. She sent 'flirts' to the three men she had selected. Clicking on another user's flirt command didn't require her to say anything. It just meant she was interested. And she was.

When she was finished online, she called the precinct and asked a clerk in the records department to run Christine Conboy, the redheaded receptionist at FirstDate. Conboy had a few old driving offenses on Long Island and a current phone number in Queens. Ellie checked the clock and saw it was past eleven, but she dialed the number anyway. A friendly voice said hello.

'Christine? This is Detective Ellie Hatcher. We met this morning?'

'Um, yeah?'

'I was hoping you could help me with something. I have a — '

'I'm not supposed to talk to you. The company says that any communications from law enforcement are supposed to go to the CEO.'

'The company says? You mean Mark Stern announced this today after we left?' Ellie took the silence on the other end of the line as confirmation. 'Just hear me out, okay? Your boss will never know.'

'Can I trust you on that?'

'Did I seem to be buddies with Mr. Stern?'

That got a laugh in response. 'I have to say, he didn't seem to be real fond of you.'

'Well, don't tell him, but the feeling's mutual.

You, on the other hand, seemed to actually care that we're trying to catch someone who killed two women.'

'Of course I *care*. I just have no idea how I can possibly help you.'

'I have a list of profile names — people who were in touch with our two victims. I just need to know who they are. If we had that, we could start trying to put some pieces together.'

'I'm the receptionist. I don't know how to get that information. Trust me, I wish I could. *I'm not just an employee, I'm a customer.*' Ellie got the reference to the old hair club ads, but the attempt at humor was awkward. 'Really. We don't have access to personal information.'

'But someone must. It's stored in your database somewhere. It just needs to be turned over.'

There was a long pause. 'I can't help. I'm sorry.'

'Can I at least talk to you in person?' Saying no is always harder in person.

'If Stern sees me talking to you, I'll lose my job. He's a total control freak.'

'He won't see us. I can come to your house. I can meet you on your break. Your lunch hour?'

'One o'clock. There's a noodle place on Rector and Broadway. Much too lowbrow for the boss.'

Ellie took down the intersection and thanked Christine profusely. Then she climbed back into bed and shut her eyes. She left the bedroom door open so she could hear Jess come home. Once he did, she fell into a deep slumber.

# 11

In the morning, Ellie found Jess lounging on the sofa, her laptop open on his chest.

'You seem bright-eyed and bushy-tailed this morning,' she said. 'One might even say you appear fully employable, and it's only eight a.m.'

'Sorry to disappoint you, but I'm still up from last night. I figured I'd take advantage of your computer before catching some z's.' He eyed her with obvious amusement, apparently waiting for some response.

'What's wrong with you?'

'Nothing. I'm just glad to see you getting out into the world, El.'

'What's that supposed to mean?'

'*Welcome to FirstDate?* Sorry, but I noticed the subject line in your in-box.'

'Get out of my e-mail!'

'Um, *hello*? Who's got their computer set up to open e-mail automatically when you log in? I couldn't help it. Besides, I think it's cool. It's about time you started getting laid again. You've got to be the only attractive woman in Manhattan who's not getting her freak on.'

'I'm sure having you on my couch will be very conducive to that. And, I hate to break it to you, but my participation on FirstDate is part of that case I mentioned.' She told him about Flann McIlroy and his theory about FirstDate. She could sense Jess wanted to say something about the wisdom of her assignment, but he kept his thoughts to himself.

'Well, I hope he's kissing luck's butt for handing him the only cop in New York who works cases off the clock. The last cop I'd want on my ass is Ellie Mae Hatcher.'

'I *am* the cop on your ass.' When Ellie first joined the department, she and Jess struck a deal meant to balance the obvious differences, and potential conflicts, in their lifestyles. Ellie made sure Jess knew the difference between keeping bad company and becoming a criminal accomplice. Jess made sure he never crossed that line. Tolerating his intermittent presence on her sofa was one way Ellie helped him to keep his end of the deal.

'Maybe there'll be an added benefit to this FirstDate research. Maybe you'll actually find someone decent while you're at it.'

'I told you. It's only for the case.'

'Um, maybe not anymore. I sort of flirted with a few guys who looked good for you.'

'You did what?'

'The e-mail from FirstDate had all your account info, and I got curious. The next thing I knew, I was sending flirts to people. I finally had to stop because it was feeling a little gay. But, trust me, I picked way better guys than the ones you flirted with.'

'Jess. I picked those men because they seemed like people who might be homicidal maniacs, not because I thought they were dreamy.'

'Sorry. My bad.'

When Jess continued to insist that there might be a personal upside to Ellie's research, she finally fessed up that her curiosity was piqued. She showed him the profile for Chef4U, the thirty-eight-year-old Upper East Sider she first noticed in Caroline Hunter's FirstDate account. He had sandy blond, wavy hair and smiling eyes.

Jess took one quick look. 'What a cornballer.' He read dramatically from the screen: '*Brainy women are sexy. It's what's on the inside that counts.*'

'What's wrong with that?'

'Because if he has to say it out loud, he doesn't mean it. Trust me. I'm a guy, I know how we operate. It's just a line to lure in women who don't think they're pretty enough to do better than him. He cooks Julia Child recipes? In Manhattan? I bet you fifty bucks he doesn't even own a frying pan.'

'As if you've got fifty bucks.'

Still, Ellie reread the profile and saw it in an entirely different light. In every other part of her life, she trusted her instincts. She never hesitated about moving to New York. She never second-guessed her decision to bypass her school plans to study criminal justice at John Jay. On the job, she read suspects, witnesses, and supposed victims better than officers with decades more experience.

But when it came to men, Ellie was as naive as she'd been in the ninth grade when she accepted her first car date with the high school quarterback Gil Morton. He opened the passenger door of his pickup and asked her what she felt like doing. *Whatever.* He suggested ordering pizza and renting *Lethal Weapon.* Fifteen minutes later, she found herself on his sofa, with no pizza and no movie, beneath one hundred and eighty pounds of sloppy kisses and groping. She walked to Quik-Trip and called Jess for a ride before things passed the tipping point, but she had never quite absorbed the lesson.

Ellie was a woman who expected men to value the same things she did. She expected men to want not just a lover but a friend, a challenge, and an equal. The problem, Jess always told her, wasn't in her expectations. Plenty of men out there met them. The problem was that Ellie, despite all her intuitive strengths, had absolutely no ability to distinguish the poseurs from the real thing.

'Here, give me that,' Jess insisted, reaching for the laptop. 'I'll find you a worthy suitor.' Jess began clicking away, and Ellie found herself involuntarily intrigued. These men were total strangers. She could develop relationships with them without ever telling them what she did for a living. They might get to know her without the hindrance of the immediate 'female cop' stereotypes. Online, she could be a completely different person.

Jess grabbed a pen and a crumpled paper napkin from the coffee table and scribbled down the names of what he called 'the keepers,' men with good jobs, at least one creative comment in their self-descriptions, and absolutely no disqualifying bullshit. Ellie snatched the running list from him and began crossing names from it.

'What are you doing, El? Those are perfectly good prospects.'

'I'm scratching out the ones who fail my litmus tests,' Ellie replied. 'Let me ask you something, Jess. You're thirty-five years old. If you were to fill out one of these surveys, what would you put down as the age range for your ideal mate?'

'For me? Um, I guess twenty . . . -four to thirty-five.'

Ellie made a noise of disgust and swatted her brother across the shoulder. 'Even you? My own flesh and blood? You are a thirty-five-year-old man with a birthday in four months, and you're telling me that you wouldn't even *consider* going out with a woman who turned thirty-six yesterday?'

'I didn't say I wouldn't consider it. Obviously if I met a woman and I liked her, and she turned out to be a little older, I wouldn't care. But if you ask me who I picture in the abstract, then yeah, I guess I picture someone my age or younger.'

Ellie rolled her eyes. 'Well, at least you include your own age. My litmus test — the men I'm crossing off — are the ones who cap their age range below their own age. Half the men on here, no matter how old they are, say their perfect woman is somewhere between her midtwenties and exactly one year younger than he is.' She continued crossing off names, clearly disgusted. 'I mean, what is it about the midtwenties?'

Jess's eyes glazed over as he hung his tongue from his mouth in mock bliss. Ellie pretended to shoot a roundhouse kick in his direction.

'All right, Gloria Steinem. But I bet you a million bucks that the women on there are just as superficial. They're just screening for different qualities. Money, power, prestige. It's market forces, little sis.'

'On that very romantic — and totally depressing — note, I think you've convinced me that my online surfing should remain strictly professional.'

The telephone rang and Jess beat her to the handset.

'You've reached the marvelous Ellie Hatcher . . . Oh, you're just the man I'd like to talk to. I hope you know how lucky you are to be working with my sister.'

Ellie smacked him on the arm and grabbed the phone. 'Sorry, Flann. My brother got out of the butterfly net.'

'I just got a call from ballistics. They got a cold hit. The gun that killed Caroline Hunter a year ago was used to shoot another woman nine months earlier. Our guy's been at it longer than we thought. There's a third victim.'

★   ★   ★

An hour later, Charlie Dixon hung up his telephone. He was angry. He did not like bad news. Only eighteen hours earlier, the FirstDate situation appeared to be under control. NYPD's investigation had nothing to do with him. They were chasing down some stupid theory cooked up by a detective known as a wing nut. He had gotten worked up over nothing.

Now this.

He picked up his telephone again, punched in a familiar number, and asked for his boss. He tried to calm his nerves while he listened to the Muzak.

'Mayfield.'

'I'm sorry to bother you, sir, but there's been a development.'

'I heard. Snow by six.' Dixon's boss had a dry way about him, even in the face of stressful developments. That trait might explain where he sat in the hierarchy. Barry Mayfield oozed confidence, able to control any situation and the people involved in it without ever changing the serious but restrained tone of his voice.

Dixon, in contrast, honestly did not have the best personality for this job. Two years ago, during a particularly unpredictable turn of events, he ripped himself an ulcer that felt as if his intestines were marinating in Tabasco. Now Dixon was thinking about that ulcer again, convinced he was starting to feel the familiar hot inside of his gut.

'It's about FirstDate.'

'I had an inkling. Those detectives again?'

'Afraid so.'

'Did they find a way to a court order? I told you before it wasn't worth worrying about. The chances of this leading back to you — '

'It's something else.' The something was worse

than a fishing expedition at FirstDate. 'I got a call from my PD source. Flann McIlroy just requested the file on the Tatiana Chekova murder.'

'Now, that is a problem.'

# PART TWO

# DATE BAIT

# 12

Entering the eighth floor of one police plaza, Ellie was as excited as a four-year-old on Christmas morning. She was anxious to catch a first-hand look at the department's fancy new Real Time Crime Center. It might not wear a plush red suit or sport a jolly white beard, but the center was the high-tech feather in the department's crime-fighting cap, a vast computerized clearinghouse to link information gathered throughout the city's many precincts. The idea was to place a wealth of databases — parole records, prior complaints, 911 calls, tattoos and aliases, criminal histories — at the fingertips of detectives, in one centralized location.

Ellie thought the location looked just as it should, like the hub of an intergalactic star chamber. She marveled at the various maps blinking from at least twenty different flat-screen televisions hanging from a single wall.

'That's the data wall.'

Ellie turned from the screens to find a smiling woman about her own age, with shiny, straight blond hair held back from her face by a barrette.

'I'm Naomi Skura. I've got your partner over there.' She gestured down an aisle of cubicles, where Ellie saw Flann peering out at her.

'What am I looking at?'

'Those maps track every piece of action going down in the city right now, in real time. Every

109

911 call, every arrest, every call-out. If we know about it, it's there.'

It was the twenty-first-century version of the 'hot spot' policing that had made Rudy Giuliani and his crime-reducing efforts nationally famous, even before September 11. Ellie followed Naomi Skura past the data screens to a long row of cubicles, one of which held a waiting Flann McIlroy.

'Did you tell her?' Flann asked excitedly.

Naomi gave a small laugh. 'I haven't exactly had time.'

'Naomi's one of the crime analysts here. She works her tail off making sure the databases hold what they're supposed to.'

The blond woman interrupted to clarify. 'The commissioner unveiled the center before all of the databases were up-to-date. It was a good move — makes sure all of the new information going forward is entered and accessible. But we're still working on configuring all of the old databases so we can get maximum accessibility. One of the databases that isn't quite up-to-date is for tracking ballistic images.'

Ellie was vaguely familiar with the technology. 'That's where they break down information about a bullet so it's something like a fingerprint?'

Naomi nodded. 'During the manufacturing process, the metal of a gun's barrel is shaped and molded. When a bullet is subsequently fired through that barrel, the gun leaves its individual mark — a fingerprint, as you said. We used to compare bullet fragments and casings by hand, under a microscope. The idea behind ballistics tracking is to computerize the ballistic finger-print, so comparisons can be made in a matter of milliseconds.'

'That's amazing.'

'But,' Flann interjected, 'I've been told it's not a priority.'

Naomi rolled her eyes at what was obviously a familiar conversation. 'Hey, in theory we could have a federal database containing the ballistic images of every gun sold in the United States. But the gun lovers say that's too close to gun registration. We here in the socialist republic of New York don't have a problem with that, however. We just don't have the money.'

'Like I said, not a priority. The point is, despite all that, Naomi went out of her way for us. After I put Caroline Hunter's case together with Amy Davis's, I asked Naomi to run the bullet from Hunter through the database. No hits, but she told me how the database was backed up. So I put her to work looking for vics of a similar profile. If a gun was used, maybe the bullet hadn't been tracked for ballistics yet.'

'I looked at unsolved murders of white women between the ages of twenty-five and forty, killed on the street in the last three years. Your two vics were in Manhattan, educated, upper middle class. I found a couple of similar cases, but they're suspected domestics still under investiga-tion. Most of the other victims were demographically dissimilar — drug users or working girls. But since Flann was ragging about our substandard ballistics tracking' — she smiled at him — 'I went ahead and took the bullet information from those women and added them to the database.'

'And it paid off,' Flann said.

'I ran Hunter again and got a match. Her name was Tatiana Chekova. She was shot almost two years ago — with a .380 semiautomatic, just like Caroline Hunter. I haven't had it verified by human eye yet, but the computer says the two guns were one and the same.'

'And the computer's reliable?' Ellie asked.

'More so than the human eye, in fact, but the technology's new enough that we still do it the old-fashioned way for the lawyers. Want me to send it to ballistics?'

'Does John Daly love chicken wings?'

'Who?'

'See what I mean? They go right over the head.' Flann cut his hand over his head to mark the point. 'Just have ballistics call me when they're finished.'

\* \* \*

The first of the three men with whom Ellie had flirted on FirstDate called himself Mr. Right. Despite the oh-so-original name, Ellie had chosen him because his etiquette was oh-so-wrong, filled with inappropriate innuendo. When Amy said she liked independent films, Mr. Right took it upon himself to ask whether she meant 'snooty highbrow movies with subtitles or tastefully artistic home videos for personal use.' And then there was that comment about the picture she'd sent him of herself at Mardi Gras: 'Did you show off your ta-tas?'

The traffic on the FDR was heavy this time of day, so Flann used his lights until he found them some clear road. He checked the rearview mirror before switching lanes, then asked Ellie about the other two men she'd honed in on during the previous night's perusal of FirstDate profiles.

'A guy named Taylor. Quasi stalker. From what I can tell, Amy met him once for coffee, then blew him off. He e-mailed her a few times the next week, asking her what was wrong, insisting they had a real connection, wondering if she was afraid of commitment — that sort of thing. Then it looks like she blocked him from her account.'

'You can do that?'

'Yeah. There's a block function on the FirstDate Web site. It's as simple as typing in the other person's user name, and voilà, they can't e-mail you anymore. Taylor's the only user name on Amy's block list. She cut him off about a week ago, so, yeah, we're interested in him. I also sent a flirt to a guy who calls himself Enoch.'

'*Eunuch?* He's advertising a lack of balls?'

'No,' she said, laughing. '*Enoch.* Could be the name of his first dog for all I know. At first, he didn't stand out. His online profile's about as bland as you can get — one cliché after another.'

'Yeah? And what's considered cliché in the online world?'

'Oh, come on. We both read a hundred of those trite profiles yesterday. *Looking for a partner in crime. Tired of the bar scene. I want a girl who can go from pearls to blue jeans. No drama queens.* Gag me. I mean, you've got two paragraphs to say something interesting about yourself and what you're looking for in life, and this is what they come up with?'

'And what should they say?'

'Something original. Something interesting. My god, even just something that doesn't sound cribbed from a high school yearbook might be nice. But everyone writes the same stupid stuff. That's what got me thinking about Enoch. In a sea of profiles filled with the same banal platitudes, his stood out almost like a prototype. At first, I just thought it was lame. But then I reread the e-mails between him and Amy, and there seemed to be a disjoint between his profile and the e-mails. As generic as his profile was, his messages were specific. He was one of the few men to ask for her name immediately, which I take is a bit taboo in the online world. He wanted to know where she was from, where she went to school, what was the worst thing she'd ever done — that kind of thing.'

'A bit too curious?'

'Yeah. And intense. When I went back and read his profile again in light of that intensity, it was almost like he was in on the joke, using all of the standard lines. I don't know. A long shot but — '

'That's the nature of risk,' Flann said, pulling the car to a stop in front of the precinct. 'The long shot's the only way to the jackpot.'

★　★　★

Ellie went straight to Flann's computer, pulled up her account on FirstDate, and immediately laughed out loud. In response to Flann's curious look, she explained. 'I have eight new messages and ten flirts.'

'You must have slapped together some profile.'

Ellie began clicking on the messages in her in-box. 'My alter ego, otherwise known as DB990, already got a response from Mr. Right. Nothing from the other two yet. What's next? This isn't the part where you tell me I'm supposed to go on dates until we catch the bad guy, is it?'

'No. Despite the moniker, I never intended to use you as date bait.' He apparently caught the significance of her user name.

'Phew,' she said, wiping her brow. 'I thought I'd have to haul out my best Pacino. *Hoo-ah!*'

'Hey, *Sea of Love* is still classic Pacino compared to *Scent of a Woman*. Nice impersonation there, by the way.'

Ellie gave a mock stage bow. 'Thank you, thank you. And thank god for the next generation of personal ads. No personal contact necessary. I'll just do what Amy would've done. Get a couple of e-mail exchanges and be receptive to a phone call?'

'Sounds good. In the meantime, I see archives sent down the file on Tatiana Chekova.' He held up a navy blue binder that was waiting for them on his desk. 'This should keep us busy awhile.'

* * *

115

Individual detectives can justify different ways of organizing a file. Chronologically to show how the investigation unfolded, piece by piece. By type of evidence — witness statements separate from forensics. But the investigating detectives on Tatiana Chekova's case used no apparent filing system whatsoever. Initial interviews, follow-ups, crime lab reports, victim info — all of it was commingled. Some sheets of paper hadn't quite made it through the hole-puncher and were jammed into the notebook's worn plastic pockets. Random handwritten notes were left unexplained and indecipherable. Ellie had never seen an NYPD murder book, but she took better care of her files on Podunk cases.

According to the initial report, Tatiana Chekova lived in Bensonhurst but was shot outside of Vibrations on the West Side Highway in Manhattan. The report filed by a Detective Ed Becker euphemistically referred to the establishment as a 'gentlemen's club.' Ellie did a double take at the name typed at the bottom of the police report. Something about it seemed familiar. She'd come across it recently in another context but couldn't place it.

It was two in the morning on April 22 when one of the members of a bachelor's party ducked to the edge of the parking lot to take a leak during a smoking break and spied bare legs behind a parked car. Assuming the legs belonged to a hooker, passed out after turning a trick, he waved his friends over for a free peep show. Her raincoat had fallen open to reveal a jeweled bra and thong. A closer look revealed a less titillating picture. Most of the woman's brain matter had spilled to the parking lot concrete.

The bouncer at the door confirmed that the body, outfit, and butterfly-tattooed ass belonged to Tatiana Chekova. She worked part-time as a waitress and, when money fell short, as a reluctant lap dancer on the floor. She'd been employed at Vibrations for six weeks. Sadly, no one at the club claimed to know her well.

Considering she devoted more words to a typical burglary, Ellie thought the report fell woefully short. The detectives supposedly questioned everyone who was still at Vibrations when they arrived, but the report tersely concluded that 'there were no witnesses to the shooting.' Details of the interviews were omitted. Even names were missing, except for the manager on duty, the drunken groomsman who found the body, and the lucky husband-to-be.

It was piss-poor police work.

The background information the detectives gathered on Chekova wasn't any more impressive. They quickly determined she was a Russian immigrant, in New York for almost five years. They ran her record: three prostitution pops her first two years in the country; more recently, a bust for credit card fraud and heroin possession three months before her murder. According to a computer printout, the officer arrested Chekova for the fraud, then found heroin in her bedroom. The case was declined for prosecution. Ellie guessed that the search was bad. Arresting a woman in her apartment usually didn't require a search of her bedroom.

As she turned to the ballistics reports, Ellie fished out her jar of Nutella and spoon from the cardboard box she'd stashed underneath Flann's desk. The crime lab reports were considerably more thorough than the detectives'. Two bullets, fired into the back of the victim's head, close range. A lot of damage.

'What's that smell?' Flann looked up from his reading. 'That's something you're *eating*?'

'Nutella. A little bit nutty, a little bit of chocolate. It's culinary perfection.'

'Smells like something you'd scoop from the bottom of a pigpen. Not to mention it's barely ten in the morning.'

Ellie helped herself to another scoop and smiled. 'You've looked at the murder book on Caroline Hunter, right?'

'Yeah. Not much there. Her purse was stolen, so it looked like a robbery gone bad. No neighborhood witnesses. The trail ran cold — fast.'

He looked up at Ellie, apparently waiting for her to come up with the right question. He'd also seen the crime lab reports on Chekova.

'What about the gunshots?' she asked.

'Two of them. Back of the head.'

'Close range?'

'Ballistics' best guess was two to three feet.'

Just like Tatiana Chekova. Same gun. Same shots. Same number of bullets. Chekova was killed nine months and ten days before Caroline Hunter. Twenty-one months and ten days before Amy Davis. No reason to suspect a FirstDate connection. No reason to dismiss

118

it either. The original investigators had no cause to look for it. Even if they had, they might not have bothered. A Russian heroin addict, living in Bensonhurst, stripping in Manhattan.

'I was hoping to avoid this,' Flann said, 'but I think we need to talk to one of the investigating detectives on the Chekova case.'

'Afraid of a turf battle?'

'There's no turf to fight over. Barney Tendall is dead — shot, off-duty, when he tried to stop a robbery. Ed Becker took retirement two months later. I guess Becker talked to Tendall on the phone a couple of hours before it all happened and couldn't get past it — like he was supposed to stop his partner from grabbing a beer.'

Becker. Twice Flann had spoken the name now, and twice it had rung a distant and annoying bell in the back of her mind. She closed her eyes and tried to remember but couldn't pull the connection forward. She wrote it off as a common name she must've run across in the newspaper.

'Becker's sour on the job?' she asked.

Flann paused before answering. 'God no. Ed Becker loved being a cop. He just wasn't very good at it if you ask me. And we're about to point that out to him by asking the questions we can't answer from these notes.'

Ellie sensed a discomfort in McIlroy that went beyond having to ask a retired cop about a cold case. The man was definitely elusive with his thoughts.

'Is there any more to it than that?'

'We worked out of the same precinct a long, long time ago. Let's just say that when it comes to Ed Becker, I'd prefer that you do most of the talking.'

# 13

Ed Becker lived in a modest Brick Tudor in Scarsdale, just north of the Bronx in Westchester. Despite the proximity, Westchester was nothing like the Bronx, and upscale Scarsdale was one of the least Bronxlike of its enclaves.

Ellie had called ahead, and Becker met them at his front door before they knocked. He was a big man — tall, thick, substantial, with a barrel chest. His skin was ruddy, his hair a light gold only just beginning to thin. He greeted them with a friendly smile.

It wasn't just Ed Becker's smile that was friendly. It was the hearty way he clasped Flann's shoulder, the enthusiastic shake he gave to Ellie's hand, and the boisterous manner in which he waved them into his living room. It was the small things that Ellie noticed, like Becker's metal sign reading Retirement Parking Only, which hung over an overstuffed reclining chair.

'Nice sign,' Ellie said.

Becker's smile grew wider. 'Yeah. Some of the boys got a little carried away with what you might call the novelty gifts when I left the job. That was about the only one that was appropriate for public display. From the looks of you, you've got quite a lot of years left with a shield before you'll be having a party.'

'Oh, every day's a party when you're part of the NYPD.'

Becker chuckled. 'I like that. Every day's a party. I like this one, McIlroy. Keep her around.'

'We plan on it.'

Based on Flann's comments, Ellie had expected Ed Becker to be an ogre. Now that she'd met the man in person, she wondered whether Flann the infamous loner perhaps had the same suspicious response toward all cops.

'So what brings you up to Westchester?'

Becker directed his question toward Flann, but Ellie answered. 'We're looking into a possible connection between the deaths of two women in Manhattan, Caroline Hunter and Amy Davis. They were killed exactly one year apart, both after dates they had arranged online.'

'That Internet dating is big stuff. My son met someone a couple of years ago. They're getting married this spring. Oh, speaking of which, Mac, how's that daughter of yours?'

The friendly question did nothing to change the scowl Flann had worn since stepping into Ed Becker's home. 'She's good, Ed. Thanks for asking.'

'Anyway, Internet dating. I'll admit, I've been tempted to try it myself. Read all about it, in fact. An old geezer like me, though — '

'You'd be surprised,' Ellie said.

'I'm sure I would. Maybe not in a good way though, you know what I mean? Wake up one morning and your pee burns and your pet bunny's been boiled. But I suspect you didn't drive all the way up here to kick-start an old guy's love life.'

'No sir. It's about an old case of yours. We just

discovered that the gun that killed one of our victims was also used to shoot Tatiana Chekova. You worked that one, right?'

'Chekova, huh?'

'Russian woman, found in the parking lot of a strip club.'

'Right. Vibrations. Some name, huh? We never cleared that one. We got names off the credit cards in the club, but no one jumped out at us. Definitely wasn't anyone in the bachelor party that found her. Two of those guys were puking their guts out on the West Side Highway.'

Ellie saw the frustration on McIlroy's face.

'Um, I pulled the file this morning,' she said gently. 'It didn't contain a list of names from the club. Or at least I didn't see it.'

Becker looked puzzled. 'It should have been there. Records ain't always the best about holding cold cases. Anyway, it didn't get us anywhere. With her background, we assumed it was a trick gone bad.'

'The M.E. found no signs of sexual activity.'

'I remember. Her coat was open though, and the shots came from behind. Close range, right?'

'Yeah.'

'See, I can remember a thing or two.' He tapped his temple for emphasis. 'Barney's theory — Barney was my partner. He figured the guy might've been groping her from behind, started to get going, and then something went wrong. She wasn't ready yet, or he couldn't get it — he couldn't complete the act.'

'Not a crazy theory.'

'Not a crazy theory. But I never quite bought

it. The manager said the vic didn't want to dance. She only did an occasional lap dance when she was desperate for a few extra bucks. And her vice pops were old. My theory was she was trying to get out of the life.'

'By working at a strip club?' That was like going on a diet by taking a job at Baskin-Robbins.

'You know, staying just at the edge of it, but not wanting to pull tricks anymore. She walked to the parking lot with someone, but then decided to go for the money without giving up the quid pro quo. Two bullets, back of the head.'

It was a better theory than Barney Tendall's. And it described a kind of murder that was nearly impossible to solve.

'That was my theory. Barney had his. Neither of them got us anywhere.'

'Flann told me about your partner. I'm sorry.'

Flann finally broke his silence. 'He was a good man, Ed.'

'Great partner too. It was rough for a while there, what happened to Barney. Looking back on it, I was in a fog my last couple of months on the job. I knew if I stuck around, I'd be chained to a desk by the year's end. The union got me an early retirement package, and I moved out here. After all those years living in the city, watching the crime rate yo-yo, I just couldn't take it anymore after Barney.'

'I can't even imagine,' Ellie muttered, knowing her words fell short.

'Aah, what are you gonna do, right? Anyway, we never closed on Chekova. That was one of our last cases together. I tried working it on my own after I was reassigned, but — well, I wasn't doing anyone much good by then. Maybe that's why I didn't get further with it.'

'Can you think of any suspects we should be looking at?'

'No, we never homed in on anyone.'

'We've been looking at this Internet dating connection between our two victims. Any chance Chekova was using a service? Did she have a computer?'

Becker shook his head. 'Not that I can remember. She was sort of transient. Moved around a lot. Staying with whatever guy was getting her high that week. Not exactly the technological type. I think I'd remember if she'd had a computer. It would have seemed out of place.'

'I hope you'll understand if we have to look at her again with new eyes. Try to find the connection between her and our victims.'

'It'd be sloppy work not to.'

'Can you remember anything that might help?'

'The file should have all my notes.' This time Becker must have caught Flann's frustrated expression as well. 'You can always call if you need anything specific.'

'Do you remember if she had family? Someone who might know if she was using FirstDate?'

'Now that I can't remember. But the vic didn't seem close to anyone, so we were pretty sure it wasn't a domestic. We worked the club angle. It's not in the file?'

'No sir.'

Becker shook his head. 'I was out of it back then, but I thought I left behind my notebooks all right.'

'I'll look again,' Ellie offered.

'Yeah, okay.'

'You a full-time retiree now, Ed?' Flann's tone was cordial enough, but the question struck Ellie as odd.

'Oh yeah,' Becker said. 'I'm not one of those second career guys. You never know how much time you got, right?'

'That's the way to do it,' Flann said.

'Well, like I said, call if I can help. I got a pretty good memory, at least for the stuff that seemed to matter.'

★   ★   ★

McIlroy was quiet during the ride back to the city.

'You okay, Flann?' Ellie asked.

The question bounced right off of him. 'That was a really nice house. Brick. Nice block. Good shape inside. How much you think that goes for in this market?'

'I'm too impoverished to bother browsing the real estate section. Why?'

'Just seems like an awfully nice house for a retired cop without a second income.'

'He did say he got a retirement package. Maybe the union got him something extra because of his partner.'

Flann's lips remained pursed in a straight line,

126

his blond eyebrows furrowed. He kept his eyes on the traffic, both hands firmly gripping the wheel. By the time they hit the Hudson, Ellie was fed up. She was grateful for a murder assignment, but McIlroy's tight lips were getting ridiculous. He was her partner, at least temporarily, and she believed that meant something. They should at least get to know each other.

'You never mentioned you had a daughter.'

McIlroy sighed loudly. 'No, I didn't. I'm sure glad lazy old Becker did.'

'I'm sure he was trying to be nice.'

'He was trying to get under my skin.'

'Odd way to get under someone's skin.'

McIlroy sighed again. 'I don't get to see her much. We were never married, her mother and I. Becker knows all that, and he asks about her anyway.'

'That must be rough.'

'All these single moms out there trying to get a daddy involved in the picture, and this one prefers I walk away. She thinks one way to do that is to make it hard for me to see my kid.'

'What's her name?'

'Miranda. Oh, you meant my daughter. Stephanie. Stephanie Hart, not McIlroy. She's thirteen. Thirteen-year-old girls need their fathers, you know?'

Ellie nodded. 'I was fourteen when my father was killed. He wasn't even fifty yet.' If McIlroy was going to open up to her, it was only fair that she did the same.

'I know some of the details already,' Flann

said. 'I read about you last year.'

'I assumed that had something to do with the special request. It's not true, most of what they said. I didn't always know I wanted to be a cop, and my father didn't start training me when I was five. Quite the opposite in fact. He always pushed my brother in that direction, but me, he humored. If he'd been around when I finally decided to take the leap, he would have tried to stop me.'

'Fathers can be protective that way.'

'You've probably figured out by now I'm not the high-tech bill of goods they were selling.'

He nodded. 'They wanted to use your story to talk about the next generation of law enforcement, which they'd like to think is all about the high-tech solutions they see on *CSI*. I've learned over the years not to trust the media's spin. In fact, I've learned to use it to mutual advantage.'

Ellie thought about that. Mutual advantage. That's precisely what she had tried to do with all those interviews and profiles she'd agreed to last year. 'Hope I didn't disappoint.'

'Not at all. Your supposed expertise in modern crime fighting wasn't the reason I called you.'

Ellie did not interrupt the silence that followed.

'You work homicide as long as I do and have nothing else going for you but the job, it can be hard sometimes to hold it together. To keep waking up in the morning and going to sleep at night — I don't want to sound morose, but even though I rarely see her, my daughter's the closest thing I've got to someone who cares whether or not I come home each night.'

'Flann — '

He held up a hand and shook his head. 'That's just the way it is. When you described to that reporter how haunted you've felt all of these years — even about the *suggestion* that your father might have left you by his own hand — well, I remembered the story. I needed a damn good cop who'd be open-minded enough to follow this one through. You seemed to fit the ticket.'

'I'm glad you asked for me.'

'And I'm glad you let me tell you why.'

# 14

Charlie Dixon watched the detectives pull into a parking spot in front of the Thirteenth Precinct. The female detective waved to McIlroy as he hopped out of the car and walked into the precinct. The woman then climbed behind the wheel and restarted the engine. She took Twenty-first Street west to Park Avenue, then turned left to go south.

Once she cleared the corner, Charlie pulled into traffic. Trailing people in the city was easy. The streets carried too many cars for one to stand out. In any event, his light blue Chevy Impala made for ideal urban camouflage. He'd followed the detectives all the way to Westchester and back without a hitch.

Traffic was heavy, so it was easy to stay a few cars back. He tried to tune out the sounds of trucks, rattling buses, and honking horns as he followed her down Broadway, past City Hall Park. It was time for midday deliveries. Double-parking was high, and so were tensions. His head was starting to throb, and he could swear that the burning in his stomach was back.

Two blocks short of Battery Park, the detective stopped in a loading zone and threw something on the dash, undoubtedly a police parking permit. Charlie allowed himself to get locked in behind a UPS truck in the middle of a delivery. Watching her on foot would be trickier.

Fortunately, she didn't stray far. She dashed across the intersection at a catty-corner, glancing up at the sign above a Vietnamese restaurant before entering. Charlie wasn't sure what to do now. For all he knew, she was meeting a girlfriend for lunch. Maybe McIlroy was the one doing the legwork, while he was spinning his wheels watching the girl just because she left the precinct first.

It had been just over twenty-four hours since he learned that the NYPD was asking Stern for the personal information of FirstDate users. Two women were dead, and a Detective McIlroy seemed to be working a serial killer theory. Apparently Mark Stern was convinced that the theory was nonsense. According to Dixon's source at the company — a nice-enough guy with a nasty penchant for recreational coke — Stern even sounded slightly smug about the coincidence. From the singleminded perspective of a successful entrepreneur, two murder victims tied to his company in a twelve-month period demonstrated just how ubiquitous the service had become among New Yorkers.

Nevertheless, Stern was firmly committed against handing over private information to the police. The promise of anonymity, he emphasized, was FirstDate's most valuable asset. He circled the wagons and made sure that his employees understood that any inquiries about the matter should go directly to him.

In the end, it was Dixon who helped get the cops off Stern's back. A few discreet calls revealed McIlroy was known as a loose cannon, a

131

detective who conjured up wild fantasies out of imaginary evidence. His nickname was McIl-Mulder, for Christ's sake. The higher-ups were letting him run amok on this theory to reward him for getting lucky on an earlier case. Once this indulgence ran its course, his star would fall.

So Dixon had made the call. It was risky. He could have let the NYPD get the information it was looking for. Once they realized it was a dead end, they'd move on. But he had too much at stake with FirstDate. If Stern got nervous — even about some wild theory — he might change his habits while Dixon was still trying to figure them out.

But now apparently McIlroy and his partner had done enough digging to turn up Tatiana. First they had requested the police reports, then they'd driven all the way to Scarsdale to see that sorry excuse for a detective who never even scratched the surface of Tatiana's murder. Why in the world were they asking about Tatiana? Was it part of the serial killer theory, or had they moved directly into his territory?

Now that Tatiana was on their radar, her death might give them a direction, something to focus their attention on. She wouldn't fit easily into their serial theory, so they'd have to dig further. Work from the victim outward, that would be the goal. It would be the smart way to investigate. It was also a problem. If McIlroy and his partner were even half decent cops — not like that other one — the trail could lead right back to Dixon.

His stomach was starting to burn again when he saw another woman he recognized walk into the Vietnamese restaurant. He had never seen her in person, but he had her driver's license photograph on his dining room wall — the wall on which he had mapped out the corporate structure of FirstDate. She was prettier in person.

The pain in his gut was subsiding. She was down at the bottom, both literally on the wall and figuratively in the corporate hierarchy. She was the receptionist. What was her name again? Conroy or something.

He'd already dug into the backgrounds of everyone at the company. The redhead was clean. Dixon also knew a bit about her boss. Mark Stern was a control freak. No way did he let his receptionist know anything about the company. She was there strictly to answer telephones.

If Detective Hatcher was spending her lunch hour on a liaison with her, they were definitely still working their serial killer theory, still trying to get a list of the men who contacted that woman who was strangled this week. They hadn't begun to connect the dots that actually connected Tatiana Chekova and FirstDate — the dots that drew a line back to Special Agent Charlie Dixon of the Federal Bureau of Investigation. A line that had nothing to do with the jurisdiction of the NYPD. A line that hopefully they would never find.

He called the FBI field office to report the good news to his boss, Special Agent in Charge Barry Mayfield.

'Stay on top of it,' Mayfield warned. 'You're

sure your source at FirstDate won't mention your side project?'

'Positive,' he said. *Ninety-five percent certain.*

'And make sure to get rid of anything that could tie you to that dead girl.'

Dixon hated hearing Tatiana referred to as *that dead girl*, but he was in no position to correct Mayfield under the circumstances.

⋆ ⋆ ⋆

Ellie didn't get much time with Christine Conboy. The receptionist made it clear she'd talk as long as it took to walk out with her pork noodle bowl and a spring roll, and no longer.

'I want to help you. I do. Nothing scares me more than the idea of someone hunting down single women. But, like I said, no one I know can directly access user information.'

'What about the employees who handle the billing?'

'They only have access to the billing information — how much to charge, and what credit card to charge it to. They'd know people's real names but wouldn't be able to match those to the profile names you have. Trust me. I tried.'

'You told them it was for the police?'

'Are you kidding? No way. Stern sent a memo out yesterday saying that police were conducting an inquiry that related to the company — but only indirectly. He was clear about that. He was also clear that all communications from police were to go through him. I know billing can't help you because I started getting serious with someone online a few months ago, and I got suspicious. I begged my friend in accounting, and she swore she couldn't help me.'

'I'm not just spying on a new boyfriend, Christine. I'm looking for a killer. Can't you at least ask around and find someone who can help?'

Christine hushed Ellie with a pat on the forearm, checking again to make sure she didn't recognize anyone in the restaurant.

'So you can pressure them? You don't seem to get what I'm saying. We don't have civil service protection. We don't have a union. Mark Stern will fire any one of us at the drop of a hat, and the job market's rough out there. Not that you would know.'

Ellie had made the mistake of momentarily forgetting that she was bullying an innocent person. It wasn't the bullying that was wrong; it was the forgetting. Ellie was asking Christine to put something important on the line for a cause that was not hers, and she had acted as if it were owed to her.

'Look, Christine. I'm sorry. I appreciate the help. I appreciate your time. I appreciate your meeting me. Did I mention that I appreciate you?' Christine smiled. 'I'll find some other way.'

The woman at the cash register called out a number, and Christine raised her hand. 'That's me. I'm sorry if I'm a little testy. I'm sure my job seems Podunk, but it's all I've got.'

Christine stopped Ellie as she was heading toward the door. 'You know, if you want some help from someone who's not afraid of Stern, there's one guy you might want to talk to first. Jason Upton. He worked at FirstDate for a long time. He left about a year ago when the company got a little too big for him.'

'You know this guy?'

'Yeah. He was one of the early programmers. Stern's always saying how fond he was of Jason and what great friends they were, so Jason's probably not afraid of him either. If there's a way to pull together the information you need, he might at least know who in the company can do it. He went to Larkin, Baker & Howry to run their I.T. department.' Ellie recognized the name of one of the city's largest law firms. 'He's nice too. Nicer than Stern. I'm sure you can track him down.'

'I'll do that. Thank you.'

Ellie watched Christine throw a set of chopsticks and two packets of chili sauce into her lunch bag. She left the restaurant just as snow was beginning to fall.

# 15

Three months before Tatiana Chekova was murdered, a man named Eric Rivero found a charge on his American Express card that he had not made — the purchase of a television from Circuit City. That discovery eventually led to Tatiana's arrest and to the police report now waiting for Ellie back at the precinct. She gave it a quick read.

Unlike most credit card owners, Rivero had reported the unauthorized charge not only to American Express but also to the police. And he had been smart. He asked Circuit City where the television had been delivered and then filed the police report in the corresponding Brooklyn police precinct. An ambitious rookie patrol officer found the time to follow up and stopped by the address where the television had been delivered.

The first thing the officer saw when Tatiana Chekova opened the door was a fancy new plasma screen in the living room. Tatiana consented to a search of the rest of the apartment, and the officer found heroin in Tatiana's nightstand drawer. It was a straightforward case, put together with a self-investigating citizen, good police work, and a bit of luck.

When Ellie was finished reading, she turned to Flann. 'Tatiana gave a sister as her contact information when she was arrested a couple of years ago. The sister also lives in Bensonhurst, or at least she did back then.'

'Good. Maybe she'll know if Tatiana was using FirstDate.'

'I've been thinking about that,' Ellie said. 'How well did you smooth things over with Stern after I left his office yesterday?'

'He stopped talking about siccing a lawsuit on us, but he's probably not about to invite me over to meet the missus. Why?'

'Because even in his self-righteous indignation about customer privacy, he did offer to cooperate if we had a narrower request backed by a better reason.'

'And now all we need to know is if Tatiana was a FirstDate customer,' Flann said.

'How much more specific can we be, right? It's certainly worth a phone call.'

'Nah. I better see him in person. He might check, find out she's in his system, and then lie about it.'

'He struck you as that evil?'

'He's the CEO of a corporation that's about to go public. A few taps on his keyboard might just confirm that some bedbug out there is using his customers for urban hunting.'

'Enough said.' Confirmation of three victims linked to FirstDate, two of them killed by the same gun, would send Mark Stern's stock values plummeting. 'You know what I can't figure is why the D.A. kicked Tatiana's case.'

'Bad search?' Flann asked.

'That's what I assumed, but it looks textbook. She said the TV arrived in the mail, and she just assumed it was a gift. Give me a break.'

'And the drugs?'

'She gave consent to search, then admitted the horse was hers. Looks like a slam dunk.'

Flann shrugged it off. 'Maybe the prosecutor didn't think it was worth the hassle. A gullible jury might've bought the story of a television miraculously arriving to a working girl's doorstep. And the heroin was a first-time drug pop.'

'But enough quantity to trigger a hefty sentence.'

'You know how judges can be about so-called consent searches. Maybe the prosecutor didn't want to push it.'

'Too bad for Tatiana. If she'd gotten some jail time, she might not have been in the Vibrations parking lot three months later.'

Ellie was interrupted by the chirp of her cell phone. She didn't recognize the incoming number. 'Let me get rid of this. Hello?'

'Hatcher, it's Ed Becker. I hope you don't mind me calling your cell. They didn't have you on the roster at Homicide for some reason, so I played the old retiree card with some friends and got this number.'

'Not a problem, Ed. Thanks again for your time this morning.' Flann threw Ellie a curious look, and Ellie shrugged.

'I've been thinking more about the Chekova case, and I'm not feeling good right now about how I handled it. Looking back, I might've missed something on that one.'

'I'm sure you did what you could. We're just

taking a fresh look in light of the new killings. You never know what could break it, right?'

'You're a real nice girl — woman, sorry — but I'm in a better state of mind now compared to back then. I'm pretty sure I did a piss-poor job. But, hey, I'm not calling so you'll feel sorry for me or anything. I want to help.'

'Help how?'

Flann's look moved from curiosity to anger. He shook his head quickly at Ellie. On the other end of the line, Becker laughed.

'Don't worry. I know the last thing you and McIlroy need is me nipping at your heels. I was just thinking about our talk yesterday. I told you we eliminated the bachelor party at the outset. In retrospect, though, I can't remember whether we really looked at them or not. We just went with our gut — '

'And the fact that they were spilling their guts on the side of the road?'

'Exactly,' Becker said with another laugh. 'Not a bad judgment in the beginning, when you're prioritizing. But when we didn't have any other leads, we should have gone back and taken a closer look. After what happened with my partner, well, I don't think I ever did. You might want to check them out after all.'

'All right, we'll do that. Thanks for the call.'

'No problem. I mean it, if there's anything I can do, let me know. Hell, I know I can't be much help anymore, but it's just eating at me. Promise me you'll let me know if I missed something — '

'Stop assuming that. It's just a new set of eyes

is all. And of course I'll call you if we get anywhere.'

Flann threw her another cross look.

'I'll be here waiting. I'm just sitting up here in Westchester getting old.'

When Ellie flipped her phone shut, an obviously unhappy Flann pressed her for every detail.

'He can find out the results of our investigation when we publicly announce an arrest. We're not about to partner up with Ed Becker.'

'Nobody's talking about *partnering up*.'

'Sharing information, talking about the old days, whatever. I don't care what he says, but that phone call's about covering his ass. I'm not getting involved, and, trust me, you shouldn't either.' Flann stood and started to pull his coat on.

'I don't get it, Flann. What is it with you and Becker? He's being a hell of a lot nicer than most retired detectives would be about someone working an old case, and you find something wrong with every step he makes.'

'That's because with a guy like Ed Becker, nice always comes with a price. Now, I'm going down to FirstDate to see Stern. You coming?'

'No, after yesterday's fireworks between me and Stern, you should go alone. Besides,' she said, looking at her watch, 'we're supposed to go see that computer guy. Just meet me at his office when you're done with Stern.' Jason Upton, the former FirstDate programmer, had agreed to meet with her at two o'clock at his office.

Once Flann was gone, Ellie checked her FirstDate account. Eleven new messages, not including flirts. She had a message from Mr. Right. He was the one she thought of as dirty birdy, who'd used such subtle sexual innuendo with Amy Davis. He was nice enough to leave a phone number. She also had a message from Taylor, the one she'd mentally dubbed as stalker-guy. He was interested in meeting for a drink. Still no word from bachelor number three, Enoch.

She pulled up the message from Taylor, hit Reply, and typed, *Taylor, How about a phone call first? Give me a number where I can call you?'* Twenty seconds later, she received a message from Taylor with a telephone number, complete with the desperate comment that he had plenty of free minutes on his new CellularOne plan. That was the nice thing about stalkers. They were good about returning messages.

Then she found herself reading another message, this one from one of the 'keepers' to whom Jess had sent a flirt on her behalf. *Hey. It's pretty funny they call hitting a little button on their Web page flirting. Doesn't flirting usually involve lingering glances across a crowded room, a gentle graze of the forearm after a subtle joke, deliberately placed lips on a wine glass . . . Whoops, sorry, got a little carried away there. Wow, is it hot in here? Anyway, thanks for flirting with me. If you get a chance, tell me a little bit about yourself. How's this for an ice-breaker? My name's Peter. Hey, don't* laugh. *My name really is Peter. Seriously.*

The message was enough to make Ellie laugh — twice — so she clicked on Peter's profile, amazed that she was even remotely curious about a man her brother had selected. She read the brief introduction he'd written about himself. *It's official. I'm a hypocrite. I shake my angry fist at the publishing industry that fails to recognize my manuscripts as the future classics of American fiction, and yet I have no idea what to say about myself in this little box. I have a salaried writing job by day but dream of making it to the walls of Chumley's. I guess that makes me a writer manqué. I consider myself a non-British, much better-looking version of Nick Hornby, so prepare yourself for endless conversations involving randomly inserted allusions to culturally significant popular icons such as the Clash, the Simpsons, John Waters, so-bad-it's good reality TV, and on and on till the break of dawn. Sounds fun, right?*

Ellie smiled, then found herself typing a response. *Peter, Thanks for the note. About that mental digression of yours, I hope I was good. Manqué? I looked up that fancy SAT word in the dictionary and it sounds a little bit like a wannabe. You shouldn't be so hard on yourself.* She paused, knowing that she should say at least something about herself. *I'm not a writer but I do like to read. I overheard a woman in a bookstore the other day tell her friend she really loved books, 'but not the reading kind.' Besides reading and eavesdropping on strangers in stores, I like kickboxing and watching my*

143

*brother's band play. Wow. That made me sound really butch and boring. Hopefully I'm neither. If I had to pick one, though, I guess I'd go with the former.*

Ellie paused again. *You need to sign an e-mail, don't you?* She typed DB990, then erased it. *Ally.* Close enough. She hit send. *Your message has been sent to Unpublished.* Too late to back out now.

She checked her watch. Jason Upton was expecting her in forty minutes. She'd have to wait to learn more about Peter, but she had just enough time to do a little research into the men who called themselves Taylor and Mr. Right.

# 16

Ellie waited for Jason Upton on a squat, shiny black leather sofa in the Midtown lobby of the law firm of Larkin, Baker & Howry. She took in a Jasper Johns silkscreen on the wall across from her as she sipped a coffee fetched for her by the receptionist.

'Detective Hatcher? I'm Jason Upton.'

The man who offered his hand did not fit the stereotype of a computer geek or tech-head. He was probably in his midthirties and dressed fashionably in a pair of loose khaki pants and a striped open-collar shirt. His frame was full but fit. His dark hair managed to be simultaneously neat but tousled. His accent was northeastern and uniquely moneyed.

'Thanks for making time for me. My partner should be here shortly, but we can start without him.'

Jason asked the receptionist to bring McIlroy to them when he arrived, and then led the way to a more modest office two floors down.

'Big change in scenery,' she commented.

'Welcome to the fifty-seventh floor, land of word processing, printing, and I.T. No clients means no interior decorators. Just cubicles, copy machines, and lots of computers. I'm lucky to have walls.'

'I think I prefer the art in here,' Ellie said, gesturing to a framed poster from *Pulp Fiction* as she took a seat in Jason's sole guest chair. She got straight to the point, first covering the possible link between two murder victims and FirstDate, then moving on to the effort to determine the true identities behind all of the user names. 'We started an account ourselves and are trying to get ID's on a few of the men by contacting them directly, but it would be a lot easier if someone with access to the company's computers would just hand over the names.'

'The police department has an online dating profile?' he asked, laughing.

'I meant more like a royal we, as in me.'

'Usually I have this spiel I give my female friends before they try the online dating thing, but I assume this is strictly for investigative purposes?'

'All business, I'm afraid.' A thought of Peter the wannabe writer flashed through her mind. 'Go ahead and give me the spiel anyway.'

'Don't get me wrong. I wouldn't have worked to start the company if I didn't think it could serve a good purpose. Love's a beautiful thing, right? Mark and I really believed that the Internet held the potential to transform the way a couple interacts when they first 'meet,' so to speak. People open up on e-mail in a more honest way than when they're face-to-face with someone they're trying to impress. Then, by the time you see each other in person, there's already a connection there. A bad outfit, or the beginning of baldness, or a few extra pounds — those physical imperfections that might have been deal killers if you met in a bar — they become something you get past.'

'You make it sound so — ' Ellie wanted to say *sickening* but instead she opted for 'pure.'

'Well, those upsides were what we had in mind when we started. But we also knew there could be downsides. We did our best to warn customers up front so they could be smart, but, frankly, not everyone's so smart.'

'I see a lot of that in my job.'

'So you can imagine what I'm talking about. People handed over their real names and phone numbers to total strangers. They met for first dates at their homes. One guy said he lived in Arizona and needed money to move up to New York to pursue the relationship. Of course, he lived in Hoboken and gave the same story to twenty different women. Really stupid stuff. I left when our customer base was relatively small, but we were already getting a ton of complaints about unwanted e-mails, phone calls, whatever.'

Ellie was reminded of Amy Davis's problems with Taylor, the man who couldn't take no for an answer. 'That's why you've got that Block function, right?'

'We programmed that in after the first few *weeks* online. We had that many problems. It's a quick fix, but only for customers who are smart enough to stay anonymous — no names, phone numbers, any of that.'

'And not everyone's smart.'

'Exactly. Then of course you've got all the same problems you have out there with good old-fashioned dating. One guy I worked with was

147

juggling five different women in any given week. Each of them thought their boyfriend was working so hard he could only see them once a week on date night. Now, in the old-fashioned world, a guy like that would eventually get caught juggling women in his building, or from work, or who were friends of friends — the girls might put the pieces together. And if he did get caught, there'd be the embarrassment factor if he had to keep running into them. But FirstDate introduces people who share absolutely no preexisting links. As a result, there's no accountability if someone gets caught being a dog.'

'This dog from work — he doesn't happen to be Mark Stern?'

Jason laughed. 'Mark? No, definitely not. Very happily married.'

'So it's not just a marketing image? I thought maybe he hired someone to pose for that perfect wedding picture on his desk.'

'You're a very cynical woman, so I'm sorry to disappoint you. He's actually as happy as he appears to be.'

'Just not fair,' Ellie said dryly.

Knuckles rapped against the office door frame.

'Hi. Flann McIlroy.' Ellie noticed that her partner was carrying a pair of brown sheepskin gloves and a laptop that looked a lot like Amy Davis's. He laid the gloves on Jason's desk and shifted the computer into his left hand as he offered Jason the other. 'The woman upstairs said it was all right to come down.'

'The more the merrier,' Jason said, making

room to roll a stool from the hallway into his small office.

'Did you get what you wanted downtown?' Ellie asked. She was eager to know what Flann had learned from Mark Stern. If Tatiana also had an account, they'd have a stronger argument for getting a court order giving them access to FirstDate's records, and they wouldn't even need Jason Upton.

'I got an answer to the question, but it wasn't the one we wanted.' Flann did his best to make it sound innocuous, but Ellie could tell he was disappointed. So was she. Chekova was killed by the same gun as Caroline Hunter but wasn't using FirstDate. Maybe they were hurtling down an entirely wrong track.

★　★　★

'I was just about to ask Jason why he left the company,' Ellie said.

'For all of this,' Jason said, holding his arms out wide. 'Money, prestige, power.'

'We have all the same rewards in our job.'

'I left because Mark was more ambitious than I was. I liked the work we were doing, the freedom of self-employment, breaking new ground. I had a trust fund, though, and Mark didn't. He was a few years older. He was the entrepreneur, the one with the M.B.A. and the big plans. Honestly, I wasn't willing to do the corporate side of the work. I mean, come on. I was a computer science major, archaeology minor at Tufts. What do I know about business?

Maybe if I'd pulled myself up by the bootstraps, I'd be more like him, but what can I say? Dot-com's were all going bust so I got out. Mark had the cojones to stick with it.'

'You left on good terms?'

'Oh yeah. Mark's a little uptight, but we always got along real well. He was nice enough to act heartbroken when I left, but he was probably happy to be able to take the company in his own direction. We worked out a nice little deal for both of us. I got to move on to other things. Mark kept his stock and got to live his dream.'

'He strikes us as more than just a little uptight,' Ellie said. 'He pretty much threw us out of his office when we asked him to give us some customer names, then threatened to sue us if the story leaked. And he's apparently got all of his employees too scared to help us behind his back.'

'Like I said, he was always more corporate than I was.'

'Feel like taking your old job back, just for a few days?' Ellie asked.

'Sorry. I hope that's not your reason for being here.'

'Actually, I was hoping you might at least be able to point us in the right direction. Do you know someone at FirstDate who could pull the information we need?'

Jason shook his head. 'I don't know most of the people there now. The company's grown, and we always had a lot of turnover. You've got to understand. It's not like there's this public file in the network at FirstDate that links customer names to their profiles. Very few people have access to that. Otherwise, you get one bad employee, and every married man hooking up online would get blackmailed. Only a few people are likely to have access, but I've got to be honest — my guess is they'll toe the party line if Mark has put his foot down on this one.'

'Which he has,' Ellie made clear. 'I don't suppose you still have some magic password you can use to log on to the system?'

Jason smiled and shook his head. 'Sorry. I'm afraid it doesn't work like that.'

'I figured you probably would have mentioned it by now.'

'I've got a question,' Flann interjected. 'Any idea how someone could get into a woman's FirstDate e-mails and print one of them out?' Flann explained how they found a FirstDate message that apparently wasn't printed by the victim. He placed the laptop he was carrying on Jason's desk and opened it. 'This belonged to one of our victims if you want to take a look.'

'Well, let's start with the easy stuff. You said you have a list of FirstDate connections, so that means you managed to get into this woman's account. How'd you do it?'

Ellie explained how she requested a lost password and answered the so-called security questions on the FirstDate site. Jason nodded.

'Okay, so there's one way right there. You knew enough about the victim to have the password sent directly from the Web site provider. A higher tech way to get a password is by stealing a person's cookies.'

'English please,' Flann said.

'A cookie is a tiny piece of data sent from a Web server to a Web browser. So when you use a browser like Internet Explorer to go to a Web site like eBay, eBay sends a cookie to your browser, then it's stored on your computer so that eBay will recognize you the next time you visit the site from that same computer. What people don't understand is that computers don't just hang on to the stuff that you intentionally tell them to save. They also hang on to all kinds of data on a temporary basis. Here, take a look at this.'

He had logged Amy Davis onto the law firm's wireless network and then pulled up the popular search engine site Google. He clicked on the empty text box provided for users to type in their Internet search. A menu of text appeared.

'With just one click on an empty box, we can see all of the different Google searches she ran since the last time she cleared her search history.'

He scrolled down the alphabetical list. American Idol. Black wedge boots. Cat toys. Dwight Schrute.

'That information is all stored in the computer temporarily. Same thing with her Internet browser.' He hit a separate button to display Amy Davis's history on Internet Explorer, then scrolled down to point out all of the Web sites she'd visited recently.

'You could erase all of this data just by hitting Clear, or by scheduling your computer to do it every day automatically. The same is true with all the cookies that get sent to your computer from Web servers. So what a cookie *tracker* does is send the victim to a link that's disguised as a legitimate Web site. But instead of being whatever site it purports to be, the link lets the bad guy steal the cookies off the victim's computer.'

'And cookies are worth having?' Ellie asked.

'Sure, if they contain anything of value to the person who steals them — things like passwords, user names, sites visited, old searches. A good hacker can steal all kinds of information through cookies. Or cookies could be used to create a profile of a person, by monitoring their activities across a number of different Web sites. It's like someone stalking while you surf.'

'Can you tell if anyone did that to Amy Davis's laptop?'

'No, but a computer like this is a hacker's best friend. Her privacy levels are low. She hadn't updated the security on her system for more than a year. It also looks like she was using an unprotected home wireless network to connect to the Internet.'

'And what does that mean?' McIlroy asked.

'Half the people in Manhattan do it,' Ellie explained, 'including me. Wireless home networks are designed for houses, which means that in a city apartment, you can mooch off your neighbor's connection and not have to pay for your own.'

'It also means there's about fifty different ways someone could have known what Web sites she was going to,' Jason explained. 'They also could have gotten into any files she downloaded from the net, including that message.'

'And with all that clicking around you're doing there, you can't tell us which of those methods was most likely?' McIlroy asked.

'Nope. But what most people fail to realize is that the biggest risk of losing privacy online isn't from the technological potential of the Internet. It's carelessness.'

'What do you mean?' Ellie asked.

'Like one way for a black hat to get a white hat's account password is to know them well enough to figure it out. People use birth dates, their kids' names — amateur stuff. You pulled off a more sophisticated version when you answered all her security questions that backed up her password. Or they can hack it. Super computer nerd stuff. But the black hat could just persuade the white hat to turn it over. A phone call. *There's been a problem with our records,*' he said, holding an imaginary telephone to his ear. '*It's possible that someone else has recently changed your password. We need you to verify your account information.*'

'So the idea is to scare the person with a threat that doesn't really exist, so they suddenly trust this stranger on the phone,' Ellie said.

'Precisely. Now imagine doing it not with a phone call, but with an e-mail sent to thousands of potential victims at one time. That's what they call *phishing.*'

'I bet the fraud unit sees cases like that all the time,' Flann added. 'Why go for an e-mail password when you can say you're American Express and need to verify the customer's account number? It's a very simple con.'

'Exactly,' Jason said. 'But the technology provides the incentive. The black hats can hit thousands of potential marks with a single e-mail. The stolen credit card numbers can be used to wire money to a Western Union, where it's picked up using a fake ID.'

Ellie knew that the profitability of identity theft had created a vast market for the sale and purchase of personal information. 'So the same simple tricks people use for identity theft could've been used by our guy to access a victim's FirstDate account,' Ellie said.

'Yep. Or, like I said, it could be super low tech if her password was obvious.' Jason shut down Amy Davis's computer and handed it to Flann. 'At first I thought you meant someone was using FirstDate to find women, like a big search engine. But if he was actually snooping through her account — I'm not a psychologist, but isn't that, you know, sort of obsessive?'

'That's what we thought,' Ellie said. 'Not just killing, but stalking first.'

'If that's the case, he probably did a lot more than read a few of her e-mails. Do you have any idea how much you can learn about a person without ever leaving your office? Even here,' Jason said, 'the attorneys ask me to do research on opposing parties all the time. I can pull up a person's divorce records, income levels, real estate transactions, an entire life picture. Pretty helpful stuff when you're trying to figure out how deep a person's pockets are or where they're hiding money. And it's all publicly available, thanks to data-mining companies that aggregate information from the public domain and pop it up on the Internet for all to see. Now imagine if someone with competent hacking skills decided to break the rules.'

★ ★ ★

Down in the marble lobby, men and women in thousand-dollar suits bustled through at fast clips to make the elevator, Starbucks cups in hand. Corporate types were always in a hurry, Ellie thought, but they always seemed to have time to stand in line for a five-dollar cup of coffee. Once they made it through the crowd, Ellie asked Flann about his visit to Mark Stern.

'He was actually cooperative. I told him how we connected Tatiana Chekova to Caroline Hunter through ballistics. He immediately saw why we'd want to know if she was a customer. I watched over his shoulder while he checked, and, unfortunately, Tatiana's name was nowhere in the system. He double-checked by calling accounting to see if anyone named Chekova had ever been billed by them. Nothing. He looked pretty relieved.'

'So where does that leave us?' Ellie asked. If Stern was relieved, it meant he was even more convinced that FirstDate was unrelated to the murders. She was having some real doubts about their theory as well.

'Same place we were before. We keep working all the angles and hope something breaks.'

'On that note, I've got real names for both Taylor and Mr. Right.'

'How'd you manage that?'

'They both sent me phone numbers.'

'Jesus, it really is easier for women, isn't it?'

Ellie removed a small notepad from her handbag. 'I ran the numbers through the reverse directory, and voilà. Mr. Right's real name is Rick Newton.' He was the one Ellie thought of as dirty birdy, so fond of double entendre. 'He's got a drunk and disorderly three years ago at a bar in Tribeca. I took the liberty of calling him. I told him it was about some found property. He's coming into the station this afternoon.'

'And Taylor?'

'Taylor Gottman. Two different women have obtained restraining orders against him in the last five years.'

'Ding ding ding,' Flann said, touching the tip of his nose.

'No arrests, but he's definitely interesting. Him, I think we need to surprise.'

Flann stole a glance at his watch. 'No time like the present.'

'Sounds good.'

On the way out of the building, Ellie pulled on her gloves and looped her scarf around her face.

'Doggone it,' Flann said, patting the pockets of his coat. 'I left my gloves upstairs.' He headed in the direction of the elevators. 'I'll be right back. Can you do me a favor? I don't want to waste the rest of the day trying to find this guy Taylor. Call his cell, make up some story, and figure out where he is?'

'I'm supposed to do all that while you go fetch

157

your gloves? Maybe I'll get myself a manicure while I'm at it.'

'See the confidence I have in you,' Flann said, his ruddy face beaming. 'Oh, and, no pressure, but my lieutenant called. He wants a briefing this afternoon so we'd better nail down something soon.'

Right, Ellie thought, flipping open her phone. No pressure.

★ ★ ★

'May I please speak with Mr. Gottman?' Ellie had dialed the number Taylor Gottman had e-mailed to the woman he knew as DB990.

'This is him.'

Ellie fingered Jason Upton's Larkin, Baker & Howry business card. 'This is Larkin Baker calling from CellularOne. Can you please verify your home address and telephone number for identification purposes?'

'What is this about?'

'There's been some recent activity on your cellular account that we need to confirm for security purposes. Can you please verify the address and home telephone number on the account?'

Taylor rattled off a Brooklyn street address and a 718 area code number.

'And can I get a work number for you while I have you on the line?'

He recited a 212 number that she added to her notes.

'Okay. And in the event we're disconnected, is

the work number where I can reach you now? Great.' She circled Gottman's office number. 'I'm calling because we recently received a request to add cellular telephone insurance to this account. Was that request made by you?'

'No, it wasn't,' Taylor said, sounding alarmed. 'I don't even know what that is.'

'All right. There's no need for concern. That's why we make these phone calls, to make sure there's no fraudulent activity on the account.'

'Fraud? Someone's using my phone?'

'No, sir. Everything's fine. The insurance covers the replacement of your telephone in the event that it is lost or stolen. Unfortunately, some people have been adding insurance to accounts, then making claims in our branch stores for very expensive telephones. Now we call customers to ensure that the insurance and any claims are authentic. Since we caught it up front, there's nothing to worry about.'

'Okay. I guess I should be grateful you guys are on top of it.'

'We try our best,' Ellie said, hitting the end button on her phone. A quick call to the precinct for a reverse phone directory search of Taylor Gottman's work number yielded a Midtown address. She was clicking her phone shut as Flann emerged from the elevator with his gloves on.

'We ready to roll?' he asked optimistically.

'Taylor Gottman's office is six blocks from here.'

# 17

SMO Media occupied four floors of a midsize office tower at Forty-ninth and Lexington. The marketing firm's receptionist was a young lithe brunette with full lips and flawless skin — undoubtedly an aspiring model when she wasn't wearing that headset. She was squinting at Ellie and Flann, polite but clearly confused.

'I'm sorry, who is it you're looking for?' A well-polished fingernail ran again down the pages of names on the desk in front of her.

'Taylor Gottman,' Flann said.

'Do you know what department he's in?'

The man's FirstDate profile described his job as 'marketing/advertising/other' and his annual income as more than one hundred thousand dollars. 'We're pretty sure he's one of the marketing or advertising executives,' Ellie said.

The receptionist's big green eyes roamed the phone list again as she shook her head bewilderedly. 'No. I'm sorry. I don't see him here. You're sure he works here? SMO? You know, there are a bunch of other marketing groups in this building.'

Damnit. Had Taylor been tipped off by Ellie's phone call? No way, Ellie thought. No way did he pull a phone number of another marketing company out of his ass like that.

Ellie pulled a small notebook from her jacket pocket and looked at the notes she had taken

160

from Taylor's profile. 'He's five eleven. Brown hair, brown eyes.' She tried to recall the online photograph. 'Sort of short hair. Thin face.'

The receptionist shrugged her shoulders, and Ellie realized her description was no better than the junk she usually got from eyewitnesses.

'Do you have Internet access on that?' Ellie asked, gesturing to the flat-screen computer panel in front of the receptionist.

'Of course,' the receptionist jiggled the mouse on her desk and the Web site for *Entertainment Weekly* appeared on her screen.

'May I?' Ellie asked, already stepping behind the desk. She logged on to the FirstDate Web site, clicked on her connections, and pointed to a photograph of Taylor. 'Does this man look familiar?'

'Um, I'm not sure.' The model moved her face closer to the screen and looked again. 'Oh my god. Is that . . . *the mail room guy?*'

'What mail room guy?'

'Some creepy guy who works in the mail room. I don't know his name. He stares at me when he's up here. A couple of times he noticed me catch him at it. He apologized, but then told me how pretty I was.'

'That sounds like our guy. Do you know where we can find him?'

She gave them directions to the mail room two floors down and pointed the way to the stairs.

'The mail room, huh?' Flann said on the way down. 'Last I heard, that wasn't a six-figure job.'

Ellie feigned shock and fanned herself like a southern belle. 'Oh my lawd. Call the papers. A

161

man lied about his income.'

They found their way to a large room in the back corner, where a bulky man sat at the front counter, placing labels on a series of envelopes.

'Can I help you?'

Ellie scanned the office and saw a man resembling Taylor sorting manila interoffice envelopes into folders hanging from a file cart. She shifted her jacket, revealing the NYPD badge clipped at her waist.

'We're looking for Taylor Gottman. Is that him?' She nodded her head toward the back of the room, and the big man's gaze followed hers.

'Yeah. What'd he do?'

Ellie noticed the response. *Is everything all right? Did something happen?* That's what she was used to from employers, coworkers, neighbors — people who knew the suspect. But not with Taylor Gottman. *What'd he do?*

'Absolutely nothing,' she said confidently. 'We're just here about some unauthorized activity reported on his cellular account. We'll need him to file a report.'

'Yo, Taylor. Cops for you.' Taylor and his four coworkers all turned in response to the man's big voice. 'Something about your cell phone.'

Taylor Gottman was tall and thin with short brown hair, full lips, and pale, smooth skin. As he made his way over, Ellie noticed he had an effeminate walk.

'Someone from the company just called me twenty minutes ago. I didn't even call the police.'

'Is there somewhere we can talk privately?' Flann asked.

162

Taylor looked uncertainly at the beefy guy with the big voice, who in turn looked at the watch on his thick wrist.

'Go ahead and take your fifteen,' the man said.

Taylor led the way to a break room down the hallway. A frumpy woman sat at the only table in the small room, eating a Butterfinger and reading a paperback romance novel. 'Excuse me,' Ellie said. The woman's eyes didn't leave her book. 'Ma'am? Hello? Excuse me.'

Finally, at least a visual acknowledgment of their presence. 'We're police. We need to take a crime report from this gentleman. I hate to interrupt you, but could you give us some privacy?'

The woman pushed some yellow Butterfinger crust into her mouth as she considered the request. 'My break's over anyway,' she acquiesced, glancing at the clock. She read a moment more, then tucked a bookmark neatly into the novel.

When she was gone, Taylor had an observation to make. 'You look familiar,' he said to Ellie. 'And your voice too. This isn't about that cell phone insurance, is it?'

'Do you know a woman named Amy Davis?'

Taylor repeated the name to himself a couple of times, as if trying to jog his memory. 'It sounds familiar. Can you tell me who she is?'

*Was. Who Amy was.* 'I think you might know her from FirstDate?'

'That's right,' Taylor said, snapping his fingers. 'What's her online name again?'

'MoMAgirl. She works at the Museum of Modern Art.'

'Right, right.' He nodded his head like it was all coming back to him now. 'We went out on a date. Must have been — I don't know — a few weeks ago?'

'A date?' Ellie asked skeptically. 'From what we can tell from your e-mails, it was one cup of coffee. And it didn't go very well.'

'Well, I considered it a date.'

'And you also considered it to be a pretty successful one. But Amy didn't agree, did she? Amy wasn't interested in having another — well, what you call a date.'

'I don't remember why it didn't go further.' Taylor brushed imaginary crumbs from his dark green pants. 'I would've said it was mutual. Whatever. We didn't see each other again. What does it matter anyway?'

'It matters,' Flann said, 'because MoMAgirl is dead.' He laid a picture of Amy's face, resting against the cold metal slab at the coroner's office, on the table in front of Taylor. 'She was killed Friday night.'

Apparently Taylor wasn't one for reading newspapers. He didn't take his eyes from the gruesome photograph, but the color left his skin and for a second, Ellie thought he was going to be sick. He finally looked away, shaking his head adamantly. 'No. No. You can't possibly — That's ridiculous. I didn't even know her.'

'You wanted to though. We've seen the e-mails, Taylor.' Ellie leaned forward, moving herself closer. 'We need to understand what happened.'

'Nothing.' Taylor used his hands to push his

chair back from the table subtly, giving himself space from Ellie. 'We went out one time.'

'You have a problem letting go.'

'That's not true.'

'Of course it's true. But — '

'It is not.'

'What do you want me to say in response to that, Taylor? *Is so?* We can go back and forth like that all day if you'd like. But ultimately, I'm going to win. Why? Because in addition to all those e-mails you sent to Amy Davis — so many that she had to *block* you from her in-box — we also know about the restraining orders. Two of them. From two different women. Even the receptionist — that pretty girl upstairs — says you stare at her all the time.'

'You make me sound like some kind of . . . vulture.'

'No.' Ellie's voice was firm. 'I said you had a problem letting go. I didn't judge. That woman upstairs? From what she told us, you complimented her. Told her how nice she looks. Did I say there was anything wrong with that? I mean she obviously tries to look good. It's not your fault she's offended when someone notices. I'm just saying you can be — tenacious. That doesn't mean you hurt Amy. That's what we're here to understand.'

'You talked to Monique?'

Ellie said nothing.

'The girl at the front desk. Her name's Monique.' He appeared to struggle to find the right words. 'She's — she's nothing. All looks. Nice skin, pretty hair. She smells good. But

165

there's no substance.'

'What about Amy?' Flann asked. 'She was different, wasn't she?'

Taylor nodded slowly. For the first time since he'd seen the picture, he looked genuinely sad. 'So completely different. She was smart and funny and confident. Did you know she graduated in the top ten percent of her class at Colby? Then she had a fellowship in Washington, D.C., with the National Endowment for the Arts. She sat on the board of a nonprofit here in New York that took poor kids to Broadway shows. She knew a ton about art. She was good to her friends.'

It was an odd way of describing the dead. More like the rundown of a résumé than a personal account of the woman. And they had already determined that Amy didn't have many friends in the city — just girlfriends from college who'd moved on to motherly lives in the suburbs.

'You know. She was the kind of girl who organized her five-year college reunion. And she'd been a bridesmaid a few times. You could see by the way her friends smiled around her that she had a real impact on them.'

It all clicked for Ellie as she listened to Taylor reminisce. 'How do you know these things about her?'

'What?'

'How do you know she did all of these things, Taylor? And when did you see her with her friends if you only went out once for coffee, just the two of you?'

He was silent, staring at the table in front of him.

'You researched her. You snuck around and learned those things about her on your own. She never told you any of it. She didn't even know you. How'd you do it? Follow her? Talk to her friends?' Ellie knew the answer but wanted to hear it from Taylor.

He was shaking his head. 'It wasn't like that. Not at all. All I did was Google her.'

'And you didn't think that invaded her privacy?'

His brow furrowed and he looked up at Ellie. 'Googling someone? You mean to tell me that you wouldn't pop in the name of a new boyfriend on the Internet? Everyone does it.'

'How did you even know her last name?'

Silence again. Ellie stared at him until he answered. 'I didn't. But I knew she went to Colby and worked at MoMA. That was enough. Google's amazing.'

'You did all this work to learn about a woman who didn't want to know you. And now she's dead, Taylor.'

'I didn't do it. When was it? You said Friday night. What time?'

Ellie looked to Flann. 'Around midnight.'

Taylor's knee jiggled under the table.

'Let me guess,' Ellie said. 'Sitting alone at home watching TV.'

'In my bed, sleeping. Alone.'

'On a Friday night?' Flann asked.

'Yeah.' He seemed to realize it sounded pathetic. 'Look, I'm not perfect. I'm — how'd you say it — I don't like letting go. But I was totally over Amy. I promise. I didn't understand why she wouldn't see me again, but — well, there's someone else now.'

'A girlfriend?'

More knee jiggling. 'You know, someone else I'm paying more attention to.'

Ellie realized what he was telling them. His obsession — his myopic focus on one particular woman who didn't return his affections — was homed in on a new target.

'Who is she?'

'From FirstDate. I can log on to my account if you want. You can see all the messages.'

They followed Taylor back to the mail room and asked the behemoth of a supervisor for some privacy at his computer terminal. 'We need to get some information off his cell phone account,' Ellie explained.

Taylor logged on to the FirstDate Web site and pulled up a list of messages he had sent. Forty-five in the last five days alone, most of them to a woman calling herself Dragonfly. Nothing to Amy Davis for eleven days. Taylor appeared to have moved on.

One message to Taylor's current project was transmitted just after eleven the night Amy was murdered. It mentioned a mock interview that Ellie recognized from that night's episode of *The Daily Show*. If Taylor had been watching television at his apartment in Prospect Heights, it would have been possible for him to get into Manhattan to kill Amy an hour later, but not likely.

Flann gave Ellie a look that said he felt it too. Taylor Gottman was a creep, but he wasn't their creep.

'What's her real name?' Ellie asked. 'This new woman, Dragonfly. The one you're e-mailing with.'

'Janet.'

'Janet What?'

'Janet Bobbitt.'

'All right. You're not going to e-mail her anymore.'

'What?' Taylor quickly lowered his voice to a whisper, avoiding the attention of his coworkers in the mail room. 'But you were here about Amy — '

'And we're going to leave you alone about her.' His worried face was immediately washed in relief. 'And in exchange you're not going to e-mail Janet. And you're going to stop using FirstDate. As soon as we leave, you're terminating your account. And I'm going to go back to the precinct and make sure you've done it.'

Taylor no longer looked relieved but he wasn't fighting them either.

'I shouldn't even help you.'

'You haven't,' Ellie said firmly.

'But I can. You have to promise not to get mad at me.' Taylor was whispering again.

'Get *mad at you*? What do you think this is, Taylor? Kindergarten?'

'You know what I mean. You can't yell at me, or arrest me or something.'

'What did you do? We can't promise not to

arrest you if we don't know what we're talking about.'

'Nothing illegal. It's nothing. It's just — well, I — I followed Amy a few times.'

Ellie sighed and shook her head. 'Depending on what we're talking about, that's stalking. It's the same thing that got you those restraining orders.'

'Fine. Arrest me then. I'm trying to help you. For Amy. I followed her and — well, I saw someone else. I saw another man. Twice. First I saw him looking at us when we met for coffee. He was outside. I felt sort of proud, like another man was noticing me with a woman as beautiful as Amy. But then I saw him again, standing under the fire escape at her building.'

'When?'

'I don't know. About two weeks ago, not long after our date. I even tried to e-mail Amy about it, but she had blocked me. Look — I can show you.'

He turned to the computer and pulled up a message sent to MoMAgirl eleven days earlier. *Amy, I know you're not interested in seeing me, and I know this will sound really weird. I was in your neighborhood visiting a friend and noticed a man in the alley by your building. DON'T FREAK OUT. I only know you live there because I happened to see you walk in once. Anyway, I think I saw the same guy watching us at the coffee shop. I know it sounds crazy, but please be careful. I promise not to contact you again.*

It was indeed the last message he'd sent her,

and it had been bounced back to him with a notification that he'd been blocked from the user's FirstDate account.

A man beneath Amy's fire escape, in the same alley where her body was found. 'What did the guy look like? The one you saw in the alley.'

He shrugged his shoulders. 'I don't know. Tall, I guess. Not big, though. He was all bundled up in the cold. I think I'd recognize him if I saw him again.'

Ellie tried having Taylor look at Amy's connections on FirstDate in the hope of jogging a memory loose, but it was no use.

'I should have done more,' Taylor said. 'I could have called her or something.'

Ellie took a final look at Taylor Gottman, slumped at his boss's computer, staring at the messages supposedly sent by a successful advertising executive.

'It wouldn't have made a difference, Taylor. She wouldn't have believed you.'

# 18

Special agent Charlie Dixon stared out at the Hudson River, but saw something else altogether. He saw the smiling face of Tatiana Chekova framed by long, loose, honey brown curls, blown by the winds that rushed over the Hudson River on an unseasonably warm spring afternoon almost two years ago.

Charlie had called in sick that day so he and Tatiana could take a sightseeing cruise. The champagne-pouring, sailor-hat-wearing tour guide was corny, but they both knew this was the closest they could come anytime soon to fulfilling Tatiana's dream of a real luxury cruise. He thought of the glee on her face — the utter carefree abandon — as they waited among the tourists to board at Pier Eighty-three. The way she pushed her cheek into his hand when he reached for her. The one time he had touched her in public. That's what Charlie remembered now as he stared at the water.

They had met two months earlier when Charlie drove to the precinct in Brooklyn to debrief a Russian female who had just been arrested for heroin possession and credit card fraud. His friend and supervisor Barry Mayfield liked to say that Charlie 'got played' by Tatiana. It was easier for Mayfield to think of it that way — to think of Charlie as the victim instead of Tatiana. In Mayfield's view, Tatiana had

172

immediately spotted an easy mark.

Charlie used his federal authority to cut her loose from the state felony charges she was facing. But instead of giving cooperation, she gave Charlie fake stories and false promises that led to nothing except the violation of a number of Justice Department guidelines — enough to lose Charlie his job and his pension, if not his freedom. In Mayfield's view, Tatiana was probably killed by some other gullible horn dog who was sucker enough to fall for her shit. As Mayfield saw it, Charlie was luckier for it, as long as no one ever found out about him and Tatiana.

Charlie understood why Mayfield liked that version of the story, but he also knew it wasn't true. He remembered the way Tatiana cried during that first interview. He'd seen a lot of suspects — male and female — try to cry their way out of it, but these tears were real. She was in over her head, and she had no idea how to get out.

Russian heroin importers were among the most sadistic, ruthless, and organized criminals Dixon had ever encountered. They also expected loyalty among cohorts, meting out heinous reprisals against those who disappointed. Dixon had flipped a member of the Russian mob three years ago. Six hours after the plea deal was struck, the informant's wife and three children disappeared from the family's home. Three days later, eight hack-sawed thumbs arrived in a care package mailed to the informant at his federal holding facility. The bodies were never found, and Dixon's informant backed out of the cooperation agreement and served his full sentence. Tatiana didn't want to go upstate but she wasn't about to double-cross the men who fed her drug habit.

She was in the worst position suspects could find themselves in. She was a stripper-slash-occasional hooker who wanted a television she couldn't afford. An eager-beaver cop's search for the flat-screen led to her pop with enough horse to trigger eight years under the state's Rockefeller sentencing laws. She was just dangerous enough, to men who were just bad enough, that she just might find herself killed. But she didn't have an established record of cooperation, and she couldn't corroborate anything she had to say. She was of marginal worth as an informant and was not even close to being the kind of deep player who could earn witness protection as a quid pro quo.

But Charlie got her out of the local charges anyway. He didn't have it in him to do anything else. Not this time. She was too vulnerable, too needy. She seemed too good, and it had been a long time since he'd used his position to help anyone. So he helped Tatiana. He listened to her. And to reconcile the help he had given her with his obligations as an FBI agent, he had even acted on the limited information she did provide. He set up a controlled buy with a dealer she gave up. He popped another guy walking out of a motel with nearly a hundred stolen credit card numbers.

But, on paper, he didn't document one word

about Tatiana — not the information she gave him, and not the consideration he'd shown her at the Brooklyn precinct. If he did, it would be obvious she got too good a deal for the information she gave. There'd be an inquiry. His motives would be questioned. And someone might figure out that he had fallen in love.

Everything might have been fine if Charlie had ignored the most intriguing piece of information Tatiana provided. *This one time*, she said, *I heard some guys talking about some arrangement they had with a company called FirstDate.* Charlie pressed her for more. What guys? What kind of arrangement? Nothing. He should have let it drop. But even with that vague description, he had a theory: Organized criminals had to have a means of washing the proceeds of their criminal enterprises, and it was often legitimate businesspeople who did the laundering.

He couldn't extract cooperation from the members of the criminal ring themselves, but he figured a man like Mark Stern would make a deal the minute the possibility of federal criminal charges was mentioned. So, nearly three months after he first met Tatiana, with absolutely no evidence to back him up, Dixon went to Mark Stern and told him he was a target. He claimed he had an informant who could document the use of his company, FirstDate, to hide financial transactions for Russian drug dealers.

But, to his surprise, Stern feigned ignorance, and then threw Charlie out of his office. Three nights later, Tatiana was shot in the Vibrations parking lot.

Looking back on it, almost two years after her death, he realized that Tatiana knew more than she told him. Her elusive mention of 'some guys' with 'some arrangement' was intentionally unhelpful. Tatiana wouldn't have hidden anything from him, though, unless she were truly terrified. What crushed Charlie the most was the possibility that she was even trying to protect him. She had loved him too, after all. And they both knew that the men she was talking about made the crooks Charlie usually dealt with look like Boy Scouts.

So because Charlie had not let the FirstDate matter go when it would have made a difference to Tatiana, he had vowed never to let it go. He was still trying to figure out how Stern knew his information came from Tatiana. He was also still trying to find a connection between Stern and the men whom Tatiana was wrapped up with. In short, he was still looking for a way to bring Stern down.

Stern had all the signs of a man up to no good. According to his tax returns, he was drawing only a modest salary — modest for a CEO, at least — and had no other documented income. Meanwhile, he and his strictly volunteer-work wife managed to cover the mortgage on their twenty-four-hundred-square-foot apartment, complete with keys to Gramercy Park. They blew thirty grand on a weeklong stay last winter at a five-star resort on Paradise Island. They had a private driver. They were not living on Mark Stern's salary. A hundred times Charlie had been tempted to turn what he had over to the tax division of the U.S. Attorney's Office. After all, Al Capone had been taken down for tax evasion. But then Charlie would have to explain how he knew so much about Mark Stern. And Stern would remember his meeting with Charlie two years ago. And Charlie would have to identify his informant. And then Charlie's career would be over. He might even be prosecuted himself.

So Charlie kept waiting and watching, thinking someday Stern would slip up. Charlie would catch him with the wrong person. Figure out who else was involved. He'd make it look like one of them had been cooperating with the FBI all along. It was an old lawman's trick — find out what you need to know first, then find yourself an informant to take the credit.

He'd used laws intended for terror investigations to get access to Mark Stern's financial information. He kept up an undocumented informant relationship with a marketing assistant at FirstDate — on federal parole for a little coke habit. He could lose everything but had gotten absolutely nowhere. Up until this week, the only dirt he'd uncovered was that Mark Stern lived above his explainable means. Then, yesterday, out of the blue, his informant called to report that Stern had sent out an office-wide memo about a police inquiry related to the company. And now two NYPD detectives were threatening his mission by asking their own questions about FirstDate.

Charlie reached into his pocket for the one piece of evidence that remained of his relationship with Tatiana — a single photograph of them together, purchased for five dollars that day on the sightseeing cruise. Her smile was radiant. She was clean of the drugs. She was happy. His own face was at peace in a way he hadn't felt since. He would remember that day on the boat with her — and the love he felt for her then — forever.

He took one last long look and tore the picture in half. Then he continued tearing, watching its unrecognizable pieces fall to the river below.

# 19

'Can I just say you were a lot hotter as DB990?'

'Thanks. I'll make a mental note. Now about the alibi — '

'How much detail do you need from me, Detective?'

The tone of the question was intended to be seductive. Unfortunately for Ellie, the questioner — Rick Newton, aka 'Mr. Right' — was anything but. His jeans were a size too tight, and his disheveled hair was an inch too long. He gazed at Ellie in the interrogation room over rose-tinted sunglasses the size of salad plates. His attempt to be hip was more David Cassidy than George Clooney.

'Not nearly as much as you've got in mind,' Ellie responded. 'Just a name and phone number would be fine.'

She pushed a notepad across the table in his direction, and he flipped his cell phone open to retrieve the requested information.

'I forgot the last name, but I'm sure she'll be . . . forthcoming.' Newton grinned at Ellie as the final word dripped from his lips.

'It's that kind of schtick that landed you here in the first place.'

'It's also what *landed* me with Reeva. Hey, what does a Chinese Elvis impersonator say?'

'Why do I have a feeling you're going to tell me anyway?'

'Reeva Ras Vegas.'

'That's not even how the accent — oh, forget it.'

Newton was still singing when Ellie left the room to call poor Reeva. Her last name turned out to be Stanton. She also turned out to be mortified.

'I knew it. I just fucking knew it. I *knew* that sleeping with that sleaze-meister motherfucker was going to come back to haunt me.'

Ellie stifled a laugh. 'I hate to do this to you, but could you give me a rough timeline?'

'Jesus, I'm so tempted to tell you I never met the guy. Too late, huh?'

Now Ellie snickered aloud. 'Afraid so. That whole lying to the police thing can ruin a perfectly good day.'

'Oh, yeah. *That*. Well, don't share it with the world, but I only met him that one night. At Uptown Lounge, at the bar.'

Ellie knew the place. It was an Upper East Side restaurant, particularly popular with good-looking single people.

'What time was that?'

'I got there pretty late, around eleven thirty. He was already there.'

'He, meaning Rick Newton?'

'I'm trying to repress it, but yes. Anyway, I just went through a horrible breakup, so I went out with my girlfriends. I'm following some silly book that says you're supposed to go sixty days without talking to the asshole you're trying to get over, and you're supposed to stay busy while you go cold turkey. The same book probably says somewhere not to sleep with the first loser who comes sniffing your way, but, chalk it up to four ginger martinis and a broken heart, right?'

'So, as far as a timeline goes — '

'How long was it before my inner slut took him home? A couple of hours. We left around two. He tried to stick around in the morning, but I woke up early and told him I had to go to yoga. That was probably around nine on Saturday. Then I stayed hungover in bed for another six hours. I was hoping never to hear about it again.'

'Hopefully this will be the end of it. Can I get a name of one of your girlfriends? Just to corroborate?'

Reeva sighed loudly and gave Ellie a name and number. 'She is going to give me so much shit.'

*　*　*

Flann waved Ellie over to his desk when she was finished with her call. 'What did you get from Mr. Right?'

'A nasty case of the crabs if he had his way. In a development that proves that there's someone out there for everyone — at least for an evening — Rick Newton somehow managed to get lucky Friday night.' Ellie shook her head in bewilderment. 'He looks good to go.'

'So get a load of this. My friend from the D.A.'s office called.'

'Jeffrey P. Yong the poker player?'

'That would be the man. He worked his way up the ladder to figure out why he was told to back off the FirstDate subpoena. It wasn't Stern

181

after all. It was a call from the FBI field office.'

It took a moment for the information to sink in. 'Why would the feds care about FirstDate?'

McIlroy raised his eyebrows. 'Interesting question, isn't it? Go ahead and wrap up things with your guy. Maybe you can call the feds while my lieutenant chews me out.'

'And what exactly did you do to make you chew-out-able?'

'With Lieutenant Dan Eckels, simply being Flann McIlroy is generally enough.' They shared a glance toward the man inside the glass office occupying one side of the detectives' room. Ellie could see from the way that Lieutenant Eckels's salt-and-pepper hairline barely cleared the back of his chair that he was short. Big, though. Wide. She remembered Flann telling her that his lieutenant wasn't happy about the assistant chief's decision to run with this investigation.

'Shouldn't both of us go?' Ellie asked.

'You really don't need to go to a Lieutenant Eckels chew-out session to feel like you've been there. Just imagine the mean, gruff boss in any cop movie you've ever seen. He'll lean on me, remind me for the sixty-third time we don't have the resources to run off on fantasy missions. He'll scold me when I tell him we don't have anything solid yet. And then he'll set some arbitrary deadline by which we have to catch our man or he'll shut us down. Got the general picture?'

'You sure you don't want a second body to share the wrath?'

'Nah, he's waiting for me. Besides, if all else

fails, I can use the fact that the feds are interested to buy us a little more time. Eckels might hate me, but I'm a pal compared to the fibbies. Call the FBI office and see what you can find. Unless of course you need a little more private time with Rick Newton.' Flann threw her a cheeky wink before heading to the gallows.

★  ★  ★

Ellie did call the FBI, but the conversation was short. When she told Special Agent in Charge Barry Mayfield why she was calling, she could practically hear the thud as she hit the brick wall.

'I'm sorry, Detective. Tell me again why you think our office has any involvement with this company you're talking about?'

Ellie couldn't let on that she knew the FBI impeded their efforts to get a subpoena for FirstDate's records. She didn't want to burn Jeff Yong.

'The way you let word get around, I didn't know it was a secret.'

'I know what cases my agents are working, and this one doesn't ring a bell.'

'We're working a murder case. Three of them actually. Tatiana Chekova. Caroline Hunter. Amy Davis. There's a connection to an online dating company called FirstDate. The CEO is Mark Stern.'

'I understood that the first time you said it, Detective. None of it sounds like a federal concern. Unless of course you're asking for the FBI's assistance with a suspected serial killer. In that case, I'll certainly call in Quantico. You'll have national experts there within twenty-four hours.'

'We've got our case under control. In the spirit of cooperation, I was trying to see if we had some overlap. The company's about to go public. Maybe you've got some kind of white collar investigation on it? Fraud in the initial public stock offering, perhaps?'

'Like I told you, Detective. I know the caseload out of this office.'

'Maybe it's not an official case? Perhaps you've got an agent who's friends with Stern? Asking a few questions for him about our investigation? We'd sure appreciate knowing something like that.'

'I don't keep tabs on my agents' friendships unless there's a reason to worry about them. Now if you've got some specifics, something one of my agents did that's inappropriate — '

'I didn't say any such thing.'

'I didn't think so. Thank you for calling, Detective. Good luck with that investigation. It sounds like a real barn burner.'

A young civilian aide lingered beside Flann's desk with a manila envelope. 'A messenger dropped this off for Detective McIlroy.'

'I'll take it.' The mailing label on the envelope indicated it came from the law firm of Larkin, Baker & Howry. Ellie slid a letter opener across the top and removed a half-inch-thick stack of papers. On the first sheet was a Post-it note: *Detective, The works, as you requested. Should all be self-explanatory. Fason Upton*

Ellie flipped through the documents. Financial information. Public records. Property archives. All relating to Ed Becker.

She scanned the first printout. It showed a real estate transaction almost a year and a half earlier. The title of a house in Scarsdale had transferred from James Gunther to Edward Becker. The next page documented the simultaneous closing on a house in Staten Island, sold by Ed Becker for slightly less than what he paid for his new home in Scarsdale.

Ellie bit her lower lip as she realized what McIlroy had done. Forgotten gloves? Right. He had snuck upstairs to ask Jason the wunderkind to do a background check on Becker.

Ellie was still seething when McIlroy emerged from the lieutenant's office. He failed to notice.

'Something better break for us soon,' he reported. 'I played the fibbie card, but Eckels is talking about pulling the plug if we don't start tying some pieces together. At this rate, we may not get a decent lead until our guy kills another victim.'

'You almost sound like you're looking forward to it.' Ellie regretted the comment at once, knowing it was a passive-aggressive way of dealing with what actually angered her.

'Jesus, Hatcher. I was only kidding. I forget you haven't thickened your skin yet. Any luck with the G-men?'

'No. They denied all knowledge of the subject. Are you going to do the same about this?' She dropped the stack of paper on McIlroy's desk. He flipped through the pages, nodding as he read.

'You did a background check on another cop?'
A couple of nearby heads turned, and Ellie
lowered her voice. 'I may be junior to you, but
what the hell are you thinking? Show some
loyalty.'

'You're right, you are junior to me, so don't
talk to me like I'm I.A. I don't *have* any loyalty
to cops like Becker. You saw that house up there,
in that highbrow neighborhood. When Upton
said he could dig up information that the law
keeps us from getting — '

'Well, I hope you're happy. There's nothing
there. That house cost the same as he was paying
back at his old place on the job. Oh, excuse me,
the house itself cost slightly more, but if you
check out his mortgage payments, he's actually
paying a little less per month now thanks to
interest rates.'

'His mortgage payments are in here?'

'You did ask for the works, after all. What did
you expect? An offshore account? A secret
warehouse filled with piles of cash?'

Flann's face fell. 'I don't know. A higher
purchase price on that house, for one — something too spendy for a cop's pension.'

'Well, you're not going to find it there. Or
anything else for that matter.'

'I guess some guys are just lucky.'

'Yeah, I'm sure Becker will feel real lucky
knowing we checked up on him.'

'He's not going to know, Ellie.'

'That wasn't my point.'

'Look, I'm sorry that I've offended you.
Becker's not the most wholesome cop in my

book, and the luxury digs set off my spidey senses. I didn't see the harm in having someone check it out. I should have told you before I went back to Upton's office.'

'You mean before you *snuck* back to his office?'

'Yes, before I snuck, like the snake in the grass that I am, back to his office. I should have told you the truth. Now does that tiny hint of a smile on your face mean we're gonna be okay? You're going to forgive the snake?'

'Yeah, we're fine, Flann. As long as you promise not to do a background check on me.' Ellie wasn't about to let on that she was harboring doubts about her new partner.

'I think I can live with that.'

'So, moving on to other subjects, I was thinking about trying to track down Tatiana's sister tonight. Maybe check out the club she worked at too. You in?'

Flann checked his watch. 'Sorry. I should have realized. I mean I shouldn't have made other plans.'

'That's okay. We hadn't talked about it.' Ellie had just assumed that, like herself, Flann worked past the clock, regardless of the O.T.

'It's just that — well, after our talk yesterday, I called Miranda, Stephanie's mom. My daughter's mother. Anyway, I'm going over there tonight. Stephanie and I are having dinner. I'm eating dinner with my daughter.'

'Flann. That's wonderful.' Ellie couldn't figure this guy out. One minute he seemed like a self-promoting turncoat, and the next he was a teddy bear.

'All right. Enough of that. You're going to be cooing cute noises at me soon if you don't stop looking at me like that.'

'Just gives me faith in the world. That's all.'

'Get some rest tonight,' Flann said, pulling on his coat. 'We'll take another crack at it tomorrow.'

Ellie assured him she was going straight home too, but in the back of her mind, she couldn't shake Flann's passing remark: *We may not get a decent lead until our guy kills another victim.* She was not going to wait around for that to happen.

★   ★   ★

Ellie's father always believed that the key to finding a killer was to identify his motive. *Find the motive*, he used to say, *and the motive will lead you to the man.* Jerry Hatcher had been convinced that the College Hill Strangler was motivated by masochistic sexual voyeurism. That conviction had guided his thirteen-year search for men who got off watching women in pain.

Ellie reread all of her notes on the case, wondering about motive. None of the women were raped, but the absence of sexual contact didn't preclude the possibility of a sexual motive. On the other hand, maybe she was overlooking an entirely different possibility. She found herself fixed on the words she'd transcribed politely while Amy Davis's parents retrieved Chowhound. High school boy. Changed grade. Restraining order. Call Suzanne Mouton to

188

verify. A New Iberia telephone number.

*Changed grade.* Ellie remembered that at some point in her own education, handwritten report cards were replaced by computer printouts. She assumed the same modernization had occurred in New Iberia by the time Amy Davis and Suzanne Mouton were in high school. What if Amy's parents had given her their best clue at the very beginning? Ellie dialed Suzanne Mouton's number.

'Hello?'

'I'm calling for Suzanne Mouton.' She tried pronouncing it the way Evelyn Davis had.

'This is Suzanne.'

Ellie explained who she was and why she was calling. 'We're working a lot of the leads we have locally, but we want to be thorough. Can't risk missing a thing, you know? Anyway, Mrs. Davis mentioned a problem Amy had with a guy when you all were younger, before she left for college. I was hoping you could fill me in on the details.'

'You mean Edmond?'

'I don't know the boy's name. Apparently Mr. Davis had to get a restraining order against him?'

'Yeah, that was Edmond Bertrand,' Suzanne explained. 'Just about the scariest boy a group of us girls could have imagined back then. Of course, that was before we realized how much worse people could be.'

'What exactly was the problem with Edmond?'

'A lot of what I know about the beginning is kind of secondhand. Amy and I really weren't all that close around then. I suspect she and her friends thought I was a bore. Whatever

189

happened, though, I do remember how obsessed Edmond got over her.'

'So they were high school sweethearts or something?'

'I wouldn't go that far. It was a short-lived thing. He was sort of an outcast — the kind of weird kid who only has one friend, you know? Kind of sad. Amy — well, I don't feel right saying something bad about her. It was so long ago and now she's gone.'

'Her mom said something about him changing a grade for her?' Ellie prompted.

'Well, that was what I heard. She used him, to be frank. Everyone at school knew something wasn't quite right with him. He wasn't slow enough to be in the special classes with the short school bus, but, still, something was off. He lived in one of those group homes or something. But everyone knew how bad Amy wanted to get into one of those elite colleges she was always talking about, and he started bragging about how he knew how to change grades. Amy saw a way to take care of that C in Mr. Gribble's bio class.'

'I don't suppose you know whether it involved hacking into the school computers, did it?'

'Well, that's what Edmond said he did.'

Ellie felt the beginnings of an adrenaline high. Whoever they were looking for had better-than-average computer skills.

'To tell you the truth,' Suzanne went on, 'the rest of us figured it was all talk. But the next thing you know, the rumor is Amy's letting him cop a feel behind the school fence.'

'I gather it didn't last?'

'Only until she got her college acceptance letters. She blew him off, then started complaining around town that he wouldn't leave her alone. At first we all felt sort of sorry for him, like she kind of brought it on herself, but then he crossed this line. It was like he was trying to possess her somehow — like if she wasn't going to be with him, then he wasn't going to let her move on.'

'And this continued even when she left for Colby?'

'Um, yeah, I think so. They pressed charges at one point. I think he got, like, thirty days in jail. I'm sorry. I know you're trying to be thorough, but what does any of this have to do with what happened in New York?'

'Probably nothing,' Ellie said, trying to keep her voice even, but knowing in her gut she could be on the right track. In a boy who was already unstable, seduction followed by rejection and a jail sentence could be a motive to kill, even years later. The question was whether Edmond Bertrand was unstable enough to take out a few extra people to cover his trail. 'We're just trying to make sure. There have been cases where people carry grudges for decades then reappear out of nowhere.'

'I don't think this is one of those cases. Evelyn and Hampton didn't tell you?'

'Tell me what?' Ellie asked.

'Edmond Bertrand is dead. He overdosed on heroin. I was probably a junior in college by then. I heard about it at LSU.'

Ellie looked at all the notes she'd just taken

and ran a giant, frustrated scribble across them all. 'No, I didn't realize. They mentioned that things got worse after Bertrand's arrest but — '

'They got weird is what they got. Amy always wondered if he would've been using drugs at all if it weren't for her. We tried telling her it wasn't her fault. Anyway, it doesn't matter. He's been dead for ten years.'

'I didn't realize. I'm sorry to waste your time,' Ellie said.

'I'm sorry if you wasted *yours*. You don't know who did this to her, do you?'

Ellie wished she could offer another answer to the question but could think of only one honest response. 'Not yet.'

# 20

He left work a little early. He wanted to see Megan when she emerged from her building. He wondered if watching her — getting to know the life he would eventually take from her — would be as enjoyable as it had been with Amy Davis. Amy had been special. He had taken his time setting up every last detail. It had paid off too. The plan played out without a hitch.

With Megan, everything was different. He had nothing against her personally. Not yet. At least not consciously. But following her, tracking her, secretly becoming a part of her life — it could still be fun. He was surprised at how eager he was to experience his own reaction.

He sat at the front counter of the Starbucks on Forty-sixth, sipping an Oregon chai tea, monitoring the two revolving doors of the office building across the street now ridiculously named the Avenue of the Americas. He had seen seven pictures of Megan by now. The most recent involved little more than a sheer white negligee. Still, this would be his first look at her in person — in the flesh, so to speak. He wasn't certain he would recognize her.

But precisely six minutes and ninety-eight departing employees later, there she was. She pushed her way awkwardly through the door, carrying an overstuffed canvas book tote and a Macy's shopping bag. So much for her claim of being low maintenance, the rare woman who despised shopping.

That was not the only penchant for consumption she had lied about. The photographs she sent, even the racy one, had all been conveniently cropped beneath her ample chest. There had been one full-length shot, but two rug rats — a niece and nephew, she claimed — obscured her lower body. Watching her plod away from her building, he smiled slightly. Sure enough, she was a chubster. The only 'athletic' frame she could legitimately avow belonged in a sumo ring. So predictable. So typical. Such a manipulative little liar.

Over the years he had learned that everyone lied — not just to others, but to themselves. They convinced themselves that they were good and motivated by decency. They assuaged their own guilt by conjuring excuses for their self-interested actions. Megan, no doubt, persuaded herself that all of her self-indulgences were justified. He could just picture her fat face saying, 'I deserve it,' as she shoveled in another piece of chocolate cheesecake.

That's how it was with the average person. They were dishonest and stupid, each trait feeding the other. Only a stupid person could believe the lies most people tell themselves. Only a blissfully ignorant person could be so stupid. He, on the other hand, was different. He was honest — at least with himself — and was definitely not stupid.

Megan had a not unpleasant face, with round, pink cheeks and cheerful hazel eyes — at least she described them as hazel on FirstDate — and framed by bouncy brown curls. She reminded him of a Campbell's soup kid. Or maybe one of those annoying Cabbage Patch dolls the spoiled girls collected when he was a kid.

His heart rate picked up slightly as he walked outside and adopted a pace about half a block behind her. This would be the fun part. Spying online was one thing, but he had learned with Amy that he enjoyed the live version even more.

Early on, he decided that the next victim would have to be a woman who contacted him. That way, the initial step was actually hers. He was just playing along. He had two other rules as well. Somewhere in the communications, he'd tip her off. He would give her a reason to be cautious. And third, if she ever told him to leave her alone, he would. It was that simple. He was empowering her to leave herself out of his game, if that's what she chose.

As he followed her down the stairway to the 7 train, he wondered why he had settled on Megan. It was true that she'd been assertive enough to e-mail him, satisfying his initial criterion. In her first e-mail, she suggested they had a lot in common because she also enjoyed reading *The Da Vinci Code*. But his in-box had no shortage of annoying e-mails from other women, each convinced they had found their soul mate in the most generic profile he had been able to create.

What was it about Megan that had piqued his curiosity? He had plenty of time to figure that out as he got to know more about her — from a distance.

Ellie found Jess sprawled across her couch at the apartment. He wore a wide-collared, checked shirt and a pair of weathered blue jeans. Were it not for the change of clothing and the can of aerosol cheese he was emptying directly into his mouth, she would have wondered whether he'd moved at all the entire day.

She draped her down coat on a hook inside the doorway, kicked off her fleece-lined suede boots, and grabbed a bottle of Rolling Rock from the fridge. Nudging Jess's legs, she sat next to him and took a long pull from the bottle.

'New Yorkers are a bunch of wusses,' she declared, blowing her bangs from her forehead as she stripped down further, pulling off her bulky cable-knit cardigan.

Jess used the remote control to mute a show about motorcycles. 'That's not a claim one hears too often.'

'It's the snow. A couple tiny flakes of wimpy pansy snow, and everyone goes ballistic. The drivers can't drive. The pedestrians keep on with their stupid habit of waiting *in the street* for the light to change. Then they're outraged when some dumbass who can't drive starts to slide right into them through the slush. I must've seen three near misses just coming from the subway. And don't get me started about the crowds on the train — '

'I hate to break it to you, El, but you sound like a true New Yorker. '*Yo, don't gemme started*.''

'Except I don't talk like that. And I know how to drive in snow. And walk in it. And dress in it, for Christ's sake. You know how many women I saw on the train wearing pointy high-heeled shoes? Three days of a Kansas winter, and these people would grow some sense.'

'In more ways than one.'

Ellie tipped the bottle at him, then finished it off. 'Damn. Two weeks without a cigarette and I'm still craving it. You want something?' she asked, heading to the refrigerator. He passed on the offer, and Ellie settled back onto the couch with another beer and her laptop. She told Jess that they'd cleared Taylor and Mr. Right. 'Still no word from Enoch,' she said.

'What kind of name is Enoch?' Jess asked. 'Sounds like some celebrity kid name, like Apple or Blanket.'

Ellie flipped open her laptop and Googled 'Enoch.' She clicked on an encyclopedia entry in Wikipedia.

'Turns out to have at least one thing in common with Apple. It says here the name is biblical.' She scrolled down the screen. 'The name comes up in two contexts. One was a son of Cain, as in Cain and Abel. And one was the son of someone named Jared.'

'We sure learned a lot in those Confirmation classes, didn't we?'

The Hatchers had attended mass at Blessed Sacrament most Sundays, and Jess and Ellie had been raised to say prayers every night. But other than the well-known stories of Adam and Eve, Mary, Job, and Noah, their knowledge of the Bible was limited.

She clicked on a few other links that popped up from the search. 'I guess one of them is the basis of something called the Book of Enoch, which isn't actually part of the Bible. Who the hell knows? Maybe it was the name of the guy's first dog.'

Ellie switched the computer to standby mode and lowered it to the floor.

'I need a favor, Jess.'

'Can't say I recall you ever speaking that particular sentence.'

'I mean it. It's not much of an imposition. In fact, I'm pretty sure you'll find some enjoyment in it.'

'So what's the hitch?'

'Don't make me regret asking. I need you to go with me somewhere.' She added, 'It's for the case I'm working.'

Jess paused, obviously fighting the urge to go another round with her about her involvement in the case. 'I can't say anything to change your mind on this, can I?'

'Nope.'

Jess shrugged his shoulders. 'Well in that case, don't sweat it. I was being a dick last night anyway. So where are we headed?'

★   ★   ★

Twenty minutes later, they stood in the Vibrations parking lot.

'Classy!' Jess yelled above the sound of traffic on the West Side Highway. He gestured to a

198

life-size purple neon sign of an arched-back naked silhouette.

'I don't know. She's got a little gut, don't you think?'

'I never thought I'd be going to a titty bar with my baby sister. It's so wrong, on so many levels.'

'I'm sure you won't be looking at any of the dirty stuff.'

'Of course not. I'm absolutely repulsed by the mere notion of it. The objectification of these women — it's reprehensible, is what it is. I'm just doing my civic duty at the request of a police officer in need.'

Ellie figured she'd have better luck at a club like Vibrations if she had a man with her. Since Flann had personal obligations, Jess would have to do.

Vibrations earned its name in more than one way. The kinetic bass thump of heavy metal music rumbled through the floor of the building, while women in pasties and G-strings gyrated against poles, the floor, and, to the apparent delight of one drooling man at a front table, each other. The crowd was a bizarre mix of men sitting solo, staring longingly at the dancers, and groups of rowdier men who tried to appear more amused than titillated. Interspersed throughout were a few young women, no doubt fulfilling all kinds of fantasies for their accompanying boyfriends.

The bouncer apparently assumed that Ellie and Jess were a similarly adventurous couple, throwing Jess a look that said, *You scored, dude.* His look turned guarded when Ellie asked for

Seth Verona, the manager who was on duty the night Tatiana Chekova was shot.

'Who's asking?'

'The New York Police Department.' Ellie flashed her shield.

'He's a little busy right now. We don't have no problems here.'

She took a look around the vast club. 'You mean to tell me that the pasties and G-strings always stay on in those back rooms? I won't find a guy copping an extra feel during a private lap dance? Something like that would cause you big problems with your liquor license.'

'Yeah, all right. Hey, Crystal. Crystal. Get your skinny ass over here.' A tall woman with long, dark auburn curls and full red lips came their way. She wore four-inch plastic heels, a nine-inch leather miniskirt, and a purple halter top that barely covered her enormous breasts. 'Take these guys back to Seth. Make sure you knock first.'

'I'm sure Crystal's her real name,' Jess said to Ellie as he eagerly took his place behind the towering woman.

Following a knock and a quick conversation through the cracked door, Crystal delivered them to a plain-looking man sitting at his desk surrounded by ordinary off-white walls adorned with metal-framed Monet prints. Seth Verona, with his striped, collared shirt and horn-rimmed glasses, could have been anyone working anywhere. He invited them to take seats, like a travel agent about to book a trip for the happy couple.

'We're following up on an old case. Tatiana

200

Chekova.' Ellie handed him a photograph to refresh his memory, but he shooed it away with a wave of a hand.

'I remember. Not every day we have an employee shot in the parking lot.'

'What do you remember about her?'

'Dark blond hair. Pretty. Kind of a sweet girl, really. A lot less screwed up than most of them around here. She only worked for me a couple of months.'

'She wasn't a dancer?'

'Not here she wasn't. Maybe before, at another club. I got the impression she was trying to pull her shit together. Only wanted to wait tables, even though the money's a pittance compared to the other girls. She was broke, I know that. I gave her some small advances here and there.'

'You make a habit of handing out money before the girls have earned it?'

'I wouldn't be in business long if I did. Like I said, Tatiana was different. She was like a lost little puppy finally starting to make her way. And when I did front her some cash, she always caught up.'

'Did she have any friends? Family?'

'Now *that* I don't know about. The way girls go in and out of this place, I try not to get too personal. You know what I mean?'

'What about a boyfriend? A customer who might have shown a little more than the usual interest?'

'Guys like that, they get taken in by the dancers — some girl who gives them a little extra knee time in the back rooms. The waitresses are just eye candy. There was this one guy, though. Not our usual type. Real straightlaced. Like an accountant. He'd come in by himself, but didn't come off as lonely, you know? And he never sat near the stage. Always toward the back. I only saw him in here a few times, but every time I did, he was talking to Tatiana. Come to think of it, I don't recall seeing him since what happened.'

Taylor Gottman had described the man lurking near Amy Davis's apartment as tall and dark-haired. Ellie wondered if it was the same man who came to mingle with Tatiana. 'Do you remember anything else about him? Age? Height? Hair color?'

'Nah. Could be you for all I know,' Seth said, gesturing to Jess. 'Okay, maybe not you. You, I can tell, aren't straightlaced. But I can't give you any details. I only remember the guy because I told the cops about it back then, the night she was killed.'

Another piece of information that failed to make it into Becker's reports.

'What about that night? Do you remember anything unusual?'

He chuckled. 'Unusual? Every night at this place is unusual. But, no, nothing stood out about that night. Just like I told the cops then, Tatiana seemed fine. Worked her shift, served her drinks, and left. Next thing I know, a couple of guys come running in, yelling for 911.'

'These are the members of the bachelor party?'

'One of the bachelor parties, yeah. That sounds right.'

'What about them? Did you notice any of them paying special attention to Tatiana? Or acting strangely afterward?'

'Are you kidding? Those guys? Totally harmless. Now, you tell me a girl gets grabbed a little, maybe roughed up — I've learned by now a lot of guys you'd never suspect, they've got it in them. But a gun? No way were these guys packing.'

Becker and his partner had had the same instincts.

'I'm about to see Tatiana's sister, Zoya. Her married name's Rostov. She lives in Bensonhurst. You don't happen to know anything about her, huh?'

He shook his head. 'Like I said, I don't get personal. But send her my way if she's looking for work. If I had more girls as good looking and reliable as Tatiana — '

Ellie thanked Seth for his time, and then Jess spoke up for the first time.

'Hey, I don't suppose you're hiring any guys, are you? Bar work, no dancing,' he said with a smile. 'No drugs, no convictions.'

'You're kidding me, right?'

Jess wasn't kidding. He made Ellie wait while he filled out an application.

# 21

Ellie rode the subway to Bensonhurst alone. Not literally — as she shared a seven o'clock train with the crowds of nannies, housekeepers, and other workers finally making their way home from Manhattan — but she was unaccompanied.

She had tried to persuade Jess to come along, but he had two reasons for passing, each of which he insisted was sufficient justification. He, unlike Ellie, had a personal life. He was supposed to have a drink with a woman he met at his last gig. He used the opportunity to remind Ellie that she should get around to meeting someone too. Ellie found his second reason equally frustrating. Whenever he had a Manhattan crash pad, he didn't 'do the bridge and tunnel thing.' So even though that crash pad was Ellie's, she was going solo to Bensonhurst.

There was a time when Bensonhurst was strictly Italian, famous — infamous some would say — for its mafia settlements. Ellie was in junior high when a crowd of local boys beat sixteen-year-old Yusef Hawkins to death for being a black boy looking to buy a used car in the wrong neighborhood. As hard as they'd tried to resist the inevitable ethnic changes, this was no longer the same Bensonhurst. Italians moved to the suburbs of Staten Island and Nassau County, leaving African Americans behind and making way for a melting pot of new immigrants from Eastern Europe and Asia.

She passed a Chinese dollar store, a Russian deli, and a Turkish fast food stand as she made her way to Zoya Rostov's address. Nearing the narrow brick walk-up, she spotted a familiar face heading toward her under a street lamp. The face spread into a smile, and Ed Becker offered a firm handshake.

'Detective Hatcher. I wonder which of us is more surprised. You got O.T. approved on a cold case?'

Ellie was pretty sure she topped Becker on the surprise meter. 'I'm doing a little background work in my spare time. What are you doing here, Ed?'

'I guess you could say I'm doing the same. I've been wracking my brain and shook out a recollection that Chekova had a sister. I thought I remembered where she lived, so I figured I'd check it out.'

Ellie recalled McIlroy's concerns about precisely this situation. 'We didn't mean to call you out of retirement.'

Becker laughed. 'No chance of that. Let's just say I didn't feel particularly helpful the other day. I thought I'd check the mailboxes to see if she still lives here, then give you a call. I wasn't going to talk to her. I mean, what would I say, right? *I screwed up your sister's case when I was half drunk and half crazy, and now I thought I'd solve it without a shield?* Turned out to be a waste of time. It took me half an hour of driving in circles before I found the building. There's a mess of Russian names on the mailboxes. I thought I'd recognize the sister's — '

'It's Rostov. And she's in 4F.'

Becker nodded as if he should have remembered, then pulled a set of keys from his pocket. Ellie watched as he headed toward a blue Buick Regal parked two doors down. She'd allowed Flann's comments about Becker to get to her, and now she'd made the man feel small. She took another look at Zoya Rostov's apartment building.

'You feel like coming up? It might help break the ice if she sees a familiar face.'

As Ed Becker returned his keys to his coat, Ellie thought she saw a look of purpose that hadn't been there before.

★ ★ ★

The wail of an unhappy baby grew louder as they climbed the hallway steps of the narrow apartment building. Immediately outside the door to Zoya Rostov's apartment, they also heard the delighted squeals of another child inside, joined by a man's voice, yelling something in Russian, when they knocked on the door.

'Yes. Who is it?' a woman asked.

'Police,' Ellie replied. 'I hate to bother you, ma'am, but it's about your sister. It's about Tatiana.'

The woman who opened the door was striking. She had full, peach-tinted lips and eyes the size of quarters, which peered out at Ellie and Ed through wisps of short brown hair. She gently jiggled the crying baby she held against her hip.

'I'm sorry. Who are you?' With a delicate Russian accent, she appeared to direct the question to Ellie. Ed jumped in to answer.

'You might remember me from when I worked your sister's case back then. I'm retired now, but this is Detective Ellie Hatcher. She'd like to talk to you about some recent developments.'

The man's voice rang out, again in Russian, and Zoya answered. 'It is police, Vitya.'

'The police?'

'The man from before. And a woman is with him.'

Zoya opened the door wider. A handsome man, who looked to be in his early forties, with short blond hair, sat on the floor amid a fantasy farmland of miniature people and animals. Next to him, a white-haired toddler laughed, completely unaware of his father's surprised expression as he marched a plastic cow up his resting leg.

'Ask them in. Yes, come in.' He said something quietly in Russian to his son and patted him on the bottom, and the boy ran off happily to another room, clutching his cow to his chest. 'I am Zoya's husband, Vitali. Vitali Rostov. Has something happened?'

'A woman named Caroline Hunter was killed a little over a year ago with the same weapon that was used in your sister's murder. Earlier this week, another woman was killed. She wasn't shot, but there are reasons to think her murder

207

might have been connected to Caroline Hunter's. I'm trying to see how Tatiana's case might be connected.'

Ellie focused her attention on Zoya, but the woman showed no response. Though the baby had quieted, she continued to stroke her thin hair and deliver soothing little kisses to her forehead.

'The woman this week,' Vitali asked, 'is that the museum worker that was in the paper?'

'Yes. Her name was Amy Davis. Does that name sound familiar?'

'Not to me.'

'Or Caroline Hunter?'

The man shook his head, and Ellie looked again at Zoya. It took the woman a moment to realize the room was waiting for her. She shook her head. 'No. I did not know my sister's friends. Tatiana led her own life, separate from ours.'

'Do you know if she was dating someone? A boyfriend, maybe, or even something more casual?'

Vitali let out an exasperated laugh, and Zoya threw him a disapproving glance. 'I am sorry, Zoya, but your sister — let's just say that for Tatiana it was always, as you say, casual. She had her fair share of male companionship, but nothing we wanted to know about.'

'What he means to say, Detective, is that my sister, when she was alive, was a prostitute. She was a drug addict and she was a prostitute. She did one to serve the other, and so it was.'

'I'm sorry, ma'am,' Ellie offered. 'I'm sure it's hard to be reminded of all this again. I wouldn't be here if it weren't important.'

Zoya bowed her head slightly. Ellie remembered in the earliest years of the College Hill Strangler investigation how her father dreaded having to re-question the victims' families. He said he felt like he was literally tearing off the scabs that had finally started to heal over the wounds of the people left behind to mourn. As time passed, her father stopped talking to the families altogether, unless they contacted him. Nothing he turned up ever seemed important enough to justify picking at those old sores again. But the ballistics match to the Hunter case showed a connection of some kind to Tatiana. Ellie just had to find it.

'The connection between the two other women has to do with a computerized dating company. Do you know if she used a service like that? It's called FirstDate.'

The Rostovs both shook their heads silently.

'Did she own a computer? Or have access to one?'

'Tatiana could barely afford to feed herself,' Vitali said. 'We gave her money here and there, but not enough for a computer. Even if she had that kind of money, that is not what she would have used it for.'

Ellie asked a few more questions about possible connections to Caroline Hunter's graduate school, the Museum of Modern Art, and the neighborhoods the women traveled in, but the questions only served to show how different Tatiana's life had been from the others'. The point wasn't lost on the Rostovs.

'These women,' Vitali said. 'They do not sound anything like Zoya's sister. Obviously, you are the police. But guns get lost, you know. Guns get stolen and sold. Maybe Tatiana has nothing to do with any of this, in which case there is nothing we can do to help you.'

The unspoken message was clear. *In which case, you did not need to come here and remind my wife what happened to her sister.* Ellie offered her business card, apologized again for the disturbance, and thanked them for their time.

'If it makes any difference, Mrs. Rostov, from what I've been able to gather so far, it sounds like your sister was working hard to get her life together. She was reliable at her job, and she was getting away from those activities you referred to before. That's what I've heard anyway.'

Zoya's big eyes pooled and for just a moment she looked serene as if she were remembering some earlier time with her sister. Then the pools gave way to tears, and she tucked her face into her baby's neck.

'I'm sorry, I'm sorry.' She continued to apologize as she carried the child to the back of the apartment.

Ellie didn't know what to say once she and Ed were alone with Vitali. 'She'll be fine,' he said, waving off the concerned look on Ellie's face. 'She will cry, and then she will go back to how she was this morning. Do not worry.'

Ellie asked him once again to call if they thought of anything new, or if she could help them in any way. 'I don't think that will happen, Detective. It was a long time ago now, and Zoya has accepted that we will probably never know who did this to Tatiana. But, yes, we will keep the number.'

Ellie paused in the hallway after the door closed behind them. Seconds later, she heard the Rostovs speaking in Russian. Even in another language, she could tell the conversation was tense. Urgent. Angry.

'What do you think that's about?' Ellie whispered.

'Whatever they were probably fighting about before we showed up,' he said, leading the way down the staircase. 'So what do you think?'

'I'm not sure what I was hoping for. A connection to FirstDate, I guess. I don't know — maybe we're barking up the wrong tree. Like he said, guns change hands. A trick gone bad could have shot Tatiana then sold the gun. Or he panicked and dumped it along the West Side Highway, and someone else picked it up and used it later on Hunter. I feel like I'm swimming in goop on this one.'

'That's the technical evidentiary term for it, all right. Goop.'

'What'd you think of them?' she asked, gesturing up toward the Rostovs' apartment. 'Were they like that before? Right after it happened?'

'Like what?'

'They seemed — I don't know — distant, or something. Cold? Disinterested? I mean, they didn't ask anything about the other women, who they were, what they might have to do with Tatiana. They didn't seem to care one way or another whether we ever solved the case.'

Becker seemed to take it in stride. 'You see it all the time in murder cases. By the time you deliver the news, their family's written them off as dead a long time ago.'

'But the sister. She was obviously upset. She just didn't seem to want to have anything to do with me.'

'Don't knock yourself over it. Some people, their emotions take them places they don't want to go. Who knows? Maybe she'll think more about what you said, about Tatiana getting better and everything. Maybe she'll start caring again and you'll hear from her.'

'Maybe.'

'Hey, where you going next? Let me give you a lift.'

'Just to the subway would be great.'

'You kidding me? You're gonna ride the train with the rest of the citizens when you can get door-to-door service? What kind of a lady are you?'

Ellie hesitated, reluctant to impose.

'You'll be doing me a favor. I can tell myself I was helpful, go back to the peaceful life of a retiree, and forget all about this case.'

Ellie laughed. 'All right. But only since I'm helping you out. I'm going back to Manhattan. Thirty-eighth and Park.'

'Your carriage awaits, madam.'

★  ★  ★

212

Once Becker had wound his way through the narrow side streets onto the Brooklyn-Queens Expressway, he got the conversation rolling. 'So does McIlroy still do that thing where he answers you with a rhetorical question?'

'Does Tara Reid drink beer?'

Becker smiled even though she suspected he'd never heard of Tara Reid. 'That's a damn annoying habit. The man can't just give you a simple 'yes,' you know what I mean? So other than that, how's Flann doing?'

Ellie heard the discomfort in her own voice when she said he was fine.

'I've always had the impression that McIlroy's not a big fan of mine,' Becker said. 'He might have mentioned something to you about it?'

'No details, but I picked up on some tension.'

'Sure you did. You're a detective, right? It's not like you couldn't tell when you guys were up at my house.'

'So, is there some story involving the two of you that I don't know about?'

'Aah, it's water under the bridge. I'm not the type to try to taint you on a new partner. He's a good enough guy. Smart as a whip, that's for sure.'

'And yet?'

'We're two different kinds of cops. That's all. Back in the day, it was Mac who was odd man out. But who knows. Maybe now, it's guys like me who are the dying breed.'

'Come on. You're not that much older than Flann. What? Five years?' She was being generous. Her guess was that Flann was in his midforties at best, and Ed was pushing sixty.

'Hell of a lot more than that, but I'm not talking age in years. It's a way of thinking about the job. The thin blue line. When I was a beat cop, that really meant something. At the end of the day, it didn't matter what your beef was with another cop. You were all brothers, held together by the job, by a code of loyalty. Flann's a whole 'nother breed.'

'You make it sound like I can't trust him.' She thought about Flann sneaking up to see Jason Upton without her and that ridiculous background check he ran on a fellow officer. She thought about the bond her father had felt among his friends at the Wichita Police Department, the commitment that made the city's treatment of his death so much harder for her to understand.

'I shouldn't have started running my old mouth. It's nothing like that. He's a good guy. He just sees the world different, that's all. His loyalty to the job is about doing the job itself. He follows all the rules, dots all the i's, crosses off the t's. It's not about the brotherhood. See what an old man I sound like? His way's the way of the future. And he won't have any problems with a smart one like you. You probably even went to college, didn't you?'

'John Jay.'

'How about that. A graduate degree even?'

'No, just a bachelor's. I started toward a master's in forensic psychology — even thought of going the FBI route for a while.'

'You didn't want to be a G-man? Or I guess

you'd be a G-woman, huh?'

'Whatever. No, I just was too eager to get into the real world. Studying crime out of books in a classroom never seemed to work for me. I figured the best thing I could do for my instincts was to get out on the street as soon as I could.'

Then, for reasons she didn't understand, she told Ed about Jerry Hatcher, his role in the College Hill Strangler case, and her unresolved questions about his death. And when she was finally finished, he told her he was sorry her family had to go through that. It was the only response she needed.

'I bet your old man would be proud of you, Hatcher. You're just a kid and already made detective. Working homicides, even.'

'Well, not really.' She told him about Flann's special request for her assistance, and he let out a whistle.

'Who knew Flann had that kind of muscle with the honchos. Ever wonder why he asked for you?'

She recalled the partial explanation Flann gave her on the ride back from Becker's home, but she kept it to herself.

'And he knows about that whole thing with your father. All the attention you got from the news?'

'I think so.'

Becker didn't speak until they emerged from the Midtown Tunnel. 'Flann McIlroy never was one to shy away from the media.'

215

# 22

It turned out that big-boned Megan Quinn wasn't as popular with the boys on FirstDate as Amy Davis had been. If Megan never left the house, he couldn't kill her outside late at night. So he made adjustments.

Getting into the building didn't prove to be much of a challenge. Megan lived in an enormous generic rental building on the far, far east side of the Upper East Side, in the yuppy slum of Yorkville. Unlike the white-gloved doormen in the ritzier apartments near the park, the staff at these places were strictly for show and a false sense of security. He showed up shortly after seven thirty. Evening rush hour. He pulled the hood of his jacket over his head.

'Delivery for 32M. It comes with a song, so I have to see her in person.' He made sure to hold the flowers in front of his face. The doorman was on the phone with one resident and handing a package to another.

'Yeah, okay. Go on up.'

He rode the crowded elevator with his face turned from the camera in the upper corner. He pushed the button for the thirty-second floor with his knuckle. A woman stepped off with him. He waited until she entered her apartment, then knocked on the door of 32M.

★　★　★

It had only been two nights since Jess began his latest sojourn on her sofa, but Ellie was struck by the silence and emptiness in her apartment. She flipped on the television just for the sound of it, and then settled onto the couch with her laptop and logged onto FirstDate.

More new messages and even more flirts. She had a lame two-sentence profile, but a decent if grainy picture. Maybe she'd unwittingly tapped into precisely what men valued. She scanned the list of messages. Only one user name caught her eye, and it had nothing to do with the case. Unpublished, the writer manqué whom she'd e-mailed earlier. She clicked on the message.

*Ally, You sound fun. I'd like to know more about you, but I don't like e-mail. (I know. Stupid way to try to meet someone if you don't like e-mail.) This may sound forward, but do you want to go for a drink tonight? I promise you can take one look at me and walk out if you like. I won't take it personally. In fact, I've gotten used to it. Peter.* He left a phone number.

Ellie started to delete the message, then stopped herself. Jess was out. She was alone. Her brain needed a break from the case. If she stayed here, she'd only surf the Web and feel like a loser. She clicked on the photograph posted with Unpublished's profile. Peter had dark brown tousled hair and intense green eyes, and he posed with a panting golden retriever. A caption beneath the picture read, 'Sorry, but this isn't my dog.'

She made a deal with herself, thought it through one more time, and then picked up the phone and dialed.

'Peter?'

'Last time I checked.'

'Hey, it's Ally. Um, from FirstDate. I got your e-mail. Is it too late to take you up on that drink offer?'

'No, perfect timing. I'm just leaving work. Where do you want to go?'

'How about I come to you?' She didn't need someone like Taylor Gottman cruising her neighborhood later, trying to track her down.

'There's a place by me called Delta Grill.' He gave her an address, but Ellie told him she knew the place. 'You don't mind coming to Hell's Kitchen?'

'Nope. I love it over there,' Ellie said.

'Very good. That scares a lot of people off.'

'I think that's why you're supposed to call it Clinton.' The neighborhood used to be Manhattan's ghetto for the roughneck lower middle class, but like the rest of the borough, had experienced what the real estate brokers called a 'transition.' Along with a slew of new high-class residents who couldn't quite swing their dream pad on the other side of Lincoln Center, the neighborhood had also inherited a new, safer-sounding name.

'We renters call it Hell's Kitchen. How long do you need to get here?'

Ellie considered that day's choice of work clothes — a red turtleneck sweater, gray pencil skirt, and knee-high black leather boots — and decided she was good to go. 'Is half an hour too soon?'

'Perfect. I'll be the guy in the purple velvet

jacket with a vicious case of acne.'

'Okay. I'll be in my motorcycle leathers. If you still can't spot me, I'm wearing the *pink* chain today that drapes from my nose to my ear.'

'You like Hell's Kitchen. You can leave for a drink on a second's notice. And you're not afraid to call a man out when he's being stupid. You got it going on, Ally.'

★   ★   ★

Megan Quinn was alone in her apartment when the doorman buzzed. *Ten, nine, eight, seven* . . . She scissored her legs in the air and mimicked the breathing patterns of the lithe instructor on the Pilates DVD. *Six, five, four, three* . . . The phone buzzed again. *Two, one.*

She took a deep breath and folded her knees into her abdomen. Then she hit the pause button on the remote control, wiped a bead of sweat from her temple, and pushed herself up from the blue mat unrolled on the living room floor. She ran to the intercom. 'Hello?'

'Delivery.'

'I didn't order anything, Lewis.'

'He said 32M.'

'N, Lewis. He probably said N, as in Not M. As in Never for Megan, always for the neighbor.' The guys across the hallway ordered in dinner every night, usually from multiple establishments. And half of those nights, the doormen called to tell her about it by mistake.

'Not food this time. Flowers.'

'Well, it's definitely not for me then.'

219

'Sorry.'

'Not a problem.'

Megan hung up the phone and looked in the mirror that hung beside it on the wall. She pressed her round cheeks with her palms, squishing the fat around her lips and nose. She tried to pinpoint when this had happened, and how long it would take to lose. She had been thin once. She had been confident. She sucked in her cheeks and held up the skin of her wrinkled forehead and for a moment looked like the girl who had waved from the homecoming float in Colorado while her date sang a comedic version of 'Mandy,' substituting in 'Oh, Megan.' Now she was so ashamed of how she looked that she was actually afraid of meeting any man who could possibly be *the one*. He might reject her as too heavy, and then she would have missed her chance.

She looked away from the mirror, reminding herself that her days of feeling bad about herself were numbered. She had joined Weight Watchers. She was doing Pilates. She looked and felt better every day. She even forced herself to go shopping during her lunch break to buy some transition clothes now that her fat ones were too loose. Baby steps. Three months from now, she'd reach her goal weight and treat herself to an entirely new wardrobe.

As she settled back down onto her exercise mat, there was a knock on the door. 'Who is it?' she yelled.

'Delivery.'

The delivery men didn't speak English any

better than Lewis, she thought as she climbed back up to her feet. She squinted against the peephole and saw a bouquet of flowers blocking the profile of a brown-haired delivery man.

'They're not for me. 32F, maybe.' That's where the long-haired skank with the chihuahua, pierced tongue, and all the boyfriends lived.

'Megan, they're for you. It's me. Greg. From FirstDate. I told you that if you wouldn't go out with me, I'd show up at your door one day with flowers.'

It wasn't actually the man at the door who had written that promise to Megan, but a very nice man named Greg London, who had been exchanging e-mails with Megan for a good solid week now on FirstDate. Lots of chemistry. Plenty of witty banter. Greg was one of the few men interested in meeting Megan in person, but Megan was mortified at the thought of meeting a trim stranger who described his perfect match as slender. Megan had been putting him off, racing to shed a few more pounds before the big introduction.

And now Greg had made good on his promise to surprise her one day with flowers. She did a panicked check in the mirror, then decided that sweat became her. She looked happy and healthy, and, screw it, she was finally going to meet Greg.

'How on earth did you find me?'

★　★　★

The man standing outside 32M pictured the round face pressed against the peephole. Flowers

221

and brown hair. That's all she'd see. *How on earth did you find me?* He heard locks turning in the door, and then Megan smiled and welcomed him and his cheap bouquet of flowers inside.

Megan did not live long enough to learn the answer to her eager question. Just as she closed the door and locked it behind her, the man who called himself Enoch realized that Megan looked a lot like one of his foster mothers. He was still thinking about the absurdity of that when he grabbed her.

# PART THREE

# ENOCH

# 23

The delta grill has a Louisiana theme, complete with wood-planked floors, New Orleans bar signs, and live zydeco music. Ellie made her way past the band in the bar, searching for a face that matched the picture posted on FirstDate by Unpublished. They spotted each other simultaneously.

Peter stood up from a small table in the back to shake her hand. 'I hope you don't mind sitting here. I figured we could hear better.'

'No, it's good. So I've taken one look at you. Is this the part where most of the girls run away?' Ellie asked.

'Yeah, but that was before someone told me about that whole using-soap-while-you-shower thing. I'm better now, I think.'

Ellie took a seat.

'Does this mean you're staying?'

'Stop it,' Ellie said. 'Yes, of course I'm staying.'

'Admit it. You're relieved.'

Ellie kept a serious face for all of two seconds before she broke. She was in fact relieved. Peter was even better looking in person: small-framed, but not too small, and he had a cute smile that turned up more on one side than the other.

'I was a little nervous,' she admitted. 'I've never gone out with someone from FirstDate before.'

'That's what they all say.'

Ellie insisted she was telling the truth, but Peter waved her off. 'I'm just kidding. This is my first time too. I just signed up a few weeks ago and wasn't real happy with the kinds of responses I was finding out there.'

'*Looking for a partner in crime? I just loved The Da Vinci Code?*'

'Exactly. What is up with that? Anyway, you actually got my ridiculous sense of humor, so I figured I had to persuade you to meet me at least once before I canceled my membership.'

A waitress came by and asked what she could get them to drink. She plugged the hurricanes as the house specialty.

'A hurricane it is, then,' Ellie said.

'Make it two.'

The waitress was back in a flash with a dangerously tasty concoction of sugar and alcohol.

'So who's the Golden?' Ellie asked.

Peter's expression was momentarily confused, then he smiled. 'Ah, the very attractive canine in my online photo. He would belong to my sister, Erica. She's good people, and her dog Boggle's the closest thing I have to a nephew.'

'And what about your great American novel? The adventures of a dog named Boggle?'

'No, although I can see the commercial potential there,' he said with a squint of mock concentration. 'It's actually about the trials and tribulations of a thirty-five-year-old reporter who lives in Hell's Kitchen. He writes his columns. He struggles to publish a book. He tries like hell to find a woman who gets him. Pretty darn original, huh?'

226

'Don't knock it. Your female counterparts have spawned several bestsellers writing about being single in the city. You might introduce a whole new genre: Call it dick-lit.'

Ellie usually had a better filter between her brain and her mouth, at least with strangers, but Peter seemed to appreciate the comment.

'Are the two of you ordering dinner?' The waitress was back. Ellie and Peter exchanged looks across the table, and then laughed.

'Nah, that wasn't awkward at all, was it? Um, just give us a second,' Peter said.

The invitation had been for drinks, but every dater — even Ellie — knew that was just a ruse. If all goes well, drinks evolve into dinner.

'I tell you what.' Ellie took two napkins from the tabletop and grabbed two pens from her purse. 'We each write down either dinner or drinks. We'll stay only if it's mutual. No pressure.'

They scribbled notes on their respective napkins, then showed their cards. *Dinner,* Ellie had written. Peter's napkin read, *Dinner! For the love of God, just one dinner!* He called the waitress back and asked for two menus.

★   ★   ★

Three hurricanes, one crab cake, and an oyster po-boy later, Ellie was stuffed and red in the face from the laughter and the booze. Based on the crooked smile on Peter's face, she thought he was having a good time too. But it was nearing midnight, and Peter caught her looking at her watch.

227

'It's late, huh?'

'Yeah, unfortunately.'

Ellie felt a twinge of regret about the deal she'd struck with herself at the apartment. She'd learned over time that it was better to set boundaries for herself and then stick with them. When she quit smoking, for example, it had been cold turkey. And before she allowed herself to pick up the phone to accept Peter's drink invitation, she had vowed it would be a one-time occasion.

She was tempted to break her own self-imposed contract, but knew she would not. She hadn't set this rule for herself arbitrarily. She wasn't ready for a new relationship, and this one in particular would be off to a bad start from the beginning. She'd lied to him online and then compounded it all night as she rattled on about her work as a paralegal for a real estate attorney. He didn't even know her *name*.

Even worse, between all the banter, she'd learned that Peter not only was a reporter, but a crime reporter. He was Peter Morse, the name she'd seen splashed across the byline of crime stories in the *Daily Post*, a newspaper that sold papers by out-sensationalizing, out-tabloidizing, and out-scandalizing all of the other local rags. She couldn't even begin to explain why she'd been misleading him all night without tipping him off to the FirstDate investigation.

She told herself not to be disappointed.

'Can I walk you wherever you're going?' Peter asked.

'No, let's be unconventional. I'll walk you home.'

'Oh, you *are* butch.'

The truth was, Clinton — né Hell's Kitchen — could still be a sketchy neighborhood. Peter was tipsy himself, and, despite the gender difference, Ellie was pretty confident that she had the better defensive skills. Plus she wanted a few more minutes with him before she said good-bye.

They walked side by side until they reached a storefront on West Forty-fourth. Peter stopped in front of the graffiti-laden metal gate that shielded the store entrance. 'This is it.'

Ellie gave him a skeptical look. 'Is this like when you told me you'd be wearing a purple velvet jacket?'

'Nope. It's one of the last places in the hood zoned for mixed use — live and work. I took the top from some guy who sold tourist tchotchkes downstairs. He got busted two months ago for selling counterfeit goods. They're trying to give me the boot, but I've got a lawyer working on it.' He gave her a name, wondering if she knew him from her paralegal work. The question only made her feel bad.

'It's hard, losing a good place in the city.'

'A home, I wouldn't have a problem with. But this is like a second office. It's only a few blocks from the paper, and I can come here and have a beer and write in peace. I can even file copy from my home computer. I think it's part of the paper's goal to phase out our desk space entirely so they don't have to pay the overhead.'

Peter mistook Ellie's sad expression for boredom.

'Sorry. I'm rambling. And you, madam, probably have to get home. Thank you very much for the walk. You're quite chivalrous. You sure you're all right? Let me at least hail you a cab.'

'No, I'll be fine. I can walk from here.' She said it, but her feet weren't moving anywhere.

He took a step closer to her and wrapped her sagging scarf around her shoulders. Then he placed the softest, most gentle, perfect kiss on her lips. 'Can I see you again?'

'Um — no, you can't.'

Peter made a face that said, *There you go again*, until he realized she wasn't smiling. 'I'm sorry. Did I misunderstand — ?' He looked back toward the restaurant as if to make sure he hadn't imagined the entire evening.

'I know this sounds really crazy. But I shouldn't have gone out with you. I shouldn't have even e-mailed you. It's too complicated to explain, but I just can't ever see you again.'

'Well, if you really mean that, obviously I'll respect that. Is there anything I can do that might make you reconsider? Anything legal, I mean? Not kidnapping. That would be bad, of course.'

Ellie gave him a sad smile, wishing he'd be less likeable. 'Trust me. I'm saving you a lot of trouble.'

'If it makes any difference, I'm incredibly disappointed — pathetically, really. I'm going to go upstairs and wallow. Like seriously wallow. Ice cream, sweatpants, Lifetime television, the works.'

Ellie smiled and kissed him on the cheek. 'Thanks.'

As she walked away, she heard him entering a combination into the electric keypad near a narrow door adjacent to the graffiti-covered gate. She turned around to face him again.

'So, that whole thing I just said about not being able to see you again?'

'I think I remember that,' Peter said, nodding.

'There's no reason our one night has to be over yet. I've got a bit of a soft spot for Lifetime myself.'

He walked her upstairs to the apartment he called his second office. There was no ice cream, no television, and definitely no sweatpants. Ellie closed her eyes and enjoyed the night for what it was, trying to convince herself that one anonymous night with a stranger was exactly what she needed. And every time he gently whispered *Ally*, she pretended it was close enough.

# 24

'Earth To Hatcher. Where's Your Head At?'

Ellie snapped from her daydream. 'I'm sorry. What?'

'Lieutenant Eckels might send you back to where you came from if we don't come up with something today.'

They'd already brought in Seth Verona, the manager of Vibrations, to look at booking photos and FirstDate profiles, but the clean-cut man who used to visit Tatiana wasn't among them. They could find no other common connections between Tatiana, Caroline, and Amy. This was supposedly a brainstorming session, but Ellie held her pen against a blank pad of paper. She looked at her watch — eleven o'clock in the morning.

'You using a patch or something?' Flann asked.

'What are you talking about?'

'To quit smoking. You're not fiddling with your pen today.'

Ellie assured Flann it was a matter of pure willpower, but she knew what was different about today. She had already noticed the newfound steadiness in her hands. She also noticed that she hadn't craved a cigarette once since her date with Peter. Maybe Jess had been right that she'd been craving something else all this time.

'Nah, it's something,' Flann pestered. 'You've got a funny look on your face. Are you sneaking candy bars or something? Maybe an extra little spoonful out of that nasty jar of junk you keep in that box of yours?'

Ellie felt her face begin to flush but was saved by the ring of Flann's cell.

'McIlroy . . . You heard correctly. The company's called FirstDate . . . Yes, my partner is very pretty.' Flann threw a look to Ellie and smiled. 'What's up, Antoine? . . . Eighty-sixth and First? All right, we'll be right there.'

Flann flipped his phone shut. 'Grab your coat. We've got another body.'

★   ★   ★

They pulled in front of the high-rise Yorkville apartment building twenty minutes later. As they made their way to the entrance, Ellie spotted a NY1 van screech to a halt at the curb. She nudged Flann when a man holding a camera climbed from the back.

'How can they know already?'

'A big building like this? Someone tells someone else, and before you know it, they call their friend at the news station. Word spreads. We'll have a mob up here before long. Quiet time is over. This is about to hit the big leagues.'

Ellie thought she detected a note of excitement in his voice. They waited to speak with the doorman, who was busy helping a well-dressed tenant push a box onto the elevator on the opposite side of the lobby. They could have easily walked right in without notice, but waited anyway.

Ellie used the time to check out three small, black-and-white screens that rested beneath the check-in desk. On the middle screen, she recognized the well-dressed tenant and his package. When the doorman returned, Ellie asked if the security cameras were attached to a recorder, or only used for monitoring.

'We record,' he said. 'I don't know how long but — '

Ellie knew that most apartment buildings, if they sprung at all for recording, only retained a limited duration of footage — twenty-four hours max. 'We need whatever you've got from the elevator that goes to the thirty-second floor. As soon as you can do it.'

He assured them he'd grab the tape ASAP, then promptly left the lobby unattended and unsecured.

* * *

The body in apartment 32M belonged to Megan Quinn. An hour after she should have been at work, writing copy for *Travel & Leisure* magazine, her housekeeper found her face up on the living room floor, a disheveled bouquet of flowers strewn beside her. Placed neatly on her torso was the piece of paper that had led to the phone call Flann had received about her murder.

It was a printout of an e-mail, sent through FirstDate, to the account of MeganMay, from the account of GregUK. *You sound terrific.*

*Enough e-mails. I really want to meet you. If you won't tell me when and where, I might just have to show up at your doorstep one day with a bouquet of roses.* It was signed *Greg*. He left his phone number.

Antoine Williams, the homicide detective from Manhattan North who originally caught the call-out, had heard rumors that Flann was working a case full time that was somehow related to Internet dating. Flann had long ago learned to stop asking how his name and his cases came to be discussed among other detectives. He was grateful Antoine made the connection so quickly.

'I suppose we should call Greg. Nail down his story,' Ellie said. Flann nodded, but they both suspected what they'd find. GregUK would be a decent guy who had nothing to do with any of this, other than unwittingly providing a killer access to a woman he had really hoped to meet.

Flann beelined to a good-looking black man with a short Afro and a groomed goatee, who stood over Megan Quinn's body. 'Antoine Williams, this is Ellie Hatcher. Hatcher, Williams. What have we got?'

Megan wore a gray Lycra tank top and black yoga pants. Tiny red splotches marked her eyes, cheeks, and neck. Bleeding beneath the skin had led to petechial hemorrhaging.

'We're still waiting on the M.E., but looks like asphyxiation. No bruising or ligature marks on her neck though, so I think we're talking smothering. We pulled a pillow off the couch with her lipstick and mascara on it. Creepy shit.

Looked like a death mask. No doubt we'll find saliva on it with her DNA.'

'What kind of pillow?' Ellie asked.

'Like the matching one over there.' He pointed to a moss green throw cushion on the upholstered tapestry couch.

Ellie took a closer look at the body. 'No scratches. No cuts. No bruises. Only the petechiae. He just covered her face with a pillow and smothered her.'

'I'm sorry,' Williams said, not sounding sorry at all. 'I thought that's what I just said.'

'No, I know that's what you said. It just strikes me as odd. This is victim number four, but he's changing his M.O. with each murder. The first woman, Tatiana — '

Williams interrupted, holding his hands up in a capital T. 'Mac, I can see you found yourself a suitable partner. If this is about to be a whole big picture kind of conversation, I may as well get on out of your all's way. All I been doing so far is checking on the crime scene. We good here?'

Flann assured him they were and thanked Williams once again for connecting them so quickly to the case.

Ellie didn't bother with good-byes. 'So Tatiana. She's an outlier from the other three simply because of the demographics. Shot in the parking lot of Vibrations with a .380 semiautomatic. Two bullets to the back of the head. Caroline Hunter's a higher-class victim, but same method of killing. Two shots, back of the head, same gun.'

'So far, so good,' Flann said.

'Right. But exactly one year after Caroline, we've got Amy Davis. You could say it's a similar victim profile to Hunter, plus you've got the FirstDate connection, but look at the method of killing. No gun. Instead, we had those horrible black bruises all across her neck and face. He strangled her with his bare hands. He crushed her larynx. He literally squeezed the life out of her.'

'So maybe he ditched the gun as a precaution, then decided to try something new when he got the urge to kill.'

Ellie shook off the suggestion. 'Uh-uh. This guy plans. He chooses his victim. He stalks. We know he stalks. He gets into their e-mail accounts. And Taylor Gottman says he saw a man watching Amy. He's not an impulse killer. If shooting is what he likes to do, then he'd get another gun. If we stopped with Amy Davis, I would have said he was seeking a more personal connection with death as he escalated. At first it was enough to pull a trigger and walk away quick, knowing he was powerful, knowing he was the one who ended a life. But then with Davis, he gets closer. He draws it out. It's more physical. More intimate. He wants to savor the moment and literally feel it pass through his body.'

'But now we've got poor Megan here.'

'Exactly. You see my point. He's past the doorman. He's in the apartment. He has access. Why so impersonal? Why hide her face beneath a pillow? Why not watch her choke — see her pain? It's like he's regressing. He's taking a step backward, getting more distance after Amy's murder.'

'Maybe. But this is the first time he's gone inside a victim's home, into a big apartment complex. Maybe he was worried about the noise. The pillow covers her mouth. It keeps her from yelling.'

Ellie squinted, trying to picture it, then shook her head. 'He's too meticulous. He watches, he stalks. If it was important for him to touch her, to feel her in his hands, to look into her eyes while she died — he would have figured out a way. But for some reason, with Megan, it didn't matter.'

Flann didn't seem to share her concern. 'The kill's quicker this time too. We had exactly a year between Hunter and Davis. Now, not even a week. Maybe he got such a high from Davis, when he did get a hands-on feel for it, that he couldn't wait this time. He rushed it, realized he had a noise problem, then had to use the pillow.'

'I just don't see it. He's a planner. He was careful enough to remember to leave an e-mail behind for us to find. You and I both know we won't find anything on the building's security tape. He wouldn't be so cautious and then deprive himself of the pleasure he wants.'

'So what's your theory?' Flann asked.

'Well, he could be evolving. Experimenting. Trying to find a comfort level between quick and dirty assassination, and something as personal as Davis.'

'That also might explain the timing. He feels guilty, somehow tainted, by the violence of the

238

Davis killing. So now he's trying again?'

'There could be another explanation, Flann. Maybe he got more personal with Davis because something about *her* made it personal.'

'We already checked out the people who knew her. She was squeaky clean.'

'I didn't say he knew her. Maybe she just reminded him of someone. But some kind of connection could have set off the rage we saw in her murder, something he doesn't generally need in order to feel satisfied. It could even be someone who knew her in the past — someone you haven't checked out yet.'

'And he appears all these years later in New York, and takes out a few extra people while he's at it?'

'We should at least look into it. The D.C. Sniper mastermind was out to kill his ex-wife, remember? All those poor victims were just camouflage.'

'Jesus Christ. This guy stepped up the pace with no notice, and we've got nothing. We've got mystery men from strip bars, ghosts from the past. No. This stops now. We're going back to where we should have been all along.'

'Mark Stern.'

'Does the pope work Sundays? Damn straight, Mark Stern.'

★   ★   ★

According to his assistant, Stern was out of the office. When Flann pressed, she said he was out for a meeting with the company's lawyers. When

239

Flann pressed still harder, mentioning the possibility of the company name being plastered across the front page of tomorrow's *Daily Post*, she gave him Stern's cell phone number and the name of the law firm handling FirstDate's public offering. At the mention of the *Daily Post*, Ellie tried not to think about Peter Morse.

Despite more calls, Stern was nowhere to be found. After some legal babble about attorney-client privilege, the law firm revealed that Stern departed twenty minutes earlier. Urgent messages left on his cell phone went unreturned.

Flann finally gave up and clamped his phone shut. 'Asshole. Megan Quinn might be alive right now if that guy had a heart half the size of his wallet. And the rest of the city's about to find that out.'

★   ★   ★

By the time they left the building, three other news vans had joined NY1's, and patrol officers had restricted the entire block from vehicle access. Several reporters lined the wooden barricades, notebooks or microphones in hand depending on the medium. Ellie scanned the line briefly and was relieved not to see Peter.

As soon as the reporters caught sight of McIlroy and Ellie, the questions began, each louder and more inflammatory than the previous. *Can you confirm there was a homicide? Is this related to last weekend's Lower East Side murder? Is it another single woman? Did the victim know Amy Davis?* McIlroy waited for the most daunting question: *Detectives, is New York City looking at another serial killer?*

Flann looked directly into a camera bearing a NY1 logo. 'As you know, there's little I can provide in the way of details at this early stage. There are leads to follow, witnesses to interview, and family members to notify. I *will* tell you this: We will find the person responsible, and we will not tolerate anyone who gives criminals safe harbor. Members of the media, you are our partners in this. Help spread the word that we need the good people of New York to help us with our investigation. Anyone with information should call the New York City Police Department. They can ask either for me, Flann McIlroy, or this is my partner, Ellie Hatcher. H-A-T-C-H-E-R. That's all I can say right now. A formal statement will be made later.'

★   ★   ★

Ellie started a mental count to ten once they were inside the Crown Vic. She unleashed at five. 'Are you going to tell me what that was all about, or are you just waiting to see if I'm smart enough to figure it out?'

He threw her a perplexed sideways glance. 'Don't sweat it. Cops make generic statements like that all the time. I wanted to send a quiet message to Stern with that safe harbor line. We've established a relationship with the media early, and we'll throw him to the wolves if we have to. He will give us our information, or I'll turn him into this city's next great corporate

241

villain. Leona Helmsley will look like Mother Teresa. But don't worry — it was subtle enough that we won't get any heat.'

'Flann, I'm not talking about departmental policy.' All media inquiries were supposed to go through the NYPD's Public Information Office. 'The reporters? The news vans? The cameras and the microphones and the spotlights? I asked you when we pulled up how they could have heard about the murder already. But then they had all those questions — such *knowing* questions. I don't think someone from the building could have tipped them off about a connection to Amy Davis.'

'What are you trying to say?'

'*A serial killer, Flann?* You expect me to think they came up with that on their own?'

'So I might have made a call or two before we came up here.'

'And once again, you didn't think to tell me about it,' she said.

'I didn't tell you because I didn't want you in the crapper with me. Stern'll be pissed. The department might — '

'Knock it off. I'm not as naive as you've been playing me. And I'm pretty sure I care a lot less about department rules than you do.'

'I know what I'm doing. You need to trust me,' Flann said.

'Hey pot, have you met my buddy, kettle? When are you going to get around to the rest of it?'

'Really, Ellie. We have other priorities right now.'

'I know. That's why I'm in the car with you, letting you drive, and trying to get this over with as quickly as possible. So just go ahead and admit that this is what you had in mind all along. This is why you put me on the case. *Ask for me or Ellie Hatcher?* You just had to get my name in there.'

She had been stupid enough to believe that she had earned an early career as a big-time homicide detective. Now it turned out that she was just bait after all. She was here not because of any talent she had as a detective, but because the media would salivate at the idea of the little girl obsessed with the College Hill Strangler growing up to hunt a serial murderer of her own. She was here to get Flann McIlroy just a little more press.

Flann merged onto FDR Drive, the siren howling above, and then finally spoke.

'When I came up with this idea about FirstDate, it got me thinking about the mind of a serial killer. For some reason, I started making connections to the College Hill Strangler case, and then I started thinking more about your story. I told you the truth when I said I was touched by it.'

'So touched you decided to use me as bait — just not in the way I thought.'

'I figured that if this guy was into the Internet, it wouldn't take long for him to pull up the stories about you and your dad's history. Maybe he'd get inspired by all those letters Summer wrote, the way he kept police after him for all those years. It was the contact from the killer that finally worked in Wichita. It's also how they caught the D.C. Sniper — a line of communication between us and him.'

'I'm not asking you to defend the plan, because here's what's really ironic. I would've done it if you'd asked, Flann. If you had a valid reason for wanting to titillate the press, I would've said, *Go for it. Do what you need to do*. But I had a right to know I was being used this way.'

'I couldn't have known that then.'

'You should've known it by now. That's your problem. Maybe it's why the other guys have nicknames for you, why you're an outsider. You don't trust other cops. You think you're better than the rest of us.'

'I'm not better,' he said.

'I know. You're not.'

'Ouch.'

'Obviously you're a good cop. You've got better instincts than anyone I've ever seen. But you can't be an independent contractor. You can't act like you're all by yourself on a little island. Drawing the killer out to communicate with you — that's a great idea. But you needed someone else to help you.'

'That's right. I needed you.'

'And if you need other people, you've also got to trust them. You can't just use them for your own purposes. This job we have — it only works if it means something to you other than a job. It's got to be your life. Your second family.'

'Why do I have a feeling you've heard those words in a more positive light than I have?'

244

Ellie didn't respond.

'Well, when I've heard talk like that at the NYPD, it always comes from some cop who's the poster child for not trusting other cops too much. You've asked me about the problems between me and Ed Becker? Let's just say that back in the day he was one of the poster children.'

'Why didn't you tell me?'

'It was a long time ago. What was I going to say? Fifteen years ago when I was a rookie, I saw him take some protection money from a video arcade in Brooklyn? Maybe people change. If we're talking about trust, maybe I decided to trust your instincts on that one instead of mine.'

'More like trust, but verify,' Ellie said.

'I guess so. I'm sorry I didn't fill you in on the background check. Or on the news leak. It took me a few days to realize I finally found a partner with a little faith in me — someone to share my little island with.'

Ellie saw no use in pursuing the issue any further. She'd been brought to Flann to serve one purpose, and now that purpose had been served. After this case, she'd go back to her precinct and remain, as she always said, quite happy with her everyday garden variety felonies. But until that happened, only one thing mattered: Finding the asshole who killed Megan Quinn on her watch.

'This better fucking work.'

# 25

Megan Quinn's murder was the lead story on every local network. Ellie flipped from channel to channel on a small TV set in the precinct lunchroom, finally settling on Fox 5 News. The white-haired male anchor introduced the story.

'We lead tonight with the murder last night of a young woman, killed inside the safety of her apartment, located in a usually quiet section of the Upper East Side. Police say it's too early to speculate, but in light of another killing last weekend on the Lower East Side, some New Yorkers are already asking, *Is the city looking at the activity of another serial killer?* We go to Anne Vasquez for more.'

'Thank you, Roger.' The reporter was attractive, with thick layers of black hair, dark eye makeup, and deep mauve lipstick. Ellie guessed the hushed voice was meant to connote the seriousness of the story at hand. 'I'm standing in front of an apartment building in the Yorkville section of the Upper East Side. Normally, this neighborhood is a quiet haven for the largely professional population that resides here. But this morning, Roger, that sense of solitude — and safety — was shattered by a startling murder.

'Sources tell me that the victim is a thirty-three-year-old single woman who resided alone in this doorman building. The woman was found smothered to death in her apartment. Police believe the murder occurred last night. We are withholding the victim's name pursuant to a request from the NYPD, but according to both the neighbors and the police, the woman was unlikely to have been killed by anyone who knew her.

'Her death follows the strangling murder last weekend of Amy Davis, another single woman of approximately the same age, who also lived alone, killed on the Lower East Side outside of her residence. Police believe she was killed by a stranger as well.

'Although we have not received official confirmation from the police department, we are able to report to you now that the police are investigating a possible connection between the Davis murder and the murder inside this building last night.'

'Anne, if both women were killed by the same stranger, are you saying that these murders are the work of a serial killer?'

'Our sources have been careful not to use those words' — even though Channel Five wasn't — 'but we do know that one theory the police are looking into is that both women were customers of the same company. We have not confirmed the identity of that company, but apparently it is a common link between the two women. Obviously, we here at Fox 5 News will bring it to you as soon as we know.

'On another note, Roger, there's an intriguing connection between this case and one of the investigating detectives, New York City Detective

Ellie Hatcher. Now, according to our sources, Hatcher has been a detective for only one year and was brought into the homicide unit specifically for this case.'

'Have you been able to determine the reason for that, Anne?'

'The police don't usually share such information with us, but it's certainly raising questions. We do know that Detective Hatcher is herself a thirty-year-old woman, not dissimilar from these two victims, so perhaps she can offer some insight from that perspective. But a more intriguing explanation is Detective Hatcher's connection to a serial killer in her own personal background. You might remember a couple of years ago, Roger, when police in Wichita, Kansas, arrested William Summer, the College Hill Strangler.'

'That was an awful story, wasn't it?'

'Well, Ellie Hatcher's *father* was one of the lead detectives on that College Hill Strangler investigation. Maybe the NYPD is hoping tonight that the apple didn't fall far from the tree.'

'Interesting and scary stuff there, Anne. Thanks for the report, and keep us updated.'

'I will, Roger.'

'Also tonight, fire marshals investigate a blaze in Queens that — '

Ellie hit the power button on the television. An awkward silence filled the room as a civilian aide who had just removed a Snickers bar from the vending machine stared at Ellie, as if obligated to say something.

The young woman finally settled on, 'Who knows? Maybe the killer will be jealous of all the attention you're getting. Come out of the woodwork.'

Ellie threw a look at Flann. 'Huh . . . we hadn't thought of that. That would be interesting, wouldn't it?'

'You never know,' the woman said, unwrapping her candy bar and fleeing while she had the chance.

'You all right?' Flann asked.

'Yeah, I'm fine. Just give me a second.'

'No problem. I'm going across the street for some decent coffee. You want anything?'

She shook her head. 'But thanks,' she added as he walked out.

She wanted the time to mull over her thoughts. To her surprise, they were filled not with concerns about her renewed status as a media target, but instead by the nagging feeling that they were missing something important. It had to be related to Amy. All of the other murders had been quick — relatively painless as far as murders go. But with Amy, he'd been brutal. She remembered the deep bruises and contusions in the morgue photograph, reconstructing the struggle that must have taken place to leave those injuries. She mentally compared those images to what she'd just seen at Megan Quinn's apartment. Something about Amy had been special.

Before bringing in Ellie, Flann had eliminated from consideration anyone in Amy's current life, and she trusted Flann not to miss an obvious suspect. That left Amy's past.

The fact that Amy had a restraining order against a boy from her hometown kept jumping out at her. Lots of women had problems with ex-boyfriends, but how many required a court's intervention? And then there was the fact that the boy in question had been so computer savvy. An obsessive person with techie skills was precisely whom they were looking for. She pictured a personality like Taylor Gottman's. Was it so far-fetched that something could reignite an obsession a decade later?

She looked at the notes she'd made — and then crossed out — from her conversation with Suzanne Mouton. Edmond Bertrand had been looking like a prime suspect until Suzanne said that he had died. *He overdosed on heroin. I heard about it at LSU.*

Ellie realized then that she may have been too quick to write Bertrand off. Suzanne hadn't lived in New Iberia when he supposedly overdosed. She *heard about it*, undoubtedly from someone who repeated a secondhand story. And people embellish when they repeat, and then other people embellish further. Like in a slumber party game of Operator, news of a bad drug trip one night in New Iberia might have turned into a fatal overdose by the time it hit Suzanne Mouton's dorm on LSU's Lafayette campus.

Ellie left the solitude of the break room and pulled up the New York DMV database on Flann's computer. No New York driver's license or identification card. She tried crime reports.

250

No New York arrests or convictions. She went next to the NCIC database, a national clearinghouse of records like fugitive warrants, missing person alerts, and sex offender registrations. She ran Bertrand's name and got a hit.

Edmond Bertrand, date of birth, October 16, 1974. Arrested in Boston six years earlier for forgery. Bertrand no-showed for his arraignment, and was never picked up on the warrant.

According to Suzanne Mouton, the Edmond Bertrand who'd stalked Amy Davis had overdosed ten years ago. She found Suzanne's phone number and called.

After apologizing in advance for the bizarre nature of her question, she asked Suzanne if she were certain that Edmond Bertrand's drug overdose was fatal.

'Um, you warned me to expect the bizarre. It's not like I saw the body or anything, but, yeah, that's what everyone said.'

Ellie took another look at the six-year-old Massachusetts arrest warrant on the computer screen in front of her. 'And you're sure about the timing? It couldn't have been in the last six years?'

'No. I was definitely at LSU. I'm pretty sure I was a junior; maybe even a sophomore.'

'Did you actually see an obituary? Or do you know anyone who went to the funeral?'

'What's this all about?'

'It registered after we hung up last time that you had heard about Bertrand's death second-hand while you were in school. I thought I'd verify it wasn't just a rumor — just to make sure we didn't jump the gun counting him out. That's all.'

'I guess I never questioned what I heard. I know that Amy and her parents heard the same thing.'

'That's fine. I'll call around down there and have someone check the death records, just to be sure.'

'I'll tell you what. I've got a neighbor down the road who works for the sheriff's office. He can get you all the details. Do you have a phone number or e-mail or something?'

Ellie rattled off her number and e-mail address. 'And can you also ask him to look up Edmond Bertrand's date of birth? It's important.'

★   ★   ★

The woman at the records division of the Boston Police Department was able to pull up the information Ellie requested in less than a minute.

'The only entry in our database for an Edmond Bertrand is that one arrest. And, unfortunately, there's no booking photo coming up on that. But a picture from a six-year-old forgery might not have made it into the computer anyway.'

'So is there somewhere else I could get a photograph?' Ellie spotted Flann heading her way, coat still on and coffee in hand. He looked excited and gestured at her to cut the call short.

'My guess is on a charge like that, the officer

252

probably cited and released him, in which case we wouldn't have either a picture or prints. The only way to know for sure is from the police report. Want me to put in a request for you?'

'I'd appreciate it.' Ellie gave her the fax number at the precinct and hung up.

'What was that?' Flann asked.

'A favor for a friend.' Ellie wasn't sure whether she fibbed to gloss over the long-shot phone call to Boston, or because of lingering resentment toward Flann for his own secrecy. Either way, it didn't seem to warrant discussion in light of Flann's eagerness. 'What's up?'

'I told you media attention would be our friend. I just got a call from a very apologetic Mark Stern, who assured me he called the moment he got our messages.'

'He's finally willing to help?'

'Greg UK's real name is Greg London.'

'And we both know he's not going to be our guy, just like Amy Davis's date wasn't our guy.'

'That's why he's going to pull up all the names of the men who contacted Caroline Hunter, Amy Davis, and Megan Quinn while we have a little chat with Mr. London.'

* * *

Greg London had absolutely no criminal history, was fully employed as a lighting technician for Broadway shows, and insisted that on the night Megan Quinn was murdered he was at home reading a Truman biography. Although no one could vouch for his whereabouts, they were nevertheless able to exclude London from suspicion: The man in the security video from Megan's apartment building was six feet tall. Greg London was five foot eight.

Ellie wasn't particularly disappointed, and she certainly wasn't surprised. The killer would never make it that easy.

★   ★   ★

Like a losing politician who gives verbal hugs to the candidate he spent fourteen months trashing, Stern welcomed them into his office as if he had never been their adversary. 'I've got the names of every account holder who ever contacted Caroline Hunter, Amy Davis, or Megan Quinn — just like you asked. But there's one guy you're going to want to check out first. His name's Richard Hamline.'

'What puts him at the top of the list?' Flann asked.

'Because I cross-referenced the lists. He's the only user who's been in contact with two of the women: Amy Davis and Megan Quinn.' Stern directed their attention to the flat-screen monitor on his desk. 'I pulled up a dummy of his account. We're basically seeing what Hamline would see if he pulled up his own account, but I'm able to go through the back door without actually logging in. That way, he won't be able to tell someone else is in his account.'

The screen displayed Hamline's FirstDate connections. Stern clicked first on Megan Quinn, opening up a series of e-mails, then on

Amy Davis. Ellie shook her head in disbelief.

'We had him in front of us the whole time, Flann. The user name. Check out the user name.'

Richard Hamline was the real name behind the pseudonym Enoch, the one with the generic profile and very specific questions about Amy Davis. The one who never did return the flirt from Ellie. The one using the biblical name she was going to ask about if he ever contacted her. The killer had contacted the two most recent victims through the same FirstDate account. He had to know they would make the connection. He was engaging them. Ellie took a hard look at the dark-haired, blue-eyed, fair-skinned man smiling at her from the screen and wondered if Hamline was bold enough to use a real photograph.

'What else can you tell us about him?' Ellie asked.

Stern handed her a sheet of paper. 'That's his name, billing information, and e-mail address from the account. I called one of our I.T. people to pull up his I.S.P. information.'

'You called in a what for a who?' Flann asked.

'I called an information technology staffer to locate the Internet service provider. Like most commercial Internet sites, we automatically collect every user's Internet service provider each time they visit the site. We also get their I.P. address.'

'And an I.P. is — '

'An Internet protocol address,' Stern explained. 'Like most of our customers, Hamline used an easy-to-get, free e-mail address to open his account with us. You don't have to provide any kind of verifiable identifying information to open that kind of an e-mail account. But that's where the I.P. address is helpful. Every device that links to the Internet — whether it be a computer, or a printer, or a router — has a unique number. It's used to identify the device and to communicate with other devices. I'll get someone to track that down for Hamline.'

'And how is that useful?' Flann asked.

'We can use the number to geolocate the device. Just think of the I.P. address as a computer's street address or a phone number. It identifies a unique, specific computer. In most cases, we can actually use the I.P. address to match the computer to a physical location.'

'And every Web site keeps track of them? So much for privacy,' Ellie said.

'Not only do we do it. We *have* to do it under the Patriot Act. I'm sure the ACLU is overjoyed.'

'Well, I say thank God for Big Brother,' Flann said. 'How soon can we get that information?'

'My I.T. guy's on his way from Jersey City. Should be forty minutes or so.'

Flann didn't waste any time asking questions. 'Let's go ahead and work it like the twentieth century. We've got a good old-fashioned name and date of birth.'

★　★　★

Richard Hamline's name and date of birth appeared only once in the NYPD's records — in a police report he'd filed two years earlier after a man who was never identified grabbed his gym bag from his shoulder as he left work shortly after midnight. According to the report, Hamline worked as a corporate lawyer at a Wall Street law firm and lived in a seventeenth-floor apartment adjacent to Battery Park.

Ellie held the police report in one hand and a copy of Hamline's driver's license photo in another. The picture was nearly eight years old. Although it bore a slight resemblance to the photo accompanying Enoch's profile, Ellie suspected the better-looking photo on FirstDate was bogus.

'This doesn't feel right,' Ellie said. 'He gives his real name on an account he uses to contact two of the victims? It's too easy. This is just going to be another cycle in the game.'

'Do you have any other suggestions?' Flann asked. A judge had already issued a telephonic warrant to arrest Hamline. The spreading media hysteria about a possible serial killer no doubt gave them an edge in the probable cause balance.

'Nope. Just making sure we're on the same page.' It was not yet eight o'clock at night — early by a corporate lawyer's standards. 'We should try his office first.'

# 26

'I was wondering if you might call me in, Boss.' Charlie Dixon's tone was friendly but resigned. He settled himself into one of the hunter green leather guest chairs across from Barry Mayfield's enormous mahogany desk. The windows behind his boss were flanked on either side by the flags of the United States and the Department of Justice. He looked out toward the old World Trade Center site.

'You ever worked a serial case, Charlie?'

'I'll treat that as a rhetorical question.' Most agents who were merely adequate — agents like Charlie — worked bank robberies and gun cases their entire careers. With a decent amount of ass-kissing and a touch of good luck, Charlie carried a semirespectable fraud caseload, but Quantico reserved its serial cases for the superstars.

'I worked one about fifteen years ago,' Mayfield said. 'You want to talk about ulcer-inducing, get involved in one of those bad boys. You literally have a clock ticking over your head, with an unknown number of minutes on the timer. Miss one angle, act a few hours late — bam, you got another body.'

Charlie sat silently, staring at a crystal golf ball clock on the desk, knowing that Mayfield would get to the point in his own time and in his own way.

'I don't think we can write this off as one cop's lunatic theory anymore, Charlie. It's all over the news: The NYPD officially has a serial case on its hands now. When that female cop called the other day, she had three victims including your girl Tatiana. This new one makes four. Apparently they're convinced that FirstDate's got something to do with it all. Without knowing more, I suspect most of their work right now is about finding commonalities among their victims. What do you think?'

'Like I said, I never worked a case like that before, but that sounds reasonable.'

'Not knowing everything you can about a victim can really throw things off. If you treat her as just another part of the series when she's actually the most important . . . or you throw her in the mix when she really doesn't belong in the pattern. See how something like that could muck up the picture?'

Dixon was growing impatient but did his best to conceal it. 'I can see the problem.'

'So how does Tatiana figure into NYPD's case?'

'Don't I wish I knew.'

'It's pretty fucking weird that she said something was screwy with FirstDate, and now they got three other dead women somehow related to that company. You've had your bee all up in a bonnet over Mark Stern. Could it be him?'

Charlie didn't miss a beat. 'No. He's a crook, but he's not that kind of wrong. You know, one way to find out would be to take the case, Barry.'

Charlie leaned in to make the argument he'd been rehearsing at his desk. 'A case like this would be good for the bureau — show we've still got room for our meat and potatoes even with all the terrorism investigations.'

'Except that ain't exactly true now, is it? You know as well as I do where the priorities are these days. And I've thought about it. It's better this way. It's like a Chinese wall between them and us. If anyone finds out about you and that girl, no one can say the relationship tainted the investigation — not if we're not the ones conducting it.'

'You assume they can solve it.'

'The NYPD's good at these cases. They'll find the guy, and they'll do it without us.'

'But maybe we'd have a better chance, knowing what we know.'

'And therein lies the rub,' Mayfield said. 'I thought about this awhile, and it always comes back to the fact that we know something they don't. And that's why one of us needs to change that situation.'

'You want to tell them?'

'Actually, I thought it was more fair to have you do it.'

'Tell them what?'

'You really don't see an opportunity when it's handed to you, do you, Charlie?' He smiled at his old friend when he said it, but it still pissed Charlie off. 'You go to them, you talk to them, you find out what the fuck's going on. And then you tell them anything you know that might be relevant. Is the fact that you were nailing that dead girl going to be relevant?'

'No.' It was all Charlie could bring himself to say at that moment. He'd been in love with that dead girl. He hadn't made love to another woman since.

'All right then. That's what I meant by an opportunity. You get to control the message. But you better make sure the message gets across.'

As Charlie turned to leave the office, he heard Mayfield call out behind him, 'You're welcome, man.'

*Screw you, man,* Charlie thought. He knew damn well why Barry Mayfield was sending him to the NYPD alone. If the shit hit the fan, he'd deny all knowledge. Charlie would be a rogue agent with a hardon for that dead girl.

★ ★ ★

Richard Hamline's law firm occupied nine floors of One Liberty Plaza in the financial district. The receptionist insisted that Mr. Hamline was unavailable. He was overseeing a major closing.

Through a long wall of glass windows adjacent to the lobby, Ellie spotted a thin, dark-haired, blue-eyed man at the head of a large, rectangular conference table lined with men in suits, with a few women scattered in between. Ellie recognized the speaker from Hamline's driver's license.

Yes, the receptionist confirmed, that is Mr. Hamline. And, no, they could not interrupt.

The arrest warrant signed by Judge Bernie Jacob shortened the rest of the conversation

261

considerably. Ignoring the receptionist's protestations, Ellie and Flann breezed into the conference room. Hamline held a laser pointer in one hand, and a binder of notes in the other. He gestured with the laser to a series of numerical figures projected onto a screen behind him, while the rest of the table followed along from matching notebooks. Taking a closer look at the man, the doubt in Ellie's stomach burrowed further. The photograph posted on FirstDate was definitely not his.

'Wrong room, guys.' Hamline was momentarily startled by the open door and two strangers, but then turned his attention back to the screen. 'Now if you look at the aggregate values of the two stock classes on page seventeen — '

'New York police, Mr. Hamline.' Ellie held up the shield she'd hung from her neck to keep her hands free. She felt the comfort of the 9-mm Glock against her hip. Better safe than sorry. Muscle memory kicked in as she visualized the twist-then-up motion that would unholster the pistol from the leather. 'Something's come up, sir. We need to talk to you in the lobby.'

A look of concern flickered across Hamline's face, but then he smiled at his table of listeners. 'I appreciate the good service, officers, but we're putting a deal together here.' A few members of his audience laughed, appreciating an inside joke that two civil service employees would never understand.

'It's urgent, sir. Please don't make me ask you again,' Ellie said.

'Now wait a second, officer — '

'Hands,' Flann cried out, responding to Hamline's quick movement as he dropped his notes to the table. 'Keep your hands where they were.'

Flann had his gun in his right hand now, but kept it pointed at the floor. Several of the people in the room huddled closer to the table, as if that subtle movement could shield them from whatever confrontation was about to take place. A couple of others gasped. Someone said something about calling building security. No one stood up.

Hamline hunched his shoulders, palms toward them. 'Okay, um, okay. There's apparently some misunderstanding. I'm, I'll — what did you say? The lobby, right? Okay, I'm coming out.' He edged his way around the table, keeping his hands by his face. 'Um, I'll be back as soon as I can. Tim, go ahead and cover the stock values.'

Flann placed his left hand on Hamline's back and guided him toward the door. 'The rest of you all might want to plan on finishing your work without him,' Ellie said politely, closing the door behind her.

'Richard Hamline, we have a warrant for your arrest.'

Flann continued with Miranda warnings while Hamline insisted this was all a colossal misunderstanding. By the time he'd been marched through the lobby to the elevator bank, Hamline realized this wasn't going to get taken care of on his home turf.

'Libby,' he barked back to the receptionist, 'call Michele Campbell. Call her *now*.'

Ellie left the building knowing in her gut that she and Flann had just arrested an innocent man.

★ ★ ★

The most seasoned criminal lawyer at Hamline's firm was not happy to find her colleague in an interrogation room at the Thirteenth Precinct speaking with two homicide detectives.

'What is going on in here? I'm sure you're not questioning my client, because, unless I'm mistaken, a witness to his arrest heard his express request for counsel. That is, after all, how I came to be here — eventually. Sorry, Rick. Detectives, Michele Campbell.'

Michele Campbell wasn't like any of the criminal defense attorneys Ellie had ever encountered. Her dark shiny hair fell perfectly into a broom-straight bob. A black suit fit impeccably over a hot pink sweater and what appeared to be a terrific set of legs. Her reprimand of their interrogation was firm but surprisingly friendly. She made a damn good first impression. Unfortunately, her client, despite his profession, had made the same rookie mistake all defendants made.

'Sorry, counselor. Your client invoked his rights, then promptly initiated contact with us.'

Campbell threw a frustrated look at her client for verification.

'Chele, they arrested me for *murder*. Some

serial killer or something. On an Internet dating site.'

'*You* started talking to *them*?'

'The silence was killing me. All I asked was what they were arresting me for. Then they said murder. You weren't here. I wanted to know what the fuck was going on.'

Campbell exhaled loudly. 'I guess corporate lawyers read the stock page during crim pro. Sorry to ruin your fun, Detectives, but this stops now. You tell me what's going on, and he doesn't say another word until I okay it.'

'Two women have been murdered in one week,' Flann explained. 'Evidence left near the bodies linked both to an Internet dating site. Your client is the one and only person, out of tens of thousands of users, who managed to have recent contact with both victims. As you can imagine, we're looking for an explanation.'

'It's not me,' Hamline interjected. 'I told you. It's not even my picture.'

Campbell shushed her client.

'What evidence do you have that it's his account?'

'The account is in his name,' Flann said. 'It lists all of the correct identifying information, including his precise height and date of birth. And he paid for the account a month ago using his own credit card. If he's not our guy, he should be willing to clear up the misunderstanding. We were just starting to cover the details before you got here.'

'Give us a second?'

Through a one-way mirror, they watched the

two attorneys huddled close at the table. Campbell placed her arm around Hamline's shoulder and gave him a squeeze, then she turned and pulled the blinds closed.

'Think he's our guy?' Flann asked.

'Nope.'

'Too normal?'

'No such thing as too normal. I just don't think our guy would have made it this easy.'

Michele Campbell knocked on the window of the interrogation room, and they reentered.

'Although I never thought I'd let a client talk to law enforcement, I think the quicker we can get this cleared up, the better for all of us. What do we need to tell you for Rick to go home?'

'Tell us about this Internet profile.' Ellie laid a printout of the profile's home page on the table in front of Hamline.

'I don't know anything about it. I've never seen it, and that's obviously not my picture.'

'Have you ever used FirstDate?'

'No. I know what it is — their ads are everywhere. But I got divorced about a year ago, and I've been happily seeing someone ever since.'

'Can we get a name?' Ellie looked at Michele Campbell as she asked the question.

'Dating a colleague would be against the internal policies of my client's law firm,' Campbell said. 'Our law firm. Let's just say that should you need to talk to his girlfriend, I can definitely tell you anything you need to know.'

'The credit card that was used to open the account was an American Express.' Ellie read the numbers off quickly from her notes. 'Is that yours?'

'I don't know. I'd have to check. Are you going to shoot me if I reach for my wallet?' His tone was bitter, but Campbell lightened the mood with a quiet laugh.

'No bullets. We promise,' Ellie assured him.

Hamline opened a thin black leather billfold, removed a platinum card, and slid it across the table. 'That's my only Am Ex.'

'Not according to the credit card company.'

'Well, check and see when it was opened, because that card in your hand is the only Am Ex that I ever applied for.'

According to FirstDate's records, the Enoch profile was created not quite a month earlier. Ellie had a feeling they were going to find out that the credit card in question hadn't been around much longer.

'Do you have any idea how someone could've gotten the information they'd need to open both a FirstDate account and a credit card in your name? Or why they'd pick you? They'd need your name, height, hair color. For a credit card, they'd need your Social Security number.'

Hamline shook his head. 'Who the fuck knows.' Michele placed her arm around the back of his chair, and he appeared to calm down. 'I don't know. This is one of those identity theft things, isn't it? I can't frickin' believe this. The only thing I can think of is that I got my wallet stolen two years ago — right after Christmas. People weren't as cautious then. Like an idiot, I had my Social Security card in there. As time passed, I assumed whoever stole it grabbed the cash and tossed the rest. I guess not.'

It was total speculation, and unhelpful in any event. Grab and runs were impossible to solve two days after the fact, let alone two years.

'Let me ask my question again,' Campbell said, again firmly but in a friendly way. 'What do we need to tell you for Rick to go home?'

Usually a defense attorney's attempt to steer the direction of a conversation in the interrogation room would have provoked threats of high sentences, cherry-popping cell mates, and death row. But under these circumstances, Ellie shared Campbell's desire to clear Hamline as quickly as possible.

She looked at her watch. It had been more than an hour since Mark Stern had called in the employee from Jersey City to track Enoch's computer usage by location.

'You bill your hours at the law firm, right?' Ellie asked.

'Unfortunately,' Hamline said.

Ellie knew from her ex-boyfriend that corporate lawyers were obligated to keep detailed records to account for their professional time in six-minute increments. At five hundred bucks an hour, clients tended to complain about rounding up. Ellie had a feeling that a comparison of Hamline's billing records against Enoch's log-ons would exonerate him.

'Give us a second, and we'll see if we can't clear this up.'

★   ★   ★

Ellie reached the credit card company while Flann called Mark Stern to ask for a report of Enoch's log-ons to FirstDate. The card had been opened only a month earlier. Whoever opened the account used Hamline's home address as his residence, but asked that the credit card and all bills be sent to a post office box at a Mailboxes Etc. No doubt they'd find out that the box had been rented with Hamline's stolen ID.

'Were there any charges on the account other than to FirstDate?' Ellie asked the woman at the other end of the line. By tracking down purchases, they might locate the purchaser.

'No, ma'am. Just the two charges to FirstDate, each for thirty dollars.'

'I'm sorry. You said there are *two* charges?' Thirty dollars covered a one-month membership, and Enoch had not yet been a member for a full month.

'That's right.' She provided two dates to Ellie. One corresponded with the day Enoch enrolled with FirstDate. The other payment was made three days later. Ellie thanked the woman for her time and flipped her phone shut.

She found Flann at his desk, reviewing a fax from Mark Stern. It was the computer-locating information for Enoch.

'Thanks to this,' Flann said, 'we've got a timeline of Enoch's online activities, matched with physical locations. We need to cut this Hamline guy loose. Almost all of Enoch's connections to FirstDate were made from three different cybercafés throughout Manhattan: one downtown, one in Murray Hill, and one in

269

Midtown. The one exception was when he logged on last night from a café on City Island.' Ellie recognized the name of the town, a seaport community off the western edge of the Long Island Sound. 'I'm still waiting on the billing records, but that firecracker in there already vouches that Hamline was taking a dinner break downtown last night, not frolicking on City Island.'

Ellie told Flann what she'd learned from American Express. 'If Enoch made two payments to FirstDate in the last month, he must have another profile, using another name to contact who knows how many other women. We need to call Stern.'

'Good. You do that while I wrap up Hamline's alibi.'

★   ★   ★

To Ellie's surprise, Stern sounded downright gleeful to hear from her. 'Did you get the I.P. data I sent?' Mark Stern, citizen extraordinaire, fighting crime wherever it was found.

'Yes, thank you. It's proving very helpful. Look, I'm calling because we need one more thing. It turns out Richard Hamline's credit card paid for two different memberships this month. Can you check on that?'

'No problem.' She heard fingers tapping on a keyboard. 'Huh. That's odd.'

'What?'

'The other membership. Wow, that's really weird.'

'What's weird?'

'The charge was for Amy Davis. Richard Hamline paid for Amy Davis's membership.'

Ellie paused, trying to process the information Stern was giving her. 'Are you sure?'

'Positive. I'm looking at it right here.'

'But Amy had a free membership.'

Stern laughed. 'Sorry. Free membership's an oxymoron at FirstDate.'

'But I saw the offer on her computer. It was a thirty-day trial membership.'

'Not for FirstDate, it wasn't. The marketing types have proposed it, and I've held firm. If people think they can subscribe for free, they'll stop paying me.'

Ellie was certain of what she'd seen in Amy's e-mail account. She described it in detail to Stern, who didn't seem to be surprised.

'It's fishing,' he said.

'Fishing for what?'

'No, phishing. With a ph. It's a doctored e-mail, so it looks like it came from a legitimate company. It probably contained a link to a Web site that looks like FirstDate's site, and then asks the recipient of the e-mail for information about themselves. I can tell you one thing, though — if it offered a free account, it didn't come from us.'

Ellie thanked Stern for his time and hung up in a daze. Flann was walking toward her, a piece of paper in his hand.

'Hope you don't mind, but I went ahead and sprang Hamline. His billing records all checked out. The guy's barely got time to take a leak, let alone hang out in cybercafés all day long. You okay?' Before Ellie had a chance to answer, he offered her the paper in his hand. 'This fax came for you. An old police report on an Edmond Bertrand?'

According to the Boston Police Department, Edmond Bertrand, date of birth, October 16, 1974, had been arrested for forgery six years earlier. Cited and released. No booking photo and no fingerprints. He had been arrested after trying to use a stolen credit card number to pay for a suit at Brooks Brothers.

Ellie needed to call Suzanne Mouton again.

# 27

'I'm sorry to bother you at home, Detective Robi — ' Ellie stumbled over a seemingly unpronounceable Cajun last name.

'Just call me Dave.'

'Sorry. Your neighbor Suzanne Mouton gave me your number. I believe she might have told you that I was interested in Edmond Bertrand?'

'I was just fixing to give you a ring.'

'Do you know the details of his drug overdose? He had some problems years ago with a homicide victim we've got up here.'

'Oh, I'm pretty sure this fellow can't be up your way. He's dead.'

'You're sure?'

'Suzanne told me you'd probably be asking that, so I checked the death records. It was no rumor. Edmond Bertrand died of a fatal drug overdose. Says here his body was found on Avery Island.'

'I'm just being thorough.'

'Don't apologize. I had a partner who was just as tenacious, and now she's the sheriff.'

'Did you happen to get a date of birth for me?'

'Five, twenty, seventy-seven.'

The man arrested in Boston had given his birth date as October 16, 1974. The easiest explanation was that the man arrested in Boston had no connection to the Edmond Bertrand who had died in Louisiana nine years ago. But the name was so unusual, and Ellie couldn't ignore the fact that the Boston Bertrand had been arrested for unauthorized credit card activity. Tatiana's initial arrest involved the same crime, and Enoch's FirstDate membership was paid for through credit card fraud.

'Do you know anything else about Bertrand?'

'I asked around after Suzanne called. You sure you want to hear this? It's the kind of story that'll put snakes in your brain.'

'Trust me. They'll find plenty of company.'

'You know the Davis family had a problem with him?'

Ellie reeled off what she knew about Edmond's unwanted attentions toward Amy and the restraining order issued against him.

'Well, the warning didn't take. He followed her at the shopping mall when she was home from college, and he went down for a ninety-day stint. Bertrand had been known as a neighborhood character, mentally challenged but fairly harmless. From what I've learned, two recidivists got hold of Bertrand in his cell and violated him. By the time he got out of jail, he was using heroin to self-medicate. Within a year of his release, he OD'd on the full-tilt boogie.'

Ellie sucked in her breath. She had more than snakes in the brain. She had a lump in her throat and an intense feeling of anger at Evelyn and Hampton Davis — even at Amy. She used a boy to get a grade she hadn't earned, and his punishment was a sexual assault and a deadly heroin addiction. In the wrong person, she could imagine that kind of treatment developing into a dangerous and obsessive hatred.

'Is there any chance the body wasn't Bertrand's?'

'Pardon?'

'Well, does the death certificate indicate how the ID was made, or what shape the body was in?'

'It doesn't include that level of detail, but I know the coroner who signed off on it. He's a good man. Conscientious too. And Bertrand's prints would've been on file. You can bet the ranch on this one.'

Ellie realized her questions must've sounded crazy, but she wasn't ready to let the subject drop. 'Do you have a number for the coroner?'

'You weren't kidding when you said you were thorough.' He paused, then read off a Louisiana telephone number.

'Did Bertrand have family? Anyone close to him who might've identified the body?'

'He was raised by a widow named Helen Benoit. She never had children herself, but she brought in the damaged ones like stray animals. She may be able to tell you more.' He gave her another phone number.

'Thank you for your time, Dave. I appreciate it.'

'No problem. You need anything else, you can always call your podjo down in old New Iberia.'

★ ★ ★

Ellie dialed the number for Dr. Ballentine Clarke, the coroner who had certified Edmond

Bertrand's death certificate. She was greeted by an answering machine for the county coroner's office and left a message asking Dr. Clarke to call her back as soon as possible. She noticed Flann pulling on his coat and she hung up the phone.

'Where are you going?'

'I don't know about you,' he said, 'but I need a break. We've done everything we can do tonight. We'll take a fresh look tomorrow.'

'But what about this?' She held up the fax from the Boston PD, and Flann laughed.

'That was your thing, remember? I seem to recall being told that you were requesting that report as a personal favor for a friend?'

'Sorry about that. It was just such a long shot.'

'Exactly, and now all you've got are two unfortunate people who share the same cracker name.'

'But the so-called free membership from FirstDate changes everything. Enoch obviously had something against Amy Davis. He sent her that fake e-mail to lure her onto the Internet.'

'I agree. But Amy's beef with Bertrand was ten years ago — '

'But — '

'Grudges can last decades. I know. And that's why you had good instincts thinking it could be him. But you've checked now, and the guy's dead. Even in Louisiana, coroners know how to identify a body. Tomorrow we take another look at everyone who knew her.'

'Coroners make mistakes. Maybe he didn't bother with fingerprints or dental records. Visual

ID's can go wrong. Remember that car accident last year where the girl's family ID'd the wrong body? Turned out their daughter was alive and well.'

'Until the error was discovered a week later. Edmond Bertrand has been sleeping with the fishes for ten years. I think someone would've realized by now if there'd been a problem. Besides, the birthdays don't even match.'

'If Bertrand doesn't want to be found, he could have given Boston PD a fake date of birth.' People who use aliases often juggle multiple names but use their own dates of birth. Edmond Bertrand could be doing the reverse.

'Go home, Ellie. There's nothing else to do tonight.'

She watched Flann's back move toward the exit. 'I'm calling Helen Benoit.'

He threw her a departing wave. 'You're waking up an old lady for nothing, Hatcher.'

Ellie looked at her watch. It was an hour earlier in Louisiana, but still late for a call to a stranger. On the other hand, sometimes being a member of law enforcement called for poor manners. She punched in the telephone number for Helen Benoit.

'Hello?' The woman's voice was quiet. Her accent was similar to Evelyn Davis's, but she sounded older and less genteel.

Ellie explained who she was, then said she was calling about Edmond Bertrand. Silence fell on the line.

'Mrs. Benoit?' Ellie prompted.

'Edmond?'

'Yes. Edmond Bertrand. I was told you brought him up?'

More silence. Then, 'I haven't thought about Edmond for a very long time. I was his foster mother.'

'I'm sorry to bring it up, but his name has come up in a matter related to Amy Davis.'

'That *horrible* girl.'

'That horrible girl is dead. She was murdered this week in New York.'

Ellie heard the old woman gasp, as if she might literally suck the words back into her mouth. 'Well, I hadn't heard that. I'm surprised I wasn't told. At least, I don't *think* I was.'

'I know that this sounds peculiar, but we're trying to make sure this doesn't have anything to do with all the trouble that happened down there between her and Edmond.' Ellie hoped that New Iberia social custom wasn't so different from Kansas, where every piece of nastiness could be alluded to politely as *all the trouble.* 'We have to check out every possible avenue.'

'Edmond was blamed for a lot of bad things, but this one I'm sure he had nothing to do with. Edmond passed on some time ago, right?'

'I'm aware. Losing him that way must have been very hard on you.'

'Well, I tried not to get too attached to any of them. I was not their real mother, you know, just a temporary caregiver.'

Ellie could tell by the tone of the woman's voice, nearly a decade after Edmond's death, that, as hard as she might have tried, professional detachment had eluded Helen Benoit.

'I was wondering whether you might know how Edmond's body was identified when he passed on. Did you see him?'

'Oh no. The state took care of all that. I think he was cremated. There were no services.'

She did not appear to understand what Ellie was asking. 'I was wondering if perhaps the coroner had you come in to identify the body before he was cremated.'

'He was an adult by then.' As a foster mother, Helen's legal guardianship over Edmond would have terminated when he turned eighteen.

'Did he have another family member who might've handled the identification process?'

'Children wind up with me when they don't have any other family.'

'I see. So you're not sure how they knew it was Edmond.'

'I never thought to ask. Why does any of this matter now?'

'I'm just trying to nail down a few things about what happened with him and Amy. Do you happen to know if Edmond was good with computers?'

'Edmond? I don't think so. He was slow, wasn't he?'

Ellie noticed this was the third time that Helen seemed to be asking questions of Ellie instead of the other way around.

'I don't know, Mrs. Benoit. That's why I was calling you — to ask you about Edmond.'

'Well, then, he was slow. I guess that's what they'd call it. He wasn't good at many things, other than looking for people to care about him.

And the children who came and went through here had all kinds of hobbies — I couldn't always keep track — but Edmond and the computers? I don't think so.'

'What about someone close to him? Did he have a friend, or maybe another child in the house, who knew about computers?'

'There was another boy — maybe Jasper, or was it Tommy or Dean? But the one I'm thinking of didn't live here when Edmond was around. Or at least I don't think so. Oh, darling, I just don't know. It's been so long, and I'm on in years myself. I cared for more than thirty children, and I can't remember what all of them were interested in.'

'What about religion? Were any of them particularly religious?' Ellie rattled the cages of her memory searching for the information she'd read on the Internet about the name Enoch. Two biblical meanings. One, the son of Cain. The other, the son of someone else, and the source of something called the Book of Enoch.

'I took them all to church with me every Sunday. Can't say whether it stuck with any of them, to tell the truth.'

'I don't suppose the Book of Enoch sounds familiar to you?' It was a shot in the dark. Religious fascination often morphs over time as people move from church to church, sect to sect, and text to text, seeking the satisfaction that continually eludes them.

'The Book of what?'

'Enoch.'

'Now that one I haven't heard of. That's not in

the Bible. This is a Christian household.'

'Does the name Enoch sound familiar at all? Maybe even a pet or something?'

'Oh no. I never let the children have pets. I had enough of a time watching the kids.'

'Would you mind if I spoke to some of the other kids who were in your care with Edmond?'

'I'm afraid they don't stay in touch with me. That's one of the hard parts of being a foster parent.'

'Can you give me their names? I can track them down from there.'

'Well, I'd have to go back into my picture albums to see who was here, when. Would pictures be helpful? I could mail you some pictures, and you could look at those.'

Helen Benoit sounded excited and Ellie realized that the woman was reaching an age where she was losing her memories and was offering the one form of assistance she could provide. Ellie hated the fact that her questions were forcing this woman to confront her inability to remember the children she had reared in her own home.

'Maybe someone who went to school with the kids could help — '

'Yes, ma'am. I'll see if I can't track someone down.'

Ellie added that pictures would be nice, then spelled out her home address to avoid the black hole that was the police department's interoffice mail system. 'And I'll make sure the photographs get back to you safe and sound.'

Ellie hung up the phone picturing Flann as he

waved good-bye. He was right. She had bothered Helen Benoit for nothing.

★   ★   ★

Jess was watching the late night news when Ellie finally got home. The look on his face told Ellie he wasn't happy.

'You didn't return any of my calls, so I'm watching TV trying to figure out what the hell my sister's gotten herself into.'

'Sorry. I've been moving nonstop since I woke up.' She went directly to her laptop.

'Where were you last night?'

'Working. I slept at the precinct.'

She felt bad lying to Jess, but she didn't have the energy to get into her love life when he was clearly upset by what he must have seen on the news.

'Why are they dusting off old stories about William Summer and our family? What does any of that have to do with your case, Ellie?'

'Obviously it has nothing to do with it. But we haven't released any details. We had a suspect for about five minutes, but then we had to let him go — without anyone knowing about it, thank god — because this asshole keeps sending us on wild-goose chases. The reporters have nothing to say, because we've got nothing to tell them. But they know they've got a good story, so instead they talk about little old me and our family's interesting background.'

She stared at the computer screen, willing it to power up faster, then gave up to grab a beer from the refrigerator.

'Please tell me you didn't do this just to get Dad back in the news again. You tried that before. You gave yourself high blood pressure, got way too skinny, and Mom's still broke and half crazy.'

She took a few big gulps from the bottle of Rolling Rock, then gave Jess a long stare. 'No, Jess, that's not what happened.'

'So why would you put yourself out there? How'd your name even get out? Why would you let that happen?'

'Stop talking to me that way. If it's good for the case, I really don't mind if a bunch of mindless talking heads want to haul out old news.'

'*If it's good for the case?* What are you talking about?'

She sighed. 'This guy might not be too happy if they start comparing him to someone better known, who's gotten more victims, who's more notorious. Maybe it'll draw him out. We want him to talk to us.'

'Jesus, Ellie. Talk about psychological suicide. Every once in a while, you really should think about yourself.'

Ellie refrained from telling him that the idea was Flann's, self-executed without her prior permission.

'I don't need this right now, Jess. I need to figure out what we've been missing. This guy finds these women, he knows who they're talking to online, he knows when they're meeting them.'

'And that's another reason why you don't

283

want him knowing who you are. I'm not just worried about your psyche here. This guy sounds like he's one hallucination away from Charlie Manson, and, from what I hear on the news, he takes a liking to pretty women in their early thirties. Sound like anyone you know? And you're trying to draw him out? What's going to get him more attention than going after the sweet, attractive cop whose daddy was killed by the College Hill Strangler?'

Ellie blocked out his words with her own. Ellie knew it was natural to worry about her own safety at some level, but she could never let those concerns come first. The minute she let fear control her, she'd never be the same kind of cop. 'He uses bogus names, untrackable Internet connections, stolen credit cards. He's a ghost, and we've got nothing.'

Jess had learned early on not to try to engage her in anything else once she hit this mind-set. He went silent as she furiously tapped away at the keys of her computer.

'You look absolutely, diagnosably OCD right now.'

'You're not going to believe this, Jess. He was one of the three. He was one of the guys I picked from the very beginning. Enoch. I should have kept pushing. When he didn't write back, I should have pressed him.'

'So he'd send you some trite bullshit on his e-mail? Then what would you have done? Kept exchanging messages with him until he decided you should be his next victim? Until that schmuck at FirstDate was willing to give you the names behind the accounts, you couldn't do anything.'

'Well, now the schmuck is cooperating, and we still don't have anything. I'm tracking down that stupid user name. It was something biblical, remember?'

'This is terrific, Ellie. The fringy religious crazies are the craziest of them all.'

'This guy really does like the head games. There are two Enochs in the Bible, both in the bloodline of Adam. One's the son of Cain, and then there's another one who's the basis of something called the Book of Enoch. The Bible says Enoch lived for sixty-five years, and then for another three hundred with God. I guess in the lineage, he was Noah's grandfather, like from Noah's Ark.'

'Him, I've heard of.'

'I can't believe this. The most accepted translation of the Book of Enoch is by R. H. Charles. The fucker used the fake ID for a guy named Richard Hamline to open his FirstDate account — R. H.'

'There's no way you could have figured that out,' Jess said.

'No, but it's yet another thing he did to piss us off once we were on his trail.' She shook her head in disbelief as she continued to read the material on her screen. 'The Book of Enoch is all about these fallen angels called the Watchers, who mated with mortal women.'

'Sounds like my kind of scene.'

'This is truly bizarre stuff. I guess most of the established religions say that the book was wrongly attributed to Enoch, but I don't know — a couple of these sites make it sound like the book is inspired by God. Apparently these people think it's apocalyptic.'

As Ellie moved from Web site to Web site — each quite amateur, and each devoted to analyzing the supposedly lost biblical text — she grew increasingly angry at herself for not looking into this earlier. If she'd read any of this sooner, she would have known to pay more attention to Enoch.

'Promise me you won't stay at this all night.' Jess began pulling his coat on over a sweater.

'Where are you going?' Ellie asked.

'Work.'

'Where are you playing tonight?'

'I'm not. Or at least it's not that kind of playing. I got that job at Vibrations.' Jess delivered the news with a grin.

'You have got to be kidding me.'

'You're the one who's always after me to get a real job. This has the kind of hours I can deal with. Decent pay too. The views aren't bad either. I'll be pulling my first full shift tonight.'

'Oh, shit, it's late. I forgot to call Mom again.'

'I figured,' Jess said. 'Don't worry — I called her. I knew you had your hands full and would worry about it later. And, no, I didn't mention anything about your case. I told her you had a date.'

'Why, Jess Hatcher. You called our mother. And you did it all on your own.' *For me*, she thought. Ellie was surprised at how touched she was.

'Hey, I gotta run. My dream job awaits. Oh, and Ellie, bolt the door behind me. Don't open it. Don't talk to strangers. Keep the blinds drawn. Gun near the bed. Polo mallet as a backup.'

She threw a pillow his way. 'Because I have so many mallets at the ready. I'll be fine, you. Get out of here.'

He continued mumbling safety advice as the door closed behind him. An hour later, Ellie was still surfing the net, reading about the Book of Enoch, when her eyes began to close involuntarily. She took a last look at Enoch's FirstDate profile. *Active within 48 hours!* the screen announced. He hadn't logged on today. Mark Stern had promised they'd be paged the minute Enoch accessed his account, but Ellie knew that he was too smart to log on again — at least, not as Enoch.

She could not resist the temptation to sneak a peak at Peter Morse's profile while she was at it. *Active within 48 hours!* He hadn't signed on today either. She wondered if that meant anything about the night they'd spent together. She looked at Peter's picture, wondering if some other woman out there would snatch him off FirstDate. Some other woman who didn't follow her self-imposed rules was going to end up with the man who could have been her next boyfriend.

She exited the FirstDate Web site and went to Barnes and Noble's site, which promised twenty-four-hour delivery in Manhattan. She had a copy of *The Book of Enoch*, translated by

R. H. Charles, sent to her attention at the police precinct.

★   ★   ★

An hour later, the man who called himself Enoch was sitting at his special laptop, composing a letter. He could tell from the media coverage what the police were trying to do, but he was going to kick it up a notch. That's what that fat, hairy TV chef liked to say. One of the ladies down the street — the one who always harped on him about smoking in the alley — used to have his cooking show on at all hours. Kick it up a notch. Bam! He'd kicked it up scads of notches when he'd bammed the old bag's spoiled cat in the alley with his boots. *Car accident, my ass.*

He reread the words on his screen. This was the perfect way to rattle that blond detective's cage. He'd been tempted a few times to respond to that ridiculous little flirt she'd sent his way. He'd even thought about making her the last victim instead of Megan. But this letter was better. For now.

He was careful to save the letter to his hard drive before pressing the print command on his keyboard. Then he pulled on a pair of latex gloves, removed the piece of paper from the printer, and folded it into an envelope. He used some water from the tap to moisten the seal with his knuckle, and found a phone number for the *New York Daily Post.*

# 28

'You're not really going to read that entire thing, are you?'

Ellie was sucking on a spoonful of Nutella, using her free hand to hold open the paperback edition of *The Book of Enoch*, which Flann eyed suspiciously.

'Nonsense goes surprisingly quickly,' Ellie said. 'I'm just trying to get a feel for what we're dealing with.'

'And do you have a full-blown criminal profile ready for us to distribute to the fine citizens of New York City?'

She shot him a mock glare. 'My inclination is that he's *not* actually a religious zealot. He's been too clever, too meticulous, and too tech-savvy to be some homeless schizo inspired by the Book of Enoch.'

'Agreed.'

'Okay, so then why does he use the name Enoch? Because he's a game player. He wants a cat-and-mouse chase with us. He waits a full calendar year between Hunter and Davis, to create a pattern. He even puts a copy of Davis's FirstDate e-mail in her coat pocket, to give us another hint. By the time he kills Megan, all subtlety is gone. He places the FirstDate note right on top of her body, but then never signs on again. He knew that once we found Megan, we'd know that Enoch had contacted both her and

Davis. He knew signing on under that account would be too risky. But the user name itself is another layer in the game. He had to have picked it intentionally.'

'I was skeptical at first, but you're on to something. The name's peculiar, but you noticed him in the first place because the profile itself was so generic.'

'Right. Absolutely vanilla. No personality. But instead of the standard lame handles — Looking for Love, Sleepless in SoHo — he picks an oddball name like Enoch. And using Rick Hamline's credit card to pay for the FirstDate account?' Ellie flashed the book cover toward Flann. 'This is the established, accepted translation. It's been around nearly a century. Notice the name of the translator.'

'R. H. Charles. You think that was intentional?'

'It's enough to make me wonder. And that's exactly what this guy wants us to do — to sit around wondering what makes him tick. He's screwing with us.'

'So aren't you falling for it by reading that ridiculous book?'

'Do you have any other suggestions? He won't log in as Enoch again, so we'll never get a hit from the computer tracking. The mailbox rented to open Hamline's credit card account was a dead end. And we got nowhere with the Internet cafés.'

Flann and Ellie had spent the entire morning interviewing the employees at the various locations Enoch used to access FirstDate. Each of the employees regularly noticed customers logged on to FirstDate, but that kind of computer activity was so commonplace, they didn't bother to note who the people were, let alone remember them. So, until they came up with a better plan, Ellie was reading *The Book of Enoch*, and Flann was reviewing all of Caroline Hunter's notes again looking for a link to Enoch.

'My current theory is that there's something 'cute' about the book from his perspective. The most famous part of the book is the legend of the Watchers, who came from the highest level of angels. But when they descended to Earth — supposedly for the purpose of watching over the mortals — they lusted for human women and ended up mating with them. Enoch tried to intercede with God, but to no avail. God sent the Great Flood to punish the Watchers — to force them to witness the slaughter of their offspring with mortals.'

'Yeah, I see what you mean about 'cute.''

'Like I said, from *his* perspective. Something clever. One possibility is that he's trying to say something about the process of judgment, or the risks of lust. He's the fallen angel lusting for these women on FirstDate.'

'And how does knowing that help us?'

'It doesn't. The other possibility, though, is that he sent us to the Book of Enoch not just as a clever reference to his motivations but because that's where we're really going to find the game. Another section of the book has Enoch learning all of these mysteries embedded in astronomy and the calendar, then he has these dream visions that supposedly prophesied some of the most significant events in the Bible. Some people believe it's all a puzzle — that you can align the calendar to Enoch's lunar calendar and track significant dates in Christ's life.'

'So maybe the year-long gap between Hunter and Davis is an allusion to that?'

'I thought you said I was crazy to read this book.'

'You forget you're talking to McIl-Mulder. I don't think anything's crazy.'

'I keep going back to something my father always said: *Find the motive, and the motive will lead you to the man.*'

'Not a bad maxim.'

'The problem I'm having is making the leap from motive to the man. On my dad's case, he thought the motive was sexual, so he spent a lot of time in the red light district and responding to calls of peeping toms. And on your psychiatrist case last year — '

'The key was figuring out that the killer was obsessed with the number eight.'

'And from there you went to the homeless shelters to find the neighborhood crazies. But if our guy thinks he's following a pattern that's related to the Book of Enoch, I have no idea how that leads us to the man. There's talk in here about twelve winds, the four quarters of the world, seven rivers, the moon, the sun — there's no way to know how someone might twist that around to pick the date of the next murder, or the next victim, or whatever it is he might be using the book for.'

'So stop trying to predict what the killer's

going to do next. You forget that on the number eight case, I did the most obvious thing. Once you think you know what makes the killer tick, you use that information to resolve the clues you already have — the clues on the crimes he already committed.'

'So if the Book of Enoch is a clue about his motives, then he must have a copy of the book. I ordered mine off the Internet. I wonder where he bought his.'

'Now that sounds like something you can work with.'

⋆  ⋆  ⋆

Peter Morse slurped his coffee — it was a little too hot — while he admired the morning's *Daily Post*. Side-by-side photographs of Amy Davis and Megan Quinn graced the front page. Davis had shoulder-length brown wavy hair, pale skin, and dark lips. Megan had shorter, curlier hair. She was chubby but cute, with freckles and bright eyes. He had had to persist with the families in that unctuous way he always found uncomfortable but had come up with great pictures of both women by deadline. He took another look at the banner headline running across the top of the page: Two Beauties Slain: More to Come?

Peter had reported some bombshell stories before, but this one had the potential to be legendary. Murdered girls came and went from the front pages of newspapers, but another serial killer at work in New York City? Jimmy Breslin had worked the Son of Sam case, and he was a journalistic god. Granted, his iconic status came from something other than receiving that renowned letter from Berkowitz, but still, you couldn't talk about Breslin without mention of the summer of 1977.

That's because the story about Son of Sam was about more than just Berkowitz or the lives he claimed. It was a story about an era. It was a story about an entire city — a great city — made vulnerable by one man, a man who could *be* any of us and could *choose* any of us as his next victims.

Peter opened the paper to the article he wrote yesterday afternoon when he first got the tip that the two murders were related. This one had potential. This one would have legs. Flann McIlroy called in the tip himself. That was unusual. It meant he wanted the story out there, which could only mean that he didn't have any leads. If he had a suspect — a landlord, a mutual boyfriend, the bartender who closed a watering hole shared by the two women — the cops would be worried about scaring a suspect off. But McIlroy also must have had a feeling in his gut about this one. And from what Peter knew about the detective, that was saying something.

He flipped through the pages of notes he had put together for tomorrow's article. Hopefully it would be the next entry in a long and meaningful series, the beginning of what would ultimately become a book. He sorted his material into two piles.

One pile related to Detective Ellie Hatcher.

The *Daily Post* had run a story about her in a sidebar a year ago, presenting the local angle to the College Hill Strangler case. She might make a good front-page story for tomorrow — assuming that another victim didn't turn up in the meantime. Haunted by the death of her father, raised under the fearful influences of a killer and the hunting instincts of his pursuer, not too dissimilar in her demographics from the victims themselves. Peter could picture the story and he liked what he saw.

The other pile related to the murder of a woman named Caroline Hunter. She was about the same age as the other victims. Her murder also remained unsolved. He'd written a couple of stories about her case last year, before the city's attention — and his — moved on to other things. The date of her murder was precisely one year earlier than Amy Davis's.

He had a strategic decision to make about whether to focus on one story or both. If the public's interest stayed hot, it was better to dole out a new angle each morning — keep the papers moving from the stands. But if the police were going to announce an arrest tomorrow night, he was better off shooting his wad at once, before the focus turned to a suspect.

He stuck with the feeling in his gut and decided to use just one story for now and save the other for the following day. The Caroline Hunter angle was risky. His speculation could be totally off-base, and there was no guarantee he could come up with sufficient corroboration by deadline. On the other hand, with risks came rewards. He might be the only reporter to make the connection, while the TV news had already tapped into Ellie Hatcher's backstory.

Maybe he'd let photogenics break the tie. His editor always said that pictures sold papers. He studied the head shot of Caroline Hunter that had run the morning after her murder. Even prettier than Davis and Quinn, she'd be awfully hard to compete with, especially by some cop. He pulled up Google on his computer and ran a search for images under the name Ellie Hatcher.

The screen changed to a display of twelve thumbnail photographs, most of them of the same award-winning quilt apparently designed by a woman named Ellie Hatcher. Toward the bottom of the screen was a small photograph of a blond woman in a white blouse and dark jacket. The text beneath it read Family of College Hill Strangler Detective Cries Cover-Up, followed by a link to *People* magazine's Web site. He double clicked on the link.

He'd followed the College Hill Strangler story at the time, but not closely enough to remember the accompanying photograph two years later. Gazing at him from the screen with big blue eyes, full pink lips, and a heart-shaped face was the woman he'd been thinking about every twelve minutes for the last twenty-seven hours: Ally, last name unknown, whom he promised never to contact again.

'Who's the hottie?' Peter looked up to find the smiling face and dark eyes of Justine Navarro, the intern from NYU with a pierced tongue and an uncomfortably revealing wardrobe. Today's ensemble was the usual hip-hugger pants and a clingy off-white sweater with a plunging neckline.

'Believe it or not, she's apparently an NYPD detective.'

'I wouldn't kick her out of bed.'

Peter had no idea whether Justine was a lesbian, bisexual, or simply the free-spoken product of a generation that had no qualms about checking out members of the same sex. He knew better than to spend too much time thinking about it. She had good taste though. He hadn't kicked Ellie Hatcher out of bed either, even if her presence there came with the horrible condition that it was a one-night deal. Man, he could not stop thinking about this woman.

'Hey, I'm sending a call back in about sixty seconds,' Justine said. 'You better pick it up.'

One of the interns' jobs was to answer the general public's crime beat calls. The reporters had lobbied for the change, fed up with constant and absolutely unnewsworthy bitching about abandoned cars, noisy dance clubs, street-level drug dealing, and the occasional illegal exotic pet. Granted, sometimes an apartment-reared lion made good copy, but the interns were perfectly capable of passing along a worthy tip.

'I always take my calls,' Peter said.

'No you don't. You say you do, but I catch you cheating all the time.'

Peter was only in his midthirties, but increasingly he found himself thinking that youth was a pain in the ass. 'Well, it never seems to matter, does it?'

'On this one, it might. The guy says he's got something on that serial killer case. An exclusive tip only for you.'

Peter didn't bother to get his hopes up. This call would be just one of many he and other reporters around the city would receive from various whack jobs. He kept his eyes on Ellie Hatcher, wondering if she was getting the same kind of phone calls. 'So transfer him already.'

'I tried. I pretended to look for your number while I tried getting your attention. He said he'd call back in exactly ninety seconds and expected to be transferred immediately.' She rushed back to her desk, yelling, 'We've got about five seconds left.'

This could be interesting. Peter watched the digital clock tick away on the LED readout of his phone. He kept an eye on Justine, who was at her desk now, with one hand on the phone. Five, four, three, two, one. A millisecond of a phone ringing, then Justine's voice. '*Daily Post* . . . .Right away.'

She gave Peter an urgent look and pushed a few buttons on her phone, then Peter's phone rang.

'Peter Morse.'

'Did that young thing with the pretty voice tell you why I was calling?' The voice had a southern accent. Not a twang, but something southern. Raised in the northeast, Peter couldn't place it any more particularly.

'She said it was about this week's murders.'

'That's right. Amy and Megan.' The names oozed like warm caramel. 'There's more you need to know about what got them killed. Something the police are hiding. You got a pen? Write this down. 455 Fifth Avenue. Third floor.' He read off a series of numbers followed by letters.

'Is that some kind of code?'

'You mean to tell me that an accomplished journalist like yourself is unfamiliar with the Dewey Decimal system? I promise, it'll make good reading.'

'Wait. Who are you? How can I get ahold of you?'

Peter heard a click in his ear, then hung up as well. He rolled out his keyboard drawer and Googled the address the man had recited. The mid-Manhattan public library. He reached for the pile of notes on Ellie Hatcher and flipped to a summary of the College Hill Strangler case that he'd printed from a Web site called Crime Library. He found what he was looking for on the third page:

*The first of several communications by the College Hill Strangler to Wichita authorities was in October of 1974. A reporter at the* Wichita Eagle-Beacon *newspaper received an anonymous telephone call from a man who claimed to have killed Rhonda Cook and her two children. The caller said the reporter would find a letter detailing the crime inside a copy of Michel Foucault's* Discipline and Punish. *The reporter discovered the letter, as promised, tucked inside the pages of Foucault's graphic description of a public execution.*

Peter was already pulling on his coat as he finished reading. If his caller was a whack job, he certainly was a creative one.

# 29

Locating copies of *The Book of Enoch* was no easy task. With a recently published title, they could have tracked shipments from the wholesale distributors, then looked for sales with the city's major book retailers. But the ancient text of the Book of Enoch, unprotected by copyright, could be found reprinted in a dozen different books. Used copies could be purchased in myriads of untraceable ways.

Ellie was on hold with a clerk from the Strand bookstore when her cell phone rang. The screen read, Caller Unknown.

'Ellie Hatcher.'

'Detective Hatcher, this is Agent Charlie Dixon of the FBI. I understand that you're working on this murder case involving Megan Quinn and Amy Davis.'

She cradled the handset of the desk phone against her shoulder and tossed a pencil toward Flann to break him away from Caroline Hunter's notes. 'That's right, I'm working on both of those cases. How can I help you, Agent Dixon?'

She had Flann's attention.

'It's more a question of whether I can help you. Can we meet somewhere?'

'You're more than welcome to come on in. We're doing some desk work now.'

'Sorry, I'm not a big fan of local police

stations. It's turning into a nice, bright day outside. You feel like taking a little walk? Somewhere near your station — I don't want to put you out.'

It was a typical federal ploy for power, but Ellie figured she'd find plenty to argue about with Dixon later. 'Sure. There's an Italian place just around the corner. Lamarca on Twenty-second and Third. How long do you need?'

'I can see it from my car. I'll be waiting for you.'

★ ★ ★

It wasn't hard to miss the tall man in a suit, trench coat, and wool cap, settling into a corner table at Lamarca. He had thinning dark hair, small brown eyes, and a puffy, unshaven face. He also had a tray with three coffees and several pastries. They exchanged introductions and handshakes as they unbundled from their coats.

'No partner?'

'Like I said, we're tied to our desks right now.' The truth was that Flann had so many choice words about the FBI and their penchant for poaching good cases that Ellie had ultimately insisted on meeting Dixon alone.

'I won't waste your time then. It's my understanding you're looking into the murder of Tatiana Chekova as part of this suspected serial killer case. Here, take one of these coffees. And dig into these bad boys too. I didn't know what you'd want so I — '

'It's your understanding, huh?' Ellie helped

herself to a hazelnut roll. 'And how exactly did you come to have this understanding about one of our cases?'

'I know you're new to this, Detective, but you do realize, don't you, that if we don't like the kind of cooperation we get from you, the FBI can always take this case away. Patternistic multiple homicides are a Quantico specialty.'

'Yeah, I don't think that's really going to happen though. I already spoke to your Special Agent in Charge. What's his name — Barry Mayfield? Anyway, he knows we're working this case. I asked about Tatiana — and a company called FirstDate too, by the way — and he has to have gotten wind of yesterday's news by now. If he wanted jurisdiction, he'd take the case. He'd at least come talk to us. You wouldn't be here. So let's make this a two-way street: Why are you so interested in Tatiana Chekova?'

Dixon smiled. 'Honestly, I don't want to get into a jurisdictional pissing match with you. Let's start fresh. I got coffees, I got treats, I'm trying to play nice with you in our little law enforcement sandbox. So why don't we get past the part where you pretend to be surprised that the FBI — and the NYPD — find ways outside of official channels to know what other agencies are working on. I know you guys pulled Chekova's cold case file. I just want to know why so I can figure out if I have any information that might be helpful to you.'

'That's one way to proceed. Or you could start by sharing whatever information you have, and I can decide whether or not it's helpful.'

'So much for avoiding the classic pissing match.'

'At least we've got tasty snacks to mitigate the unpleasantness.' Ellie took another nibble from the hazelnut roll, and then reached for a chocolate something-or-other. 'I'm not trying to be a bitch. If you've got information, we want it. But I might have been a little more forthcoming before Megan Quinn was murdered. I called your boss trying to find out why you guys were keeping us away from FirstDate.'

'At the time, it seemed like you were fishing. I hope you don't mind me saying, but your partner's reputation didn't help much in that regard. We didn't want you guys screwing up a long-term investigation because of some mis-guided tangent.'

'And you no longer think it's a misguided tangent?'

'I don't know. That's why I'm here. The fact that you've got another body suggests you might have a pattern. I'm trying to figure out how Tatiana Chekova fits into it, and whether we might have information relevant to your investigation.'

'Fair enough. I'll go first. Counting Megan Quinn, we now have three women killed in the last year, all of whom were enrolled on FirstDate. The most recent two had notes at the crime scenes referring to FirstDate, and the same two had been in contact with the same man using the service. We're doing our best right now to ID the person behind the online persona, but he's done some work to cover his trail.'

'And what made you look into Tatiana Chekova's murder?'

Ellie realized then that Dixon didn't know about the gun that linked Chekova and Hunter. He was arrogant enough to assume she and Flann had their heads up their asses, but whatever source he had in the NYPD wasn't thorough enough to tell him about the gun match. When she dropped the bomb about the common weapon used to kill both women, his frustration was obvious.

'You never thought the connection would be that concrete, did you?' Ellie asked.

'I didn't know what you had. Like I said, it's why I'm here.' He was playing it cool, but Ellie detected a discomfort in his expression that was more than just frustration. It was pain, almost betrayal. She resisted the urge to remind him that he could have obtained the information sooner if Mayfield had been more forthcoming when she called.

'So now I've shared,' she said. 'Maybe you should start by explaining why you got the D.A.'s office to back off from a subpoena against FirstDate.'

'I've been watching that company for two years. I had a confidential informant who said something was shady there — some connection they'd heard about between Russian criminals and the company.' Ellie noticed his ungrammatical use of the gender-ambiguous pronoun *they* to describe a single informant. 'It wasn't a good enough tip to get a search warrant or a wiretap — but I believed it. Still do.'

'What kind of something shady?'

'Like I said, no details — just some nefarious connection between the corporation and a criminal element. My theory is that it has to be money laundering — buy and sell stock to outsiders, and structure the deals in a way that hides the source of the cash. The company's going public in less than two weeks. There's extraordinary opportunity there to wash money through stock options and the I.P.O.'

'So why isn't the S.E.C. involved?'

'We don't have enough for them to launch an official securities proceeding.'

And yet, Ellie thought, you have enough to keep an eye out on the company for two years, and to justify keeping the NYPD away from your turf.

'And how does Tatiana Chekova fit in?'

Dixon took another sip of coffee, taking time to blow on the hot liquid that he'd drunk comfortably just a minute earlier.

'She was your informant?' Ellie prompted.

Dixon nodded. 'We never even put her through the system officially — for her protection, obviously. She gave us some minor players here and there, but no one who could dime up FirstDate. We always assumed that she was too afraid to give us whoever knew about that connection directly.'

'Did her cooperation with you have something to do with her arrest in Brooklyn a few months before she was killed?' It would explain how a perfectly decent bust got dumped from the system, a fact that had been troubling Ellie all along.

Dixon nodded again. 'She told the arresting officer she had major info to trade on, but would only work with the feds. No NYPD.'

'Did you ever figure out why?'

'She told me later that the people she knew had cops in their pockets.'

'But she didn't give you the cops, just like she didn't give you whoever could flip on FirstDate. Did it ever dawn on you that she was lying? Suspects with no information to trade have been known to fabricate when necessary.'

'Fine, if you think she was lying, then I guess nothing I have to say is relevant to your investigation. Sorry I've wasted your time.' He moved to put on his hat, but Ellie stopped him.

'Come on, that's not what I meant,' she said. 'Obviously it's got something to do with the bigger picture. I'm just trying to understand why you would have believed her back then.'

⋆ ⋆ ⋆

Dixon was starting to wish he'd called McIlroy. This probing into his personal motivations seemed uniquely female. McIlroy would have looked for conspiracy theories involving Tatiana and FirstDate, but Hatcher's questions were taking him into the very territory that he was trying to avoid.

'To tell you the truth, I doubted it at times. And, even when I believed it, I still knew I'd blown a lot of time on the case without getting anywhere. The bureau can't abide that these days. That's why I went to Mark Stern and told him I knew something was up and that he needed to consider coming forward with a complete confession implicating any other members of a criminal enterprise he might be involved in.'

'I'm sorry. You did what?'

Dixon had figured this would look bad if it ever came out, but saying it aloud now he realized just how ridiculous it sounded — how desperate he had been back then to close the door on the investigation. He reminded himself of Mayfield's warning: Control the message.

'We've got a full plate these days, trying to stay ahead on terror cases. That takes time away from solving crimes after the fact. Our entire case stats — white collar, fraud, even drugs — are down. I wasn't going to work this FirstDate thing much longer, so I rolled the dice. I tried to bluff him.'

'And it didn't work.'

'Three days later, Tatiana was killed.'

Finally, he used his informant's name. Not Chekova, not the girl, not the C.I. acronym for a confidential informant. *Tatiana. Tatiana was killed.* Just as Dixon tried to read Hatcher's face to see if she'd noticed, Hatcher reached for the cell phone on her belt and flipped it open.

'Sorry,' she said, pushing a couple of buttons on it. 'It's set to vibrate — '

'You can take it if you need to.'

She returned the phone to her waistband, shrugging it off. 'If you thought a federal informant was murdered for her cooperation, why didn't the FBI take over the homicide investigation?'

Again, Dixon thought, more questions about his motivations.

'If we couldn't put together probable cause for a conspiracy involving FirstDate, how could we show that she got killed as part of it? We decided it was best to leave the investigation to the NYPD.'

'And now two years later, McIlroy and I are working on it.'

'You're clearly better than those other lazy sacks. How didn't anyone make a gun match earlier?'

'The case fell through the cracks. One of the detectives, Barney Tendall, was shot off-duty. His partner sort of fell apart after that.'

'Huh-uh. I know you guys like to defend your own, but I don't think so. We might not have taken over the investigation, but I kept an eye on it. That Ed Becker was the worst cop I ever saw — his partner too. They didn't do shit. They worked their other cases just fine, but Tatiana — Chekova,' he said, catching himself, 'she was just a dead cossack stripper to them. They never even worked the case.'

Hatcher clearly was not inclined to follow this line of conversation. 'So here's the big question now: If Tatiana was killed for cooperating with you, how does that fit with our other three murders?'

'If I knew, I'd tell you.'

'Come on now. If you *knew*, the FBI really would take the case.' She gave him a friendly smile, which he found himself returning. 'So what else can you tell me about the people who might have had a grudge against Tatiana?'

'Two men were prosecuted based on the information Tatiana provided.' Dixon handed the detective a manila folder containing a Form 302, used by federal agents to summarize interviews. Clipped to the 302 was a booking photo. 'I made two busts based on tips from Tatiana. One of them was a controlled buy for heroin out of a club she used to work. The guy's name was Alex Federov. You don't need to write that down, because Federov was killed in prison two months into his sentence.'

Hatcher's curiosity was clearly piqued. 'Any chance that was related to Tatiana's murder?'

Dixon shook his head. 'No. I checked on that. Turns out Federov took a shiv to the stomach in the yard — get this — for preempting an inmate who was ahead of him on the library waiting list for a Harry Potter book.'

'And so that leaves the second guy.' Hatcher unclipped the photograph from the 302 to take a closer look. 'This is him?'

'Lev Grosha. He was sneaking credit card numbers out of a Brooklyn motel. He paid the clerk at the front desk to run the cards through a scanner. Massive fraud potential. With the U.S. Attorney's Office leaning hard on him, we assumed he'd cooperate. It's pretty much the only way to get a sentencing break these days.'

'And instead?'

'Grosha pled to all charges and took the full guideline term.'

'Where's he serving his time?'

'MDC Brooklyn. He's got a sick mom or

something, so the Bureau of Prisons kept him local.' The Metropolitan Detention Center was just off the Gowanus Expressway near the bay.

'Can you put me on his visitor's list?' Hatcher asked.

'No problem,' he said, making a note of it. 'Do me a favor? If you find anything that leads straight to Stern, will you let me know? I don't think he's your doer, but something doesn't add up with that one. My impression is he's got way too much money based on what he's bringing in.'

Given the illegal investigation tactics he'd used to keep an eye on Stern, Dixon was relieved when Hatcher didn't press the question of how he'd formed his 'impression.'

'Sure,' she promised. 'And, hey, thanks for calling me. And for the sweets.'

Dixon rose from the table and pulled his coat on. He left the café satisfied with the way he'd controlled the message. He'd given the NYPD the information they needed, and his hands were clean. Hatcher seemed like a decent cop. Maybe she could carry the burden now, and he could finally put all of this behind him.

\* \* \*

Ellie watched Charlie Dixon walk to a blue Impala down the street, then she pulled her cell phone from her waist, flipped it open, and pressed the camera button. Charlie Dixon popped up on the small screen, in color, his coffee cup held just below his chin. It wasn't a bad photograph.

She left Lamarca with a small box of tiramisu wrapped in string, a surprise for Flann. Unfortunately, a very different kind of surprise awaited her. Just outside the precinct entrance, a mere eighty feet away, stood Peter Morse. She could not believe her luck. Millions of people had reckless evenings of casual sex with strangers. She did it one time — only once — and the guy wound up literally at her doorstep.

She ducked down a metal staircase leading to a basement laundry shop and stifled a scream when a rat scurried across her foot. She watched as Peter pulled open one of the precinct's glass double doors. How long was she willing to stand here in the cold, with this stench, to avoid him? Until she saw him leave, she decided — no matter how long it took.

Her cell phone jingled at her waist. She flipped it open and recognized Flann's number.

'Hello?' She whispered as if Peter could hear her from inside the walls of the precinct across the street.

'Are you almost done with the elusive G-man?'

'Yeah, I'm done. I'm just, um, yeah, I'm on my way back. What's up?'

'Just get back here.'

'It might be a sec — '

'If this is about the apparently prescient reporter named Peter Morse, he's standing right here and warned me you'd try to avoid him. Get back here please. The sooner you talk to him, the sooner he'll leave.'

# 30

Peter Morse followed Ellie's sheepish entrance with a pleased expression. Flann shot her eye daggers.

'I brought tiramisu,' she said, offering Flann the dainty bakery package. She offered Peter her hand, playing it cool. 'Hi. I'm Ellie Hatcher. But it sounds like you already know that.'

'I know now.' Ellie couldn't tell if he was angry, amused, or both. 'I hope you don't mind, but I told your partner that I really needed to talk to the two of you together.'

'I tried pushing him off on the Public Information Office,' Flann said, 'but he insisted you'd want to hear this. The two of you know each other?'

'Oh yeah, we go way back,' Peter said. 'Good times. Good times. So anyhoo, I got a phone call this morning from your killer.'

Ellie and Flann exchanged skeptical looks. Reporters contacted cops to suck up information, not to dole it out.

'It was probably just a prank,' Flann said. 'Routine on high-profile cases.'

'That's what I assumed too. It was at least a clever crank. He told me to go to the public library to find a letter he left there for me. Sound familiar?'

'That's how William Summer delivered the first of the College Hill Strangler letters,' Ellie

313

explained to Flann. 'He hid a letter inside a book at the library, then gave a tip to a reporter.'

'I guess I play the role of the reporter.' Peter handed them a piece of paper sealed inside a plastic bag. 'I watch *CSI*.'

*Dear Mr. Morse, Congratulations. You found this letter. Now here is your reward.* The letter continued with a detailed description of the killings, down to the shrill mews of Amy Davis's cat while he strangled her and the tapestry pattern on the sofa where he found the pillow used to smother Megan Quinn. *They were sinners and fornicators and temptresses, but that is not why I killed them. The police are covering up the real reason. They were liars, using deception to trigger lust in honest men. They used FirstDate, then took their Last Breath. 'And behold! He cometh to execute judgement upon all, and to destroy the ungodly, and to convict all flesh of all the works which they have ungodly committed.' Three down and many more to go. Enoch.*

'You probably recognize that last line about how many more,' Peter said, looking at Ellie.

Of course she recognized the reference. In 1982, the College Hill Strangler wrote a letter to police asking how many people he had to murder before he would get some media attention. In his postscript, he wrote, 'five down and many more to go.'

'He's fucking with me,' Ellie said. 'He saw the news coverage mentioning my connection to

William Summer, and now he's intentionally fucking with me.'

'I'm sorry.' Peter Morse sounded like he actually meant it.

'You can't run the story,' Flann said.

'What?' Peter exclaimed. 'That's not your call to make. I only came here to give you evidence and to see if you have any comment.'

'He's escalating,' Flann explained. 'It's all about his ego. He wants notoriety. If you give it to him, it'll only up the ante. He'll kill again to prove that he can live up to the reputation.'

'That's not enough to justify holding the story. If publication presented an imminent threat — '

'Don't hold the story,' Ellie said. 'Get it out there as soon as you can.'

'Ellie, this is not your decision.'

'I'm sorry if I'm being insubordinate, Flann, but I will not be part of hiding this from the public. I grew up in a town where every couple of years a woman would be tied up in her home and slowly tortured to death. The police knew about it and kept us in the dark. Then they said he was gone, when they should have known he wasn't. Some of his victims might have lived if they'd known to be more careful. Peter's right. You're just speculating about what Enoch will do. He might be more likely to kill again if he *doesn't* get the press he wants. The only thing we know for sure is that women might be more careful if they know what they're dealing with. He should go with the story.'

'He signed the letter Enoch,' Peter said. 'Is that a name that means something to you?'

It was clear the train was leaving the station. Flann had no way of stopping Peter from running the story — he of all people was not going to report Ellie to the department for cooperating with the press — but that wasn't going to stop him from salvaging some secrecy. 'Any way we can persuade you to at least hold back the name?' he asked.

'I already know it's from the Book of Enoch. The reference librarian tracked down the quote in the letter for me.'

'Off the record for a second?' Ellie asked.

'Sure.'

Ellie told him about the FirstDate user who called himself Enoch. 'His profile is still online. It's a real long shot, but we've got it monitored so we can locate him in the event that he logs back on to his account.'

'Okay. That's good enough reason for me. The name won't go in. Neither will the quote.'

'Really?' Ellie tilted her head.

'Even reporters can be reasonable, Detective. I need to do more work on the Book of Enoch angle in any event. Just one more question, back on the record. What do you want me to say about you? About the fact that he's apparently trying to push some buttons in your background?'

'I think that letter gives you enough for a day's newsprint. You can say we believe that one man has used FirstDate to kill at least three women and that we believe the letter is authentic.' She chose her words carefully when she described *at least three* victims. The letter detailed the

Hunter, Davis, and Quinn murders, but didn't mention Tatiana Chekova, and Peter apparently didn't know about her. She wanted to be truthful, but no more forthcoming than necessary to protect the public. Flann nodded his approval. 'We have no further comment about any other details.'

'Yeah, okay. I've got enough to run with for now. You'll give me a break in the future, I hope. For holding back the Enoch thing?'

'No problem,' Flann said, already turning his attention back to his desk.

Ellie offered to walk Peter out. She finally spoke once they reached the sidewalk. 'You probably hate me. I'm so sorry — '

'I don't hate you. I'm intrigued. And, with tremendous guilt given the circumstances, I'm actually happy to have an excuse to break my promise never to call you again.'

'I'm not the kind of person who lies, who tells stories — '

'Hey, if you want to make it up to me, promise me you'll stop apologizing. It's not like I regret anything that happened. And if you really, really want to make it up to me, rethink that whole never-seeing-each-other-again agreement. We've both got a ton of work to do — yours more important than mine, obviously — but if you get a chance, even just for a drink, call me tonight.' He scribbled a number down on a business card and handed it to her. 'Hopefully I'll talk to you soon.'

* * *

On the way back to the detectives' room, Ellie checked her reflection in the glass door to make sure it didn't reveal the few seconds of giddiness she allowed herself. Nope, plain old normal Ellie, even though Peter Morse knew who she was and what she did for a living. He didn't hate her. He wanted to see her again. He agreed to hold back the name, without even a fight.

Flann wasted no time getting back to the task at hand. 'I sent the original of the letter down to the crime lab, but it'll be a while before we hear anything.'

'They won't find anything anyway.' Enoch hadn't left prints behind on anything yet. 'I think I've got a better lead from our friendly neighborhood FBI agent.'

Flann ate tiramisu, nodding occasionally as she walked him through her chat with Charlie Dixon.

'So Chekova was killed for flipping for the FBI, but then the same gun used on her is used to kill our first victim? That doesn't add up.'

'It does if Enoch is somehow tied to whatever criminal enterprise Tatiana had knowledge of.'

'So we're looking for Russian heroin dealers, or, more interestingly, we're looking at Mark Stern. You think Stern's got it in him?'

'Anyone can be evil. But I don't think it's Stern. I remember the momentary look of panic on his face when we first told him that someone was using his company to pluck off young single women. He wasn't panicked because he was our guy; he was freaking out because that piece of information, made public, would ruin his company. If he wanted to go on a killing spree, why drag his livelihood down with it?'

'So that leaves somebody connected to whoever wanted to silence Tatiana. Maybe he kills her to shut her up, gets off on it, and then continues to use FirstDate to find more victims and to develop his Enoch persona?' Flann immediately saw the flaw in his own theory. 'But if he's on a learning curve and using FirstDate to play, how do we explain him luring Amy Davis onto the site?'

'I know,' Ellie said. 'None of it adds up. But we've got to track down this Tatiana angle. We don't have any other leads.'

'The doorman at Megan Quinn's building said the man who delivered the flowers didn't have an accent of any kind, so my guess is he's not a Russian.'

'And Peter Morse said the guy who called him had a southern accent. Maybe the Latino doorman couldn't tell the difference between a southern accent and a plain old generic white boy? We're looking for a man with a southern accent, connections to Russian criminals, and a fixation on an obscure religious text? Piece of cake.'

Ellie reached across Flann's desk for the bakery box and caught a glance at Caroline Hunter's open notebook. Flann had marked a single page with a neon orange Post-it note.

'What's this?' she asked, turning the notebook toward her.

'See for yourself.' In the margin next to the orange sticky was a handwritten notation: *MC Becker*.

Ellie recognized the scrawl. When she'd first read the police reports on Tatiana Chekova's murder, she knew she'd recently come across the name Becker. What she hadn't realized at the time was that she'd seen the name among the miscellaneous doodles of Caroline Hunter's research notes.

'It's my old buddy from Scarsdale,' Flann said.

Ellie wasn't surprised that Flann would jump to conclusions when it came to Ed Becker. 'You don't know that, Flann.'

'He's been in front of us the entire time. He caught Tatiana's murder. Now his name's in Caroline Hunter's notebook. And accents are easy to fake.'

'It's a common last name.' Ellie took another look at the note. 'And the way it's written there, it might even say McBecker. It's hard to tell.'

'Looks more like MC Becker to me. According to Dixon, Tatiana said the men she knew had NYPD cops on the take, and I know firsthand that Becker's got that kind of thing in his background. MC could've been shorthand for a meeting place.'

'Or maybe it's his son's initials? Becker said his son met his fiancée online. Or it may be totally unrelated. I could call him. Ask him about it.'

'He'll say it's a coincidence, and then what? No, we've got to look into Becker without him knowing.'

Ellie hated the idea that the man who wrote that letter, the man who killed these women, could have given her a ride home. She didn't want to believe that her instincts could be so wrong. But no matter how she shaped the ideas in her mind, she couldn't shake Flann's reasoning. Flann might be jumping to conclusions, but the possibility had to be pursued, especially when she considered Charlie Dixon's other troubling comment. 'Dixon said that Becker was slacking on Tatiana's murder case from the very beginning, before his partner was killed. Apparently they were working their other cases just fine.'

'That doesn't jibe with what Becker told us.'

'I know, and it does a lot to explain that train wreck of a murder notebook he left behind. It bothers me.'

'One of us needs to look at Becker's old files for comparison. See if he really did bury Tatiana's case.'

'I'll do it,' Ellie offered.

Flann shook his head. 'You won't know what to look for. This is your first homicide case.'

'Fine. You do it. But promise me you'll run anything by me before you whisk off and arrest him or something, okay?'

'Aye, aye.'

'I'll go out to Brooklyn to talk to Tatiana's sister again. See if she knows anything about the deal with the FBI. If there's time on the way back, I might stop by MDC to see Lev Grosha.'

On the way out of the precinct, Ellie used her

telephone to send the digital photograph of Charlie Dixon to Jess's e-mail account. She followed up with a text message: 'See if anyone at Vibrations knows him. Start with the manager. C U 2nite.'

# 31

In the narrow, white-tile hallway that led to Zoya Rostov's apartment, Ellie recognized the familiar baby's cry and toddlerlike squeals of happiness she'd heard on her first visit to Tatiana's sister. She wondered if perhaps children were born with fixed temperaments, one sibling content and playful while the other fussed stoically. But when Zoya opened the apartment door and Ellie glimpsed the young faces of the baby and the boy, she realized how inchoate their identities were; their current emotional states fleeting — just momentary phases in a child's development of days, weeks, and years. These two little lives had so much more to experience before anyone could guess what their future adult selves might become.

Zoya invited Ellie in, then locked the door behind her, securing the chain in place.

'Your husband isn't here?' Ellie asked.

'Vitya is working.'

'What does your husband do for a living?'

'He is a security guard at a storage warehouse. He usually is on night shift, but lately he has overtime to work.'

'Staying home with both of the kids all those hours has to be hard,' Ellie offered.

'I never see my children as work. Other people's children — that was work. In Russia, I was a schoolteacher. The children, they were good, nice children. But every day, I thought, how much work it is to take care of all of these children in one little room. Keeping them from hurting themselves, getting them to behave — that was all work, let alone trying to teach them anything. Now that I have my own? I cannot imagine anyone else thinking of them as work.'

'Did you ever think of being a teacher here in the United States?'

Zoya nodded. 'Of course. At first. But I found nothing. Not even teaching Russian. Too many licenses and requirements. I looked for other work. Some girls, they learn how to style hair or become house servants. I was offered a job at a massage parlor, but I could see from one visit what went on there. I made the mistake of telling Tatiana about it. And now here we are.'

'What do you mean by that? *Here we are.*'

'I got lucky. I marry a good man, a good father. I have children and am happy. Tatiana, she worked at massages and never got lucky like I was. Now she is dead. She never even got to meet her little niece. Her name is Tanya,' she said, jiggling the calmed baby toward Ellie. 'It is like a nickname of Tatiana in Russian.'

'That's really nice, both the name and the sentiment.'

'Vitya, he fought me on it. He made jokes that he did not want our daughter to turn out like Tatiana. But I told him this is what I wanted, and that was the end of it.'

Ellie noted the sound of pride in Zoya's voice

and decided it was well deserved as she pictured this tiny waif of a woman standing up on behalf of her sister's good name.

'You probably figured out by now that I came back to talk to you about Tatiana.'

Zoya nodded.

'Did you know that she was an informant for the FBI?' Zoya's eyes widened, and Ellie pulled out the booking photograph of Lev Grosha that she'd received from Charlie Dixon. 'Do you recognize this man? His name is Lev Grosha. He's in prison based in part on information that Tatiana gave to the FBI.'

Zoya held the picture and stared at it blankly.

'I take it you had no idea how serious her legal problems had gotten.'

'This man is in prison because of *Tatiana?*'

'That's my understanding. We just heard about it ourselves.' Ellie pulled her phone from her waist, flipped it open, and showed Zoya the picture she'd taken of Charlie Dixon. 'This was the FBI agent she was working with.'

Ellie could not read Zoya's silence, but it seemed more troubled than surprised.

'This man,' she said, jutting her chin toward Ellie's phone, 'he is an agent for the police?'

'Well, not for the police, but for the Federal Bureau of Investigation. They're — '

'Yes, I know what is the FBI. I just say police. But he works for FBI?'

Ellie nodded, and Zoya worked her lips nervously between her teeth. Her eyes moved between the grainy digital photo of Dixon and the booking photo of Lev Grosha.

325

'Have you seen the FBI agent before? With your sister?'

'Yes, I think so. She came here, not long before — she came and asked for some money, just a little bit, like always. I have to ask Vitya, you know. But we give her some money, and then she leaves. Vitya and I, we go out a few minutes later to take Anton to the park, back when we had just the one child. A car passed us and Tatiana was inside. Vitya, you know, he was bothered, like she had come asking for money but was running off with some strange man anyway. He made a big fuss over it is why I remember. This man on your phone, I think he was the man who was driving.'

'I can imagine what your husband must have thought when he saw her in a new car with a man who was probably wearing a suit and tie. But he wasn't a client. She was providing information to law enforcement.' Ellie kept her suspicions about the nature of Charlie's relationship with Tatiana to herself.

'Did your partner know that?'

'Excuse me? My partner?'

'The man you came here with before. Mr. Becker, right? Did he know my sister was working with the FBI?'

'No. He's retired now. He couldn't have known she was an informant for the FBI. They're totally separate from the city police. What about the man in the other photograph? Do you recognize him? Lev Grosha?'

Zoya shook her head but still looked rattled.

'Can you think of how your sister might have known Lev Grosha? She told the agent that he was part of a larger criminal conspiracy. Grosha was arrested for credit card fraud, but there was also heroin dealing involved, maybe money laundering.'

They both jumped at the sound of a key in the lock. Zoya pushed Grosha's photograph back into Ellie's hands. 'You must go.'

'What's wrong, Zoya?'

'Nothing. I told you, I saw my sister with that man on your phone, but I did not know who he was. Now, please. Do not cause problems.'

'What aren't you telling me?'

Ellie heard the door slam against the closed chain and the sound of a friendly holler in Russian. Zoya released the chain for her husband. Vitali — whom his wife called Vitya — fell silent when he walked into the room and saw Ellie. 'Detective. I did not realize we had company.'

'Not for long. I was just stopping by to apologize for upsetting your wife the other day. In light of some developments on the case, we don't think the killings are related to Tatiana's death after all. It's probably as you said: Guns change hands. I'm just sorry to have brought up bad memories.'

Vitali nodded and thanked her for the information. Behind him, Zoya stood silently. Ellie apologized once again before leaving.

Just as she had on her first visit to the apartment, Ellie paused outside the door. She heard Vitali wrestle with their son, Anton. She heard Zoya speak in Russian, then an abrupt response from Vitali. Zoya spoke again, more urgently, then Vitali, sounding angry. By the time Ellie headed for the stairs, the pitch had reached full-scale verbal combat.

Ellie wondered if the Rostovs were one of those couples who fought around the clock, despite all that talk from Zoya about how lucky she was to have found a loving caretaker. If not, then something about Ellie had that effect on them, and that made Ellie wonder what kinds of secrets Zoya and Vitali Rostov had hidden beneath their happy veneer.

★ ★ ★

Ellie arrived at Brooklyn's Metropolitan Detention Center just after five o'clock. Evening visitors' hours had just begun, and a line wrapped around the concrete bunker of a building. As Ellie made a beeline for the security checkpoint, she felt the resentful eyes of wives, girlfriends, mothers, and children fall on the light-haired, light-skinned woman of authority cutting ahead of them in the dark cold.

The corrections officer at the entrance was a young man with a skin-close haircut, probably just out of an enlisted military stint. 'I'm here to see Lev Grosha. Special Agent Charlie Dixon should have added me to his visitors' list.'

The guard checked the computer in front of him and nodded. 'You need some privacy?'

'If that's possible.'

'I'll put you in one of the attorney visiting areas. Just be advised. The conversations are monitored by the Bureau of Corrections.'

'The defense attorneys don't have a problem with that?'

'You think John Ashcroft was thinking about them when he changed our regs? Take a seat at one of the tables in the back. Grosha will be right out.'

The man brought out moments later resembled the man in Lev Grosha's booking photo but had a roughness to him that she had not anticipated. He was thinner, harder, and more wiry than the pale-skinned, pink-cheeked blond who'd entered MDC eighteen months earlier. As he settled into the seat across from her, she noticed the bottom half of a dark green swastika peeking from a rolled-up shirt sleeve. She waited for the guard to leave.

'Good afternoon, Mr. Grosha. I'm Ellie Hatcher. I'm a detective with the New York Police Department.'

'And you are sure you are here to see me?' His accent was Brooklyn, still tinged with a hint of the old Russian. 'The statute of limitations must have run out on anything I might have done before my arrest. Two years, right?'

'Sorry. It's at least five on most felonies.'

'This is what happens when you listen to jailhouse lawyers.' Behind Grosha's faint smile, Ellie saw a closer resemblance to the photograph she carried in her purse.

'Not to worry in any case, because I'm not here about anything you might have done. I'm here regarding some murders that have taken place during your incarceration.'

'I'd say I have an ironclad alibi.'

329

'Yes, you do. We've had three women killed in the last year, all of whom were using an Internet dating service called FirstDate. Does that company mean anything to you?'

'No. I mean, yes, I think I have heard of it. You know, people saying that's how they met. Some even in here, so maybe that's not the best advertising. But it does not mean anything special to me in particular.'

'We have reason to believe that one man killed all three of these women, and we think it might be someone who — well, let's just say he might be within your circle of professional acquaintances.'

'And what makes you think I would know this man?'

She had to be cautious here not to reveal too much about Tatiana's connection to his prosecution, or her murder's connection to the recent serial killings. 'A piece of evidence that has come up in our investigation bears some relation to you.'

'What do you mean, a piece of evidence?'

'The details really don't matter, do they? What matters is whether you can help me find the guy who's doing this. A multiple murderer compared to the handful of stolen credit card numbers you swiped? I can get you substantial consideration with the government if you point us in the right direction.'

Ellie hadn't actually run this part of her pitch past Charlie Dixon, let alone the federal prosecutors who would need to make the deal, but she was pretty sure they'd be able to swing it if Grosha proved helpful. She also knew she had Lev Grosha's attention. He did not look like a man who enjoyed prison.

'All you've told me is that some man is killing women, and that a mysterious link ties the two of us together. That does give me a fair basis for helping you.'

'The man we're looking for hates women. He judges them. He would be uncomfortable with promiscuity, most likely with women generally. He may also think of himself as religious. He is fascinated with something called the Book of Enoch. You might have seen him reading religious text, or quoting spiritual verse. He may do this either because he truly believes it or is a cynic who uses religion to justify the things that he does. We also know that he has an acumen for computers. He uses public Internet connections so he is not traceable. And — this is right up your alley — he used a stolen credit card to create an account with the company I mentioned, FirstDate. Does any of this remind you of anyone?'

Grosha was staring at her with an amused expression.

'I can keep your name out of it. We just need a lead. He's murdering innocent women.' She placed pictures of Caroline Hunter, Amy Davis, and Megan Quinn on the table in front of him.

'The only thing that sounded vaguely familiar from anything you mentioned was the use of another person's credit card. That, as you know, is something I am familiar with. But the people I run with? We are what you might call believers in the capitalist system. We break rules to make our way, to make money. These three women, you said they were innocent. They did not buy drugs or steal or con?'

'No.'

'In that case, the men I know? If they saw these women, they might try to fuck them, but hurting them — what would be the point of that, you know? And religion' — he waved a hand dismissively — 'I do not know anyone who gives a fuck about that.'

'How about Vitali Rostov? Do you know anyone by that name? Or he might go by Vitya Rostov.'

His eyes were calm, but she noticed a slight left-leaning head tilt. 'Vitya is what you'd call a nickname for Vitali,' he explained. 'But no, I do not know a man by that name. He is the man you think is hurting these women?'

'No, probably not. Just a name that's come up. You're curious for someone who doesn't even know him.'

'You have me intrigued. A serial killer. Like Hannibal Lecter, no?'

'Without the cannibalism or the bad face mask.'

Grosha laughed, caught off guard by the humor. 'Like I said, I do not know anyone like the man you described, nor do I know any Vitya — what name did you say?'

'Rostov. Vitali or Vitya Rostov,' Ellie clarified.

Grosha shook his head slowly. 'I'm sorry. I cannot help you. But it has been nice to meet you, Ellie Hatcher. You are the kind of visitor that a man in prison does not mind seeing, even under these circumstances.'

'Well, since you don't mind the company, and since you asked a question out of mere curiosity, maybe you won't mind if I do the same.' He gave her a slight nod of consent. 'When did you get the ink?' She glanced at the green bars of the swastika on his forearm.

'Three months after the United States government put me here.'

'Looks like pretty decent work for a prison tat. Your jacket didn't say anything about having white ethnic pride.' She used the white supremacists' preferred euphemism for racism.

Grosha double-checked the empty area around them before speaking. 'I don't give a fuck what color people are. Even the men you Americans call white look brown compared to me. But inside this place, you cannot be alone. I learned that quickly. The brothers, they do not want to take care of a man who looks like me. This?' He pulled his sleeve to cover the ink. 'This was the easy way. I have it removed later. Big deal.'

'You do what you have to in order to survive.'

'Exactly.'

'Not unlike the way you refused to tell the U.S. Attorney's Office who you were feeding the credit card numbers to after you got them from the motel clerk. That was about survival too?'

'Like I said, the tattoo was easy. You know that I cannot say any more than I have. But I promise you this. I am telling the truth when I say I do not know any man like the one you are looking for. If I did, you would not need to give me — what did you call it — *substantial consideration*. I would help you, or I would kill the man myself. Men like that in Russia, they do not get away with hurting women, not like in this country.'

On the way out of the prison, Ellie stopped to see the young, short-haired guard at the entrance.

'Did you get what you needed from your Russian?' he asked.

'Unfortunately, I didn't, but I was wondering if maybe you could help me with something. In order to see anyone in here, you've got to have your name on the inmate's visiting list, right?'

'Yep. It's got to all be done in advance. No such thing as a pop-in at a corrections facility.'

'Can I get a list of Lev Grosha's visitors?'

'No problem.' He hit a few keys. 'It's a short one.' The printer churned out only five names, including hers. The other four were Russian, two females and two males. One of the women, probably his mother, shared the Grosha surname. The two men were named Ivan Ovinko and Mark Jakov. Neither name was familiar to Ellie, and neither Zoya nor Vitali Rostov was on the list.

★　★　★

Stuck in stop-and-start traffic for over forty minutes on the Gowanus Expressway, Ellie felt too antsy to return to Murray Hill for a quiet night alone in her apartment. She was close to a

334

breakthrough, she could tell, but she couldn't piece the tangents of her wandering mind into a coherent thought. Tatiana's sister knew something. Ellie had seen the unspoken concern on Zoya's face, and knew that it had something to do with her husband. The woman also seemed a little too interested in Ed Becker, betraying more than just idle curiosity when she asked if he'd known about Tatiana's cooperation with the FBI. And all those connections that Flann had pointed out between Becker and their case — how did they fit in? And how did they relate to FirstDate and all of the women who'd been killed?

She dialed Flann's number on her cell. 'Hey there, it's me.'

'You're all done seeing the sister?'

'I talked to her, and I also went to see Lev Grosha at MDC. I think there's something more to what Zoya knows. She might not know how it fits into her sister's death, but I said something to her that — I don't know, confused her or something.'

'No idea what it was?'

'She's hard to read. She said she didn't recognize Grosha, but it's possible she's lying. She remembered seeing Tatiana with Dixon, but I don't see why that would be so upsetting. The one thing I did find curious was that she asked if Becker knew Tatiana was an informant. At first I thought she was upset because Becker should have told her, or should have connected it to her murder. But I don't know, she still seemed troubled even when I told her we didn't know until today. Then Vitya came home, and she basically made me leave on the spot. I'm wondering if maybe Vitya's involved in whatever criminal activity Tatiana was pointing the FBI to. She gave up a couple of people, but not her own brother-in-law.'

'And what did Lev Grosha say?'

'That he'd never heard of Vitali or Vitya Rostov. But, again, I think he was probably lying. He did this weird head tilt.'

'Ellie Hatcher, human lie detector.'

'Did you find anything more about Becker's old cases?'

'Charlie Dixon was right. Becker and Tendall carried a pretty high clearance rate, and Becker's remained above average even after Tendall died.'

'So if he was slacking on Tatiana's case, it's not because he'd lost it altogether, like he told us.'

'Exactly. But, again, as with everything, we still don't know how it ties into our case. My spidey senses are going off though. That note in Hunter's binder is about Ed Becker.'

'Well, I hope you're wrong. A *cop* involved in something like this?'

McIlroy said nothing in response.

'I'm on my way back from Brooklyn. Do you have time for a drink or something? We can throw all of this around, see if something comes out.'

'Sorry, I can't tonight. I want to wrap some things up here at the desk, then I need to go.'

'Hot date?'

'No,' he said, then after a pause, 'I'm seeing my daughter again.'

'Oh, Flann, that's great.' Ellie kept her tone upbeat but the silence on the other end of the line had her wondering. 'Well, I guess tomorrow morning it is, then.'

'Yeah, I'll see you tomorrow.' He sounded distant.

'Is everything okay, Flann?'

'Yeah. Just end-of-the-day fatigue is all. Enjoy your youth while you've got it, Hatcher.'

Ellie flipped her phone shut and spent the next twenty minutes of the drive pulling at the threads of information they had. Tatiana was plugged into a ring of Russian criminals who had some connection to FirstDate. Ed Becker — who dropped the ball on Tatiana's murder, who'd been so eager to give Ellie a hand, whose surname was in Caroline Hunter's notes. Stolen credit cards — used by Lev Grosha, by Enoch, by Edmond Bertrand six years ago in Boston. Zoya and Vitya Rostov, who saw Tatiana with Charlie Dixon.

She called Jess's cell number.

'Yo, sis. What up?'

Ellie heard the thumping of Def Leppard's 'Pour Some Sugar on Me' in the background. 'Please tell me you're at Vibrations.'

'You don't think Dog Park should try playing a little Def? I could wear my hair all big, slip into some leather, and ride the eighties revival.'

'Did you get the picture I e-mailed you?' She wanted to know if the club manager, Seth Verona, recognized Charlie.

'Hello? Why do you think I'm here? I don't start my shift for three hours, but I'm trying to

337

catch Seth before he leaves. Who's the stud muffin?'

'An FBI agent named Charlie Dixon. Remember when we talked to Seth, he said he remembered a straightlaced guy who would come in and talk to Tatiana? I want to know if that's him.'

'All right. I just got here, so give me a while.'

By the time Ellie reached the precinct and returned the fleet car, she still wasn't ready to go home. She needed to think about something other than the case. She needed to clear her head and come back to it later. She could think of only one person to call. She found his business card in her jacket pocket, took a deep breath, and dialed his number.

★  ★  ★

Thirty minutes later, the man who called himself Enoch hung up his phone, disappointed. The game was going to have to end earlier than intended. He had planned to wait, at least for a few days of headlines about the FirstDate murders. But now there was a problem.

He had only now learned that police were asking questions about Tatiana Chekova, not just Caroline Hunter, Amy Davis, and Megan Quinn. They were asking questions about information Tatiana had given to the FBI. They were trying to figure out how Tatiana fit into the pattern.

He should have realized they would make the connection. It was the one mistake he'd made during an entire year of planning. He needed to put an end to those inquiries.

Fortunately, there was no harm done if the game had to end early. The letter left in the library would ensure a front-page story the following morning about the FirstDate murders. And he knew precisely how to halt the investigation. He closed the laptop on his kitchen table and thought about what else he needed to bring with him. He was expected on City Island in two hours.

# 32

Ellie met Peter Morse at Half King, a pub he chose in Chelsea. He wore faded jeans, a long-sleeve black T-shirt, and a crumpled charcoal gray blazer that would have looked formal on another man, but worked just fine on Peter. He greeted her with a friendly kiss on the cheek, and Ellie caught a group of women two tables over taking notice. Peter had those kind of looks.

'Great place,' she offered.

'A writer friend of mine owns it. They've got a regular reading series, and, as you can probably tell, it's a favorite place for writers to gather and look for inspiration.' Ellie noticed a few customers scribbling in open notebooks. 'Me, I can only write in total silence. I come here to eat and to drink.'

'That makes it my kind of place.'

'I'm really glad you called, Ellie.' He emphasized the first syllable of her name.

'Me too,' she said, meaning it. It felt good to hear him use her real name.

'And with perfect timing. I just finished filing the article with my editor right before you called. I put the focus on the letter from the library. It's the first time I've become a part of my own story, so it was tricky, but I think I got the tone right.'

'That's good.'

'Of course, I couldn't write the story without including a little bit of your own background. The parallels to the College Hill Strangler case were so obvious that the connection had to be explained. I hope it's something you can live with.'

'I guess we'll find out in the morning.'

'I thought about running it by you, but — '

'I wouldn't even think of it,' Ellie said. 'You've got your job, and getting prior permission from me isn't part of it.'

'Thanks for understanding. I guess the same has to be true for you too — keeping your work life separate from the personal.'

'That's right, so you better hope I don't find that meth lab you've got stashed away in your bedroom closet.' His comment had been a clear invitation to discuss her reasons for trying to preempt a relationship between them, but she wasn't ready for that conversation. She wasn't sure what she wanted to talk about, in fact, and was second-guessing her decision to call him. She wanted to see him in part because she needed to be with someone with whom she would not — could not — discuss the case.

'If it helps any, I turned it in with a blurred photograph of Enoch's letter, instead of a picture of you. Hopefully the editor won't make any changes.'

'I hope you didn't make that decision just because of me.'

'Nah, a threatening letter from a sex-phobic religious zealot is much more ominous than a beautiful police officer. Macabre sells. I was

341

thinking about following up with a story fleshing out the computer angle. Maybe interview some experts about how the killer might have been able to access the e-mail accounts of his victims.'

Ellie liked that angle. It wouldn't involve any details of the actual case, and it had absolutely nothing to do with her. 'I know just the guy for you. He used to work at FirstDate and knows a lot of stuff. Very helpful.' She fished around in her purse and found Jason Upton's business card.

Peter fingered the edges of the card. 'A guy who knows a lot of stuff, huh? Should I be worried about the competition?'

'Nope. He's a little too Waspy for my taste.' The truth was that until she met Peter, she thought she went for preppy men.

'An upper-crust computer nerd?' Peter feigned skepticism.

'A rich kid with a hobby as a day job. And he likes *Pulp Fiction*. You'll like him.'

Peter thanked her and placed the card in his wallet, and Ellie took the opportunity to change the subject. 'So what's good here?' she asked, opening a menu.

'Ah, nice transition. So either you're starving, or that's a sign that we should declare your current case and my current story a conversational no-no.'

'Both actually, if that's okay with you.'

'More than okay. And you can't go wrong with the menu, but your first time here, I'd go with either the shepherd's pie or the fish-and-chips.'

When the waiter came, Ellie ordered a Johnny

Walker Black and shepherd's pie. Peter opted for a pint of Guinness and fish-and-chips.

'So can I ask you how you wound up in New York from Wichita, Kansas, or will that inevitably lead to verboten subject matter?' he asked.

'That's well within limits. I came here because I have a very funny and crazy and irresponsible big brother who dropped out of college so he could hit it big as a rock star. He'd call Mom and tell her he was opening up for big names at CBGB's — as if she even knew what that was. But I knew my brother, you know? When it came time for me to decide what I wanted to do, my high school teachers laid it out for me: What's it gonna be — KU, K. State, or WSU? I stuck it out at Wichita State for a couple of years but eventually it hit me: I'd only lived one place my entire life, and there was absolutely no reason for me to stay. My mom needed me, but most of what she worried about was my brother. So I finished the semester, then came up here.'

'And your mom's still in Kansas?'

'Yep. I call her every night. Just spoke to her before coming here in fact.' Ellie had tried not to let her mother's continued attempts to pull Ellie into a visit to Wichita get to her.

'She's got a good daughter. You went to John Jay right away?'

The rhythm of the conversation should have been awkward. Here they were, having what was essentially a first date — at least for him to get to know the real her — but he already knew so much about her past, and they'd already been together physically. In a strange way that she didn't understand, she felt completely at ease with him.

'No. I figured I'd get here, settle in, and apply to CUNY or something. I wanted to be a lawyer.'

'But then you realized you were carbon-based. Buh-dump-bum. Sorry, obligatory lawyer joke.'

'Thank you for that. So, yeah, I realized I was carbon-based, and I also realized I couldn't afford to live here and pay for school. So I was waiting tables and hanging around with Jess's crowd, and keeping his kind of hours, and I guess I realized I was a little more of a cop at heart than I realized. Like a hand-to-hand drug exchange would be going down in a club bathroom, and I'd notice in a way that most people wouldn't. And I'd see all of these disturbing things every day on the street that would really eat at me. Then one night I saw a girl, way too young even to be out at that hour, wander off from Washington Square Park with some Wall Street cokehead after the bars closed, and I just wanted to stop him from even being near her.'

'Sure.'

'I even confronted the guy — like an idiot, you know? Like, 'Hey, isn't she a little young for you, buddy?' He told me to mind my own business, and she swore she was eighteen. I couldn't do anything about it. I just watched them walk away, knowing full well what was going on, knowing the kind of life that girl was going to have. That was the moment it all clicked for me. I knew what I wanted to do, and I knew I'd be good at it. I enrolled at John Jay the next morning.'

'It sounds more like you needed to do it.'

'I guess. In training, one of the sergeants told us that being a cop should be a calling. That if you see it as just a job, you may as well go sell RV's or tennis rackets. Anyway, I've never regretted it.'

'Not even after days like today?'

'Never. How about reporting? Is that your *calling*?' she asked dramatically.

He thought about it for a second. 'No. Writing might be, but the reporting is just a part of it. I'd like to do more. I've been working on that novel for a few years now, but I'm never quite willing to call it done. It's probably some deep-seated fear of failure, undoubtedly traceable to my parents. Someday, when I'm over it, I'd like to be able to say I'm an *author*, not just a reporter, but I certainly don't regret the journalism. I just wouldn't want it to get in the way of my friendships with anyone I might come to care about.'

Ellie knew he was trying to ease her fears, but she wound up laughing. Some whiskey trickled down her chin. 'Sorry,' she said, wiping the dribble with a napkin. 'Very attractive, I'm sure.'

'Delightful, actually, but I should be the one to apologize. A little over the top?'

'No, I'm sorry. It was incredibly sweet.'

'And sweet makes you spit whiskey?'

'No, it was just really funny to me.'

'Oh good. Funny's what I was going for.'

'It's just that, here we are, saying that maybe we'll wind up being friends, and we've already slept together. I'm sure it's perfectly normal, but if you had any idea what a nun I've been. My stupid idea about having one anonymous night of passion — I just realized how funny it is.'

Ellie found herself laughing uncontrollably. The stress of the case, her nervousness about seeing Peter again, and the surreal quality of this second first date all culminated at once. To her inestimable relief, Peter joined her.

Two hours later, lying next to each other in Ellie's bed, they were both still smiling when Ellie's cell phone rang.

'Ignore it.' Peter pushed a strand of sweat-dampened hair from her forehead and kissed the newly revealed spot on her face. For a second, Ellie was tempted. She could let it ring. She could pretend she was Ally the paralegal, who wasn't in the middle of a murder investigation. But the thought lasted only a second. She flipped her phone open on the third ring.

'Hatcher.'

'Detective Hatcher, this is Officer Griffin Connelly, Tenth Precinct. I'm sorry to bother you after hours.'

'Not a problem.' Ellie sat up and pulled a sheet over her naked body. Peter smiled and pulled it off of her with one finger.

'They can't see you over the phone,' he whispered.

Ellie was so distracted by the thing Peter was doing to her stomach that she almost missed what the officer said next.

'I'm at St. Vincent's Hospital with a Jess Hatcher. He says he's your brother?'

⋆ ⋆ ⋆

Officer Connelly was a thin man with fair skin and light brown hair. He waited for Ellie outside of a treatment room in St. Vincent's emergency care center. Peter had initially insisted on coming with her, and to her surprise, she actually wanted him to. But she ultimately persuaded him to go back to his apartment. If whatever happened to Jess had anything to do with the case, she didn't want to find it on the front page of the *Daily Post*, and she didn't want Peter to be in the position of keeping it quiet before they'd reached an agreement about how to balance his job with hers.

'Thanks for waiting for me, Officer. I just wanted to make sure someone was with him until I got here.'

'I had a hard time explaining it to my sergeant. Is there something more to this than meets the eye?'

'Nothing but a protective little sister. Please thank your sergeant for me.'

According to the statement Jess had given to Officer Connelly, two men had jumped him outside of Vibrations before his shift. He didn't recognize either of the men and was too busy getting his ass kicked to give a helpful description — two white men, average height and weight and, in Jess's words, 'apparently royally pissed off at me for reasons unknown.'

She felt a knot in her stomach as Connelly related the story.

'Lucky for your brother you're on the job. Bouncer at a strip club, random assault in the parking lot? We were searching him for drugs when he told us to call you.'

'You can finish up if you think it's appropriate, Officer.'

'Not necessary. Just get your brother whatever help he needs.'

Ellie found Jess reclining on a narrow hospital bed. He tried to sit up when she walked in, but winced from the movement. The smile he forced onto his face seemed to pain him as well.

'Note to self: Cracked ribs hurt.' He eased himself back down into the bed.

'What happened, Jess?'

'It looks like I finally found a beating I couldn't talk my way out of.'

Ellie always saw Jess as younger than his true years — always happy, never worried, almost invincible. But she hated the way he looked right now — tired, too old to be in this position, and extremely vulnerable.

'They just attacked you in the parking lot for no reason?'

'I went outside to call you, and there they were. Could this have something to do with the picture I showed the Vibrations manager? Seth thinks it was the same guy he saw with Tatiana, by the way.'

Ellie wondered how she'd managed to endanger Jess by verifying the relationship she suspected between Charlie Dixon and Tatiana

Chekova. Had she read Dixon entirely wrong? Then Jess asked her if the man in the picture was Russian.

'Why? The men who did this to you were Russian?'

'Russian, Czech, Romanian, Ukrainian. Slavic, whatever. One of those. When I left the apartment, I noticed a couple of guys standing across the street. I didn't think much of it, but I'm pretty sure they were the same ones who did this to me.'

'Why didn't you say something to the officer?'

'Because my beat down came with a warning, Ellie. And if it was only for me, I would have told them to fuck themselves. But it was about you. I don't know what you've gotten yourself into, but they said to back off. Next time we're both dead. And they know where you live. Ellie, please, you've got to get off this case.'

# 33

Ellie's calls were all put through to Flann's voice mail. When he didn't return three back-to-back messages, she tried to tell herself that the policing could wait until tomorrow. She tried to sit and comfort her brother like any other family member of an assault victim. But she couldn't stop thinking about the Slavic accents of the men who had beaten Jess.

She wanted mug shots. She wanted a positive ID from Jess. She wanted to track them down and, in an ideal world, find them resisting arrest. She wanted an excuse to act on her rage.

But while she worried about protecting her brother, he was still trying to shield her from the threat that had been delivered through him. He refused to let her pass the information on to Officer Connelly, promising that if she did, he would stick to his bogus cover story. So she kept coming back to the same dilemma: Either she needed to leave Jess's side to print some pictures of suspects for him to ID, or she needed to find Flann.

She tried Flann's cell phone one last time, then dialed directory assistance and requested a listing for Miranda Hart. She'd apologize to Flann later for bothering the mother of his child but, at that moment, all she could think about was her own need to get some help. The operator connected her directly.

'Hello?' The woman sounded distracted. Ellie heard water running in the background and the faint sounds of a television.

'Ms. Hart?'

'Yes?'

'I'm sorry to bother you. My name is Ellie Hatcher. I'm Flann McIlroy's partner at the NYPD. I really need to find him, and he's not answering his phone.'

The running water stopped. 'I'm not sure why you have this number. He doesn't live here. He never has.'

'I thought maybe he was there with your daughter. Or maybe you could tell me where he took her for dinner?'

'I'm sorry. There's some misunderstanding. He saw her earlier in the week.'

'He told me he was having dinner with her again tonight.'

'No. We agreed to take things slow. I want to ease him into Stephanie's life.'

'But I just talked to him a few hours ago. Wasn't he supposed to see her?'

'He told you that? No. We talked a long time after he brought Stephanie home the other night. He's supposed to call to schedule something next *week*. I haven't talked to him since.'

Ellie thanked Miranda for her time, cut the call short, and began redialing Flann's number. Once, twice, three more times. Straight to voice mail. His phone was turned off, and she was beginning to worry. Her brother was in the hospital. Her partner had lied to her and was missing. If they had gotten to Jess, could they have gotten to Flann too?

She sat at the edge of Jess's bed. He looked at her like he didn't know whether to laugh or scream at her. 'Just go, Ellie. Seriously, do what you need to do, but you've got to promise me to be careful. I got a good thing going with the Vicodin here, and all your stress is seriously harshing my mellow.'

After a few minutes of repeated 'are you sure's?' Jess threatened to have the attending nurse call security if Ellie did not leave him to rest.

'If I arrange to fax some pictures here, do you think you can find the energy to take a look at them and maybe give me a text message?'

'Now that's my baby sister. Yeah, I think I can handle it. I didn't get enough punches in to hurt these babies,' he said, wiggling his fingers.

★   ★   ★

Ellie splurged for a cab to the precinct, not wanting to lose her cell phone signal on the subway in case Flann called. As she checked her phone for incoming calls one last time before she paid the driver, a thought suddenly hit her, and she felt stupid for not realizing it earlier: Flann's phone might be going directly to voice mail simply because he was somewhere without a signal. It still left her questioning why he lied to her about seeing his daughter, but at least it shifted her thoughts from the more unnerving possibilities she'd conjured.

She settled herself in front of a records

terminal and began printing out copies of the photographs she wanted Jess to see. Vitali Rostov was first. He had no criminal record, so she pulled his New York driver's license photograph. Next, she ran off the photographs of the two men who were on Lev Grosha's list of approved inmate visitors: Ivan Ovinko and Mark Jakov. She numbered the photographs with a pen — one through three — then faxed them to the hospital along with a note for the security guard who had promised to shepherd the fax to Jess's room.

As she watched the pages feed through the fax machine, she took a deep breath. Now came the hard part. Waiting. She checked her phone. No new calls. She tried Flann again. Still straight to voice mail. Where was he?

A folder rested on Flann's desk, its contents spilling out slightly. She recognized it as the folder Jason Upton had sent to the precinct after running a background check on Ed Becker. She opened it and found three documents that had not been there originally.

One was a copy of a New York DMV boat registration for a 1995 Gibson 5900 Cabin Yacht, registered to Ed Becker. The second was a copy of title information on the same boat, documenting ownership transferring from a man named Luke Steiner to Ed Becker the previous March. The third document was a fax addressed to Detective Flann McIlroy, dated that afternoon, from the law firm of Larkin, Baker & Howry, where Jason Upton worked.

On the cover sheet was a handwritten note:

*Got your message. Sorry I missed you, and sorry I missed the boat. Goes to show there's always somewhere else to look. Here's the registration if you don't already have it. Call me if you need anything else.* He had left a telephone number with a cellular phone area code, followed by the initials J. U. Attached was a copy of the same DMV boat registration that Becker had apparently printed out on his own before receiving Upton's fax.

Ellie tried to call Flann again. Still straight to voice mail. She stared at the registration for Ed Becker's 1995 Gibson 5900 Cabin Yacht, then Googled 'Gibson 5900' on Flann's computer. She double clicked on the first result and pulled up a listing of a 2002 yacht. Asking price: a quarter of a mil. She let out a whistle, then checked a few more listings. The cheapest 1995 she could find was still $160,000. How did a retired cop afford a boat like that? It certainly explained why Flann had been curious, but what led him to ask Jason Upton about the boat in the first place?

She remembered Upton's computer tutorial about cookies. She used the computer's mouse to click on the history of Flann's Internet Explorer, then clicked on a folder marked *today*. Beneath an entry for 'images.google,' a name popped out at her: Ed Becker. She clicked on it.

The screen changed to a collection of small photographs. A number in the top right-hand corner of the screen indicated that she had pulled up more than five hundred matches. She searched Google Images again, this time for 'Ed

Becker New York.' That narrowed it to a manageable thirty-two matches. She browsed the photos. A kid graduating from high school. A paleontologist reconstructing the skeleton of a T. rex. Some guy with a smile and a rifle next to a really dead Bambi.

She clicked over to the next page of photographs. Between a head shot of a bankruptcy lawyer and a poster for the movie *City Hall* was a group photograph that caught her eye. It was too small to make out faces, but the text beneath the picture read, Bronx Yacht Club Activities. She clicked on the photograph to enlarge it.

Retired NYPD Detective Ed Becker stood third from the left, beer in hand, on the deck of a sailboat. A description beneath the picture read, Blue Cup Regatta.

Ellie returned to Flann's history and saw a listing for the Bronx Yacht Club. She clicked on the link to pull up the club's Web site. The home page announced, 'Welcome to the site of the Bronx Yacht Club, located in the nautical community of City Island, New York.' A separate entry in Flann's browser history showed that he also visited a Web site about City Island itself.

City Island. City Island. Where had she just seen something about City Island? She rummaged through the clutter scattered across Flann's desk until she found what she was looking for: the list of Internet café locations that Enoch used to access the FirstDate server. Every spot was in Manhattan, except one — an

355

Internet café called JavaNet on City Island, New York.

She opened Mapquest, then entered the address of the Bronx Yacht Club and requested directions to JavaNet. Only a quarter of a mile separated the two.

She continued scouring the papers on Flann's desk, hoping to find something to confirm her suspicions about where her partner had gone. Resting inside his top desk drawer was a sealed envelope marked 'Ellie.' She ripped it open and read the note inside:

*Ellie — Tomorrow morning I will tell you whatever I learn tonight about Ed Becker, and you will undoubtedly be angry that I did not invite you on my snooping adventure. I will explain my reasons, and you will accuse me of holding out on you once again. Then I will show you this note to prove that, unlike some moments in the past few days, I am sharing my island with you. I have every intention of sharing any and all information with you, but I have good reasons for acquiring it on my own. I know you hope I'm wrong — I do too — but I need to check on Becker. As you know, the NYPD can be a harsh place for cops who check on other cops. There's no need for you to be associated with my snooping. But I promise, I will tell you everything I know tomorrow. Now that you've read this, do you forgive me, or shall we go another round? Your partner, Flann.*

She read the letter again, so frustrated she wanted to tear it to pieces. *I hope you're wrong.* That's what she'd said to him when she called him from the car and he voiced his concerns about Becker. He'd written this note after that phone call.

She dialed Flann's number again, but this time it did not go into voice mail. It rang. Then an answer. A loud humming sound in the background, then Flann's voice: 'Can't talk,' followed by a click. She hit redial immediately, but the call went directly into voice mail this time. She tried twice more, but no luck. Flann must have turned off his cell after Ellie had finally made it through.

The noise in the background had been familiar. And loud. She pulled up a map of City Island on the computer screen. The Bronx Yacht Club was near Pelham Bay Park, not far from LaGuardia Airport. It was also not far from Westchester, where Ed Becker lived.

She pulled up the yacht club's Web site again and clicked on the link for directions. The #6 subway line ended at the Pelham Bay Park station. Ellie tried Flann's phone again. It was still off.

She walked downstairs to the car checkout desk. Behind the counter, a gray-haired woman with black-framed glasses and very red lipstick read a paperback called *To the Power of Three*.

'Hi, I'm Ellie Hatcher. I'm here this week working with — '

'I know who you are, sweetie.' The woman looked up at her over the tops of her reading glasses.

'Would you mind checking to see if McIlroy has a car out?'

'I can tell you for a fact that he does not. I saw him walk out of here — what, it must have been an hour and a half ago.'

Ninety minutes. It was about the length of the ride on the #6 train to Pelham Bay Park. Flann was out there alone, with a significant head start and without a partner.

'I need to check out a car.'

# 34

With the occasional help of a siren, Ellie made good time, crossing the small, green City Island Bridge only forty minutes after leaving the precinct. But she was still at least forty minutes behind Flann, and his phone was still turned off.

She started at the Pelham Bay Park train station and drove from there to the Bronx Yacht Club. The roads were dark, empty, and still. Ellie felt like she had driven hours away, to the eastern seaboard, but she was only twenty miles from Manhattan. She drove slowly, checking both sides of the street for signs of Flann.

It was her fault they were separated. *I hope you're wrong.* She should have said more when he voiced his concerns about Becker. She should have at least made it clear that she'd back him up no matter where the leads took them, even if it was to the boat of a former cop, docked off City Island, just a quarter mile from the Internet café used by a man who called himself Enoch. Maybe if she had said all that, he would not be out there alone. The only way to make it right was to find him.

When she reached the yacht club, she parked along Hunter Avenue and walked toward a stately white-columned building with a wrap-around porch. On her way to the large double-doored entrance, she passed two silver-haired men resting against the nearby deck railing, smoking cigars and drinking from lead crystal highball glasses.

The interior of the clubhouse was ensconced in high-gloss dark wood and white leather, as if the building itself were on water. In a large ballroom toward the back, a crowd danced and mingled to big-band music. Ellie made her way to a mustached man behind a discreet reception desk on the left side of the lobby.

'The Meyer wedding?' His tone was friendly even as he eyed her cable knit sweater, black pants, and bulky parka skeptically.

'No, sir.' She showed him her shield and a picture of a Gibson cabin yacht that she'd printed from the Internet. 'I'm looking for a potential crime witness. Can you tell me if you've seen this boat?'

'I'm sorry, ma'am. If you need information about one of our members, you'll have to talk to our director in the morning.'

'Pretend you're down the street on your coffee break, and I'm just asking you as a private citizen who works on City Island if you've ever seen this boat. Please. I'll keep your name out of it.'

He checked out the lobby for interlopers, then leaned in close to whisper. 'The truth is, hon, I don't know a damn thing about boats. They're all the same old hunk of wood and rope to me.'

Ellie zipped her coat as she left the clubhouse, prepared to walk every pier of the island to find Ed Becker's boat and her partner. The thinner of the gray-haired duo with the highballs stopped her on the way out.

'Snoozeville with the septuagenarians in there, right?'

His heavier friend placed a hand over his heart. 'Please make my day and tell me you're a whiskey drinker.'

'On another day, I would be. I'm looking for this boat and was hoping someone at the clubhouse could help me.' She unfolded her picture of the cruiser.

'If you're asking about boats, you've come to the right place. I'm Bud, and this is Jim.' The heavy man pointed to himself with his cigar-holding hand, then pointed to his friend.

'Ellie.'

'Tell you what, Ellie. I'll answer your questions about that boat if you have a little sip of whiskey with us. Our goal is to finish this bottle, and we could use the help.' Bud offered her the bottle, no glass.

Johnny Walker Blue. Very expensive. Very tempting. And arguing with these guys would take far longer than swallowing a quick drink. She grabbed the bottle and took a sip.

'Come on now,' Bud said. 'Take a real drink, then we'll talk.'

She took a long draw this time, and she felt the warmth of the liquid fill her stomach.

'Now that's a whiskey drinker,' Bud said with approval. 'So, here's the thing about your boat. That's a Gibson Cabin Yacht, one of the big ones.'

'A 5900 series, I think,' Jim added.

'It's a hell of boat.' Both men nodded, sure that they were in agreement that it was a damn fine boat.

'I know what kind of boat it is.' Ellie tried not to sound too testy. 'I really need to find it.'

'You got a scavenger hunt going with that other guy or something?' Bud asked.

'What other guy?'

'I got a confession for you,' Bud said. 'Me and Jim don't know squat about cabin cruisers. We're sailboat men ourselves. But we were down by the marina about half an hour ago. A guy asked us about Gibson Cabin Yachts and showed us a picture a lot like that one and said it was a 5900.'

'Red hair, not too tall?' Ellie asked.

'Yeah, sort of a funny-looking fellow if you ask me,' Bud said.

'He's a friend of mine. We're both looking for the same boat. Like I said, it's urgent.'

'I don't suppose you want to tell us your friend's name?' Jim asked. 'The one who owns the boat?'

'It's not like any guy's going to be embarrassed about having a visit from a woman like you,' Bud added.

'Ed Becker. Do you know him?'

'Now why didn't you say that in the first place?' Bud said. 'Walk past the yacht club's slips, then you'll get to the marina. Ed's on the fourth row — is that right, Jim?'

Ellie thanked them and was already heading toward the water when Jim called out behind her, 'The fourth row of slips to the east. Then take a left. He's about halfways down, on the right. Drag your buddies on back here. We'll get another bottle.'

★　★　★

Ellie followed their directions along the shore-line, walking at first, and then breaking into a fast jog along the boardwalk. Cold air burned her lungs, and a damp heat began to build inside her zipped coat. When she reached the boat slips at the marina, she slowed her pace, mindful of the sound of her heavy breaths and footsteps on the concrete beneath her.

She counted as she walked, four rows. Scanning the marina, she wondered if she had a good enough eye for boats to recognize Ed's, even with a picture. As her eyes ran across the boats moored to the right side of the pier, she compared each to the features that stood out to her from the picture. Big. Windows. Raised cabin. They all looked the same.

As she neared the middle of the pier, the job of identifying Ed Becker's boat became consid-erably easier. Her eyes were still adjusting to the absence of streetlight, but a man's dark figure stood out against the white back of one of the boats. He was leaning against the outside of the boat's cabin, peering through the edge of a set of double doors that led inside. Even with the moonlight as her only illumination, Ellie recognized that profile. It was Flann McIlroy.

She exhaled the breath she hadn't realized she'd been holding. Flann. It was Flann. She'd found him, and no one with a Slavic accent had put him in an emergency room.

Ellie waved, trying to get his attention, but Flann was fixated on whatever he was watching in the cabin. She walked slowly toward him, each gentle step sounding louder than the last among the unoccupied, darkened boats. With four boats between her and Flann, she was reluctant to move any closer. Presumably Ed Becker was inside his boat, and Flann did not want him to know he was being watched. Walking along the pier, Ellie felt as if she glowed in the dark.

She lowered her body to the ground and began to crawl along the right edge of the pier so any view Becker might have of her would be blocked by other boats. She also got a better look at Flann. He held his weapon at his chest, hands set to fire if necessary. She crawled faster.

As she quickened her pace, her leg caught a loose nail head protruding from a plank in the pier. She sucked in her air to suppress the cry in her throat, then continued her crawl. Just two boats away now, but Flann was too focused on whatever he was watching to feel her eyes on him.

She was still watching Flann when a high-pitched chirp penetrated the silence. It was coming from her hip. She smacked the side of her cell phone and saw the incoming text message through the small window. *#1 Jess.* Jess had identified as one of his assailants the first of the photographs she faxed to him. Number one was Vitali Rostov.

Just as Ellie slapped her phone, she heard Flann move on the boat in front of her. He'd made a sound, on Becker's boat, just feet away from Becker. She watched Flann pull his body back from the glass doors of the boat. She didn't dare move as she watched him freeze too. He waited three beats, then leaned to look inside the cabin again. She held her breath and convinced herself that Flann could talk his way out of the situation if Becker saw him.

It happened so fast that she had a hard time later remembering what Flann had said. Flann swung his entire body to the right, stepping directly in front of the boat's cabin entrance. Then he cried out. She would replay the video in her head over and over again on an endless loop, but the sound was lost. It was loud though. Urgent. Panicked. Abrupt. Maybe he had yelled, 'No.'

By the time Flann rushed through the double doors, Ellie was moving too, out of her crawl stance and into a full sprint. She pulled her gun from her holster. Twist, then up, the Glock was at the ready. She chose speed over silence now. She jumped from the pier onto the boat's stern, but as the weight of her body landed, she heard a louder noise than she'd prepared herself for. It wasn't the sound of her boots on the boat. It was a pop, followed by two more. Three shots. Three gunshots.

Moving quickly through the cabin entrance, Ellie found herself alone in a sleeping cabin. She walked more cautiously to a doorway at the end of the bulkhead, then held her breath as she slowly pushed the door open from the side. To her left, Ed Becker had collapsed on a small couch. The bottom of his face was gone, replaced by a hollow red cavity of bone and skin. To her right, Flann sat with his back against the wall, his legs splayed in front of him. One dark red hole pierced his neck above his left shirt collar. A flower of red blossomed across the right side of his shirt.

There had been one, two, three gunshots. Her senses competed for her complete attention. As she tried to comprehend the visual, she heard different noises. In front of her, then behind her. A scurry along the right side of the deck, past the cabin, and then gone. The department would try to convince her later that she should have looked — that if she'd really heard the noises she described, her instincts would have carried her out of the cabin, down the pier, after whoever it was who was responsible for making those sounds. But in that moment, all she could think about was the hole in Flann's throat, the wound in his stomach, the amount of blood that indicated massive internal damage.

Her instinct was not to chase the noises. All she could do was fall to her knees beside Flann. She pulled off her coat and pressed it against his belly, then held him tight while she punched 911 into her cell phone. She screamed at the dispatcher, '10–13, Officer shot, City Island marina, fourth row of slips on the east. 10–13. He's shot. Hurry. Please.' And she screamed at Flann. She held him and rocked him and pleaded with him not to die.

# PART FOUR

# GREED, JEALOUSY, LUST, REVENGE

# 35

Four mornings later, Ellie confronted her reflection in the bathroom mirror. She dabbed more concealer under her swollen eyes, but nothing could cover the circles that had grown darker every day since Flann had died in her arms on Ed Becker's boat. She ran a brush through her hair, knowing that her appearance would do nothing to change what was going to happen at this meeting.

Jess had gotten up early to fetch coffee and breakfast sandwiches from the deli down the street. Ellie tried to wave off the food, but he insisted that she'd feel better if she had a little energy when she went in to work. This would be her first trip back to the Thirteenth Precinct. According to standard protocol for police homicides, she'd been driven that night from City Island to the precinct to meet with an appointed police union representative. With this stranger by her side, she had sat in an interrogation room for three hours with Lieutenant Dan Eckels and two homicide detectives whose names she no longer remembered.

She gave them a detailed timeline of the entire FirstDate investigation, from the moment she met Flann McIlroy to the moment an ambulance carried his body away. She made sure to tell them about Stephanie Hart, and her mother, Miranda. Flann had a daughter. Someone needed to tell her that her father was dead. She would miss him. She should get his benefits. She should get his Siamese cat. Then Lieutenant Eckels sent her home, and the union representative delivered the news that she was officially on administrative leave. Again, it was standard protocol, she was assured.

In the three and a half days since she walked out of the precinct, the New York Police Department had erected a wall between her and the investigation into Flann McIlroy's murder, Ed Becker's apparent suicide, and the tying together of the connections between Becker and four dead women. Despite the occasional urge to smash down the wall and continue investigating on her own time, she forced herself to steer clear. She did not want the department to blame any shortcomings in its conclusions on her interference. She'd spent four nights and three full days completely shut off from the case that had been all consuming until those three shots. Pop, pop, pop.

She found other ways to keep busy. She was back to her kickboxing schedule, cheered for Dog Park at an open mic night in the West Village, and finally visited the top of the Empire State Building. She even went to Miranda Hart's house and told her how much it meant to Flann to see his daughter for dinner. But still, she couldn't rid herself of the image of Flann, dead on the floor of Becker's boat. The finality of his death seemed to feed like parasites at her heart.

After three days of silence, Lieutenant Eckels called to say he wanted to see her first thing in the morning. When she asked if she would be going back to work, he informed her they would discuss it in the morning. He reminded her of her right to bring not only union representation but an attorney of her choice. For three days, she had heard nothing — no request to question her again, no appointment with the D.A.'s office, and no estimation for when she would return to work. Now, the department wanted to see her, and the request was accompanied by none of the expected assurances — *just a formality, one last interview, you'll be back on duty tomorrow.*

The way Ellie's union representative explained it, the department's questions would be about her competence. She could lose her detective designation. She could lose her shield. She was a new enough cop that they could even strip her of her pension. But as the union rep pored over the potential consequences, all Ellie could hear was her own internal voice. *I deserve to lose it all. Flann was alone on City Island to protect me, then I forgot to turn off my phone and got him killed.*

★　★　★

Ellie walked alone into the Thirteenth Precinct. She felt the eyes of the homicide bureau — the detectives who worked with Flann McIlroy, the ones whom she never had a chance to know — follow her to the office of their lieutenant, Dan Eckels. Eckels was waiting for her. His salt-and-pepper hair was cut close to a large head that perched on a short, squat body — a fire hydrant topped with a Brillo pad. Ellie smiled sadly, remembering Flann's depiction of him as the gruff boss in a Hollywood cop movie.

To Ellie's surprise and relief, she recognized another face in Eckels's office. It belonged to the man who had warned her not so many days earlier about getting too far ahead of herself in a homicide assignment. 'Lieutenant Jenkins,' Ellie said with a nod.

'Detective.' Randy Jenkins's tone was formal, but he returned the nod. Ellie found the gesture from her own Midtown North supervisor comforting under the circumstances.

Eckels directed Ellie to a chair across from his desk, and then moved straight to the business at hand.

'When I spoke to you yesterday, you were adamant about waiving your right to have either a union representative or an attorney here on your behalf. I take it from your arrival here alone this morning that you continue to proceed without representation?'

'Yes, sir. I'm fine on my own.'

'Very well then,' Eckels said. 'Two of my detectives have worked around the clock putting together a report of the City Island incident.'

Ellie stifled a wince at his use of the word *incident*.

'As with all police homicides, a grand jury will hear the facts of the case, probably not for another couple of weeks, but we do not anticipate any problems here. I thought it fair, Detective Hatcher, to share with you what we've learned since we spoke last.'

'I appreciate that, sir. Thank you.'

'The evidence very firmly establishes that Ed Becker, a former detective of this department, is the man that you and McIlroy were looking for.'

Ellie had come to that realization herself four nights earlier, but hearing it said aloud as an official determination still sounded surreal. A former homicide detective had killed four women. The man who called himself Enoch had given her a ride home.

'As you learned before going to City Island,' Eckels continued, 'Ed Becker kept a boat not far from the cybercafé used two nights earlier by Enoch. He appears to have ignored the Tatiana Chekova investigation that he conveniently headed, and his name was found in Caroline Hunter's notes. We have learned more in the last three days. We have confirmed that the laptop found on Becker's boat is the same computer used by Enoch to sign on to the FirstDate account. The Internet usage matches up with Enoch's, and a copy of the letter left for Peter Morse in the Midtown library was saved to the hard drive. We also found a marked-up copy of *The Book of Enoch* in Becker's possession. It looks pretty straightforward. Becker saw McIlroy on his boat and realized it was all over. He fatally shot McIlroy, then shot himself.'

'But why?' Ellie asked. 'Why did he do all of this?'

Eckels was clearly put off by the question. 'You of all people should know you can't make sense of the motivations of a serial killer.'

Jenkins offered a suggestion. 'Obviously I'm

not one of the leads on this, but maybe he had some kind of relationship with Tatiana. She was a prostitute. Some cops have been known to sample the trade. If she was trying to get out of the life, as you said the club manager indicated, maybe she was shaking down Becker, trying to find another way to support herself. He shoots her, then realizes he likes it. He used FirstDate as his outlet.'

'I spent the entire weekend mulling all of this over and came up with the same theory. But what I can't figure out is why I found him at the Rostovs that day in Brooklyn. He claimed the loose ends he left behind on Tatiana's murder were bothering him. If he's the one who killed her, then why was he outside of her sister's apartment?'

'I've got to hand it to you,' Eckels said. 'McIlroy would've been proud of you, Hatcher, trying to get into the head of a sociopath. We can make up motivations for him all day long. Did you ever think he might've gotten off watching her sister? Maybe he sat out there every day for the past two and a half years, like revisiting the scene of the crime. When you ran into him, he provided a convenient cover story.'

'Or maybe there's more to this. We know the killer somehow got into Amy Davis's and Megan Quinn's FirstDate accounts. And he doctored that phony e-mail to get Amy to sign up in the first place. Becker didn't strike me as someone with that kind of computer sophistication. Becker must have had a partner, and it obviously has something to do with Vitali

Rostov. My brother was assaulted just a couple of hours before Flann was killed. He says Rostov did it and included a warning for me to back off. Clearly something I said to his wife touched a nerve. And Becker's got that expensive boat. If he was dirty, taking money from the Russians, then we don't know the whole story yet.'

Eckels looked at her like a gnat he wanted to squash. 'There's no corroboration of that account, Detective. Officer Connelly was left with the impression that the assault against your brother was drug related.'

'I'm the corroboration. I know what my brother told me.'

'So you're saying you permitted your brother to file a false police report?'

'He told the truth to me, and the last time I checked, I was also a cop.'

'A cop who might have a hard time admitting the true nature of her brother's problems. Have you ever considered that your brother told Officer Connelly the truth about what happened in the parking lot, and told you what you wanted to hear?'

Ellie pictured Jess lying on that hospital cot, pleading with her to stay safe, and fought the urge to tell Eckels precisely what she thought of his theory. She needed to focus on getting the investigation back on track.

'Where did you find *The Book of Enoch*?' She hadn't seen it in the yacht's cabin before she was physically pulled away from the scene.

'On the deck.'

Ellie nodded, picturing the layout of the boat. Doors in the back of the cabin. Another set of doors on the right side of the front bulkhead.

'Was it on the right? The side by the doors?'

'I believe that's correct. On the starboard.'

'He left a book on the deck of his boat at night in the winter? The right side is where I heard the noise. The footsteps. If someone dropped that book there for us to find, that explains the footsteps. And the shots. I told the detectives. It was like one pop, then a pause, then two more, closer together. Someone else was on that boat. Someone shot Becker first — one shot — *then* Flann.'

Eckels gave Jenkins a *told you so* look.

'That's one of the things we need to talk about, Ellie.' Jenkins placed a protective hand on her shoulder. 'I'm sure you heard something that could have sounded like footsteps from your position. You were in an unknown place, under incredible stress. And the sounds of bullets can be very misleading. You said yourself that things happened quickly.'

Ellie quietly shook her head, disappointed. She hadn't brought a lawyer or a union rep, because their only role would be to protect her. They wouldn't care about getting the department to do the right thing. With Jenkins's unexpected appearance, she'd hoped to have an ally. But here he was, trying to throw her a lifeline, yet willing to cover up the truth.

'So what you're both saying is that you want me to fall in line and get with the official story. Ed Becker acted alone. The serial killer's dead now, and the women of New York can feel safe once again.'

'What we're telling you,' Eckels said, 'is that you're in no position to contradict the very clear evidence in this case. Ed Becker put two bullets from a .38 into McIlroy, then ate one in the mouth. The ballistics back it up. It's that simple.'

'You tested for GSR on his hands?'

'As soon as we're done talking here, the assistant chief will be making a public statement. This case is closed.'

'So you're just glossing over all the details,' Ellie said. 'You're going to wrap this whole case up with a nice little bow without ever answering the hard questions about why Ed Becker would do these things, how he managed to pull it off, and what it all had to do with the information Tatiana Chekova was giving to the FBI. Call the press, everyone — the NYPD saves the day.'

Eckels pursed his thin lips. 'Listen up, young lady. If you think the department comes out of this looking good, you're a lot stupider than I thought. One of our own did this. A cop murdered four women, then took another cop out with him. And don't think for a second that the assistant chief won't face some hard questions about why he let McIlroy pull *you* in to a case like *this*.'

Ellie noticed the throbbing vein on Eckels's neck. Flann's description of a chew-out session from his lieutenant had been right on the mark. Ellie swallowed, wishing Flann was here with her, realizing how much she missed him. He would not have stood for this. He would have pushed back, no matter the consequences. The thought helped steel her resolve.

'The department should face harder questions than that,' she retorted. 'If Becker killed Tatiana because she could implicate him or the men he worked for, then that raises serious doubts about the kind of cover he was giving to Russian organized crime while he was on the job. It should also make you wonder about his partner's death. Tendall could have been wrapped up in whatever Becker had going on with Rostov, or maybe he had concerns about Becker.'

'You're dragging Barney Tendall into this conspiracy theory now? You realize how hysterical you sound?'

'I believe that was Freud's term for 'female.' Why don't you go ahead and make it transparent? Haul out the B-word and the C-word while you're at it.'

'I think we could all use a break — '

Eckels waved off Jenkins's attempt to mediate.

'As I said, the case is closed. Experienced detectives have been working it tirelessly. We owe you no further explanation. The decision you have to make, Detective Hatcher, is how you want to be depicted in the formal account of this closed case.'

'And what precisely are my choices?'

Lieutenant Jenkins interrupted again. His voice was gentle but assured. 'Can I give you some friendly advice, Ellie? Why don't you take some credit for the hard work you and Detective McIlroy did. Take some credit, and then take some time off. You're automatically entitled to paid leave. You'll return to detective borough in a month or so under my command. We're eager to have you back where you belong.'

'Listen to your lieutenant,' Eckels continued. 'McIlroy comes out a hero this way. You get to stand by the side of the assistant chief as he announces the end of a killing spree that could have become another Son of Sam.'

'And the other way?'

Jenkins worked his jaw as Eckels spelled it out for her. 'Both you and McIlroy abandoned protocol. McIlroy went to City Island on his own, not bothering to notify his own partner, let alone call for backup. When you realized what he'd done, you worsened matters by following him, again, totally on your own, without backup. You made the trip, in a department vehicle, despite the fact that you'd been drinking that night — '

Ellie opened her mouth to interrupt, but Eckels only raised his voice.

'*And* you continued to consume more alcohol once you got to City Island.'

'I told the detectives I took two sips because — '

'You were a rookie detective, in over your head, without backup. You'd been drinking. Your judgment was impaired, and your partner was murdered right in front of you. Not to mention you've got some demons in your past that might keep you from accepting the department's conclusion that your friend Ed Becker committed suicide.'

'That's a low blow,' Ellie said quietly.

'And it's precisely what the media will say if you try to derail the closure of this case. There is no one-armed man that we have yet to chase down, Detective. Ed Becker killed those women, and he killed Flann McIlroy.'

'Are we done here?' Ellie asked.

'The assistant chief expects you to stay for the press conference,' Eckels said.

'No thank you.' Ellie stood to leave.

'What exactly are your future plans with respect to this department, Detective?'

'Am I required to answer that in the course of my duties?' Ellie looked to Randy Jenkins.

'No,' her lieutenant said quietly. 'You're entitled to paid leave regardless of what you do. And you cannot be forced to attend a press conference.'

'Well, then. Lieutenant Jenkins, I guess you'll be hearing from me when my leave is up. Thank you for taking the time to be here for me this morning. I really do appreciate it.'

Jenkins urged Ellie to stay, but Eckels cut him off. 'You're wasting your time, Randy.'

'That, Lieutenant Eckels, was the strongest show of leadership you demonstrated all morning.' Ellie walked out of Eckels's office and out of the Thirteenth Precinct without looking back. The media vans were already lined up on Twenty-first Street for the assistant chief's forthcoming announcement. She had a decision to make.

But she had already made the decision six years ago, that night under the Washington Square Arch. She had decided that sitting with blissful ignorance on life's sidelines was not in her nature. She decided to become a cop. For the last three days, she had been fighting her nature, filling her schedule with back-to-back activities in an attempt to ignore the questions eating away at her like cancer. She had waited for the department's conclusions. Now that she'd heard them, it was time to follow her instincts. She owed this to Flann and to herself. She was going to find out what really happened.

She pulled up the hood of her coat, swaddled herself in her scarf, and headed away from the cameras while she dialed the number for the FBI field office.

# 36

'You know this is blackmail, don't you?' Charlie Dixon stood behind his desk with his arms folded, looking out the window at lower Manhattan.

Sitting in a guest chair across from his desk, Ellie Hatcher uncrossed her legs and shook her head in mock disappointment. 'Is that how far the FBI has gone astray from its traditional law enforcement concerns? You consider it *blackmail* now for a local police officer to share information about criminal activity and expect some modicum of cooperation?'

Dixon turned to face her. 'When it's accompanied by threats if I refuse, then yeah, I consider that blackmail.'

'All I said was that if you couldn't help me, I'd have to find someone who could. And the fact that you were previously seen, multiple times, at Vibrations with Tatiana Chekova — a very attractive federal informant, by the way — might be relevant.'

'You're blackmailing me.'

'Tomato, tomahto.'

'And how exactly am I supposed to help you find out the truth about Ed Becker if the NYPD's not interested?'

'I need two things from you. The first is a federal arrest warrant for Vitali Rostov, Tatiana Chekova's brother-in-law. My brother was assaulted Friday night by two men in the Vibrations parking lot. He can ID Rostov as one of the assailants. Rostov did it so I'd back off the questions I was asking about Lev Grosha.'

Dixon shook his head. 'There's no federal jurisdiction for a garden variety assault. And even if he intended to send a message to you, it's not a federal offense to interfere with a local investigation.'

'What about the fact that they took his wallet?'

Dixon had seen this before in local cops. Just because the FBI had stepped in on one of their robbery cases in the past, they mistakenly assumed every robbery was a federal concern. 'Robbery falls under the Hobb's Act but only if it affects interstate commerce.'

'Oh, for Pete's sake. My job is so much simpler. See person do bad thing? Haul out the handcuffs. What does that mean, *affecting commerce?*'

Dixon hardly understood the nuances of federal jurisdiction himself, so he tried to make it simple. 'It could mean a lot of things, but we usually only go that route when it's a commercial robbery. Then we show that the money that was taken from Home Depot or wherever would've been spent in commerce.'

'Well, okay then. There you go. Jess spends money in commerce all the time. There's your jurisdiction.'

Dixon frowned.

'I don't care if he's charged or not,' Ellie said. Once a suspect was in the box — even if it was for jaywalking — no limits existed on what a guy just might tell a cop. 'I just want him in custody. Can you get an arrest warrant under the Hobb's Act?'

'Yeah, I could get a warrant. What's the purpose, though? I'm sure you're pissed about your brother, but I thought you were interested in finding out more about Becker.'

She seemed to choose her words carefully, as if she knew how much her words would pain him. 'I think Vitali Rostov was the person Tatiana was protecting when she was your informant. When I showed Zoya a photograph of Lev Grosha, I think she might have recognized him. Then a couple of hours later, Rostov is beating up my brother in a parking lot, telling me to stop asking questions. And when Tatiana told you that the people she knew had sources in the NYPD, I think she was talking about Ed Becker. Flann told me that he saw Becker take protection money once back in the day. If Becker was in bed with Russian OC, it explains how he managed to own a yacht.'

Dixon fell into his office chair, digesting the information. 'It would also explain why he did nothing on Tatiana's murder case. Damnit, I never even looked into Tatiana's family. She was always talking about how straight and perfect they were — how her sister was so proud of living the immigrant American dream with her devoted husband.'

'When Tatiana said all those things, she was probably trying to steer you from the truth. Zoya *is* proud of her life, but she turns a blind eye to the way her husband makes a living. Tatiana held out on you to protect her sister.'

'And you think Rostov and Becker found out that Tatiana was an informant and killed her for it?'

'There's something else, Charlie.' It was the first time she'd called him by his first name. 'Zoya remembers seeing you with Tatiana. It was only once, but she said she saw Tatiana in the passenger seat of your car one day after she went to them for money. You were driving. And her husband saw you with her too.'

Dixon swallowed hard. 'I drove Tatiana there once. She wanted to see her nephew.'

'When you visited Tatiana at Vibrations, did you ever check for tails? Someone could have followed you from there and found out who you were.'

He turned his head toward the wall. 'This is hard to hear, you know?'

'I was ten feet away when my partner got shot four nights ago. We all do things we wish we could try again.'

'If they killed her because of me — '

'Not because of you, Charlie. Because she flipped and gave information on them.'

'But if they killed her for that, then what about the other women? Where do they fit in?'

'I don't know. Tatiana told you she overheard someone — probably Vitali, maybe Lev Grosha — mention FirstDate. Let's say Stern was laundering money for them, or was somehow involved in their criminal enterprise. Maybe he backed out, and they did this to get to him by ruining FirstDate?'

'Murder three innocent women to scare away customers from a company? That's a pretty sociopathic reason to kill.'

'But maybe that's precisely what we're dealing with. All along, this whole Book of Enoch thing has felt wrong to me. Look at the reasons why people kill.'

Dixon ticked off the classics on his fingers. 'Greed, jealousy, lust, revenge.'

'Exactly. A sociopath kills innocent people out of those same motivations, but with an underlying logic that makes sense only to them. One of my forensic psychology professors gave us the following problem. A woman goes to her mother's funeral. While she's there, a man stops and offers his condolences. Even though she's never met the man, she falls in love with him on the spot. She's convinced they're soul mates. But she never finds out who he is, so there goes her chance at love. A month later, the woman kills her sister. Why?'

Barry Mayfield would know the answer. The guys chosen by Quantico to work serial cases would know. Dixon was left guessing. 'Because she found out her sister was dating the mystery man?'

'No. Your mistake is assuming that the dead sister has some rational connection to the killer's motive. You're looking for some reason that the sister deserves to die. The answer is that the woman killed her sister hoping the mystery man would come to the funeral. Only a sociopath would think that way. He sees nothing wrong with using totally innocent people as a means to serve his ends. And if that's what we're dealing with, then this could be a case that's all about greed or revenge. That's why we have to figure out the relationship between Vitali Rostov, Ed Becker, and FirstDate.'

When Hatcher showed up in his office just as he was leaving for lunch, Dixon was inclined to hear her out only in the hope she'd keep quiet about Tatiana. But if Ed Becker didn't act alone — if Vitali Rostov had something to do with what happened to Tatiana — then Dixon was in this for his own reasons. For two years, since the first night Tatiana slept in his bed, he had managed to convince himself he was an honorable man. But he had been a coward, motivated solely by his desire to hide his relationship with the kindest woman he'd ever known. He was done worrying about himself.

'How else can I help?'

'And I thought I was going to have to blackmail you some more,' Hatcher said with a smile. 'Would a proven connection between Rostov and Becker help shore up a federal case against Rostov?'

Dixon nodded. 'We could use the fact that the NYPD takes federal funds. Or even if Rostov and Becker used the mail or the phone to deprive the public of Becker's honest services, we could go with conspiracy to commit mail or wire fraud.'

'Excellent. That's the second thing I need. Can you get Ed Becker's laptop from the NYPD? You'll have to make it sound like your interest is a modest one. You're just making sure that Tatiana's murder wasn't related to her being an informant, and you want to check the laptop to verify there's no connection between Becker and the criminal conspiracy Tatiana was giving information about. If you make it sound like you're questioning Becker's guilt for the FirstDate murders, they'll fight you tooth and nail about releasing the evidence.'

'No problem.'

'Good. I'm going to try to talk to Zoya one last time before her husband's in custody and her lucky world comes crashing down around her. Call me when you've got the laptop in hand. What I really want to see is whether Becker actually hacked into the victims' FirstDate accounts. If not, our killer's still out there.'

'Wait a second. That's going to be a problem. We'll need a computer analyst for that, and I don't trust any of my people to keep their mouths shut on something that big. And like you said, if the NYPD realizes we're second-guessing their conclusions, I'll get squelched.'

'That's why we're not using your analysts. I know a computer guy who will help us. We'll take a little sneak on our own, and then bring in your analyst if there's something there to show federal jurisdiction. I just want the laptop.'

'That's not exactly kosher, bringing in a private citizen to look at evidence.'

'Do you plan on telling anyone?' Ellie asked.

'Nope. The question is whether I can trust you.'

'Given where we stand right now, I'd say you don't have much of a choice.'

Tatiana, Caroline, Amy, Megan, and now Flann were dead, and they all had friends, lovers, and family to mourn them and yearn for answers. But only Charlie and Ellie were in a position to do anything about it.

★ ★ ★

'Jason, it's Ellie Hatcher, your friendly neighborhood detective. You haven't blocked my number yet?' There was a pause on the other end of the line, and Ellie hoped she hadn't overestimated Jason Upton's willingness to help.

'Sorry, it took me a second to realize who this was. How are you, Detective? I was sorry to hear about your partner.'

'Thank you. It's been a rough few days.'

'I just saw the news a few minutes ago on the net. The whole office is talking about it. I couldn't believe it when I read the name Ed Becker. I was like, *Hey, I know that name.*'

Apparently the assistant chief had already held his press conference, but it didn't change what Ellie wanted to do. 'I was wondering if you might be willing to help out again?'

'I'm not sure how I could possibly help.'

Ellie had hoped Upton would be eager to help out of curiosity. Massaging this was harder than she expected.

'If I get Becker's laptop, will you be able to see if he hacked into any FirstDate accounts?'

'Don't you have people there who know how to do that?'

'Yeah, we do. But since Becker was also a cop,

I'd rather get a first look from someone who's not part of the department. Would you mind? Obviously I'd have our people take another look officially, but I'd feel better getting an initial lay of the land.'

'Uh, sure. I guess I can at least look. I might not be able to tell anything, though. It depends how good he was at cleaning up his tracks.'

Ellie thanked Upton, then estimated the time it would take for Dixon to get an arrest warrant for Rostov and to negotiate the release of Becker's laptop from the NYPD. 'It probably won't be until tomorrow. End of today at the earliest.'

'That should be fine. I've got a pretty flexible schedule here.'

'Thanks. And we can keep this between the two of us? You can understand how sensitive this is.'

'Sure. Mum's the word.'

Ellie was taking a risk trusting Jason Upton, but she'd thought it through carefully. If Upton were the kind of person who wanted attention, he would have already sold to the highest bidder everything he knew about FirstDate and the help he'd given McIlroy on Becker's background check. He hadn't. This call helped confirm her impression: Upton would not go to the media. She thanked him once again before saying good-bye.

Another call came in just as she flipped her phone shut. 'Hatcher.'

'Detective Hatcher, this is Barbara Hunter, Carrie Hunter's mother? I hope it's okay to call you. Your partner gave me both of your numbers last week, and, well, I know from experience you're going through some very difficult times right now, but I didn't know who else to call. I'm sorry, I'm rambling.'

'That's okay, Mrs. Hunter. Of course you're welcome to call me whenever you'd like.' Ellie looked at her watch, feeling the minutes slipping away, along with the high of the momentum of ideas and energy she'd felt in Dixon's office.

'I saw the news about that police officer on CNN. He's the man who killed Amy?'

'Yes. I'm sorry. Someone should have called you before the press conference to tell you personally.' Apparently Lieutenant Jenkins's penchant for rudeness extended beyond Ellie and departmental politics.

'I'm calling because I've seen that man before. He came to see my daughter at her apartment. I was there for a visit, and I never forget a face. I'm sure it's the same police officer.'

Ellie pictured the note in Caroline Hunter's binder — *MC Becker*. 'You can confirm that Becker met your daughter on FirstDate?'

Then, even before Mrs. Hunter corrected her, she realized what she'd been missing.

'No. He went there as a detective. He took a report from her, a report about her credit card.'

Ellie felt the high coming back on. She knew in her gut that this was related to the motive — not religion, not the Book of Enoch, but greed, jealousy, lust, or revenge.

'He didn't go see her about FirstDate,' Ellie said.

'Well, I guess it was about FirstDate to some extent. She opened a new MasterCard, used it on FirstDate, and then within a month, she got a bill for a refrigerator purchased in Houston, Texas.'

'And she reported the fraudulent charges?'

'Oh, sure she did. The credit card company wiped it right off her bill once she swore she didn't make the purchase, but Carrie wanted them to look into it. You see, she'd only made one charge with that card, and it was to FirstDate.'

Credit cards. Tatiana's heroin bust started as an investigation into unauthorized credit card use. Lev Grosha paid a motel clerk to run credit cards through a scanner that stole the numbers. FirstDate had access to thousands of customers' credit cards. And Ellie was still trying to tie this strand together, but someone named Edmond Bertrand had been arrested for credit card fraud as well.

'Credit card companies rarely launch their own investigations into fraud,' Ellie explained. 'They just cover the loss, like you said.'

'That's what they told her. So she called the police, but they gave her some hooey about the report needing to go to the police down in Houston unless she had evidence of criminal activity in New York.'

'So do you know how Detective Becker came to take her report?' Ellie asked.

'Well, she started complaining to FirstDate. I remember because, in light of her studies, you know, she was so fascinated that she could not for the life of her get on the phone with a real person. All of the company's business was conducted on the Internet. So she sent a message to them on their Web site, telling them that their — well, I don't know what it would be called — '

'Their server?'

'Something like that. But she said something wasn't secure because she'd only used her card one place and was sure she hadn't lost track of it physically. Then the detective showed up. I don't know if he came because of the report to FirstDate, or to MasterCard, or to the precinct, but I'm sure the man was Ed Becker.'

'And what happened?'

'Nothing. He took the report, but told her that chances were, nothing would come of it. He told her most of the fraud cases just fall into a black hole.'

It was a true statement, but Ed Becker would have had no legitimate reason for being the one to deliver it. Caroline's complaint wouldn't have triggered a home visit, and Becker wasn't in the fraud unit in any event. And Flann had run Caroline Hunter's name through the NYPD system, and no credit card complaint appeared. If Becker had gone there to talk to her about her suspicions, it hadn't been on the NYPD's behalf.

'Did she continue complaining after the report was taken?' Ellie asked.

'I just don't know. I left town and she never mentioned it again. This has something to do with her murder, doesn't it?'

'I honestly don't know, Mrs. Hunter. But I'm trying to find out.'

'Will you please tell me if you learn something new?'

'I promise.'

If Caroline Hunter was killed because she was jeopardizing a credit card fraud scheme, it explained why she and Tatiana were killed by the same gun. Both women had gotten in the way, so both women were silenced. It also explained why they were the only victims who were shot — two bullets to the back of the head, quick and easy — while Amy Davis and Megan Quinn were asphyxiated. It explained why Amy Davis's murder had been so brutal, so intimate — it was, in fact, the *first* of its kind, not the third. And if Amy Davis's murder had been personal, it might also explain why Peter Morse detected a southern accent in the caller who told him to retrieve Enoch's letter from the library.

All along, they'd been looking at two patterns, not one. Tatiana Chekova and Caroline Hunter. Amy Davis and Megan Quinn. Four women, two patterns. She needed to go to Brooklyn again.

# 37

Ellie phoned the Rostov apartment from the building stairwell. 'Hello. This is Laura Liemann calling from the American Red Cross. Is Vitali Rostov in?'

Once Zoya confirmed that her husband was unavailable, Ellie made her way upstairs and knocked on the Rostovs' door. She heard a shuffle behind the peephole, but no one answered.

'Zoya, it's Detective Hatcher. I know you're there. Open up.'

She heard locks tumbling, then Zoya's face appeared in a crack in the doorway.

'Please, go away.'

'We need to talk. I know you're having some doubts about your husband right now. Denying your suspicions is not going to make them go away.'

'Vitya is not a perfect man, but he would not do the thing that you are suggesting.'

'I never suggested anything, Zoya. If you think he's connected to your sister's death, then you came to that on your own. Let me in. If you're expecting your husband to come home, we can go somewhere else to talk. I can help you with the kids.'

Zoya opened the door. 'Vitya is working late tonight, and Anton is napping. If we must talk, then we should do it now.'

The apartment was quiet, a first. The baby, Tanya, sat happily in a bouncy seat, popping bubbles of spit with her lips. Ellie took a seat on a black leather sofa across the room.

'When you said your husband couldn't have done whatever it was you thought I was suggesting, what were you referring to?'

Zoya shrugged but held Ellie's gaze. 'I do not know. I figure, the police keep coming to our door. They must think Vitya did something wrong.'

'Or it could have something to do with the fact that the two of you saw her with an FBI agent right around the time that two of Vitya's friends went to federal prison.'

'I told you that I do not know the man in your picture.'

'I know what you told me, Zoya, but I saw your expression when you asked if Lev Grosha went to prison because of Tatiana. You recognized him. My guess is you also know a man named Alex Federov. Did Vitya tell you he was killed in prison?' Zoya said nothing. 'When you found out that the man in the car with Tatiana was an FBI agent, it was the first time you realized that your sister was responsible for Vitya's friends being arrested. And now you're wondering if she was killed for it.'

'But she was my sister — '

'I know you don't want to believe it. I wouldn't want to either. But your husband is in this a lot deeper than you've ever admitted to yourself. The man who was here with me when I first met you, Ed Becker? Do you know that he's dead?'

Zoya's eyes finally left Ellie's and dropped to the floor. 'Yes. I saw it on the news.'

'Let me guess. Vitya was watching very attentively.' Ellie took Zoya's silence as confirmation. 'You knew him before I ever walked into this apartment with him, didn't you? I remember, when I came here that first day, you asked, *Who are you?* But you weren't looking at Ed Becker. You only looked at me. And when your husband asked who was at the door, you said it was the police: *the man from before*, plus a woman — me. Becker was here talking to your husband, wasn't he? He was here alone, and then came back up with me.'

'He was a friend of Vitya.'

Ellie shook her head, wondering how the last week might have unfolded if she'd realized earlier that Becker was not arriving at the Rostovs' apartment the day she saw him on the street, but leaving.

'*Friends?* If they were friends, why did the three of you hide the fact that you'd just seen each other five minutes before I knocked on your door? You need to tell me what you know, Zoya, or I'll go to the FBI, and they'll ask the U.S. Attorney's Office to open a grand jury investigation.' Zoya could not be forced to testify about her communications with her husband, but she didn't know that. 'Let me see if this gets you started. Vitya doesn't work as a security guard. He might work at a warehouse some-where, but it's a cover for widespread criminal activity that includes dealing in heroin and stolen credit card numbers. When Becker was on the job, he was on the payroll.'

Zoya pushed a loose strand of hair out of her face and turned toward Ellie. 'Vitya is a good provider. He works at the storage warehouse like I told you. They do imports and exports out of there, but I do not know the details.'

'You make a point of not knowing the details. But Tatiana didn't have any reason to keep her eyes shut, did she?'

'As much as Vitya enjoyed insulting Tatiana's lifestyle, yes, I always suspected that acquaintances of his might have shared some of her — bad habits.' She was still distancing her husband from the criminal activity, but at least she was talking.

'And it didn't strike you as odd when your husband's pal Ed Becker turned out to be the lead detective on your sister's murder case?'

'Vitya told me that Becker took the case because he is our friend — that he would find out who killed her. I had no idea she was working for police.'

'And now what do you think, Zoya?'

A tear fell slowly from the corner of her eye, down the bridge of her nose, and stopped at her lips. She brushed it away. 'I do not know what to think. Vitya, he is the father of my children.'

'And Tatiana was your sister. I talked to Charlie Dixon. He's the FBI agent in the picture I showed you. He knew Tatiana was holding something back. She was protecting Vitya. She was protecting you and your son. She didn't want you to have to earn a living the way she did, and it got her killed. If she hadn't cared so much about you, if she had simply told Dixon everything she knew, Vitya would have gone down, and Tatiana would still be alive right now. Are you really going to be able to forgive him for that?'

Zoya took short quick breaths, trying to fight back tears, but then broke into a full sob. Across the room, her baby's brow furrowed, and the bouncy seat came to a halt. Ellie told herself she should feel no sympathy for this woman. If anyone, *anyone*, ever hurt Jess, she knew exactly where her loyalties would lie.

'Tatiana told Agent Dixon that FirstDate had something to do with your husband's friends. What's the connection? You know now why your sister was murdered, but the families of three other women still don't have the truth. If you can tell me how FirstDate fits into this, I might be able to give them some answers, and I could leave you out of this.'

Zoya shook her head frantically in her hands. 'I told you, I don't know anything. He doesn't tell me anything. I am his wife. I am mother to his children. It is not like American marriage, these people on TV who talk to each other and share their secrets. He goes to work, he sees his friends. I do not ask what goes on, and he does not tell me.'

Ellie could no longer stomach being part of a conversation that Zoya was using to cement her misguided feelings of victimization. 'I hope you can live with the choices you've made, Zoya.'

\* \* \*

'I got Zoya to admit her husband knew Becker.' Ellie called Charlie Dixon on her way to the subway station and gave him a quick update. 'Barbara Hunter says her daughter used her new MasterCard only one time before an unauthorized charge turned up in Texas. Want to guess where she used it?'

'FirstDate.'

'You got it.'

'Damnit. *That's* how FirstDate was involved,' Dixon said. 'I assumed all along it was money laundering. Whenever you see white collar guys like Stern wrapped up with the kinds of scumbags Tatiana was involved with, it's either because they're using or pushing dope, or they're washing money. Stern never struck me as a junkie — '

'But he could very well be a thief. You said he lives above his means, right? Well, he's got access to a steady stream of credit card numbers. He hands those to Rostov and his buddies in exchange for a piece of the pie. Tatiana must have heard Rostov talking about FirstDate, but didn't want to give him up directly because of her sister.'

'But then Rostov saw her with a guy like me and realized something was wrong.'

'Rostov followed my brother to Vibrations before the assault. He probably found a way to follow you to the federal building.'

In the momentary silence that followed, Ellie sensed that Dixon was forcing himself to hold it together, delaying the complete meltdown that would come if he allowed himself to contemplate his role in Tatiana's death. 'So Rostov killed Tatiana for cooperating, and then killed Caroline Hunter as a precaution? Or do you think Becker pulled the trigger?'

'Becker was on duty when Tatiana was killed,' she said. 'I think Rostov's the shooter; Becker made sure to take the call-out. That would mean Rostov's probably the shooter on Caroline Hunter as well. Becker saw her death in the paper and figured out it wasn't just a robbery. He took title to that boat just a month after Caroline's murder. Want to bet it was the payoff for his silence?'

'I'll see what I can learn about its previous owner. Maybe it'll give us another link back to Rostov.'

'Thanks.'

'So if Tatiana and Hunter were killed to cover up a fraud ring, how do the other two FirstDate murders fit in?'

Four women. Two patterns. 'I don't know yet, but I'm about to ask Mark Stern that exact question.'

★　★　★

For the last three days, while the media had futilely dug around the NYPD for leaks, Peter Morse was the only reporter in the entire world who knew for certain that the City Island murder-suicide involving two members of the NYPD family was related to McIlroy's serial killer investigation. To Peter's surprise, the decision not to report the connection earlier had been an easy one. Even the reporter in him knew that it was simply off-limits to use information he had deciphered from Ellie's circumstances, at least before the two of them had a chance to agree on some ground rules.

In some ways, the last few days had been a vacation from the real world as he and Ellie got to know each other while agreeing not to talk about the case until the police department made an official statement. Now, that statement had been made.

When the assistant chief announced at this morning's press conference that Ed Becker was the FirstDate killer, the rest of the reporters in the room were as shocked as if they had just learned the Dalai Lama had a nasty porn habit. Mentally, Peter had a head start wrapping his brain around the facts, but he hadn't allowed himself to begin writing until now.

He needed help understanding the technological aspects of the case. A critical turn in the police investigation was the tracking of the locations that the killer used to access the Internet. Peter had tried fifteen different ways of glossing over the details but was still not conveying the gist of it well enough.

He tried his usual go-to contact on computer issues, but the lucky jerk was in Cabo. Then he remembered the source Ellie had mentioned during their dinner at Half King. He found the man's business card in his wallet. Hopefully, Jason Upton had some time to give him an Internet 101 primer. It would be ironic if Ellie wound up helping him report this story after all, despite their agreement not to talk about it since Friday night.

He hadn't heard from Ellie since her meeting this morning with the brass, and calling her to say he was going to contact her source would be an excuse to touch base. He tried her cell, but the call went directly in to voice mail.

*Hey, it's me. Sorry. Is that too familiar? It is I, Peter Morse of the Daily Post. I just got back from the assistant chief's press conference. I half expected to see you there, so I hope everything went okay this morning at the precinct. Oh, and thanks for pointing me to Jason Upton. I'm hoping he can walk me through the computer locating stuff. Anyway, I'm going to be workin' hard, as the president would say, trying to get this story done for deadline, but I'd love to see you later on. Give me a call, okay? 'Bye.*

\* \* \*

Ellie entered the lobby of the FirstDate offices, holding the door for two women leaving with boxes in hand. One of them looked like she'd been crying. The other seemed ready to punch whatever cheerful person might cross her path.

Christine Conboy sat behind the receptionist desk, also appearing glum. She mumbled a 'hey' when she spotted Ellie.

'What's going on around here?' Ellie asked.

'Layoffs. Our server's been crashing all day from the crush of people logging on to cancel their memberships.' She lowered her voice. 'I don't feel bad for Stern. It's karma paying him back for the way he stonewalled you guys. I was really sad to hear about your partner.'

Ellie nodded, acknowledging her sympathies. Christine looked toward Stern's office. 'It's not right. Instead of taking the losses himself, he's passing them down to the people with no safety net. People here work paycheck to paycheck. They won't get by without work.'

'It seems a little extreme to fire people,' Ellie said. 'I'm sure it's just a temporary panic.'

'Well, as was explained to us by the boss at an emergency meeting a couple of hours ago, *the company is not able to absorb the losses.* Men outnumber women on dating sites by more than two to one. Apparently a quarter of our female members pulled their profiles down since the news came out about the letter left in the library. Stern was hoping the damage would blow over when the police announced the case was closed, but instead it's only gotten worse. Seems women figure that if one nut job could do it, someone else might do the same. Once the men realize there aren't any women, they'll quit too. Stern says we don't have enough in reserves to make payroll, so out walk my former colleagues with nothing but a promise to keep them in mind if the situation turns around. No notice, no severance pay. And they won't qualify for those valuable stock options we've been waiting for because they're leaving before the public offering.'

'What about you?'

She shrugged her shoulders. 'I didn't get the axe in the first round, but let's just say I know enough to get my résumé in shape.'

'I need to see Stern. Is that going to be a problem?'

'Is he going to enjoy talking to you?' Christine asked with a smile.

'Oh, I seriously doubt that.'

Christine extended her arm toward Stern's office. 'Then make yourself at home.'

★ ★ ★

Mark Stern was in the middle of a hands-free telephone call when Ellie walked into his office without knocking. He looked behind her for the imaginary person who might protect him from unwanted interruption.

'Jan, I'm sorry. I need to call you back . . . Yeah, I know it's urgent. I'll call you right back.' He pulled off his headset and tossed it on his desk. 'Well, come on in, Detective Hatcher. What can I do for you?'

'What? No 'Sorry about your partner'? No 'I guess he was right. I should have helped the two of you earlier'?'

'Sorry. Obviously I'm very sorry about what happened to Detective McIlroy, but I told that to the other detectives who informed me of his death, and I've been cooperating as much as I can with the police department since then. But you've got your case all wrapped up, and I'm in the middle of a serious shit storm here.'

'Mass membership cancellations probably screw up a company's plans to go public, huh?'

'That, Detective, is the understatement of the

405

fucking century. That was my lawyer,' he said, pointing to the headset. 'He says the deal can't happen. To avoid fraud, I'd have to disclose the membership cancellations, and that's going to destroy the stock price. Fuck.' He sent a stack of documents flying from his desk.

'The company can't just ride this out?'

Stern took a deep breath and collapsed into his chair, trying to regain his composure. 'No. I definitely do not see a good riding-it-out scenario in front of me. My next phone call is to my wife to talk to her about taking another mortgage out on our apartment. That should go well.'

'I have to ask you a question, Mr. Stern, and I want you to control your temper when I do. I'm willing to keep an open mind about whatever you tell me, but after what has happened the last few days, I just don't have the energy to get into a fight with you.'

'I don't have a lot of fight left in me either. Go ahead and ask your questions, Detective Hatcher.'

'Do you know that your customers' credit card numbers are being stolen off your server?'

Stern's obvious surprise confirmed Ellie's suspicions.

'That's what I thought. I'll be honest. I walked into the building just now assuming you were involved. But seeing you try to save your company in the middle of all this chaos reminded me that every person I've spoken to who's had any encounter with you has mentioned your ferocious dedication to First-Date. You frustrated the hell out of me, in fact, with your single-mindedness.'

Stern nodded gently. 'I tell people that this company is my baby. I created it.'

'Exactly. Your baby. And stealing credit card numbers from your customers could jeopardize that baby, and you wouldn't do something like that unless the payoffs were substantial.'

'I wouldn't do it at all, Detective.'

'I'm not judging you. I'm pointing out that you don't appear to be enjoying those kinds of financial windfalls. And if you were reaping side profits from fraud, you never would have called attention to it by taking your company public. That would only open you up to the scrutiny of shareholders and financial analysts.'

Charlie Dixon had assumed that Stern was sitting on a pile of untraceable money, but the truth was, the man was broke. He was living above his means, and now the public offering that was going to save him was nothing but a fantasy.

'So you're telling me that on top of all my other problems, I've got a hole in my server that someone's hacking into? What does this have to do with Ed Becker?'

'I don't think he killed those women. I think he had something to do with two of them — it's a long story. My point is that I think someone else murdered Amy Davis and Megan Quinn, and they did it to ruin you. When Caroline Hunter was killed, all the news coverage mentioned her research into online dating. Someone with a grudge against you saw the opportunity to destroy your baby

— and you along with it. And whoever it was also had a grudge against Amy Davis. They sent her that bogus solicitation for a free membership, then used Richard Hamline's credit card to pay for it. They killed Amy exactly one year after Hunter was killed, placing a FirstDate e-mail in her coat pocket to make sure the police connected the two cases. Then, when the media still didn't name your company or you, he added another victim — Megan Quinn.'

'This is nuts. This is absolutely sick. I don't know *anyone* who would do something like that. I can't even imagine knowing someone who could concoct such a demented plan, let alone someone who'd carry it out.'

'You can't think that way,' Ellie argued. 'A man like this can be a father, a husband, a church leader, a man of the community. No matter how absurd you think this is, I need to know who might have a grudge against you, particularly with respect to FirstDate.'

Stern was shaking his head.

'It's possible it's someone who knows about computers or even has access to your server. Maybe an employee? Someone you fired?'

As Ellie listened to her own thoughts leave her mouth, she heard discordant lines of recent conversations clashing in her head. Mark Stern: *This company is my baby. I created it.* Another voice saying, *I wouldn't have worked to start the company if I didn't think it could serve a good purpose . . . Mark and I really believed . . . We did our best . . .*

She saw a pause in Mark Stern, a momentary hesitation.

'Tell me about Jason Upton,' she said.

'But how did you — '

'Because I know what happened.'

# 38

Ellie gave Stern a condensed version of the story that Upton had told her: Upton and Stern had started the company together, went their separate ways with no hard feelings, and Upton had lived happily ever after on his severance package and his trust fund. Stern offered a slightly different account.

'He was pissed. When we incorporated, he demanded equal footing in the company, and I refused to give it to him. He claimed to be a founder, and he was only a programmer. It was my idea. I found the capital. I created the structure. All he did was program.'

Ellie remembered the nostalgic way that Upton conveyed his memories of starting FirstDate with Stern, and wondered if perhaps Upton's claims had more merit than Stern was letting on.

'But he walked away from the company despite all of that?'

'He continued working as a programmer at first. Occasionally he'd make snarky, pissy remarks, but for the most part, I thought he was over it. Then he threatened to sue. Shit, in retrospect, he threatened to do a lot more than that. I assumed it was hothead stuff — blowing off steam. I'd known the guy for five years, and he never struck me as violent. In the end, I had my lawyer bring him in and offer a settlement. I swore I'd fight a penny more, and he backed down. Or so I thought. You don't really think — '

'I don't know. I'm still trying to make sense of it myself. He's got plenty of money, so why would he do all of this? Just out of pride? Because you didn't give him the recognition he wanted?'

'Don't look at me. I think this entire conversation is absurd. But I can tell you that if Jason Upton has money these days, it's not from his family, and it's certainly not from his settlement with me.'

'I know for certain he said he had a trust fund. In fact, he suggested it was the reason he didn't share your ambitions. And I remember thinking he seemed like the kind of person who'd have family money. He's got that whole preppy thing going on like he was born on the Princeton campus.'

'That's all an act. Jason went to Tufts, but it was on scholarship. His dad sold shoes, and his mom was a teacher. He grew up in Oklahoma. He developed that Waspy affectation over time because it helped him land chicks. I met him about six months after he got to New York, and he was living in some ratty old studio on the Lower East Side.'

'Tufts. That's in Boston, right?'

Stern nodded.

'And Upton would've still been in Boston six years ago?'

Stern thought for a moment, then nodded again. 'Yeah. I think he hung out there for about a year after he graduated, then I met him shortly after he moved here. That was almost exactly six years ago.'

Stern had met Upton when he first moved to New York, not long after a man using the name Edmond Bertrand had an arrest warrant issued in Boston for his failure to appear on charges of using a stolen credit card.

*Accents are easy to fake.* Flann had made the observation when he first suggested that Becker could be their man. But they had been assuming that the person who called Peter about the letter in the library was faking a southern accent, not concealing it from everyone else.

'Did you ever verify that Upton even went to Tufts?'

Stern's facial expression was answer enough. 'You don't think — '

'You're not the first employer who didn't check on a friend's references. Do you think you might have a record of Upton's date of birth?' Ellie suspected that most of what Upton had told Stern about himself was a lie, but, like many people who used aliases, he might have been truthful about his birth date. Juggling multiple names was enough work without keeping track of corresponding birth dates.

'Human resources probably has it. I can ask.'

While Stern picked up his phone to make the call, Ellie took out her cell phone to call Charlie Dixon with an update. A red flashing light indicated she had a new message that must have come in while she was on the subway. She checked her voice mail and smiled when she heard Peter's voice. Then she got to the end of the message and dropped the phone.

Enoch. The killer called himself Enoch. Reading something into that moniker had thrown Ellie onto the wrong track. She had glommed onto the Book of Enoch, just because the name Richard Hamline had been used to open Enoch's FirstDate account. R. H., like *The Book of Enoch* translated by R. H. Charles.

She had made the same mistake the D.C. Sniper investigators made when they attributed meaning to reports of a white truck near all the shootings. It was the same mistake shared by Wichitans who'd found a seeming pattern in the number three, found in the addresses of many of the College Hill Strangler's victims. But white trucks and number threes are so common that they can always be found, as long as you're looking for them. She had found a connection to the Book of Enoch because she had searched for it.

What she had overlooked was the other Enoch — the son of Cain, who betrayed and killed his brother, Abel. All along, the name Enoch had been Jason Upton's private joke, referring to FirstDate itself, the offspring of the traitorous Mark Stern.

She realized now the truth that lay beneath all of the illusions created by Jason Upton. Disgruntled with Stern's refusal to recognize him as a cofounder of the company, Upton started stealing credit card numbers off the FirstDate server and selling them in the vast black market that exists for such information. He could steal here and there and never get caught because credit card companies tended to eat the losses without investigating how the numbers were lost. But Caroline Hunter was different. He rigged the FirstDate server to get a preview of any online complaints, and Caroline's complaint would have jumped out at him. He'd made the mistake of stealing the credit card number of a customer who'd used her card for only one purchase — a FirstDate membership.

*I don't suppose you still have some magic password you can use to log on to the system?* Ellie had asked the question jokingly six days earlier in Upton's office. *Sorry. I'm afraid it doesn't work like that.*

But that was precisely how it worked.

When he read the complaint Caroline Hunter filed with FirstDate, he would have told Vitali Rostov, his contact for the buyers of the stolen card numbers. Rostov sent Becker to quell Hunter's concerns, but Becker must have left with doubts that Hunter would let the matter drop. To play it safe, Rostov killed her. After all, he'd done it once before: Tatiana.

When Upton read the news of Caroline Hunter's murder, and learned about her online dating research, he saw his opportunity. He tracked down Amy Davis to use as the 'next' victim of a serial killer using FirstDate to murder. Ellie wasn't certain yet why Upton wanted revenge against Amy, but she knew it had something to do with Edmond Bertrand.

Then, as luck would have it, the detectives searching for Enoch had shown up in Jason

414

Upton's office looking for help. He hadn't given Becker's boat registration to Flann initially because he realized it might tip the detectives off to Becker's connection to Vitali Rostov. To misdirect the investigation, he left a letter for a *Daily Post* reporter quoting from the Book of Enoch.

But when Ellie began asking too many questions about Chekova and Rostov anyway, Upton realized that his personal vendetta against Stern could jeopardize the money train. When Flann had asked for a background check on Becker, Upton saw an opportunity to pin all of the murders on him.

And because Ellie had fallen for all of these tricks, she had sent Peter Morse directly into the hands of a man who would sacrifice two innocent women as pawns in a one-sided war.

There was no answer at Peter's desk. She tried his cell. No answer. She called the general number for the *Daily Post* newsroom. A woman picked up.

'Hi, is this, um — ' Ellie blanked out on the name of the intern Peter had mentioned.

'Justine Navarro. For whom are you calling?'

'Peter Morse. This is Detective Ellie Hatcher — '

'Oh, I know all about you.'

Ellie didn't have time to pursue that one. 'I really need to find Peter. Is he there?'

'No, he left about a half hour ago. He was meeting someone at his apartment.'

Ellie thanked Justine and hung up, wondering what to do next. A taxi ride to Peter's apartment would take at least half an hour.

415

She called Peter's cell phone again. 'Listen very closely to me, Peter. Act like I'm not telling you anything special. Keep your gaze straight ahead and your expression neutral. Jason Upton is very dangerous. Don't take any chances with him. Call me as soon as he leaves your apartment.'

She dialed another number and reached yet another voice-mail recording. 'Jason, hi. This is Ellie Hatcher. I've got that laptop ready.' She worked to steady her voice. Cool and calm. 'I'm not going to be able to keep it long, so whenever you can check it out, that'd be great. Talk to you soon.'

'I take it you couldn't reach either of them?' Stern asked.

Ellie shook her head and dialed Peter's cell number again. The call went directly to his outgoing message.

'I need to ask you one more question, Mark, and I need you to give me an honest answer. How flexible are you willing to be on the details of how we figured out what we think we know about Jason Upton?'

She watched as Stern's mouth turned up slightly at one corner. 'If flexibility means getting back at the motherfucker who did all of this, then consider me extremely flexible.'

Ellie had only one way to play this.

★   ★   ★

Ellie knew the layout of Peter's apartment. She knew he was there with Jason Upton. She was fairly confident that Upton would be unarmed. She had a good cover story for showing up — she needed Jason to check out Becker's laptop and was told by Peter's intern that the two of them were holed up here. The plan was to play it cool and walk Jason out of the apartment, leaving Peter safely behind.

Of course, she knew there was a chance Jason would be waiting for her. He could have realized something was up when she called. And it was at least conceivable he had a gun. But it was precisely in those circumstances that Peter would need her intervention most.

She had done everything she could to stack the deck in her favor, but now she had no choice but to accept the odds and go upstairs on her own. She punched in the electronic security code she'd seen Peter use the past few days.

Ellie never even checked her blind spot when she stepped inside the building and considered the dark, narrow staircase in front of her. By the time she heard a sound behind her and reached for her gun, it was too late. She felt cold, circular metal against the base of her skull and immediately realized her mistake. Zoya had claimed that Vitali Rostov was at work, but stopping Ellie *was* Rostov's work. He'd been standing behind the door — not inside the apartment, but on the ground floor at the entrance.

'Uh, uh, uh. I'll take that.' She felt a hand move across the back of her waistband to her holster, then felt the weight of her Glock leave her body. 'Upstairs, Detective.'

As she climbed the stairs, Ellie considered her options. She could hear Rostov close behind her. She smelled his sweat and stale deodorant. She could almost feel the warmth of his body against hers. He was only one step behind her. A heavy rear push kick might send him falling. It might also get her shot, leaving Peter helpless. And even if she made it upstairs, it would still leave her unarmed, trapped above the bottleneck of a staircase, with an injured Rostov waiting for them below. She had to wait it out.

When she stopped at Peter's closed apartment door, Rostov ordered her to open it. He nudged her with the gun to emphasize the point.

Ellie opened the door to find Jason Upton sitting at Peter's dining room table. He slowly bobbed a tea bag up and down in a mug Ellie had drunk from the previous morning. Rostov pushed her through the apartment door.

'Good afternoon, Detective. Where's that laptop you called me about? Funny, you don't seem to have it with you.' Rostov shoved Ellie to the back corner of the room and stood next to Upton. She watched as he placed her service pistol on the table in front of him while he kept his own weapon fixed on her. 'That was a stupid thing you did, calling me like that. I was planning to deal with you later, once you got that laptop. I'd tell you what you needed to hear to go away and, well, if that didn't work, I'd find some other way.'

'Where's Peter?' Ellie asked.

'You're the one who dragged your boyfriend into this. He was in the bathroom the first time you called. I saw your name on the screen of his phone. Then you called him again. Then you left a message for me, and that's when I turned his phone off. See, if you were so hot to have me examine that laptop of yours, why would you call Peter first?'

'I don't know what you're talking about.'

'Don't insult me.' In his anger, the cultured affectation left his raised voice, and she picked up the hint of a husky southern drawl. 'You told me this morning that getting that laptop would take a while, then you call me two hours later saying you've got it already? I'm not stupid. In fact, some would say you were the one who was stupid by making this all so easy for me. I took my time tutoring your boyfriend until Vitya arrived. I knew you'd be close behind. That's what you do when your partners go missing, isn't it? Go out and look for them?'

She pictured McIlroy again, sitting on the floor of Becker's boat. Two bullet holes. So much blood.

'So you were on the boat. You got a new gun since you planted the .38 on Becker.' She looked at the double-action pepper shot Derringer that Rostov pointed at her. It held only four shots, required a manual repeat between each one, and didn't pack a ton of power. It could do some damage at close range, but still, she had caught a break when he'd opted for his own weapon over hers. 'What did you do with Peter, you son of a bitch?'

'How sweet,' Upton mocked. 'He's tied up in the bathtub. Are you into that kind of thing?'

Ellie ignored his question. She knew he was trying to break her. 'There's no reason to bring him into this. He doesn't know anything.'

'Oh, I know. We checked on that ourselves.' Ellie did not like the smile Upton gave Rostov.

'You're very good at that, Ellie,' Upton continued. 'Secrets. You've spent quite a bit of time with this man, and yet he knew nothing of the case that consumes you. Your own partner was murdered in front of you, and you hadn't even told your lover why he was killed. The problem with having secrets, Ellie, is that they make you a very easy target. If you die, so do your secrets.'

Upton gave Rostov another look, and Rostov tensed his gun arm. Things were moving faster than she'd expected.

'Wait!' Ellie called out. 'What about Peter? Use your head, Jason. You're a smart man. So far a good defense attorney could get you out of this. But you can't kill a news reporter for the *Daily Post*. The paper will put you on its front page every day to make sure a jury gives you the needle.'

'But if I spare your little friend, who's going to take the blame for shooting you?' Upton said. 'He's the easiest target, especially since you sent him an e-mail about fifteen minutes ago telling him you didn't want to see him again. He sent you one back saying he was going to kill himself if you didn't come here right away.'

Ellie opened and closed her mouth like a marionette.

'You hadn't figured that part out yet? You

really shouldn't mooch off your neighbors' wireless Internet connections. It makes it very easy for people like me to spy on you.'

'That's why you called Peter to plant the letter. You knew we'd met on FirstDate.'

'I can get whatever I want off of FirstDate at any time. I built my own personal gateway into the server before I left the company. But I know all sorts of things about you,' Upton taunted. 'The Web sites you visit. Your passwords.'

'And that's why you wrote that stupid letter about the Book of Enoch. You knew that I was researching that angle. I was visiting Web sites about the book.'

'I'm tired of this,' Upton said abruptly. 'Shoot her.'

Ellie closed her eyes and found herself praying to a god she hadn't thought of for years. She prayed that Rostov would miss, or that he'd aim for someplace other than her head. She prayed that if she had to leave this world, that Jess and her mother would be all right. She prayed for another world that followed, a place where she might even be with her father. But to her surprise, the bullet didn't come.

She opened her eyes at the sound of Rostov's voice. 'Jason wrote the letter in the library?'

'Will you fucking shoot her already? We need to do her, do the reporter, and get the fuck out of here.' All pretenses were gone now. Jason Upton sounded like he should be pumping gas and snacking on dirty rice and boudin.

With Rostov's question, Ellie realized that Upton and Rostov were not the full partners she'd imagined. Four victims. Two patterns. Two separate killers. 'You didn't know, did you, Vitya? Jason let you think there really was another killer out there who got to Amy Davis and Megan Quinn. He probably told you the only way to keep us from finding out you killed Tatiana and Caroline Hunter was to dump all four of the murders on Becker. He didn't tell you that the other women were his own personal projects?'

'She's full of shit!' Upton yelled. 'I wrote the letter so we'd have a way to set up Becker. That's why we left that retarded book on his boat. Give me the gun. I'll shoot her myself.'

Upton moved toward Rostov to take the gun, but Rostov did not turn over the weapon. Instead, he jerked his firing hand toward Upton — only slightly, and only for a second. It was not enough to create an opportunity for Ellie, but it gave her hope, and it put Jason Upton back into his seat and out of reach of her Glock, still resting on the table near Rostov.

'Think about it, Vitya,' Ellie said. 'If someone else out there killed Amy Davis and Maggie Quinn, then Jason's plan to frame Becker doesn't add up. What happens when the killer plucks off another woman from FirstDate? There's only one way he could know that wouldn't happen.' Upton was still encouraging Rostov to fire off a shot, but Ellie could tell she had Rostov's ear. 'And here's the interesting thing about that name — Enoch. It has two meanings. Enoch was the son of Cain, the one who betrayed his brother in the Bible.'

'I know the story of Cain and Abel.' Rostov

spoke quietly, eyeing his friend Upton. 'I know it because you told it to me, Jason. You said you felt like Abel, slain by your own brother.'

'So you knew how much Jason hated Mark Stern. Jason did all this — he jeopardized everything, including you — just to get back at Stern. You think killing me and Peter is going to make this go away? It's too late, at least for you, Vitya. You haven't spoken to Zoya?'

'Why are you talking about Zoya?'

'I saw her again today. She tried to protect you, but I know you saw Tatiana with that FBI agent. Tatiana wasn't just an informant, Vitya. That agent was in *love* with her. He's not going to drop this. And he knows where Becker got his boat. He's probably talking to Luke Steiner right now to find out how his boat wound up in Becker's name shortly after Caroline Hunter's murder.'

Rostov threw Upton a nervous look that confirmed Ellie's suspicion that the previous owner of Becker's boat was somehow connected to Rostov's network.

'The FBI is getting an arrest warrant for you. You're going down, and killing me won't change any of that.'

Ellie could see the veins in Upton's neck as he screamed at Rostov to put her down. Only Ellie was alert enough to see the knob turn on the apartment's front door. She gauged the distance to the Glock.

'Zoya will take the kids. You'll never see them again.' She raised her voice, hoping to cover any sounds of the door she willed to open. 'She'll probably tell them you're dead rather than take them to see their father in prison. That's all on Jason. Everything the FBI has points to you, not him. If you're going to take me out, you at least should send him with me.'

Ellie could feel the momentum changing. She was the aggressor now. In her mind's eye, she saw Rostov turning the gun on Upton. She pictured the bullet firing into Upton's body. She imagined herself diving for her weapon in the time it would take Rostov to fire another round. She visualized Peter's front door opening. And as she pictured it all, she kept on talking.

The problem was, Rostov's first shot wasn't intended for Upton. It was meant for Ellie.

The force of the bullet felt like a battering ram against Ellie's torso. She fell to the floor, landing hard against bare wood. Rostov got off a fast second shot, nailing Jason Upton squarely in the left cheek. Upton pressed both hands against the wound and swayed backward. Then like a pendulum, he swung forward again, collapsing onto the dining room table.

Just as Upton crashed headfirst into his mug of tea, Charlie Dixon pushed his way through the apartment door.

'Drop it, drop it. Drop your weapons. FBI.'

Rostov swung away from Ellie to face Dixon. Dixon reacted immediately. Pop. Pop. Two quick blasts from Dixon's semiautomatic. Rostov stumbled backward and tumbled to the floor, coming to rest beside Ellie.

Dixon ran toward Ellie and kicked the Derringer from Rostov's reach. Ellie strained to lift her head. As Dixon pressed two fingers to her carotid artery, she asked him for one more thing. 'Make sure the guy in the bathroom's all right.' Then she closed her eyes and everything turned black.

# 39

Ellie was kneeling beside Flann McIlroy, pressing her coat against his belly, while she waited for an ambulance that might save him. She heard the high-pitched squeals of a siren in the distance and pushed harder against Flann's abdomen but could still see the blood spreading beneath her parka. Her mouth was dry, her tongue was swollen, and she smelled the antiseptic odors of Jess's hospital room. She imagined her father's body slumped over his steering wheel. Pictured the damage done by the bullet fired into his mouth. Greeted by an intense beam of bright white light in front of her, she tried walking toward it. When her legs wouldn't move, she tried to run, but got no closer. She was paralyzed.

Her eyes shot open. Four round lights were mounted in metal on a vibrating wall in front of her. Then she realized that the bulbs were above her. She was horizontal, and the room was shaking. She was in an ambulance.

'You fainted,' an EMT explained. 'Your vest caught the bullet, but you're going to have a nasty bruise on your gut for about a week.'

'Hey you.' The familiar voice came from an adjacent gurney. Peter Morse looked at her through puffy, blackened eyes. A gash ran along his right cheekbone. A paramedic had wiped blood away, leaving behind a deep pink smear on Peter's pale skin.

'Hey yourself.'

'I heard the shots from the bathroom. And then the sound of your voice stopped. I thought I'd lost you.'

'A nice girl never goes to a man's house without her Kevlar.' After a quick phone call to Charlie Dixon from the cab, she'd asked the driver to make a pit stop at her apartment on the way to Peter's for the vest she kept at home.

'Good girl.'

'Hey, Peter?'

'Yeah?'

'So what exactly did you tell the intern at the paper about me?'

Peter closed his eyes as he drifted off, but he was smiling. As far as post-blackout first memories went, Ellie considered this a good one.

\* \* \*

One week later, Ellie stood next to Charlie Dixon outside a conference room in the federal building, thinking how much easier this all would be if Vitali Rostov had carried a larger gun. The power of a gun made a difference, even at close distances. Vitali Rostov took two shots from Dixon's semiautomatic and was pronounced dead on arrival. Jason Upton, however, survived the shot from Rostov's compact Derringer — which is why Ellie stood in the hallway of the federal building wishing Rostov had used a bigger gun.

Ellie knew her thoughts were morally wrong at

some level, but she couldn't control them. She wished Upton had died that day in Peter's apartment. She wanted Upton to pay the ultimate price, and inconvenient details were more easily swept away when the interested parties were dead. The NYPD didn't worry about details when it declared Ed Becker solely responsible for the four FirstDate murders. The Wichita police didn't worry about details when it labeled her father's death a suicide. But Jason Upton would not be punished until a prosecutor, judge, jury, and defense lawyer pored over the messy details created by his secrets and his lies.

In the week since the shootings, Ellie had left the job of collecting those details to Charlie Dixon. Then they had met the previous night to lock down the official version that Dixon would file in his reports and eventually repeat to a federal grand jury. And now that official version was about to get its first preview in a joint meeting called by FBI Special Agent in Charge Barry Mayfield and NYPD Lieutenant Dan Eckels.

'You sure about this?' Dixon asked one last time. A man she'd known for less than two weeks was trusting his career to her.

Ellie smiled. 'Does Britney Spears like Cheetos?'

Mayfield and Eckels were already seated on one side of the long table in the conference room, and Dixon and Ellie joined them on the other. Ellie sat patiently while Dixon explained how nearly two years earlier a federal defendant informed him that an associate named Vitya

— last name supposedly unknown — was engaged in a criminal conspiracy that related somehow to a company called FirstDate.

'What was this informant's name?' Eckels asked.

'Alexander Federov.'

'And where can we find Mr. Federov today?'

'You can't,' Dixon said. 'He was killed in prison.'

'Go on,' Mayfield encouraged.

'All I had was a guy's first name and a company name. It wasn't enough to pursue formally, and Federov made it clear he wasn't about to flip. Since then, however, I've remained curious about the tip and informally kept an eye on FirstDate.'

'What do you mean you 'informally kept an eye' on it?' Eckels asked. Ellie noticed that Barry Mayfield was leaving the questioning to Lieutenant Eckels. She hoped it was a sign of the friendship Charlie Dixon claimed he had with his boss.

'Just that. I read up on the company and its CEO, Mark Stern. Newspaper articles and advertisements would catch my eye. I was hoping to find some kind of connection to a person named Vitya. Nothing ever came of it. Then two Mondays ago, I heard from a source that Detectives McIlroy and Hatcher had arrived at Mark Stern's office asking for records as part of a criminal investigation.'

'And who was your source?' Eckels asked.

'Again, nothing formal. A marketing assistant at FirstDate was on parole for a minor drug violation and was willing to stay in touch.'

'Please, Lieutenant,' Mayfield interjected. 'If you'd let my agent tell the story, we'd get through this faster. You'll have time for questions afterward.'

The rest of the official story unfolded without interruption. At Dixon's request, Detectives McIlroy and Hatcher briefed him about their investigation into a series of murders connected to FirstDate. When they identified a woman named Tatiana Chekova as a potential victim based on ballistics evidence, Dixon was intrigued because the man who originally tipped him off about FirstDate had also been Russian. Then things took off when Dixon learned that Tatiana Chekova had a brother-in-law named Vitali Rostov. Vitya, Dixon explained, was a familiar Russian nickname for Vitali.

Dixon explained how he began following Vitali Rostov to the extent that his other investigations allowed. He saw Rostov meet at an Internet café with a man he recognized from his early surveillance of FirstDate as Jason Upton, a former programmer with the company.

'And where was this café?' Eckels asked.

Mayfield threw Eckels a look of warning, but Dixon answered without hesitation. He gave a Midtown address — one of the three Manhattan Internet cafés that Upton had used for his Enoch activities on FirstDate.

'Anyway, I recognized Upton from my early research into FirstDate, when he was still at the company. At that point, I realized that Upton had to have been the point person for whatever

430

was going on between Rostov and the company. That's when I went to Mark Stern for assistance.'

Ellie knew that Stern would have already backed up this part of the official story. She had rehearsed the information with Stern before leaving his office that day for Peter Morse's apartment. True to his word, he'd been willing to be flexible.

'Stern then informed me of the conflict between him and Mr. Upton. He also realized that Upton could have potentially given himself access to customers' credit card records. At that point, I continued to follow Vitya Rostov in the hope of witnessing an actual exchange of cash for information. That is how I wound up at Peter Morse's apartment a week ago. I saw Rostov enter the building. Then when Detective Hatcher arrived shortly thereafter, I knew I had to intervene.'

'How did you get access to the apartment?' Eckels asked. 'The lock was controlled by a combination.'

'We got lucky,' Dixon said. 'When Hatcher went in, the door didn't close completely. I just pushed it open.'

Ellie continued to listen as Dixon summarized all of the admissions that Upton made while Rostov had held her at gunpoint. From this point in the story, the official version hewed pretty closely to the truth.

Just as Ellie knew it was wrong to wish for Jason Upton's death, she knew that at some level it was wrong to lie and to have encouraged

Dixon and Stern to do the same. But they had no choice if they wanted to see Upton punished. A skeptic might take issue with some of the details in the official version that Dixon offered, but Ellie knew that in the end the powers-that-be would accept any credible lie as truth. They didn't want to see Upton walk either. And as long as that was the case, Ellie wasn't going to lose sleep over it.

Ellie tuned back in just as Dixon laid a brown mailing envelope with a New Iberia postmark on the conference table. The package was going to help Dixon tie all the pieces together. It had been delivered by the U.S. Postal Service around the same time Ellie's Kevlar vest was saving her life. Ellie found it in her mailbox when she came home from the hospital. Enclosed were several yellowed photographs of boys and girls of various ages, each picture accompanied by a Post-it note of the shaky writings of an aged hand. On one of the photographs, Helen Benoit had written, *The third boy on the left, Jasper, liked computers. He had a mean streak too.* Even in his early teens, Jasper looked a lot like Jason Upton.

Also enclosed in the envelope were copies of all of Helen Benoit's foster parent contracts with the Louisiana Department of Social Services. At the same time she'd cared for Edmond Bertrand, she'd also taken in Jasper Dupre, date of birth 10-16-74. Jason Upton had the same birth date. As did the Edmond Bertrand arrested in Boston six years ago.

Jason Upton had lied about his education,

wealth, motives — even his name. Charlie Dixon was still tracking down all of the various aliases that Jasper Dupre had used since he left Louisiana.

By the time Dixon was done telling the official version of the story, and Ellie was finished corroborating the details, it sounded like it took both of their separate investigations to come to the full truth. Ellie, of course, knew the *real* truth. She was not troubled, though, that the official version made Dixon sound more resourceful than he was, and she slightly less. Dixon needed the credit more. He was staying on the job.

*   *   *

Ellie returned to her apartment to find her suitcase open on the bed, just as she'd left it. Without bothering to remove her coat or boots, she began folding the last few pieces of clothing that remained in a pile on top of her dresser. Jess eyed her from the bedroom doorway as she placed the items in the suitcase.

'You sure you want to do this?' Jess asked.

'Yeah, I'm sure. This is what I need right now.'

Two days earlier, she'd gotten the call from the lawyer in Kansas. Now that the dust had settled on William Summer's conviction and sentence, the Wichita police were finally prepared to permit the family of deceased detective Jerry Hatcher to have a supervised look at the evidence. Ellie had booked an early-afternoon flight. She was even trying to arrange a private

433

visit with Summer at the El Dorado Correctional Facility while she was down there.

'And what are you going to do about Clark Kent?'

Ellie took it as a sign of approval that Jess had come up with a nickname for Peter. 'Lots of phone calls. He says if I'm away more than three weeks, he's flying down there himself. He's already got a story proposal in the works so the paper will pay for it.'

'What about when you get back? Don't you need to tell the department what you're doing?'

'I'll get right on that — just as soon as you know what *you'll* be doing for work in a month.'

Ellie was still on paid leave, but Lieutenant Jenkins was already inquiring as to when she might return to her old post at Midtown North. In the last two weeks, she had trusted too many of the wrong people, been suspicious of the others, and had orchestrated an apocryphal, illegal cover story because she came to believe it was the only way to obtain justice. She had watched her partner get shot, and then held him as he died. She knew better than to make a decision prematurely, but she no longer pictured herself as a police officer. At least not yet.

'And you're sure it's okay I stay here while you're gone?' Jess asked.

'Please. You know you'd stay here anyway.'

'A vacant apartment in Manhattan is a terrible thing to waste.'

Jess helped Ellie zip the suitcase and then carried it to the front door. Ellie looked at her watch.

'I better go.'

'Ellie, wait. You've thought through this decision, right? About going home? I mean, what if it turns out — you know, what if we've been fooling ourselves about Dad?'

'Yeah,' she said, nodding. 'But we need an answer. Mom needs to finally move on after all these years. And I'll be there to get her through it. I'm ready to do that.'

She heard her voice breaking, so she said good-bye to Jess one last time before she hugged him and carried her suitcase to the street. She waved down the next available cab and helped the driver load her oversized bag into the trunk. As the taxi made its way to the Midtown Tunnel, she took in the streets of Manhattan, as she had when she first arrived in the city, knowing she would miss them and that everything would be different when she returned.

# ACKNOWLEDGMENTS

As ever, I am extremely grateful to the readers and booksellers who make it possible for me to write fiction and to the many people who help me do a better job at it.

My gratitude extends to computer geniuses Gary Moore and David Joerg. What the two of you know about the ins and outs of the 'black hats' on the Internet and the havoc they can wreak on the unsuspecting is terrifying. Hopefully I've done the material justice in the translation.

I continue to be blessed by the splendid support of Henry Holt, St. Martin's Press, and Orion Publishing Group. I am especially thankful to Henry Holt's former editor-in-chief, Jennifer Barth; its vice president of Sales and Marketing, Maggie Richards; and my agent, Philip Spitzer. Jennifer is a gutsy kindred spirit who always understands precisely what I am trying to accomplish and keeps pushing me until I get there. Maggie is a fierce insomniac who will not rest until the entire world has read this book. And in Philip I have found tremendous loyalty, friendship, and family. Being me, I rarely say it, but the three of you are very special (and yes, I mean the good kind of special, not the stop-eating-the-glue kind).

*Other titles published by*
*The House of Ulverscroft:*

## CLOSE CASE

### Alafair Burke

In Portland, Oregon reporter Percy Crenshaw has been bludgeoned to death in his carport and District Attorney Samantha Kincaid attends the case. Tensions are running high after a police officer shot and killed a mother of two, prompting anti-police demonstrations. It seems that Crenshaw's death is not unrelated: soon two men are arrested after a crime spree. One of the suspects claims coercive police tactics and Samantha finds herself digging for more evidence. Her search leads her to the city's drug trade and to officers in the bureau's Northeast precinct . . . After alienating her boyfriend, Detective Chuck Forbes, and the cops, Samantha is unsure whom to trust. She tracks Crenshaw's path for clues, but it's a path that could lead to the same fatal end.

# MISSING JUSTICE

## Alafair Burke

Deputy District Attorney Samantha Kincaid is back at work after an attempt on her life and a promotion into the Major Crimes Unit. When the husband of Portland, Oregon city judge Clarissa Easterbrook reports her missing and Samantha is called on the case, she assumes her only job is to make the district attorney look good until the judge turns up. When the police discover evidence of foul play, however, Samantha finds herself unearthing secrets that Clarissa had wanted to stay hidden. And when those secrets lead to the discovery of corruption at the highest levels of the city's power structure, Samantha realizes that her quest for justice could cost her not only her job, but her life.